Adopted from birth, Pam Weaver was a nurse working in children's homes and day nurseries and at one time she was
A member of West Sussex Writers' Club since 1987, her first novel, *A Mother's Gift* (previously published as *There's Always Tomorrow*) was the winner in the Day for Writers' Novel Opening Competition and was bought by HarperCollins Avon. Pam's novels are set in Worthing during the war and the austerity years which followed. Her inspiration comes from her love of people and their stories and her passion for the town of Worthing. With the sea on one side and the Downs on the other, Worthing has a scattering of small villages within its urban sprawl and in some cases tightknit communities, making it an ideal setting for the modern saga.

Also by Pam Weaver:

The Lost Orphan
The Runaway Orphans
At Home by the Sea
Goodnight Sweetheart
A Mother's Gift previously published as
There's Always Tomorrow
Better Days Will Come
Pack Up Your Troubles
Mother's Day previously published as
For Better For Worse
Blue Moon
Love Walked Right In
Always In My Heart
Sing Them Home
Come Rain or Shine

Short stories:
Emily's Christmas Wish
Amy's Wartime Christmas
Amy's Seaside Secret

Memoir:
Bath Times and Nursery Rhymes

PAM WEAVER

A Sister's Promise

avon.

Published by AVON
A division of HarperCollins*Publishers*
1 London Bridge Street
London SE1 9GF

www.harpercollins.co.uk

HarperCollins*Publishers*
Macken House,
39/40 Mayor Street Upper,
Dublin 1
D01 C9W8A

A Paperback Original 2024
1
First published in Great Britain by HarperCollins*Publishers* 2024

ISBN: 978-0-00-854235-1

Set in Sabon LT Std by HarperCollins*Publishers* India

Printed and bound in UK using 100% Renewable Electricity at CPI Group (UK) Ltd

This book contains FSC™ certified paper and other controlled sources to ensure responsible forest management.
For more information visit: www.harpercollins.co.uk/green

I dedicate this book to all my readers. Without you, dear reader, I'm a ship without a rudder, a bike without a chain, a biro with no ink . . .

Muntham Court, 1920

Agatha stretched herself luxuriantly and lifted her face towards the early morning sun. *Ah*, she thought, *this is the life*. She was on the veranda and still in her nightgown and negligee, but she didn't care. After yesterday, it was unlikely that anyone would call on her, not at this time of the morning anyway.

Following the evening celebrations the day before, Muntham Court was peaceful and quiet. Inside the house, a team of staff were busy cleaning and putting everything back in order, but she couldn't hear them. The only sounds came from the doves – or was it pigeons (she would never get used to living in the country) – cooing on the rooftop and the odd bleat from one of the sheep in the field opposite the long drive.

Agatha smiled to herself. She had done it. Her mother said everything was lost but it wasn't. She had secured her position in society at last and she couldn't help feeling more than a little smug about it. She had it all. The big house, money, status . . . Of course it had come at a cost, but all that stress had ceased the moment she'd given birth to Charles's baby. Her confinement and the birth had been straightforward, but he would never know. Better that he thought she had had a protracted and difficult delivery. Who would tell him anything different? They wouldn't dare. She allowed herself a sly smile. No one could touch her now.

She opened her eyes as Faulkner came out of the house with the breakfast tray. She was eating light today. She'd refused anything cooked. She had to get her figure back, so it was simply toast, marmalade and a pot of tea – Earl Grey, of course. She loved the flavour made distinct by oil of bergamot, a type of orange; its connection with the one-time prime minister, Charles Grey, gave her a chance to show off her knowledge. 'It was gifted to him by the Chinese, don't you know. You may have heard of him. He was the prime minister who presided over the abolition of slavery in the British Empire.'

The butler laid the tray on the table and Agatha noted the tremble of his gnarled hands. He must be way past retirement age. It didn't look good, keeping on someone so obviously past his prime. She must remember to ask Charles what the family did with 'old retainers'. 'Thank you, Faulkner.'

'Madam,' he said, turning back unsteadily.

Agatha reached for a cigarette. 'Is my husband in the breakfast room?'

'I'm sorry, madam. The master left for London early this morning. He said he'd be back at the weekend, I believe.'

Reaching for the cigarette lighter, Agatha dismissed him. 'Thank you, Faulkner.'

As soon as the old man had gone, she poured herself some tea and relaxed again. Thank goodness she was alone. Now she could enjoy her lazy day. She yawned. A lazy and peaceful day.

The sound of a baby's cry came floating across the lawn. Agatha looked up to see the nurse striding towards the house with the child in her arms. What the hell was

2

she doing? She sat up straight and waited until the woman reached the patio. 'What do you want?' she said harshly.

The nurse, all smiles, glanced down at the squawking baby in her arms and said in a singsong voice, 'We thought we would come and see Mummy, didn't we?'

Agatha laid her cigarette on the ashtray and reached for her toast. 'Well, now you've seen me, you can go back,' she said without looking up.

The nurse blinked in surprise. 'Wouldn't madam like to hold her baby?'

'No she would not,' Agatha said coldly. 'I employed you, Nurse Cowdray, to look after her.'

'Madam is obviously tired after the birth. We'll come back later in the afternoon.'

'No, Nurse, you shall not,' Agatha said firmly. 'You feed her, you bathe her and you see that her things are washed; in short, she is your responsibility.'

'But surely . . .' Nurse Cowdray spluttered.

'But nothing,' Agatha snapped. 'Now, will you please take the baby back to the cottage and remain there for the rest of the day.' She pulled her negligee over her bound breasts but already the milk was seeping from her nipples. Damn the woman for bringing the child so near to her. The last thing she wanted was lactating mammary glands. She flushed with embarrassment. Thank the Lord that old fool Faulkner wasn't still around to see it.

'Mrs Shepherd,' Nurse Cowdray began again, 'it's really important for mother and baby to bond with each other in the early days. I know you'd rather not feed her yourself' – she had seen Agatha shudder at the thought – 'but it really is no trouble to bring her up to the house for a little cuddle. That's why I thought—'

Agatha drew herself up. 'And *I* thought I had made myself perfectly clear at your interview, Nurse Cowdray. *You* are paid to look after the baby. *You* are the one to comfort it.

3

When I want the child in the house, I shall send someone to tell you. Until then, will you please go back to the cottage and do your job!'

Visibly shocked, the nurse turned on her heel and walked back across the grass. With not one ounce of regret, Agatha shook the napkin out and laid it in her lap. For the next few minutes, she ate her toast and sipped her tea.

When she had finished, she leaned back in the chair. She would have to go back into the house in a minute. Already the leaking milk was drying into a stiff globule on her nightgown. She supposed it must have been her body's reaction to hearing the baby's cry. There was a slight sound in the doorway. Irritated, Agatha opened her eyes. A little soon-to-be three-year-old was hovering by the French doors, one foot on the patio and the other inside the sitting room. Agatha sat up. 'Hello, sweetheart. What are you doing here?'

She could see a crisp white apron just behind her. 'I hope it's all right, madam,' said Nanny Bloom, 'but Pearl spotted you from the nursery window and was so desperate to see you.'

'Of course she was,' Agatha said, her tone softening. 'Come over here, my darling. Come and give Mummy a cuddle.'

Chapter 1

26 April 1930

The cat flattened its ears back, hissing angrily, but thirteen-year-old Pearl ignored the warning. Pulling the doll's skirt over the cat's tail and back legs, she rearranged it so that it covered the animal's lower abdomen. Cleo let out a throaty growl.

'She doesn't like it,' Milly, her younger sister, cautioned.

The sisters were together in the summerhouse, which was at the other end of the extensive gardens surrounding their parents' home. An old-fashioned building, dating from pre-Victorian times, it had four rooms: a bedroom, a fairly large living area and a small kitchen. There was also a tiny boxroom for storage. Their mother had spent the whole of the previous year, when Pearl and Milly were twelve and nine respectively, refurbishing it for them. When it was finished, it looked better than some of the cottages in the village and, best of all as far as Pearl was concerned, it was the envy of all their friends.

Though none of it was new, the cottage was elegantly furnished. It had a sofa and matching chair in the sitting room, a chest of drawers painted pale grey in the bedroom, lace curtains at the windows, and an assortment of rugs on the floor. The kitchen area had everything they might need for a meal: plates, cups and saucers, pots and pans. Not that the girls cooked for themselves. Even though they considered themselves quite grown up, their mother wouldn't allow it.

'But Martha in the kitchen cooks sometimes,' Pearl had protested. Martha was only fourteen and in service. 'I've seen her boiling eggs and helping Cook.'

'You are a young lady,' her mother insisted, 'and young ladies do not work in kitchens.' So that was an end to it. Nobody argued with Agatha, so they had to content themselves with Martha bringing a box of food over from the kitchen if they wanted to eat in the summerhouse.

Now the cat, its eyes wide in terror, growled again.

'Oh Pearl,' Milly protested. 'She doesn't want to dress up. You're hurting her.'

'She's just a cat,' Pearl snapped, 'and she'll do what *I* want.' She was putting a bonnet over the cat's head. Under the skirt, Cleo's tail swished back and forth.

Pearl and Milly may have been sisters, but they weren't at all alike. They didn't even look alike. Of the two of them, Pearl was the stronger personality. Blonde with a slightly round face and green eyes, everybody agreed she was going to be tall and elegant when she grew up. Pearl was confident and authoritative, whereas Milly had a gentler disposition. Slightly on the plump side, Milly had long straight hair that was quite dark, and her eyes were brown. Her mother said her only asset was her pert little nose but, because she was forced to wear glasses, even that was spoiled.

'Dorothy Parker says, "Men seldom make passes at girls who wear glasses",' her mother had told her. At ten, Milly wasn't sure what that meant but, judging by her mother's expression, it wasn't good.

The two girls also had very different tastes when it came to the games they played. Milly enjoyed dressing up in her mother's old cast-offs. She would don one of her mother's dresses and parade in front of the long mirror in the summerhouse, or dance to the music of the gramophone and pretend she was at a ball. Right now, she was wearing an old blue and red cocktail dress which was much too long for her, while on her head she wore a white turban with a long ostrich feather at the front. She also had a pair of her mother's shoes (her whole foot fitted in the toe) which made a very satisfying click-clack sound as she walked about. Pearl never dressed up, and she had some strange ideas about what she considered 'fun'.

Milly sighed. Surely her big sister was too old to be dressing an animal. Milly gave up doing that sort of thing when she was six. It was beginning to distress her as she watched Pearl put her whole weight onto poor Cleo's body so that she could force the sleeve of a doll's cardigan over her front legs. The cat's ears flattened once more as she tried to wriggle herself away, her back arched.

'Please, Pearl . . .' Milly whimpered.

Her sister looked up crossly. 'Oh, will you shut up!'

And then it happened. With a sudden movement, Cleo jerked her body forward and lashed out with her paws, letting out a loud and angry yowl as she did so. Pearl screamed as Cleo raked her claws down the girl's face and bit her arm. Milly took in her breath noisily. There was a moment of stunned silence as Pearl let go of the cat and blood pooled on her chin.

Cleo jumped down from the sofa, pausing for a moment to growl angrily as the doll's bonnet, still tied around her neck, rolled from her head and fell to the floor. Pearl buried her head in her hands and bawled.

Milly was stunned. Her sister never cried. Never!

The cat managed to shake the cardigan off but the ribbons on the bonnet and the skirt remained in place. Milly bent to remove them, but the cowering cat spat at her and bared her teeth. Milly snatched her hand away as she watched Cleo going backwards, putting as much distance between herself and Milly as she could. By the time she'd reached relative safety underneath the chest of drawers, the offending hat was dislodged.

Milly turned her attention back to her sister. Pearl had pressed her handkerchief to her face and was holding it out to inspect it. When she saw all the blood, Pearl gasped.

'Look what she's done!' she shrieked. 'I'm bleeding to death. I shall have a scar. She's ruined my face.' As she leapt to her feet, her expression changed from pain to anger and Milly guessed what was coming. 'I'll kill her! I'll kill the stupid animal.'

Milly made a dash for the door and, as soon as she opened it, Cleo flew outside.

'Why did you do that, you stupid idiot?' her sister gasped. 'Now you've let the damned thing get away.'

'Sorry,' Milly murmured, although of course she wasn't one bit sorry. She glanced anxiously at her sister. There was every likelihood that Pearl would lash out and hit her now, but she didn't regret letting Cleo escape to safety.

Pearl stood in front of the tall mirror dabbing her face. There was a long scratch from her cheek to her chin, but it wasn't bleeding quite so much now. However, the bite on her arm looked pretty bad. Milly asked if it hurt and, by way of response, Pearl threw herself over the arm of the sofa and howled.

Milly recalled the tale she'd overheard the butcher boy telling Mrs Cunningham the cook. Apparently, Old Sam Clark (whoever he was) found a cat stuck in the 'edge but when he pulled the animal free, it scratched him. His wife had washed the wound and put on a bandage but Old Sam got blood poisoning. 'Two days,' the butcher boy said as Mrs Cunningham shook her head sadly, 'that's all it took and 'e was a goner.'

Milly was suddenly worried. Supposing Pearl got blood

poisoning? Supposing she only lasted two days? 'You should get that bite seen to,' Milly ventured. 'We need to get help.'

'I can't walk all the way to the house,' Pearl groaned. 'You'll have to fetch somebody.'

'But what if you're a goner by the time I get back?'

Pearl sat up, her eyes wide. 'Fine, but you'll have to help me,' she said dramatically. 'I think I might faint.'

Milly hitched up her mother's dress and, putting one arm around her sister, they set off across the garden. As they reached the ha-ha, a steep, manmade dip in the grass, designed to stop sheep roaming into their grounds, she was forced to kick off her mother's high-heeled shoes. Milly helped her whimpering and tearful sister over the change in ground levels and they continued towards the house.

When they got to the gravel path, they could hear raised voices coming from the house. Milly was walking gingerly. The gravel dug into her feet and it wasn't easy with Pearl leaning on her so heavily.

'Sounds like Mummy and Daddy are having an argument,' Milly remarked.

With a scoff, Pearl pooh-poohed the idea. 'Daddy wouldn't dare argue with Mummy,' she hissed. But sure enough, they could soon make out their father's strident voice coming through the open French windows of the sitting room. He was speaking in a kind of authoritative tone that neither of them had ever heard from him before.

'This is one time when I'm having my way, Agatha, so you had better get used to it.'

'*What* did you say?' their mother demanded.

'You heard me,' he replied. 'She is coming here.'

As they crept closer, the two girls saw their mother rising up sedately from her chair. 'Now you listen to me, Charles,' she said, her voice cutting the air like a knife. 'If you think I'm going to disrupt the whole household so that you can entertain your floozy, you've got another think coming.'

Outside in the garden, Pearl and Milly froze, all thoughts of Pearl's wounds suspended. They stared wide-eyed at each other, their mouths agape. Milly made to go inside, but Pearl suddenly pulled her sister under the heavy wisteria boughs and they pressed themselves close to the wall.

'What's a floozy?' Milly whispered.

'Shhh.'

'I'm not entertaining her,' their father said, his tone measured. 'I've already explained to you, she needs looking after.'

'Think of the scandal,' Agatha went on, now verging on hysteria. 'The servants will talk. Good God, we've got the fashion show to raise funds for the underprivileged in two weeks' time.'

'Agatha, it's not that important,' their father retorted. 'We can give a donation instead.'

'Don't be a fool,' Agatha snapped. 'It's far too late to cancel. The world and his wife will be here. Lady Gwendolen Fitzalan-Howard is coming to open the occasion. Have you any idea how many strings I had to pull to get her to come? No, Charles, that woman can't come here, and that's final.'

'I'm not arguing with you,' their father said resolutely.

'Charles, I have worked my fingers to the bone to get us this far,' Agatha shrilled. 'I have moved heaven and earth to get you recognition in society.'

Their father didn't reply but they heard the clink of the whisky bottle on glass.

'We've come from relative obscurity,' their mother continued, 'to being one of the most important families in the county, and now you want to throw it all away.'

'I appreciate all that you've done,' their father said. He sounded tired, defeated. 'But—'

'But nothing, Charles. I won't let you do it.'

'The girl is very ill, Agatha.'

'So?'

'So, she needs peace and quiet. She needs to be nursed. She needs to be in one place. She can stay in the east wing.' He paused, adding in a slightly lower tone, 'I owe her that much.'

'You may,' Agatha sneered sarcastically. 'But I don't.' There was no mistaking the venom in her cutting remark. 'Send the hussy to the workhouse, where people of her sort belong.'

'Do you always have to be so selfish, Agatha?' their father implored.

Milly and Pearl jumped as they heard the sound of breaking glass. 'You're the selfish one!' their mother screamed. 'I absolutely refuse to have her here!'

Pressed against the wall outside, the two girls held their breath.

What on earth was going on? For a split second there was an awkward silence, and then Pearl seized her moment. Pinching her scratches to make them bleed again, she let out what sounded like a primeval scream as she threw herself through the French doors and into the room.

Chapter 2

Milly stayed in the garden just outside the French windows. Nobody seemed to notice her silently watching them as their mother descended into a frenzy of mild panic, but that was nothing new. Milly often felt invisible.

Pearl cried and bled all over the cushions. Charles rang the bell. When the maid arrived, Pearl wailed even louder, and Agatha demanded that Martha should tell Dixon to fetch the doctor.

Charles shook his head. 'She's all right,' he said. 'Patch her up with a bandage and she'll be fine.'

Martha hesitated, unsure of what to do.

'Well, go on girl,' Agatha snapped. 'Get Dixon to bring Doctor Jennings here this minute.'

Martha fled.

Clutching Pearl to her bosom as they sat together on the sofa, their mother looked up and saw Milly hovering in the doorway. 'Did you have anything to do with this, Millicent?' she accused. 'If you've done this to your sister . . .'

Under her glasses, Milly's eyes grew wide. 'No, Mummy. No!'

'Well, I wouldn't put it past you.'

'It wasn't me, it was Cleo.'

'Cleo?' Agatha squeaked.

'I'm sure Milly wouldn't do such a thing,' Charles said mildly.

His wife rounded on him. 'And I do wish you wouldn't call her that! It sounds so common. Her name is Millicent.'

With a long-suffering sigh, Charles reached for a cigarette from the box on the table and made himself comfortable in the armchair.

Turning towards him Agatha sneered, 'Don't you care that your other daughter has been injured? You're a cold fish, aren't you.'

'And she's a drama queen,' Charles murmured.

Agatha smoothed the hair from Pearl's forehead. 'My poor baby. Tell me what happened, my darling,' she soothed.

Between her hiccups, Pearl did her best to explain the events of the morning to her mother. 'I was reading my book, Mummy,' she began innocently, the tears pooling in her eyes once more, 'just sitting on the chair like this, when all of a sudden Cleo jumped up and attacked me.'

Her father raised an eyebrow and coughed. Milly, still standing in the doorway, put one bare foot over the threshold. She had hoped that her lack of footwear would go unnoticed, but her mother's eagle eyes spotted her.

'And what on earth are you doing running about with no shoes?' her mother demanded.

'My shoes hurt my toes, Mummy.'

'Oh for goodness' sake, Millicent!' her mother snapped. 'Don't make such a fuss. I told you we're going into town on Wednesday, didn't I. They can't be that bad. You only had them at Christmas.'

Milly caught her breath and blinked. 'But they really do hurt.'

'All right, all right. There's no need to keep reminding me.' Then, turning back to Pearl, Agatha said, 'You weren't doing anything to upset the cat, were you, darling?'

'Oh no, Mummy,' said Pearl, shaking her head and blinking up at her mother innocently. 'I didn't do anything. I promise.'

Agatha looked puzzled. 'Cleo always seemed such a gentle creature,' she murmured, more to herself than anyone else.

Milly sucked in her bottom lip. 'Mummy, Cleo didn't like—' she began.

'That's what I thought,' Pearl interjected in a loud voice, drowning her sister out, 'but she suddenly jumped up to my face and scratched me. Oh Mummy, it was so painful, I thought I was going to die. I screamed and screamed then she bit me.'

'Bit you?'

'Yes, on my arm,' Pearl said. 'Here. Look.'

Agatha's expression darkened. Milly looked helplessly at her father, but he seemed miles away. There was a light knock on the door and the maid came back with the first-aid tin, a bowl of warm water, some soap and iodine.

'Is the doctor coming?' Agatha demanded.

'Yes, ma'am.'

They all watched as Martha knelt in front of Pearl and put a towel onto her lap. Although the bleeding had stopped, she was very gentle as she bathed the girl's wounds.

'Don't put that stuff on the bite,' said Charles. 'Just wrap it in a clean bandage.'

'She should have iodine on both,' Agatha insisted.

'Not on the bite,' said her father. 'That's much deeper.'

His wife glared. 'So now you're a doctor,' she said sarcastically.

'Leave it until she's seen the doctor,' Charles insisted.

Agatha glared. Pearl's scratches on her face were dabbed with iodine while she yowled with pain and tried to push Martha away. 'Ow! That stings!'

'Sorry, my darling,' Agatha said. 'We have to do it in case you get an infection.'

Milly pushed up her glasses and thought of Old Sam.

A little while later, Dr Jennings arrived. He pronounced the scratches superficial and said they were nothing to worry about. Much to Agatha's annoyance, he agreed with her husband about not putting iodine into deep wounds and suggested a little alcohol be put onto the bite instead.

'She bled an awful lot,' Agatha insisted.

'And that's a good thing,' said the doctor, eyeing the whisky bottle on the table by the door. 'Copious bleeding would have flushed everything out, you see.'

With a cotton-wool ball in her hand, Agatha reached for the brandy bottle. Once again, Pearl screeched the house down as her mother gently dabbed some onto the bite mark on her arm. Charles stood to pour the doctor a drink.

Pearl was inconsolable.

'I think Pearl should be put to bed,' Dr Jennings shouted over the sound of her wails. 'The child has obviously had a shock and a nice little sleep will do her the world of good.'

The crisis over, Agatha pulled herself to her feet to take her daughter upstairs. They left the room together, but not before she'd once again rounded on Milly. 'You can go back to the cottage and take those ridiculous clothes off,' she snapped. 'And for heaven's sake don't let me catch you walking around barefoot again.'

Before Milly could respond, Agatha turned her attention to Martha. 'And you can go and tell the gardener to search for that cat,' she barked. 'I want the wretched thing drowned.'

Milly's jaw dropped. 'Oh no, Mummy, please. It wasn't Cleo's fault. She didn't mean to . . .'

The door was closing, but not before Pearl glanced back at her with a look of triumph on her face. Milly turned to her father. 'Oh Daddy . . .' but he shook his head and motioned with his finger for Milly to be quiet.

Dr Jennings finished his whisky and said his farewell.

As soon as they were alone, Milly's father took her arm and gently led her back out into the garden. 'Are you all right?' he asked.

Milly nodded miserably.

'So tell me what really happened.'

A tear rolled down her cheek. 'Oh Daddy, it wasn't a bit like Pearl said.'

'I didn't think for one minute that it was,' he said sagely.

As the two of them strolled towards the kitchen garden, his youngest daughter told him the real reason Cleo had turned on her sister. 'Please, Daddy, please don't let Bodkin drown her. It wasn't Cleo's fault, really it wasn't.'

The gardens themselves were peppered with gravel walks. There was also an attractive fountain and, at the far end, a large greenhouse. The gardener, Bodkin, grew enough vegetables to feed the household all year round, and was locally famed for his flowers, which won prizes every year at the local flower show.

Bodkin was in the greenhouse doing some watering when Charles Shepherd called him. Snatching off his cap, he hurried over.

'My wife wants you to find Cleo and dispose of her by drowning,' Charles began.

'Oh Daddy . . .' Milly cried helplessly.

'Miss Pearl has been badly scratched,' Charles went on, 'but it appears that the animal wasn't wholly to blame. She was being teased and, that being the case, it seems a little unfair to end her life just for protecting herself.'

Bodkin nodded sagaciously.

'However,' Charles continued, 'it's also obvious that Cleo cannot be allowed to return to the house. I'm thinking that perhaps you could find someone, maybe someone in the village, to take care of her and make sure that she doesn't come back here.'

Mr Bodkin put his cap back on and touched the edge.

'Right you are, sir,' he said and, glancing down at a tearful Milly, he added cheerfully, 'Now don't you worry, miss. I knows just the place for Cleo. My sister'll 'ave her and she'll be as happy as Larry.'

Charles slipped something folded into the man's hand. Milly couldn't be sure what it was, but it looked like a pound note.

Bodkin touched his cap again. 'Thank you very much, sir,' he said, clearly delighted. 'I'll see to it right away.'

'Now let's get you back to the cottage,' said Charles, looking down at Milly. 'You have to get out of those grubby things and find your shoes.'

Milly smiled happily. While it was true that her dressing-up clothes were getting quite grubby because she kept walking on the hem, what pleased her was the thought of walking all that way with Daddy. It was unusual for her father to come to the little cottage. He'd been there once or twice, but the truth of the matter was, he seldom came home. Mummy said he was too busy working in London.

Milly hitched the dress up again and, when they reached the ha-ha, she retrieved the click-clack shoes.

Back in the cottage, she went into the bedroom to change, while her father spent some time looking around. 'Do you and Pearl play in here often?' he asked as Milly reappeared in her normal clothes.

'Only in the holidays,' said Milly.

'Of course,' said Charles with a grin. It was a foolish question. The two girls were at boarding school during termtime. In fact, they were due to be back at school on Sunday in time for the new term at the beginning of the following week.

He picked up a doll. 'Where does this go?'

Milly indicated the small wicker chair. Charles put the doll down and straightened her dress. 'I'd forgotten how nice it is in here,' he remarked.

'I don't think I want to play in the cottage any more,' Milly said miserably.

'Then perhaps you wouldn't mind if someone else came here,' her father said, lighting another cigarette. And in answer to her puzzled frown he added, 'I should like to ask a friend of mine and her daughter to stay here for a while.'

'What, live here?'

'Yes,' her father said, looking around one last time.

'But it's very small,' Milly remarked. 'And Mummy says it's not the place to do any cooking.'

Her father laughed softly. 'We'll see about that,' he said, as Milly squeezed her feet into her sandals.

He waited for her by the door and, as she came out into the cottage garden, he slipped his hand over hers. Milly looked up at him and smiled, then they both walked back to the house, her hand feeling warm and snug in his.

Chapter 3

The girls kept their distance from their parents as the bad atmosphere between Agatha and Charles deepened. That evening, Pearl and Milly were told to eat alone in the old nursery upstairs. 'Your father and I need to discuss something,' said Agatha.

'You can still do that, Mummy,' Pearl said. 'We won't listen to what you're saying,' but her mother was adamant that the discussion was private and not for young ears. Pearl made a fuss, reminding her mother that – at fourteen next birthday – she was almost an adult, but it was to no avail.

The girls were itching to know what was being said downstairs, and before long they could hear raised and angry voices. They crept along the landing and stood near the top of the stairs.

'I don't want to make a fight of it,' they heard their father say, 'but you can't always be right, my dear.'

'And you are, I suppose,' Agatha retorted.

'I didn't say that either.' Charles's voice was measured, calm.

'Look here, Charles, if we're going to continue to move up in society, we need to do it properly,' said Agatha. 'We have to be one step ahead of the rest, so that by the time the girls have their coming-out parties, we shall be well established. They deserve nothing but the best.'

'And the allowance I've given you will more than suffice. I don't think it wise to go overboard with expenses. We have to be sensible.'

Their mother scoffed. 'And this coming from the man who is investing all his money in factories making armaments.'

'That has nothing to do with it.'

'I still can't believe what you're doing,' Agatha complained. 'Have you really no idea how many pacifist movements there are in Worthing? There's the Worthing Women's Peace Crusade, the Worthing Labour Party, the youth groups . . . I myself have been asked to be on the committee of the Peace Council.'

'I happen to agree with Winston,' said Charles, 'and Lord Winterton is of the same persuasion. The whole country is walking blindfolded over a cliff.'

'We all want peace,' said Agatha, her voice rising again. 'Hitler wants peace. The whole bloody world wants peace. Everybody except you and Churchill!'

'Hitler doesn't want peace. He has a totally different agenda.'

There was an angry pause in their conversation. Pearl and Milly turned to tiptoe back to their bedroom when their father said, 'And you'd better get used to the idea. I'm bringing her here.'

There followed a loud clatter, as if someone had thrown their cutlery onto an empty plate. 'If she comes here, I'm leaving.'

'That's up to you my dear,' said Charles, 'but I can tell you now, I shall not change my mind.'

The girls eyed each other anxiously as they heard their mother shout, 'Go to hell!' The door flew open, and they only just had time to get back into the nursery before they heard her running up the stairs. A moment later, doors were being slammed and drawers were crashed shut in the master bedroom as Agatha screeched for Dixon.

Milly's heart was thumping. This was bad. Really bad.

'I hate Daddy,' Pearl declared solemnly. 'I'm never going to get married.' By the time the maid came to collect their dirty dishes, she had draped herself over the settee complaining of the throbbing in her arm.

'Tell my mother I need the doctor,' she said plaintively, her eyes tearing up again.

But when Martha reappeared about ten minutes later, all she had was a couple of aspirins and a glass of water.

'Where's Mummy?' Pearl asked.

'She said to give you these,' said Martha.

Pearl couldn't hide her disappointment. 'Didn't you tell her I'm ill? I'm in a lot of pain.'

'I told her,' Martha insisted, 'and she said you were to take these.'

Pearl scowled. 'You stupid girl! Go and get her at once.'

Martha hovered, unsure of what to do.

'Hurry up or I'll box your ears.'

'Pearl!' Milly exclaimed.

Martha hurried from the room as Pearl shouted after her, 'If you don't bring her, I'll make sure she gives you the sack.'

The two girls waited, but a few minutes later they heard the front door slam. Milly ran to the window and as she looked out she caught her breath. 'Mummy's going.'

Pearl sighed in a bored way. 'Of course she's not going.'

'Dixon is putting her suitcase into her car,' Milly gasped.

Pearl sat up, a look of horror on her face. 'But I want her here.'

Seconds later they heard the engine start, followed by the sound of wheels spinning on the gravel. Pearl hurled herself at the window, but by then all they could see was the car's taillights heading towards the open road.

* * *

21

The rest of the week was very confusing for Milly. Her sister spent most of her time either sulking in the conservatory or generally making herself thoroughly obnoxious with the servants. Her eyes were sometimes wild or, at other times, dark. She talked to herself all the time.

'We've got to do something . . . She's a she-devil . . . Daddy doesn't know what he's doing. Mummy says he's bewitched.'

Milly struggled to understand – Pearl's mumblings didn't make a lot of sense and they were scary.

Their father spent a lot of time on the telephone, then various builders turned up and were all sent to the cottage. Although their mother had left instructions with Mrs Cunningham that she and Pearl were not to go down there, a couple of times Milly sneaked over the ha-ha and hid under the eaves to see what was going on.

It soon became obvious that the builders were making some structural alterations inside. It looked as if a proper fireplace was being installed and the chimney sweep turned up. Each day a succession of vans and commercial vehicles arrived to offload everything from new bedding and furnishings to a small dining table and a vacuum cleaner. Their father was making the tiny cottage into a palace, and not only that, but a stream of would-be servants had arrived and now he was ensconced in the morning room doing interviews. There was still no sign of Mother.

On Thursday a beautiful grey enamel free-standing electric cooker arrived in a Paine Manwaring & Lephard van, and some men in brown overalls installed it. Bodkin, who was tidying the little cottage garden, came to fill the space under the eaves with logs. Milly felt a little embarrassed to be found out, but the gardener was kind enough to pretend it was perfectly normal for the child of the house to be hiding there, so she stayed to help him stack the logs.

After they had finished, Milly hurried to the house for her lunch. As she washed her hands in the downstairs cloakroom, she heard the servants talking in the kitchen.

'An electric cooker?' Mrs Cunningham exclaimed. 'Well, I'll go to the foot of our stairs. How come she can have an electric cooker while I've got to make do with this old heap?'

'Probably because the master is buying it and not the mistress,' said Dixon.

'Who is she anyway, this woman?'

Milly peered into the kitchen through the crack in the door. Dixon hadn't verbally replied but he was raising his eyebrows.

'Oh, I see,' said Mrs Cunningham.

'What do you see?' Martha asked.

'Never you mind,' said Mrs Cunningham.

'Oh,' Martha tut-tutted, clearly disappointed. 'Why is it that grown-ups are so mysterious? Why shouldn't you tell me?'

'You're too young,' said Dixon.

'That's daft,' Martha said crossly. 'I'm a working woman now.'

The two older servants glanced at each other with a grin, then Mrs Cunningham said, 'Well, if you must know, she's his fancy woman, and she's coming to live here. She's not well and he wants to look after her.'

Martha took in her breath. 'Is that why the mistress has left him?'

'What do you think?' asked Dixon.

Martha seemed horrified. 'Oh but that's awful. Poor madam.'

Behind the cloakroom door, Milly pushed her spectacles up her nose as her throat constricted. Her mother had *left* her father? Was this true? And what did it mean? When she'd asked Daddy where Mummy was, he'd only said she'd gone to the London flat for a while. Milly was going to ask Mrs Cunningham and Dixon what they were talking about but, as soon as she appeared in the doorway, everybody went back to their work and seemed to be very busy.

Milly thought about telling Pearl what she'd overheard, but Pearl was still acting strangely so she didn't dare. Anyway, Pearl would probably say, 'It's just gossip. Take no notice.'

But as the week went by, and their mother still hadn't returned, Milly became more anxious. When Martha and Dixon began packing the girls' trunks ready for their return to boarding school, Milly had a new worry. Mummy still hadn't bought her some new shoes, and she couldn't possibly manage for a whole term in her old ones. She mentioned the subject to her father, but he was in a hurry to be somewhere else.

'Your mother will sort that out,' he said, rushing through the front door. 'Ask her.' But Mummy wasn't here, was she?

On the Saturday before the girls went back to school, there was a ripple of excitement when an ambulance pulled up outside the house. The two girls rushed to the window and saw Dixon exchanging a few words with the driver before he drove off again.

'I'm going down to the cottage,' Pearl announced.

With her sister gone, Milly hid herself away in the boxroom to play her dressing-up games one last time. She never liked raised voices and rows, so she avoided them whenever possible, and it was something of a relief to know that she'd be out of the house the next day. She was in the middle of a fantasy about being Joan of Arc when Pearl burst into the room.

'She's in the cottage,' she said breathlessly.

'Who?'

'Who do you think? Father's tart.'

Milly didn't understand the expression and it must have

shown on her face because her sister threw her hands into the air. 'His *friend*,' she spat. 'His fancy woman, the bitch who has sent our mother away.'

Milly's jaw dropped.

Pearl paced up and down the room. 'Oh, I could kill her. How could she do it?'

'Perhaps she can't help it,' Milly suggested. 'After all, she is sick.'

'You are so stupid sometimes,' Pearl said, exasperated. 'Don't you understand? That woman is breaking up our parents' marriage. If that happens, she will live here with her brat and we shall have to live in some pokey little cottage miles from anywhere. We won't have servants or pretty clothes.' She tugged at Milly's dressing-up things. 'And you won't be able to play any more. You'll have to go out to work like Martha.'

Milly's eyes grew wide. Pearl threw herself onto the settee and began to cry. Milly did her best to comfort her sister, but all at once Pearl sat up and pushed her away. 'We have to do something,' she said desperately.

'But what can we do?' Milly said helplessly.

Pearl rose to her feet with a sudden determination. 'I don't know, but *something*.'

After supper, the two girls had a bath and Martha washed their hair. As always it took an age to dry but eventually they were ready for bed. Martha put their clothes on a chair ready for the morning and she listened as they said their prayers. After that, she left the nightlight in the saucer on the dressing table.

'Goodnight, Miss Pearl, goodnight, Miss Milly.'

'Goodnight,' said Milly. Pearl didn't answer.

Martha closed the door and they heard her going downstairs.

'Whatever you do,' Pearl hissed in Milly's ear as Martha's footsteps faded, 'don't go to sleep.'

'Why ever not?'
'Because as soon as they're all in bed, we're going out.'
'Going out?' said Milly. 'Where?'
'To sort this out once and for all.'

Chapter 4

Milly did her best to keep her eyes open, but the next thing she knew, Pearl was shaking her awake.

'What? What's happening'

'Shh,' Pearl said.

Milly blinked and put on her glasses. Her sister was fully dressed and she was wearing her coat. The nightlight was guttering in the saucer, casting long moving shadows over the ceiling. The house was deathly quiet.

Pearl pushed Milly's coat towards her. 'Here, put this on and be quick about it. You haven't got time to get dressed now.'

Milly was already feeling uneasy. 'Why? Where are we going?'

'Keep your voice down,' her sister hissed. 'I'll tell you when you've got your coat on.'

Milly pulled her coat over her nightie. Using the guttering nightlight, Pearl lit a long candle, swung a canvas bag over her shoulder and beckoned Milly to follow her. The two of them crept along the landing and down the stairs. In the downstairs cloakroom, Pearl put on her shoes while Milly slid her bare feet into her wellington boots. She watched as Pearl grabbed a torch and blew out the candle, which she then stuffed into the bag. With a great deal of stealth, she opened the back door and they stepped outside. It was very dark when the door closed behind them, and the two girls hurried along the wall of the house until they reached the lawn, then set off across the grass towards the ha-ha. It had been raining.

By the time they reached it, Milly was really scared. She was trembling with the cold and her heart was going like the clappers. Pearl was the first to jump the ha-ha, but Milly was frozen to the spot. She started at the sound of every strange noise: snuffling sounds, an owl hooting, and something rustling in the ditch below them. White shapes were moving about near the edge of the woods, and her heart was in her mouth until she realised they were sheep.

'I want to go back,' Milly whimpered.

'Well you can't,' said Pearl.

'But I don't like it out here in the dark,' Milly complained, her voice wobbling. 'It's spooky.'

'Come on or you can stay here on your own!'

As Milly landed beside her, Pearl grabbed her arm and pulled her closer. Look,' she spat, 'if you want Mummy and Daddy to stay together, we have to do this. Do you really want them to get a divorce and have him leave us to live with that awful woman?'

Milly's eyes pooled with tears as she shook her head miserably. 'No.'

'So come on then and keep your voice down.'

Pearl led the way with the torch. They moved as quietly as they could, although Milly's wellies made squishy noises on the wet grass.

By the time they reached the cottage, it was raining again. The only sign of life was a soft light in the bedroom. They crept along the wall but there was no room to hide under the eaves now that it was full of logs. Ducking under the window, Pearl crawled on her hands and knees until she found a small recess. Sitting with her back to the wall, she struck a match and lit the candle, then motioned Milly to join her. As they both squatted over the wet ground, Pearl pulled the canvas bag from her shoulder. Milly caught her breath as her sister took out a doll, a book and a knife.

'That's my old dolly,' Milly said surprised. 'You never asked if you could bring her. Give her back.'

But Pearl wasn't listening. She rubbed the doll's face in the mud.

'Stop it!' Milly squeaked. 'Give her back. She's my dolly.'

But her sister batted her hand away.

In the room above them, another child – a girl called Lena – lay very still. Her heart was beating faster than normal but she was doing her best to quell the fear already creeping up her body. This was the first time she'd ever slept in a house. Her mother had warned her it was bound to feel strange, and it did. Lena lived in a world of fairground rides and living in caravans, which moved from one place to another. Now she was tucked up in bed inside bricks and mortar. She didn't like the feeling of being hemmed in and now, more alarmingly, she could hear odd noises coming from outside in the dark.

Life with the travellers was never quiet. As soon as they'd pitched up on a gaff, she would usually hear the cries of the showmen claiming their patch of grass, and that was sometimes followed by an argument. Once the riding master was satisfied, the chaps would start setting up framework for the rides. Depending on who was with them, that could be anything from chairoplanes to dodgems; from knock-'em-downs to the coconut shy. While the men did the hard graft, the women, including her mother, would unpack the caravans and set up home for the next few days. The chavies like herself would put the horses out to grass, although these days horses were being used less and less. After all, this was 1930, and the motor vehicle was now the way to go.

Once everything was set up, the noise from the fairground rides filled the night air until quite late. She would fall asleep to the sound of the wheezers and maniacal laughter coming from the ghost train, or the music from the carousel and the cries of the hawkers as they tried to tempt the public to part with their money. That sort of sound didn't faze her, but the sound of scrambling and hissy whispers from under the window bothered her a lot because she had no idea who was out there.

'*Give her back. She's my dolly.*'

Lena pulled the bedcovers right over the top of her head. In December, when everybody gathered around the Yuletide fire, Big Alice would tell them spooky stories. She knew loads of them, and Lena enjoyed hearing about the Vikings who haunted Kingley Vale near Stoughton, or the dragon that lived on Bignor Hill, or the Sussex Fairies, mythical creatures who would dance on Harrow Hill or Cissbury Ring. The stories were fun when she was sitting next to her mother, Angel, and they were all wrapped up warm, but it didn't feel so good now. It was worrying to think that this house was close to Patching village and Cissbury Ring was just the other side of Findon. She shivered. Could the sounds she was hearing be the Fairies under her window? And if so, what did it mean? Every part of her wanted to run to her mother's room and tell her that she was scared. Under normal circumstances her mother would lift the blankets and she could snuggle down close to her, but she couldn't do that now. Angel was ill. Very ill.

Sucking in her lips with fear, Lena pulled the pillow around her ears.

Outside, under the eaves, the girls were still arguing. 'I don't see why you're making such a fuss. You never play with her anyway.'

'That's not the point,' said Milly, reaching out to take her doll back. 'She's mine.'

When Pearl whacked her sister on the head with it, Milly knew she'd lost the argument. She rubbed her head miserably. 'What are you going to do with her anyway?'

'Cast a spell.'

Milly snorted, but all at once she realised Pearl was deadly serious. 'Don't be silly. You can't do that,' she protested. 'It's bad.'

Pearl poked her finger in the doll's eye and it caved in. 'She's the one who's bad,' she said, jerking her head towards the window. 'The tart.'

Milly took in her breath noisily. Her sister had the big book in her hand. She didn't need to ask what it was; she had seen it often enough, although she'd never read it herself. Just the title was enough to scare her half to death. *Witches, Spells and Folklore.*

Now Milly was terrified. Every part of her wanted to get up and run away but somehow she was transfixed. Did she believe in spells? She wasn't sure, but right now she wished herself a million miles away.

'Don't make a sound,' Pearl cautioned.

Milly frowned as her sister took hold of her hand and held it palm upwards. What was she going to do now? All at once, Pearl drew the knife across Milly's palm.

'*Argh.*'

'Shh!'

Milly whimpered in pain as her blood dripped onto the open pages of the book. As she snatched her hand back and held it to her chest, Pearl ran the knife across her own hand. They both watched as her blood fell onto the book as well. Milly sucked in her silent tears. Her hand hurt. Really hurt. But Pearl wasn't finished yet. She grabbed Milly's hand back and interlaced their fingers until their blood mingled. She then began her incantation.

'Black night, full moon, I call on all nature to witness . . .'

Milly wasn't really listening to what was being said. Her only feeling, apart from the pain across her palm, was a terrible fear that at any minute God would strike her dead for what she was doing.

Pearl held the doll up with her other hand. 'May this doll bring a thousand curses upon the Jezebel who stole our father . . .'

Milly was shivering uncontrollably now. She didn't much like the doll. It had a funny snub nose, and the eye Pearl had pushed in never did open properly, but her sister was making the doll, her doll, a part of something very, very scary. It was wicked. Evil.

Milly snatched her hand away to hug her knees.

Pearl held the doll up. 'I charge you to do all in your power to bring pain and death . . .' And with that she rubbed the doll's face in the mud once more, then threw it to the back of the log pile.

At exactly the same moment, the candle spluttered and went out. Pearl grabbed at Milly's hand again. Milly gasped. 'Oh please,' she whispered feebly. 'Please, Pearl, don't.'

But Pearl wasn't listening. She pressed Milly's hand onto the book. 'Say Amen.'

'I don't want to,' Milly snivelled plaintively.

Pearl dug her fingers into her flesh and squeezed her hand really hard. 'Say Amen.'

'No. It's not right, Pearl. The things you've said, they're wicked.'

'Say it,' Pearl hissed. She began to prise Milly's middle two fingers apart. Milly held out as long as she could, but eventually the pain was so bad she had to give in. 'Amen,' she choked.

Pearl looked up at the window. 'That'll teach you, bitch,' she snarled out loud.

Milly held her sore fingers and rocked herself. Pearl wiped the bloody knife on the grass and put it back into the canvas bag. When Pearl lifted the book up, Milly could see their blood running in a trail across it. Her sister fished around in the bag and took out a much smaller book and kissed the cover.

'Now kiss this,' she said, holding it open for Milly.

Milly kissed the tissue-paper page. Her sister slammed the book shut and Milly felt sick. Pearl stuffed it in the bag. 'Come on,' she whispered. 'We'd better go. It's going to take ages to get ourselves cleaned up.'

In the room above them, Lena pulled the bedclothes down. She could still hear the Fairies whispering under the window, but then one of them said something out loud.

'That'll teach you, bitch.'

Taking a deep breath, Lena climbed out of bed and crept towards the curtain and lifted it. It was raining and it was dark, but below the window she could just make out two shapes. How weird. They were much bigger than she'd expected. In fact they looked more like people than Fairies. Children. They were two children. Two girls who looked a little older than herself.

Lena dropped the curtain and frowned. What were two girls doing outside the house in the rain at this time of night? More to the point, who were they? She waited a second or two before she lifted the edge of the curtain again and saw one girl running away. The other one was on all fours, scurrying as fast as she could behind her. Even though the only light was from the moon, Lena could see that her bottom was only covered by a wet nightie, and although she wore wellington boots, her feet were slipping and sliding on the mud. All at once, the girl stood up and turned her head towards the cottage. Lena dropped the curtain.

Pearl was running as fast as she could towards the ha-ha, but something made Milly pause and turn back to take one last look at the cottage. As she did so, she saw the curtain in the bedroom fall. Her heart went into her mouth. They'd been seen. Somebody knew what they'd done. With a whimper of terror, Milly raced to catch up with her sister.

Chapter 5

Back in the house, both girls were soaked to the skin. Milly couldn't stop shivering. Her chest was tight and her hand, especially her middle two fingers, hurt like mad. Her crying had become great gulping sounds and, much to Pearl's irritation, even her teeth chattered noisily.

'Shut up, will you,' Pearl hissed. 'You'll wake somebody up.'

'You shouldn't have done it,' Milly sobbed miserably.

But Pearl was triumphant. 'But we both did it, didn't we? We cursed that woman. She'll die now, for sure.'

'That's an awful thing to say,' Milly protested. Tears and snot ran down to her chin.

Her sister's expression softened. 'Is your hand still bleeding? Ah yes, I can see it is. Poor you.' She smirked. 'See? That's proof that you're in it as much as I am. So shut up!'

Milly wiped her eyes and blew her nose. She had never felt so dreadful. They cleaned themselves up as best they could then crept back to bed. As they passed the grandfather clock in the hall, it struck three. Up in their bedroom, they both put on dry nightdresses before getting into bed.

Unperturbed by the night's events, Pearl plumped up

her pillow and settled down to sleep immediately. Milly lay on her back, staring at the ceiling, desperately trying to get warm. Her silent tears ran down her cheeks and onto her pillow. Those awful words reverberated around in her head.

'. . . *do all in your power to bring pain and death* . . .'

They shouldn't have done it.

'*May this doll bring a thousand curses* . . .'

Not one curse but a thousand. The words wouldn't go away. Restless, Milly turned on her side. Only witches said curses. Did this mean she was a witch? She knew her father's friend was ill, but what if she died? Would that make it her fault? Was it really possible to curse someone to death? She turned over again but, still engulfed in her own misery, she couldn't sleep.

'Pearl,' she eventually whispered into the darkness, 'what was that book you made me kiss? You know, the little one?'

'The Bible, of course,' said Pearl.

And Milly's blood ran cold.

A few hundred yards away, Lena pulled the bedcovers over her head again. She wished Pa was here. She had been a bit anxious about moving to the cottage but, apart from the strangeness of being in a house, it had been all right. A nurse cared for Angel and a woman called Nan cooked their food and cleaned up after them. Lena amused herself as best she could, but she was distracted. She worried that her mother might take a long time to get better. One look at her poor skinny body was proof enough of how ill she was. Angel had a bad cough as well. Sometimes she coughed so hard she had blood on her hanky, but no one ever seemed to notice or, if they did, they never said anything. Lena didn't want to worry her mother, so she didn't point it out either.

Completely covered by the sheet, Lena wondered what it was like to be dead. Would it be like being asleep? When Granny Roe died, the vicar said she'd gone to heaven, but how did she get there? If Angel ever died, would she go to heaven? Lena hoped so, but there was no guarantee, was there. And if her mother did die, who would look after her? The fairground people were the only family she had, but she wasn't actually related to any of them. Again, she thought of Pa. Dear, loving Pa. She and her mother adored him, but they weren't with him all the time. Pa would know what to do. He would look after her – wouldn't he?

'Oh Pa,' she whispered and, burying her face into the pillow, Lena cried herself to sleep.

The next morning, Milly and Pearl woke up late. As soon as Martha bustled into the room, everything seemed to be a mad panic to get ready for school, so Milly didn't have a chance to talk to her sister about the previous evening's events.

Once their cases were packed and they had eaten breakfast, Dixon brought the car around to take Pearl to Worthing station. It had been decided that she should set off first because her school was just outside of Brighton. She was to catch the train by herself, but she wouldn't be alone. She'd be travelling with her school friends.

Milly had to go to Chichester and, being that much younger, she wasn't allowed to do the journey by herself. As soon as he got back from the station, Dixon would drive her all the way to her school.

Pearl left the house without even saying goodbye. The events of last night didn't appear to have bothered her. Meanwhile, Milly couldn't stop thinking about what they'd done. The blood-letting, the curse, and chucking her dolly with the stuck sunken eye to the back of the wood pile played on her mind. Thank goodness it couldn't talk. How could she live with herself if somebody found out? With a bit of luck, nobody had seen or heard them. There was a moment when she'd fancied she'd seen the curtain move, but it was very dark, so maybe she was mistaken.

She told herself it was all make-believe anyway – kids' stuff. Yes, it was stupid and cruel, but it was only a game. There was no way Pearl would know how to actually curse someone, but even that thought didn't make Milly feel any better.

Milly stayed in her bedroom for as long as she could. Her father wasn't home and she couldn't face the servants. She feared they'd see in her eyes that something was wrong. Besides, after being out in the pouring rain, she had a headache and a bit of a sore throat coming. If she hung around in the kitchen, Mrs Cunningham might make her stay at home until they'd called the doctor, and Milly was desperate to get away; away from the house and away from the cottage.

It was only when Mrs Cunningham called up the stairs to say that Dixon had returned from the station and was ready to go that Milly suddenly remembered her shoes. Her stomach did a somersault. Her mother had gone off to London and she still hadn't bought her a new pair. Her father had left the house the day before on business. What on earth was she going to do? Would the servants have enough money and the time to buy shoes? She hoped they would. Her father would pay them back for sure.

'I'm sorry, my dear,' said Mrs Cunningham, when Milly asked if Dixon could take her into town, 'but there's nothing we can do about it. We can't take on a responsibility like that. You'll just have to take your old shoes.'

'But they hurt my toes,' Milly protested as Cook tried to squeeze Milly's feet inside them.

'They do seem a bit tight,' Mrs Cunningham remarked.

'Here, give them to me,' said Dixon and, taking a very sharp knife, he cut away the front. When he'd finished, Milly put them on. Her toes stuck out a long way beyond the sole of her shoes and they looked pretty awful, but at least she could walk without pain. Milly could only imagine what the other girls at school would say, and now that Dixon had cut them, there was no going back. It was so embarrassing she burst into tears.

'There, there, my dear,' said Mrs Cunningham, putting her arm around Milly's shoulders. 'It'll be all right, you'll see. You just tell your teacher that your mother didn't have time to take you to buy a new pair. She'll understand. They know you're a good little girl.'

'And at least they won't cramp your feet any more,' Dixon said chirpily, 'not with your toes flapping in the wind like that.'

Mrs Cunningham gave him a hefty nudge in the ribs.

A few minutes later, Milly climbed into the back seat of the car. She didn't wave goodbye, even though Mrs Cunningham and Martha stood on the steps for her. She felt too miserable. She stared down at her feet again. She was going to be a laughing stock in the dorm, but maybe she deserved it. Mrs Cunningham thought she was a good girl, but she wasn't, was she? Good girls, nice girls, didn't go about casting curses over sick people. God must be very angry with her. Perhaps this was her punishment for what she and Pearl had done.

Over in the cottage, Lena woke up to the smell of toast, so she knew Nan was already in the kitchen. After a wash, she got dressed and hurried to her mother's bedroom, but the nurse had barred the door with a chair.

'Come back in a minute, lovey,' she called as Lena tried the handle. 'We won't be long.'

Lena knew better than to argue. The nurse would be giving Angel a wash, then changing her bed sheets and putting on a clean nightie. They didn't want Lena in the room. 'Sick people don't like anyone popping in when they're getting dressed,' Nan had said kindly when Lena first arrived in the cottage. 'Your mum will call you when she's ready.'

In the kitchen, Nan and her husband, Cyril, who acted as a general handyman, sat at the table with serious faces. Nan rose to her feet as Lena walked in.

'Ready for your breakfast, dear?' She was a cheerful woman, as round as she was tall. From what Lena could gather, she and Cyril had no children of their own but they treated her very well. They spent all day in the cottage, and one or the other of them stayed all night, even though they had their own place at the opposite end of the village near the bottom of Bost Hill. Cyril had promised to take her up the hill to see the windmill at the top of High Salvington.

Nan bustled around the kitchen and eventually put a plate of bacon and eggs with fried bread in front of Lena. A cup of strong tea followed. Lena ate everything but she struggled a little. She didn't like to ask about her mother's condition, but she knew something had changed. There was a new atmosphere in the house, one which made her feel anxious.

When she'd finished her meal, the nurse still wasn't done, so Lena put on her coat and went outside. It was still damp after all the rain the previous evening, but the sun was making a valiant effort to dry everything up. She thought again about last night. Had she really heard the Fairies or had she imagined it? Surely the Sussex Fairies weren't real. They were just a part of local folklore, weren't they? Plus, when she had looked out of the window, she had definitely seen human children. As she pondered this, she wandered around to the wood pile under the window of the boxroom which served as her bedroom.

She saw the footprints first. A few clear prints and a large number of squishy mud slides by the recess, so now she knew for sure she hadn't heard the Sussex Fairies. Whoever had made these marks was definitely human. There was a candle stuck in the mud and, right at the back of the log pile, she saw a dolly. Its legs were sticking up. It took a little effort to reach it because she had to be careful not to let the logs tumble, but eventually Lena managed to pull the dolly out. It looked a sorry sight. Its face was caked in mud and one eye had sunk right into its head. The doll's hair stuck up all over the place, as if someone had given it a very bad haircut, but it did have a very pretty floral dress, so it must have been loved once. Lena recalled a voice crying out, 'Give her back. She's my dolly.' Perhaps she should try and find the little girl who owned the doll. It would have been very hard to see it right at the back of the wood pile in the dark, and she did sound upset about it, but why did she put it there in the first place?

Back in the kitchen, Lena tried to wash the mud from the doll's face, but it was difficult because she didn't want to let too much water get into the doll's eye socket. It came as almost a relief when she heard the nurse calling her name. 'Your mum wants to see you, dear,' the nurse said, but as Lena reached the door, the woman tugged at her arm. 'Try not to tire her, dear. She's had a very bad night.'

As she entered her mother's bedroom, Lena turned and saw Nan giving her an encouraging smile but, before that, she'd caught a glimpse of the expression on her face. Nan was red-eyed and upset, and Lena had a feeling that – even though she and the nurse were smiling – something was very wrong.

Chapter 6

Milly opened her eyes slowly and frowned. Everything was swimming and she was very hot. Her head hurt too. Where was she? And how did she get here? She was in bed but she wasn't in her bedroom at home. Everything seemed to be white. The walls were white. The sheets were white. She tried to move but her whole body ached.

'Oh, there you are,' said a voice. 'You're awake.' And someone in a nurse's uniform appeared above her, starched cap bobbing on her head. The nurse squeezed out a flannel that she had dipped in a bowl of water on the locker beside the bed, and wiped it over Milly's burning face. Oooh, that was so refreshing.

Milly passed her tongue over her dry lips.

'Let me give you a little drink,' said the nurse, slipping her hand under Milly's head and bringing a glass of water to her lips. The water felt wonderfully cool on her swollen and parched tongue. Milly drank greedily. 'Steady now,' she said. 'Not too much, too quickly, or you'll be sick.'

As the nurse helped Milly lie back down, her patient tried to make sense of what was happening. Was she dreaming? No, her thumping headache told her this was real enough. A more thorough glance around at her surroundings told her she was in the school sick bay and the nurse was in fact Matron. But why was she here?

Matron stuffed a thermometer into her mouth and held her wrist as she looked at her fob watch. Milly closed her eyes again until she heard Matron say, 'That's better.'

'Have I been ill?' Milly's voice was croaky and she sounded really bunged up.

'You most certainly have. You gave us quite a fright,' said Matron, scribbling something onto a clipboard at the end of the bed. 'But not to worry. You seem to be on the mend now.' She paused for a second before adding, 'Your father is on his way.'

'Daddy?' Milly gasped incredulously. Her thoughts took off at a hundred miles an hour. Parents weren't allowed to come in term time – not unless something was very wrong, like when Katie Stewart's granny died. Had something happened to Mummy? She caught her breath. Or maybe he had found out about the terrible thing she and Pearl had done at the cottage. Her eyes grew wide with fear. Oh no! Don't say the curse had worked. That woman . . . she wasn't dead, was she?

'My dear girl, you've gone as white as a sheet,' said Matron, patting her hand gently. 'It's all right. Nobody is cross with you. You can't help being poorly. Your father is coming to take you home.'

Milly relaxed against the pillows.

'Now listen,' Matron said brightly, 'I'm just going down to the kitchen to get you a little something to eat. You haven't had anything for two days and I'm sure you must be feeling very hungry. I shan't be long.' She hurried from the room and the door closed behind her.

Two days. She'd been here for two whole days. Milly tried to remember what had happened but her mind was a blank. How had forty-eight hours of her life completely vanished? She remembered that she'd felt pretty grotty when she'd got up on Sunday morning, the day Dixon brought her back to school. The journey had been uneventful and it had been good to see her old friends again, especially Sarah Whitmore, the girl who slept in the bed next to her in the dorm. However, as the day had worn on, she'd felt worse and worse. In the end, she had gone to bed early. She'd tried to sleep but everybody in the dorm kept talking until all hours.

On Monday they'd had physical education on the front lawn, but by then she was feeling so awful it was really hard to do the exercises. Miss Averard had shouted at her a couple of times but Milly hadn't been able to follow the instructions. Her limbs had felt like lead, her throat hurt like billy-o and her head had been banging. How she'd got through the day, she never knew. Of course she'd got into hot water about her shoes . . . she knew she would. Everyone was cross with her and they seemed to think she was pretending to be ill to avoid facing punishment. She'd even got a detention for falling asleep on the desk, even though she wasn't actually asleep. It had simply become too difficult to hold her head up. She tried to tell them but nobody was listening. The headmistress, Miss Christie, threatened to ring Mummy.

'I imagine you put those shoes in your wardrobe at the end of last term and didn't say a word to your mother,' Miss Christie said icily. 'And now I have to embarrass her by telling her she must come to the school to take you out and buy some. Why you girls can't use a little more common sense, I'll never know.'

Miss Spencer, her form mistress, was the only person who showed any kindness, but even she couldn't seem to understand that Milly really and truly didn't feel well. Milly couldn't remember being sent to the sick bay. The last thing she recalled was pitching forward in the music room. Sarah had tried to catch her but hadn't been able to hold her.

There had been a lot of noise and somebody had screamed. Had she crashed into some chairs? Yes, she rather thought she had. But what had happened after that? Frustrated with herself, Milly shook her head. Everything was a blur. She couldn't remember.

Matron came back with some cold rice pudding. 'This is all I could find,' she apologised, 'but it'll have to do.'

Milly sat up and fumbled for her glasses which were on the bedside locker. Putting them on, she pulled the rice pudding towards her. She managed a few mouthfuls but the congealed stodgy pudding wasn't very appetising. It stuck to her mouth and clogged her oh-so-sore throat, making her gag.

A little later, the head came into the sick bay with her father. It was a wonderful surprise. As soon as she saw him, Milly felt a mixture of joy and apprehension – joy because she was feeling so rotten and it was wonderful to see someone who really cared about her, and apprehension because she wondered if Miss Christie had rung him to complain. While Milly struggled to sit up she felt her father's strong arms pulling her close. He was warm and smelled of Knize Ten, the gentleman's toilet water. While Miss Christie wrung her hands as she explained that Milly hadn't mentioned to anyone that she was feeling ill, father and daughter hugged each other. As they parted, Charles handed Milly a small present. It was a little stuffed dog. It was a bit babyish but, because he had given it to her, Milly loved it. She lay back on the pillow with the dog next to her cheek.

'Poor old Sweet-pea,' he said, stroking her cheek as he ignored Miss Christie's prattling. 'Sit up, darling. I'm taking you home.'

Matron offered to help Milly dress but her father waved her away. Snatching the blanket from the bed, he wrapped it around his daughter like a cocoon and swept her into his arms. With Matron right behind them, twittering on about the blanket belonging to the school, they thundered down the stairs. Dixon was sitting in the driver's seat of her father's car. When he saw them coming, he leapt out and opened the back passenger door. Milly was aware of half the school leaning out of the windows to watch the spectacle as Miss Spencer hurried outside with Milly's case. Charles Shepherd laid his daughter on the back seat and tucked the blanket around her.

'We'll soon have you home and in your own bed.' He winked and pressed the end of her nose. As he stood up, Dixon took the case and Miss Spencer handed the mutilated shoes to her father. A dark frown clouded his face as her form mistress explained why they looked as they did. Milly expected a row or, at the very least, a bit of a fuss, but her father took the shoes from her and, having examined them, he stepped aside and threw them, one at a time, to the far side of the front lawn with a first-class cricketer's bowling action. Then he climbed into the front passenger seat.

'Home, Dixon, and step on it.'

Dixon started the engine and they set off, leaving a shower of gravel and two astonished members of staff behind them. Lying on the back seat, all warm and cosy, Milly's heart sang. She still felt lousy but she was happy. *Sweet-pea.* Her father hadn't called her that in years. She was excited to get back to Muntham Court with him. Best of all, she would never have to wear those terrible shoes again.

After two more days in her own bed, Milly was feeling so much better. Mummy was still in London, so her day-to-day care was down to her father and the household staff, which was lovely because everybody made a fuss of her. Mrs Cunningham made her favourite dishes, lemon curd tart and jam roly-poly, Martha came and played cards with her and, best of all, one afternoon Bodkin, the old gardener, brought Cleo over in a wicker basket. The cat was as delighted to see

Milly as Milly was to see her, and it was lovely to hear from Bodkin about how she was getting on in her new home.

'Your Cleo's got a gentleman friend,' said Bodkin. 'She gets out at night a-singing on the wall 'ith him.' He grinned and elbowed Milly in the ribs. 'I reckon she'll be 'aving his kittens afore long.'

Once Milly was fully recovered, her father still checked in on her regularly, but he spent most of his time at the cottage. She would kneel on the window seat in her bedroom, her little stuffed dog under her arm, and watch him walk across the grass, jump over the ha-ha and head towards the woods. Milly was still terrified that someone in the cottage would tell him what she and Pearl had done but, with each passing day, nothing was mentioned, so she became less anxious.

Each evening, Milly and her father had a meal together. To begin with he came up to her bedroom but, after a few days, she was allowed downstairs.

'I should very much like you to meet someone before you go back to school, Milly,' he said lighting his after-dinner cigarette. 'Dr Jennings says you should be well enough to return at the weekend, and by that time you shall have had a whole ten days to recover.'

It was a bitter-sweet moment for Milly. She had so enjoyed being with her father and, if she was being honest, the absence of her mother, who found fault with her all the time, meant that being home was a lot more relaxing than it usually was. Best of all, for the first time in her life, she'd been thoroughly spoiled.

Her father coughed. 'In a couple of days' time,' he continued, 'we'll both go down to the cottage together.'

Milly sucked in her lips and held her breath, but luckily her father didn't seem to notice. Finishing his whisky, he stood up and kissed the top of her head. 'Night, darling. Sweet dreams.' And with that he left the room.

As she cuddled her toy dog, Milly's heart was racing and

her breathing was ragged. Did her father actually want her to meet his hussy? What if her mother found out that she'd been down to the cottage? Or Pearl, for that matter. Then there was the small matter of the woman herself. Supposing she was a witch like Pearl had said. Milly shivered. Would she be able to see through her? Would she know what she and Pearl had done?

No, she couldn't do it. She'd tell her father she couldn't possibly go down to the cottage and meet her.

She didn't dare.

Chapter 7

A couple of days later, her father told her they were going to the cottage. Milly said she'd rather stay inside, but her father wasn't having any of it. 'It's time you had a breath of fresh air,' Charles insisted. 'Don't forget that I have to get you a new pair of shoes before you go back to school.'

That was true enough. Right now she was confined to wearing either her slippers or wellies, and she certainly couldn't turn up to school on Sunday in them!

With her toy dog under her arm, Milly trailed after her father on the walk to the cottage with a heavy heart. As she passed the eaves, she felt terrible. What on earth had possessed her and her sister to say those horrible words?

To Milly's great surprise, the door was opened by a young girl. 'Pa!' she cried as she wrapped her arms around his waist.

Milly pushed up her glasses. The girl was a bit younger than herself, possibly nine or ten, with long dark hair and a small elfin face. She was very slim, with bright eyes and a smile that lit up her whole face. Milly was more than a little puzzled when her father laughed and leaned over the girl to return her hug. Who was she? Her father had mentioned that there would be another person in the cottage but why was he hugging her like that?

As their embrace ended, Milly's father said, 'And how are we today?'

The little girl grinned. 'Very-well-thank-you-sir,' she said in a well-rehearsed mantra.

'Well done.' Milly's father glanced towards the bedroom door. 'And how is your poor mother?'

'Better,' said the girl.

Milly's father smiled and patted her shoulder. 'I'll leave you two to get to know each other,' he said, before heading towards the bedroom door. He went in quietly and closed the door behind him. The two children eyed each other cautiously.

'Hello,' said the girl. 'My name is Lena.'

Lena was dressed in a strange costume, and Milly thought she looked a bit foreign. Her dark hair was held together under a minuscule floral headscarf, and she had soft brown eyes. Her face was slightly bronzed, as if she'd spent a lot of time out of doors.

Milly put her hand out. 'I'm Milly,' she said stiffly. 'How do you do?'

Without warning, the girl threw herself onto the settee with a perfectly executed somersault. She giggled at Milly's amazed expression then told her, 'We've come here to live for a while until Angel gets better.'

'I know,' said Milly.

'Where do you live?'

'In the big house,' said Milly. Lena eyed her steadily, so she added, 'Where do you come from?'

'All over,' said Lena, with a wide sweep of her arm. 'We be fairground folk. The gaffer is Rainbow George. He's really famous. 'Ave you 'eard of 'im?'

Milly shook her head and Lena pulled the corners of her mouth down. ''E's got some swing boats so we goes all round,' she went on, as if it really didn't matter anyway.

'The Lamb Fair at 'orsham, Tunbridge Wells common, Uckfield in the Bell Brook fairground and Findon o' course.' She counted them off on her fingers. 'That's where they met, at Findon.'

'Where who met?' asked Milly, slightly bewildered.

'Angel and Pa.'

Milly pushed her glasses back up her nose, none the wiser as to what the girl was on about.

'I likes your little dog,' said Lena. 'Can I 'old him?'

Milly handed the toy dog over. Lena stroked its head and kissed its muzzle.

'Do you want to see my mouse?' Lena asked and, without waiting for an answer, she took Milly to the small scullery where she pulled a round tin from under the shelf. It had once contained biscuits, but someone had drilled holes in the top. Lena sat cross-legged on the floor and pulled the lid off very carefully. Inside, a little black and tan mouse scurried under some straw.

'It's a real one!' Milly exclaimed.

Lena nodded. ''Course he's real.'

'Where did you get it?'

'I found him,' she said. 'He was ever so 'ungry. I calls him Sooty on account of his colour. Lovely, inne? You can stroke 'im if you likes.'

Milly had to agree that he was a sweet little mouse, but quite what Mrs Cunningham, or her mother for that matter, would think of keeping a pet mouse in the cottage was beyond anyone's guess. However, she stroked his soft fur and he stood up on his back legs to look at her.

They heard a door close behind them and her father was coming back. 'Ah,' he said. 'I see you two have made friends.'

Lena put the lid back on the tin.

'Now,' said Milly's father, 'how would you like to come into Worthing with us, Lena? Milly needs to buy some new shoes.'

Lena clapped her hands delightedly.

'Better get your coat and tell Angel where you're going.'

As Lena skipped happily towards the bedroom door, Milly's father smiled. 'I'm glad you both get on. I wanted you to like each other.'

Milly gave him a puzzled frown. 'Why?'

'Don't you know yet?' he said. 'I would have thought you should have worked it out by now. Lena is your half-sister.'

Milly would have enjoyed the ride into Worthing a lot more had her father not dropped his bombshell. Lena was her father's daughter? How come nobody had ever mentioned her before? Did her mother know? No, she couldn't possibly. Had she known, her mother would have been overwhelmed by the scandal. Although . . . perhaps her mother did know. Maybe that was why she had taken herself off to London. What was going to happen next? Were her parents about to get a divorce? Did Pearl know they had a half-sister? Come to that, did Lena know that she had not one but two half-sisters? Struck dumb and feeling very uncomfortable with Lena sitting next to her, Milly did her best to stay calm. As for Lena herself, she was very chatty, her words tumbling from her mouth like a waterfall.

'I've never bin to Worving before. 'Ave you bin to Worving? Rainbow George, he were born in a caravan behind the Clifton Arms in Worving. There used to be a patch of wasteground round the back and when the babby was comin', Willis 'ardham, he were the landlord, he said Rainbow George could be born there. Will we be goin' by the Clifton Arms, Pa? I should like to see 'in.'

Milly's father chuckled. 'We'll see,' he said. 'Perhaps on the way home.'

Milly turned and looked out of the window, her thoughts tossing around in her head like dice in a cup. How on earth had this happened? If the hussy was Lena's mother, that must mean that Daddy had two wives. But that couldn't be right, could it? You weren't allowed to have two wives. You could go to prison for that.

She and Lena were sitting together on the back seat of the car. Dixon was driving and Daddy sat in the front passenger seat, so Milly couldn't help giving her half-sister surreptitious glances. She did look a bit like her; they both had the same colour hair and the same brown eyes, although of course Milly's were hidden behind her glasses. She had guessed that Lena was at least a year younger than her, and she had a slightly smaller build, but there was something about her that reminded Milly of Daddy. Gosh, a secret sister.

The town was fairly busy for a Friday afternoon. Dixon parked the car near the Arcade by the seafront and their father asked him to be back by five-thirty. With a touch of his cap, Dixon turned away from them and melted into the crowd.

'First things first,' Charles said cheerfully. 'Milly's shoes.'

They found the perfect pair of boring school shoes in Stead & Simpson on South Street. The assistant seemed to know exactly what was required. 'A sensible shoe,' she said, producing her shoehorn from a pocket in her overall. 'It's well made, it has a round toe so that there's plenty of room for a little girl's toes to grow, and it has laces. Can you do up your laces all by yourself, dear?'

'Yes, I can, thank you.' Milly was slightly offended but she didn't answer back. Of course she could do up her laces. She wasn't a little kid! They all watched her as she put the shoes on. Both girls were totally underwhelmed by them, but their father was content to part with his money. Milly was just happy that they didn't hurt.

Bentall & Son's department store was next door. Their father took them in and strode towards the children's department. The three of them emerged twenty minutes later with two pretty cardigans, one each, and a dress for Lena. Milly decided that this was better than shopping with Mummy! For the first time ever, she'd actually been asked which cardigan she would like and her opinion had counted.

'Well now,' said their father as they left the department with their parcels, 'I think afternoon tea is in order. Young ladies like tea and cake, don't they?'

He took them upstairs to the restaurant. Milly could hardly believe her eyes and, judging by the expression on Lena's face, neither could she. A waitress in a black dress and the tiniest frilly apron Milly had ever seen came over to them.

'Table for three, please,' said Charles, 'a window seat if possible.'

They followed her to a table which overlooked South Street itself. The two girls sat opposite each other and next to the window, while their father ordered tea, two glasses of milk and cakes. The restaurant was fairly full and Milly couldn't help noticing that every now and then, a lady carrying a number on a card sauntered leisurely past their table. The girls were fascinated to watch as she turned this way and that in front of the tables where well-dressed women were having their afternoon tea, and then moved on. When the waitress came back she brought a whole cake stand and they were allowed to choose whatever they wanted. Lena opted for a chocolate cherry cake. Milly had a slice of iced lemon cake. Their father drank his tea and smoked his cigarette contentedly. To Milly's surprise, the lady they'd seen before reappeared wearing a completely different outfit. She carried a different number on her card, but she still did her twirl in front of the other customers.

'What's she doing?' Milly whispered.

Their father chuckled. 'She's a mannequin,' he said. 'She's

showing everyone the dress she's wearing and, if they like it, they can go to the dress department, tell the assistant the number and then they can try it on for themselves. It's a way of selling something.'

Milly stared at the mannequin with admiration.

'When I grows up,' said Lena, showering chocolate cake crumbs onto the snowy white tablecloth, 'I's going to be a nanny kin.'

Chapter 8

On the journey back to Muntham Court, the two girls sat side by side on the back seat once again, but this time Milly was more relaxed. Lena opened her parcel and took out her new cardigan. Milly thought that it was very pretty but not quite as nice as hers.

'I ain't never 'ad nuffing as beautiful and all brand new like this afore,' Lena whispered as she smoothed the dainty flowers all down the front of the cardigan. She glanced up at Milly. 'And I likes 'aving you as my sister.'

Milly returned a thin smile. She still wasn't sure about all this. Lena was nice enough, but what would Mummy say? 'Where did you say you lived before you came to the cottage?'

'I told you, all over,' said Lena, pushing the cardigan back between the tissue paper. 'We goes wherever there's a fair.'

'Yes, but where do you live?' Milly insisted.

'In the wagon, o' course,' said Lena. 'It used to be pulled by 'orses but we got a motor engine now.'

Milly frowned. 'Does that mean you're . . .?' She hesitated to say the word because she knew how her mother felt about them. Milly leaned closer towards her sister and whispered, 'Are you a gypsy?'

Lena's eyes grew wide. 'Don't be such a dinilow!' she said crossly. 'We ain't gypsies. We be travellers. Fairground travellers.'

Milly's mouth dropped open. 'You mean you and your mum actually run a funfair?'

Lena giggled. 'It's not just Angel and me. There be loads of us. We be all one family, see? We all pitches in. I does the hoopla.' She raised her voice. 'Roll up, roll up. Three rings fer a penny. Fabulous prizes. Three rings fer a penny.'

Their father turned round but only to smile. As he turned back, Lena whispered in Milly's ear. 'Can I 'old yer dog again?'

Milly handed it over and Lena stroked its head lovingly. 'And you live in the big 'ouse,' she said to the stuffed toy. 'Along wiv Milly and Pa.'

Milly marvelled that there didn't seem to be an ounce of jealousy in her. 'I'm only there in the holidays,' she said. 'I'm at boarding school most of the time.'

'What's boarding school?'

Milly explained.

'I bin to school a few times,' said Lena. 'They tried to learn me to read but I couldn't make 'ead nor tail of it.' She sighed. 'I should dearly like to read a book.'

'You can't read?' Milly squeaked.

Lena shook her head. 'I ain't been long enough at school to learn. Any-road, Rainbow George says it's a waste of time h'educatin' a girl 'cos they only gets married.'

'Well, I'm glad I'm at school,' Milly declared stoutly. 'And I shall wait until I'm really, really old before I get married. I shall make sure I'm at least twenty-three.'

They smiled at each other as if they'd shared a secret. Lena handed the toy dog back. Milly took a deep breath. 'You can have it if you like.'

Lena's eyes grew wide. 'You mean it?' she gasped.

Milly immediately regretted her hasty decision, but the

wide smile on Lena's face soon dispelled this feeling. She nodded her head.

Lena suddenly leapt at her and kissed her cheek. 'Fank you, fank you,' she whispered. 'I shall love 'e for ever.'

Dixon drove them to the cottage first. As soon as he stopped the car, Lena jumped out and ran inside. By the time Milly and her father went in, she was already showing Angel her beautiful dress and cardigan.

When she saw Lena's mother, Milly had a shock. She lay on the settee covered by a blanket and a nurse sat in a chair beside her, doing her knitting. It was clear from her features that Angel must have been a beautiful woman once, but now she was emaciated, haggard and her skin was grey. Milly knew she couldn't be much older than her own mother, but she looked older than Milly's grandmother, and *she* was positively ancient.

The nurse rose to her feet. 'And how is your patient today?' Charles asked.

'A little tired now,' said the nurse, packing her knitting into a bag. She glanced at Angel. 'Madam has done very well today. She managed to walk from the bedroom to the sofa by herself and she's been resting here since . . .' she consulted her watch, 'since three-twenty.'

'Stop talking about me as if I wasn't here,' Angel gently scolded as she held out her hand. Charles rushed to hold it. Milly stared as her father kissed Angel's fingers tenderly. She'd never seen him kiss her mother like that. Come to think of it, she'd never seen him kiss her mother, full stop.

As the nurse left the room, Milly shifted her feet awkwardly, unsure of what to do.

'And who is this?' Angel asked.

'Darling, this is Milly,' said Charles. There was no mistaking the emotional catch in his voice. 'My daughter.'

Milly gave Lena's mother a small curtsey. 'How do you do? My real name is Millicent but everybody calls me Milly.'

'Pleased to meet you, Milly,' Angel smiled. 'And I am very well, thank you.'

Milly's face suddenly grew red hot as she was consumed with embarrassment. Of course Angel wasn't very well, thank you. What on earth had possessed her to say that? How could she have been so stupid?

'Sorry, sorry,' Milly flustered. She pushed up her glasses and glanced her father's way, but he only had eyes for Angel.

Angel reached up and stroked his cheek then, turning her head towards Milly, she smiled. 'What a lovely daughter you have, Charles,' she said softly. 'So polite, so kind. You must be very proud of her.'

'I'm very proud of both my daughters,' her father said.

All at once, Lena burst back into the room wearing her new dress and cardigan. 'Look, look, Angel. Ain't it wonderful?' She twirled around the sofa, holding out the skirt so that everyone could see. 'It's the bestest dress I ever 'ad.'

Sharing her moment of joy, everybody laughed.

As Lena continued to twirl, Angel's face suddenly clouded and, looking up at Milly's father, she said earnestly, 'You will look after her, won't you, Charles?'

Milly's father raised Angel's hand to his mouth and kissed her palm. 'Upon my honour, I promise I will, my darling.'

Angel seemed relieved. Oblivious to this exchange, Lena bounced out of the room and came back with the toy dog. 'Look what Milly gave me,' she said excitedly.

Milly saw the look of surprise on her father's face. She chewed her bottom lip anxiously. Oh dear, she thought, he thinks I didn't like it.

'My father gave it to me,' said Milly, 'but Lena really, really liked it so . . .' She shrugged her shoulders.

'How kind you are,' said Lena's mother and, looking at Milly she said, 'Are you sure, dear?'

Milly felt her face colour but she nodded vigorously.

Charles Shepherd smiled. 'You've been very generous, Milly.'

After Milly and her father had said their goodbyes, Dixon, who had been in the kitchen sampling one of Nan's cakes, drove them back to the entrance of Muntham Court and took the car back to the garage. Milly couldn't wait to get indoors. Her mother's car was parked in the driveway, which meant she was back home. She had so much to tell her. Milly was about to dash in to show her mother her new shoes when her father caught her arm.

'Just a minute darling,' he said. 'I want to ask you something.'

He walked them towards the fountain, and they stood with their backs to the house. She waited as he took out his cigarette case and opened it. A moment later, he'd tapped one on the case and was searching his pocket for his lighter.

Milly stared into the depths of the fountain. It was beautiful. In the centre, there was a life-sized statue of a boy sitting in a shell which was held up by four dolphins. The boy was blowing through a conch shell, creating a jet of water which fell several feet into the basin beneath. There were other jets, smaller, coming from the noses and mouths of the dolphins. Live fish swam around the lily pads and hid in the recesses on all four corners. Milly trailed her fingers through the water.

'Listen Milly,' her father began cautiously, 'I'd rather you didn't tell your mother that we took Lena with us to Worthing.'

Milly looked up and was surprised by the troubled look on his face.

'I'm not asking you to lie,' he went on, 'but there's really no need to mention Lena at all.' He closed his eyes for a second then took a deep breath. 'Your mother knows all about her, so we're not keeping anything from her, but I'd rather she didn't know Lena was in the cottage. I just don't want Angel and Lena being even more upset, that's all.'

Milly nodded.

He sighed and said more to himself than to Milly, 'I never meant to hurt anybody.'

'Don't worry, Daddy.' Milly looked kindly up at him.

They exchanged a smile and he touched her arm. 'It was very nice of you to give your dog to Lena.'

'It wasn't that I didn't like it,' she said. 'It was just that she wanted it so badly.'

'I know,' said Charles, 'and I'm proud of you.' He paused as if he were about to say something else but then thought better of it. 'Come along now. Let's go in and show your mother those lovely new shoes.'

They turned towards the front door but, as they did, the French windows suddenly burst open. 'Charles?' said her mother's sharp voice. 'What are you two cooking up? And what's Millicent doing here? Why the hell isn't she in school?'

Almost as soon as they went indoors, her mother and father began having a humongous row.

'You should have told me the child was ill,' her mother thundered after Milly's father had explained why she was at home.

'Don't you dare play the injured and uninformed mother with me,' her father said angrily. 'I must have telephoned you a dozen times but you never once returned my calls.'

Her mother's eyes flashed. 'I-I was . . . busy!'

'Oh yes, you're always busy, aren't you, Agatha.' Milly could hear the sarcasm in her father's voice. 'Too busy for your children, too busy for your husband . . .'

'I love my children,' Agatha protested.

'But not enough to find the time to buy one of them a pair of shoes.'

'I'm sorry about the bloody shoes. I forgot. I do have other things to think about.' And rounding on Milly, her mother said, 'And if you had a ha'porth of sense in that silly head of yours, you should have reminded me.'

'Don't blame the child,' said her father, throwing himself into his chair. 'The only thoughts in your head are about what you want.'

'Oh for God's sake, don't start all that again!' Agatha snarled.

'Oh Mummy, I did try to tell you,' Milly said plaintively.

'Go to your room, Millicent,' her mother shrieked.

Milly didn't need telling twice.

Later that evening when the dinner gong sounded, Milly ventured downstairs to find her parents were hardly speaking to each other. The rest of the weekend followed the same pattern, spiteful arguments followed by long silences, and there were times when Milly felt like piggy-in-the-middle. It was obvious that this would mark a complete change in their family arrangements. Somehow Milly knew that her mother would spend most of her time in the London flat from now on. Her parents might not be getting a divorce, but to all intents and purposes they were going to lead separate lives.

It was almost a relief to be going back to school on Sunday afternoon. Her mother was having some friends over for tennis after luncheon so, as soon as the meal was over, Milly went upstairs to change into her uniform. It was all laid out on the bed and her new shoes were perfect.

Milly reached for her school hat on the dressing table. Knowing how fussy her mother was, she sat in front of the mirror to put it on correctly. That's when she saw it. Her hat was straight but as she looked into the glass, she saw something behind her left shoulder that almost made her heart stop. There on the bookshelf sat her dolly. She recognised her at once, even though she looked completely different. Her wild and uneven hair had been trimmed into an attractive bob, and she wore a pretty pink headband with a beautiful crocheted rose at the side. Her dress was floral, in a matching pink, and there was a white broderie anglaise petticoat peeping out from under the hem. Her eye had been partially restored, although it was still slightly out of kilter with the other one. The doll's face had been thoroughly cleaned.

Milly's heart was thumping in her chest. How had she got there?

'Millicent,' her mother called. 'Come down now, dear. I want to say goodbye.'

Judging by the soft tone of her voice, her mother's friends must have arrived. Milly chewed her bottom lip anxiously. Taking the doll from the shelf, she wrapped it in a blue shawl which was draped over the back of the chair, and looked around desperately, trying to find a place to hide it. Her mother must never see it and, if Pearl knew it was here, she'd only make trouble. Behind the bookcase, perhaps? No – the maid would spot it when she cleaned the room. On the shelf? No – someone would be bound to wonder why it was all wrapped up. Her gaze fell to the large drawer at the bottom of the chest of drawers. Milly pulled it open and stuffed the doll right at the back. Careful to leave everything else tidy at the front, she was confident no one would ever guess it was there.

'Millicent!' her mother called irritably. 'What on earth are you doing? Hurry up.'

Pushing the drawer closed, Milly called, 'Coming, Mother.'

She was still trembling as she hurried downstairs and, just as she suspected, the hall was filled with women in tennis outfits. Her mother gave her a perfunctory air kiss on both cheeks. 'Be a good girl, darling,' she said to the coos and approving sighs from the tennis players.

As they disappeared, Milly felt her knees give way.

'All right, Milly?' her father said as he caught her in his arms. 'No need to be nervous. I've had a word with Miss Christie and you'll soon settle into the swing of things.'

They walked outside to the car and he opened the back passenger door to let her in. Leaning in after her, he kissed her cheek. 'Did you see your dolly?' he asked innocently. 'Lena found it for you and Nan cleaned her up and made her a new dress. Wasn't that kind of them?'

Milly bit back her tears and nodded.

'I want you to write a letter to both of them to say thank you,' her father instructed. 'Address it to me and I'll see that they get it.'

He stepped back and closed the door. Dixon started the car and they set off. Milly and her father waved to each other until he was out of sight, but when she sat back she was filled with shame. The dolly looked wonderful but if Lena had found it by the eaves, it must mean only one thing.

Lena had heard everything she and Pearl had said that night.

Chapter 9

August 1937

'You won't forget to write.'

Susan Tice had run up to the car just as Uncle Neville was putting the suitcases in the boot. Milly turned around and gave her new best friend a hug. 'Of course I will – and you have a wonderful time.'

The two of them had spent many happy hours together since Milly had accepted an invitation to stay with Aunt Betsy (Milly's father's sister) and Uncle Neville during the school holidays. Now that Milly was going back home, Susan, who lived next door to her aunt, was going to Devon to stay with her grandmother for the rest of the summer.

Uncle Neville opened the passenger door of his 1930 Sunbeam and put Milly's painting things on the back seat while she climbed in. A minute or two later, he set off for the station in West Moors where she would catch the train to Worthing. Now that she was seventeen years old, she would be doing the journey on her own, including two changes, one at Brockenhurst and another at Southampton. The thought was both scary and exciting. The two friends waved to each other until they were out of sight, and then Milly settled back in her seat.

'Glad to be going home?' Uncle Neville asked.

Milly nodded. 'I've had a wonderful time,' she said politely, 'but yes, I shall be glad to be home.'

'We shall miss you,' Uncle Neville said with a chuckle. 'The place will be so quiet without you.'

Milly knew he was teasing her. She didn't get to see them very often, but she loved going to stay with Aunt Betsy. She never saw that much of Uncle Neville because he was a barrister and spent time in Dorchester at the county assizes. Also as a member of Bournemouth Council and the Parochial Church Council in his local church, he often had committee meetings. But of all her relatives, beside her father, he and Aunt Betsy treated her the best.

They had no children of their own, which was a shame really, because they would have been great parents. They always treated her so kindly and she had had a wonderful time playing with Susan next-door. Despite this, she was still anxious to get home.

If Milly had told Uncle Neville the real reason for wanting to be back in Findon, he might have been surprised. The truth of the matter was that she was looking forward to seeing Lena again.

Milly pursed her lips as she recalled the night so many years before when she and Pearl had sat in the dark under the window of the cottage and voiced that dreadful curse. Even after all this time, the horror and the shame had never really left her. There were times when she told herself she was being ridiculous – that it had been nothing more than silly, childish nonsense. Sometimes she wanted to confess everything but she was too scared. What if Lena hated her afterwards? What if her father got angry? Often the self-reproach of what she had done weighed heavily on her heart. It had been particularly bad after Lena's mother had died, in the autumn of 1930. Pearl had been elated, but Milly hadn't shared her excitement. For years she had worried that she and Pearl had actually caused Angel's death. Would she be damned to hell for what they had done? Milly didn't tell a living soul what she was thinking, not even Pearl. And she certainly could never admit her culpability. Her father had put her distress down to feeling sorry for Lena.

With her mother dead, and Lena being only nine years old, she couldn't stay in the cottage on her own. So their father had arranged for her to live with Nan Martin in her cottage at the bottom of Bost Hill. Milly's mother and sister still had no idea about Lena. Nan had no children of her own, but she was a loving and caring woman, so Charles knew that Lena would be well looked after. Milly was allowed to go to see Lena whenever she liked in the school holidays, although she was savvy enough to make sure that her mother and Pearl were never home when she biked along the new Findon bypass to Nan's place.

When Pearl left school, their mother had begun a two-year preparation period in readiness for her coming out. After spending almost a year at 'finishing school' in Switzerland, she was taken to Italy on a sort of mini grand tour. From there, she and her mother went to America. On the eve of her nineteenth birthday, Pearl received an invitation from the Lord Chamberlain in the post and, along with a great many other debutantes, she had been presented to the new but as yet uncrowned King Edward VIII, in a ceremony which marked the beginning of the social season. Right now, Milly's mother and her sister were in London going to parties, sometimes more than one a night, where eligible young women did their best to attract eligible young bachelors, who would preferably be both rich and handsome.

It was of some relief to Milly that she wasn't included. She knew she could never live up to her mother's exacting standards, and sometimes the pressure to please was crippling. No matter how hard Milly tried, Agatha was always quick to criticise.

'Sit up straight, Millicent, and for goodness' sake take off those wretched glasses.'

'But Mummy, I really can't see without them.'

'Don't be ridiculous! You look like an owl.'

Once Pearl's season was over, Milly would be expected to follow the same path. Her sister had crammed so much into her coming out preparation, but for Milly, the thought of an endless round of buying new clothes, finding the best hairdressers and getting party invitations from the rich and well connected, all designed to result in marriage to some boorish young chap, filled her with dread. However, the one thing she was looking forward to was the travel. Who wouldn't want to wander the slopes of Switzerland or go to art galleries in Florence? She would take her paints, and if possible her easel. Having been enrolled by her father in the Worthing School of Art and Science, Milly had become quite a clever artist. The course was for two years and Milly worked hard, something her father applauded even if her mother only sniffed at her work.

Even though she'd never breathed a word about what she and Pearl had done, Milly and Lena had grown much closer. With her mother and Pearl so frequently away in London, Milly was often on her own during the holidays. It gave her the opportunity to paint and to see more of Lena.

'You look miles away,' Uncle Neville remarked.

Milly sat up. 'Do I? I'm sorry. I was just remembering.'

Uncle Neville chuckled and – completely misunderstanding her remark – said, 'You and Susan certainly seemed to enjoy yourselves.'

'We did.'

'What did you do?'

'We went to Bournemouth a lot,' she said. 'We swam in the sea and went to a show at the Pavilion. Aunt Betsy took us to Ringwood Market one day and, oh, I did quite a lot of painting.'

Uncle Neville chuckled again. 'Sounds like you've had a lot of fun.' He was pulling the car into the car park in front of West Moors station and not a moment too soon. Mr Watson, high up in the signal box, was already turning the wheel to close the gates across the road, so the arrival of the train must be imminent. Uncle Neville almost fell out of the car with the suitcase, and Milly was bundled onto the platform. A minute or two later, the train thundered in. There was a frantic moment looking for the Ladies Only carriage, and then Milly hopped aboard. Uncle Neville put her case and her paintings onto the luggage rack and stepped back onto the platform. Milly pulled down the window and he stood back to wave. 'Safe journey, and remember to telephone your aunt when you get home,' he instructed. 'She'll want to know you've arrived safely.'

'I will,' Milly promised, 'and thank you.'

Uncle Neville lifted his hat and the train moved off. Milly sat down. There were two women in the carriage, one was reading a book and the other was knitting what looked like a glove on four needles. The knitter looked up and smiled. Milly nodded her head briefly before she made herself comfortable with her book to enjoy the journey to Brockenhurst.

Pearl stared at her reflection in the mirror. She looked fine; no, more than that, pretty darned good. And so she should. She'd worked hard over the past eighteen months. She had slimmed down and blossomed into a beautiful woman. Everybody said so, especially Freddie – and what a catch he'd been. Still gazing at herself, she turned sideways and put her hand on her hip. The dress was fantastic and worth every penny. Figure-hugging, it had silk flowers at the neck, on the right breast, and dotted below the waistline with the last one on her right hip. It was the colour that made it stand out. A brand-new colour; a first in the world of fashion. Shocking pink.

Pearl did another twirl. Elsa Schiaparelli wasn't as well-known as some of the other designers, but her clothes were still bought by the rich and famous – women like Daisy Fellowes, Marlene Dietrich and Wallis Simpson – and that, she told herself, was all that mattered. Pearl was desperate to be up there with the greats.

Adopting a sultry pose, she pouted a little and did another turn.

'Can I come in?'

Agatha snatched back the curtain before Pearl could answer, and put her gloved hand to her mouth. 'Oh Pearl!'

Pearl took her mother's startled expression as a compliment. 'Well? What do you think? Do you like it?'

'It's a bit . . . pink.'

The assistant glided towards them. 'Madam looks stunning,' she whispered, 'but perhaps the colour . . .'

'But it's all the rage now, isn't it?' Pearl said defensively.

'We do have an identical cream silk with pink accessories,' said the assistant. 'I'm sure it's in madam's size.'

Without waiting for an answer, she hurried away.

Agatha was looking at the price tag.

'Mother, don't!' Pearl hissed. 'It looks so vulgar. It's bad enough that we can't afford to have a complete designer wardrobe, without you reminding me that we have to shop "off the peg".'

'Darling, this is Harrods,' Agatha protested.

'All the same . . .'

While her mother wandered off to look at another dress rail, Pearl went back behind the curtain to take her dress off. It was hard to believe that she was still not engaged. Freddie was going to ask her, wasn't he? It wasn't that she wasn't accomplished. She'd spent a year in finishing school in Switzerland, where she'd learned French and how to dance. She knew how to curtsey properly, with her left knee locked behind her right so that she could bow low without wobbling, and she was comfortable in places like Ascot, Henley, and Eton's June the Fourth celebrations. She loved traditions like that. Pearl sighed. She'd been a glittering success and then she'd met Freddie. Delicious, handsome Fredrich von Herren, who was now called Freddie Herren. Pearl was quite smitten by him, especially when she discovered he had a castle in Germany and pots of money in the bank. They kept bumping into each other at luncheons and afternoon teas, even the occasional dinner party, which was why she couldn't wear the same old stuff, so right now, she was extending her wardrobe.

The assistant came back with another dress, a sleeveless Coco Chanel creation in antique gold lace over a gold-coloured silk shift. The moment she saw it, Pearl had to have it. She tried it on and it was a perfect fit.

'Shall I call madam's mother?' the girl asked.

'No need,' Pearl said imperiously. 'I'll take it – and the other one. Charge it to my father's account.'

The book was good, but Milly's mind kept wandering to memories of time spent with her secret sister. When they were younger, the two girls had played in the woods, picked wild flowers and ridden their bicycles around the countryside. As they grew older, they sometimes helped out with the harvest on the local farm. Just lately they would bike up the hill and have tea in the café under the windmill at the top of High Salvington. Lena never expected anything from Milly, so their friendship had been built on mutual love and respect. Only it wasn't as honest as it might be. Milly still harboured that guilty secret.

After Angel died, their father sent Lena to the Findon village school until she was fourteen (the school leaving age). For a while, there was talk of sending her to college, but Lena was adamant that she wanted to return to her fairground family.

'You've given me an education, Pa,' she told their father, 'for which I am eternally grateful, but half of me still belongs with my mother's people.'

There were endless discussions about it and, in the end, their father agreed that she could go back to Rainbow George and the travellers.

Because the travellers only settled wherever there was a fair, it made meeting up more difficult. Lena might be in Wivelsfield for the St John the Baptist fair in June, or Hurstpierpoint for the St Lawrence the Martyr fair in July, then perhaps in West Hoathly for the feast of St Margaret, all of them quite a distance from Milly in Findon. That and the fact that her mother must never know who Lena was, or – worse – that she and Milly were friends, made everything doubly difficult, so the two girls hadn't laid eyes on each other for almost two years. Milly had really missed seeing Lena, which was why she was so looking forward to September this year. At the end of the month, Milly was supposed to join her mother and sister in London but, before that, the Findon sheep fair would take place. Lena's relatives would be organising the fairground activities, and their father had said Milly could go along. Having heard so much about Rainbow George and Big Alice, but never actually having met them, she could hardly wait.

Milly was nervous about the change of train at Southampton. It was a much bigger station than Brockenhurst, and she had to change platforms to catch the onward connection, but with the help of a porter, she managed brilliantly, and a couple of hours later she found Dixon waiting outside Worthing station with the car. After a twenty-minute drive, the car pulled off the road to begin the approach towards Muntham Court.

With a contented sigh, Milly sat back and relaxed. The sweeping drive had lost none of its beauty. To the south she passed thick woodland and the metal railings on the opposite side, which divided the arable farmland from the fields where sheep grazed. The kitchen gardens were to the east of the house and separated from the driveway by a wall. In the distance, Milly could see glimpses of the South Downs. An avenue of mature lime trees provided the formal entrance at the front of the house, and of course the magnificent pond with its dolphins and cherubs added to the perfect setting. How she loved this beautiful house. Despite her issues with her mother, it still held many wonderful memories. Milly might have been tired after her long journey, but she was happy.

As Dixon opened the car door for her, Milly became aware for the first time just how grey he had become. It struck her that he'd lived with them as a servant for the whole of her life, and yet she knew nothing about his personal life. Bodkin the gardener had retired a few years ago, and a Mr Greene from the village of Patching had taken over. Mrs Cunningham still worked in the kitchen but, in 1932, Martha had married her sweetheart and moved to Lancing. She had been replaced by a new girl called Elsie.

'Here we are then, miss,' Dixon said pleasantly.

'Thank you, Dixon.' Milly felt her cheeks heating up as a wave of embarrassment engulfed her. How could she have lived cheek-by-jowl with these people all these years and yet know absolutely nothing about their private lives? She had it in mind to ask him something personal, but the thought was snatched away as the front door flew open and her father hurried down the steps.

'Milly!' he cried, sweeping her into his arms. 'Welcome, welcome home, my dear.'

Chapter 10

September 1937

It had been decided that Milly and her father would walk together to the fairground next to the sheep fair in Findon at noon on Saturday. It wasn't that far, and with careful timing they could avoid the thousands of sheep coming off the Downs into the village along the Horsham Road.

'I have a little business to attend to first thing in the morning,' Charles told her, 'but I should be finished long before then.'

Milly dressed carefully. Her cherry red dress was plain with a pencil skirt. There were red and white stripes on the cuff of her short sleeves which matched the belt. The dress was high at the neck, with an asymmetrical red and white striped collar in the shape of a deep 'V'. To complement the outfit, she wore white court shoes and carried a matching clutch bag and gloves.

By twelve-thirty her father still wasn't back, so Milly decided to go on her own. She knew he wouldn't like her being unchaperoned, but what could possibly happen in broad daylight? Besides, as soon as she found Lena, she'd be safe enough with her.

It was a perfect autumn day and the sheep fair itself on Nepcote Green was heaving. Since early morning, some

20,000 sheep had been penned in by wattle fences on the ground, while the buyers, some in long white coats and carrying a shepherd's crook or a walking stick with a hook on the end, wandered around to inspect them before the auctioneer arrived to conduct a sale. The whole area was a sea of bowler hats, homburg hats, flat caps and the odd fedora.

Farmers and shepherds had gathered at this time of year in Findon since the mid-eighteenth century. Back then, the large flocks had been walked across the Downs, but now things were more up-to-date. The sheep were taken to Steyning railway station, and from there transported to Findon by lorry.

The fairground was on an adjacent field, and if Milly thought the sheep fair was crowded, it was as nothing compared to the fairground. That was packed out, and felt both bewildering and exciting. There were plenty of rides and amusements, ranging from a carousel and helter-skelter, to a bumpy gangway and a tumble bug. The sideshows included a coconut shy, the greasy pole and a boxing ring, where members of the public could climb in the ring to challenge the man who had once beaten John Michael Basham before he became the British and European welter- and middleweight champion.

When she saw the crowds, Milly's heart sank. It was going to take an age to find Lena in this lot. She wandered around for ages but couldn't see her.

'You lost something, darlin'?' A man in a flat cap with terrible teeth leered at her. ''Ere, let me 'elp you.'

'No thank you,' Milly said primly as she tried to move away.

When she felt his hand on her bottom, she let out a startled squeal and pushed him away. To avoid any further contact, she headed for the other end of the field, but there was still no sign of Lena. It was only when she got there that she remembered something her sister had once told her. *We always put our pitch near the gate. That way the punters spend their money with us first.*

She'd have to go back. Milly cautiously retraced her steps when suddenly the same man stepped out of the beer tent and stood in front of her again. 'Fancy a little roll in the field, darlin'?'

Milly had no idea what a roll in the field was, but she certainly didn't want one. By now he had a tight grip on her arm and this time she couldn't break free.

Milly did her best not to panic. 'Let go of me!'

'Come on, sweetheart,' he said, pulling her closer, his beery breath making her gag. 'You'll love it.'

She became aware of someone else. Another man had pushed his way between them. He wasn't very tall and he was holding a paintbrush in his hand. 'Leave the lady alone,' he said coldly. 'She don't want it, see?'

'Sez who?' the drunk replied.

'Says Seebold Flowers,' said the newcomer.

The drunk laughed in his face. 'Well, my little flower,' he sneered, 'you can sling your 'ook. You don't scare me. Look at yer. You're 'ardly even a man. You're still wet behind yer ears.'

Now that he'd said that, Milly could see that her rescuer was not that much older than she was but, although he was only about five foot five or six, he was solidly built. However, as the drunk towered over them both, she shivered. It looked as if they were both in trouble.

A couple of other men had come out of the beer tent and wandered over to join them. 'What's up, mate?' said a man with a beer glass in his hand.

'This little runt is spoiling fer a fight,' said the drunk. 'Trying to stop me and my gal from being togeffer.'

Seebold Flowers laid his paintbrush on the top of a paint pot next to one of the rides.

'I am not your girl,' Milly said indignantly. 'I don't even know you.'

'Then let me hin-tro-duce meself,' said the drunk, leaning towards her, his lips puckered.

Milly shrieked and kicked his shin. As the drunk stumbled, he accidentally bumped the other man's beer glass, spilling the dark liquid onto the grass. Furious, the drinker turned to attack.

At the same time, she heard the other much younger man saying, 'Listen, mate. Don't waste your punches. There's a ring over yonder. For two bob, you can try your luck with the gloves on. Get through a round and you win ten bob, get through three rounds and they'll give you five quid.'

The drunk wobbled. The other man turned towards the direction of Seebold's pointing finger.

'Five quid?'

'Yep. Five quid.'

Milly forgotten, the two men appeared to be interested. Relieved, Milly turned to go, but then she heard a vaguely familiar voice calling her name. With the men distracted, the younger man took her arm and hustled her towards the hoopla stall. For a second or two, it felt as if she'd fallen out of the frying pan and into the fire, but then she heard Lena's voice.

'Milly. What happened – are you all right?'

Her rescuer was already turning back towards the men. 'Come on then, lads,' he said cheerily. 'Beat the boxer and go home rich. Five quid. That's good drinking money, that is.' And like lambs to the slaughter, they followed meekly behind him.

Lena was standing behind the colourful stall, complete with flashing lights. There was no music, but the carousel was right next door and the organ was blaring loud enough to awaken the dead. Milly felt a wave of relief. Her half-sister lifted a door in the top of the surround and Milly stumbled to safety. The two sisters clung to each other.

'What were you doing out there?' Lena gasped, putting

the three large hoops on her arm onto the counter. 'And where's Pa? I told him to wait by the caravan.'

'I came on my own,' Milly gulped tearfully. 'I shouldn't have done it. I'm sorry. Oh Lena, there was this awful man. He tried to drag me into the field and . . .'

Lena called over to a middle-aged woman on the next stall, where the punters were throwing darts at playing cards pinned to the wooden uprights. 'Hey, Lil, can you ask your Vera to take over my stall for a bit?'

As Lena put her arm around Milly's shoulder, another young girl vaulted over the barrier and picked up the three hoops from the counter.

'Thanks, Vera.'

With a nod, the girl began to call out, 'Hoopla, hoopla. Three for a tanner. Fab-ulous prizes. Roll up. Roll up. Three 'oops for a tanner.'

The two girls headed towards the end of the field, where the fairground folk had their living quarters. Calmer now, Milly glanced around at the brightly coloured caravans; some were the traditional wooden variety which would have been pulled by a horse, others were more modern, meaning that they could be fixed to a motor car. Lena pointed out her home, which was a different kind of caravan altogether. Milly gasped at the large red and white wagon. It was a solid design, made with what looked like interlocking aluminium panels. As they walked towards it, Milly could see an extra area which had been pulled out from the side. The whole thing resembled a balcony. Next to it was a flight of wooden steps, six in all, leading to the entrance. Once inside, far from encountering a pokey, cramped space, she was staggered by its size, opulence and splendour. They had walked into the kitchen, which was a world away from the humble scullery-cum-kitchen in Nan's little cottage. This one was amazing. Behind the sink and drainer was a window overlooking the fields beyond. Colourful cups hung from hooks over the sink, and matching plates were stacked on the shelves above. The sink itself had a tiled splashback. A middle-aged woman was bending to put some pots and pans into a cupboard beside the sink. She straightened up as Lena and Milly walked in the door.

"Allo, lovey,' she said to Lena. 'Come fer a spot o' grub already?'

She was neat and tidy, wearing a pink and yellow blouse and dark skirt under her colourful wrap-around apron. Her brown hair was flecked with grey and scraped into a bun on the top of her head, but little tendrils hung attractively around her face. Round her neck she wore a paisley pattern kerchief which mismatched with the pattern on her blouse.

'It's a bit early yet,' said Lena, 'but we'll stop for a cuppa.'

'Right you are,' said the woman.

'The blokes in the beer tent were getting a bit lairy,' Lena explained, 'until Seebold sorted it out.' She stepped back proudly. 'Alice, this is Milly. Millicent Ann Shepherd, my sister. Milly, this is Big Alice.'

Milly stepped forward with her hand extended. 'How do you do.'

The older woman chuckled. 'She'm very polite, 'ant she?' she said, wiping her hand vigorously down her hand-stitched apron before returning Milly's handshake.

The woman had twinkling eyes and a weather-beaten face. Milly warmed to her straight away.

'Big Alice looks ar'ter me,' Lena said, reverting back to the way she used to speak when she was in the cottage with Angel. 'I just calls her Alice.'

Milly was surprised that Lena was allowed to call an adult, no matter how familiar, by her first name. She was always expected to use the prefix Auntie or Uncle when addressing a grown-up, even though that person might not be related to her. If she spoke to someone outside the family circle, she was expected to be quite formal, and use Mr or Mrs before their surname.

Big Alice nodded. 'You go on in, lovey. George is in 'is chair. I'll bring the tea directly.'

'Can I use the toilet?' Milly whispered as they moved further down the caravan.

The bayroom, as Lena called it, was just along the short corridor. Milly was surprised to find a china sink, complete with brass taps, fresh fluffy towels hanging from brass rings beside it and plenty more on the shelves.

'This 'ere is my bedroom,' said Lena, as Milly came out of the bathroom.

Although Milly only had a moment to glance inside the room next door, she was impressed. It was snug but Lena had a full-sized box bed with a chest of drawers beside it and sliding doors underneath. The little stuffed dog Milly had given her half-sister the day they'd gone to Worthing to buy her school shoes lay on the pillow of her bed. Milly's throat tightened as the memory of that night under the eaves of the cottage came flooding back. She'd have to tell Lena, wouldn't she. She took in a breath but, as she turned towards her sister and saw her smile, Milly knew she couldn't do it. Not today.

'Very nice.'

Lena closed her bedroom door and they set off along the little corridor again. All at once, Milly leaned towards Lena and whispered confidentially, 'Why is she called Big Alice. She really isn't that big.'

Lena chuckled. 'It's because she's older than Little Alice.'

'Oh,' said Milly.

At the far end of the corridor, Milly came to a beautiful sitting area with brown mahogany surrounds, carpet on the floor and a large mirror over a wood-burning stove. On the way into the room, she'd stepped over the metal runners which enabled the 'balcony' to be pushed out. Next to the fire were two very comfortable-looking leather chairs, one facing her, the other with its back to the door. A third chair, a wooden upright, was squeezed in between. Someone was sitting in the chair with its back to the door. She couldn't see the occupant but blue smoke curled above the chair and the room smelled pleasantly of cigar.

'Milly,' Lena said proudly, 'I want you to meet Rainbow George.'

Chapter 11

The chair creaked slightly as the occupant heaved himself up. He wasn't a tall man, but he was robust. About five foot five and with a barrel chest, she could immediately see why he had the nickname of Rainbow George. Although he was dressed in a dark suit, his silk waistcoat was a patchwork of vivid colours. Reds, blues, yellows and greens blended together and a silver watchchain dangled from his waistcoat pocket. He beamed, his eyes almost disappearing as he gave her a winning smile, his gold teeth flashing. When Milly leaned forward to extend her hand, she was met with one as big as a bear's paw, but Rainbow George was gentle and his fingers were as warm as his greeting.

'Sit down, lovey,' said a voice behind her. Big Alice had followed them in with a tray of tea. Milly perched on the wooden upright chair while Lena sat cross-legged on the mat in front of the unlit fire. Big Alice put the tray onto a small table and began pouring from the large brown tea pot. The tea was almost the colour of liquorice.

'How come you'm back so early?' Rainbow George asked Lena. 'Who's looking ar'ter the stall?'

'Vera is. Milly was trashed by some chap in the beer tent,' she said, taking a cup and saucer from Big Alice.

'Actually . . .' Milly began, but Rainbow George had jumped to his feet with a roar. 'I won't have nobody makin' trouble. Not on my field, I won't.'

'Don't get yer braces in a twist,' Lena said flippantly. 'Seebold sorted it.'

Rainbow George hesitated then threw back his head with a throaty laugh. 'Good lad, Seebold. Good at mechanics and all.' Then, reaching for his hat, he added, 'I'd better go and check on 'e.'

'Sit down and drink yer tea first,' Big Alice said.

'Last I saw,' Lena said casually, 'he was takin' them all to the ring with the promise of a fiver. They all looks like dinlows so it won't take much for the boy to sort them out.'

Chuckling heartily, Rainbow George lowered himself back into his chair.

Milly leaned towards her sister. 'What did you mean when you said I was "trashed"?' she whispered. 'Nobody hit me.'

I meant that you was frightened,' said Lena. 'Sorry, it's the way we talks.'

So,' said Rainbow George, tipping some of his tea into the saucer, 'tell me all about yerself, Millicent.'

Milly, please,' said Milly. 'Everybody calls me Milly.'

Milly,' he said, his eyes shining with amusement.

As he slurped his tea, she gave him a brief résumé of her life thus far. Even though it didn't sound very exciting, it didn't seem to matter. Everyone listened attentively.

Her tea finished, Lena was anxious to be back at the hoopla stall.

'Can I come too?' Milly asked.

Lena seemed surprised. She glanced at Rainbow George and, to Milly's delight, he was nodding. 'If you really wants to.'

'Oh but I do,' Milly said.

* * *

As soon as they took over from Vera, Lena began to call the punters in. 'Get yer 'oops here. Sixpence for three. Three 'oops for a tanner.'

Milly took a deep breath and pushed her glasses back up her nose. 'Three hoops for a tanner,' she said as loudly as she dared. 'Fabulous prizes.' It sounded a little odd in her slightly plummy voice, but it certainly turned a few heads.

Lena grinned, and before long the two girls were doing a brisk trade.

'How about a kiss as well?' some punter called.

'You ain't got enough money fer one o' my kisses,' Lena snapped back as quick as lightning. 'But if you gets top prize, I'll think about it.'

The man glanced at his friend for courage and grinned. The top prize was a leather wallet perched in the middle of the tower. Milly couldn't help noticing that you'd have to be very accurate to throw the hoop over it and let it slide down to the little platform on which it stood. The punter had three goes, spending one and six on the effort but failing every time.

'No one can get the hoop over that bloody thing,' his friend said angrily. 'You've rigged it. The stand is too big.'

For a second, Milly held her breath. The man could be right. The hoops never seemed to go right over the wooden stand, no matter how hard the punters tried. But Lena wasn't fazed. She held a hoop over the wallet and let go. They all watched as it fell right over the prize and onto the wooden stand with a loud clatter. It was a tight fit, but she had proved that it was doable.

'Others might cheat you, boys,' Lena said confidently, 'but not Rainbow George. Now which one of you is gonna try his luck next?'

There was a sudden clamour for hoops, but it was some time before anyone managed to claim a prize. Sadly for the punter, it wasn't the leather wallet. It was a goldfish swimming around in a glass bowl.

The punters kept them on the go, but Milly thoroughly enjoyed her afternoon. There was a moment of sheer panic when she recognised one of her mother's friends strolling by, but she ducked down quickly as if tying her shoelace. Fortunately Mrs Jennings, the doctor's wife, didn't notice her. Had she done so, Milly had no doubt the woman would have been delighted to hot-foot over to Muntham Court with her juicy bit of gossip that Millicent Shepherd was working a fair stall like a commoner, and then all hell would no doubt break loose.

After a couple of hours, Lena handed over the stall to someone else, and the two of them made their way wearily back to the caravan. Big Alice made them some sandwiches and they had another pot of tea. Rainbow George had gone back onto the field, so the two girls had the sitting room to themselves.

'Are you glad to be back with the travellers?' Milly asked.

Her sister made a pouty face. 'Yes and no,' she said. 'I love the fairground and all that, but Rainbow George keeps on at me about being wed.'

'What, already? But you're only sixteen.'

'Almost seventeen,' Lena snapped back.

Milly laughed. 'Sounds like you're being pushed into marriage just the same as me.'

'Pa wants you to marry someone?' Lena gasped.

'Not my father,' said Milly, 'but I'm nudging eighteen now and my mother has grandiose ideas. I shall soon have to be on the lookout for the perfect husband.'

Lena giggled. 'I bet he'll turn out to be a lord or a prince or something.'

Milly went on to explain about her coming out parties, and what it meant to be a debutante. 'I'm starting a little later than usual,' she explained, 'because my mother has

84

spent the last eighteen months organising Pearl's coming out.'

'It sounds amazing,' Lena remarked.

'I wouldn't mind the travel and stuff,' Milly conceded, 'but I'm not ready for wet kisses in the garden with boys I've only just met. I want to do something with my life.'

Lena laughed. 'You and me both.'

Milly shook her head. 'People seem to think girls can't have a career, yet look at what women did in the Great War. They worked as telephone operators; they were bus conductresses and some even became bus drivers.'

Lena nodded.

'Of course the powers-that-be didn't make it easy for them,' Milly went on. 'The post office wouldn't let women deliver telegrams to certain areas, and they certainly weren't allowed to work at night.'

'Because it was too dangerous?' Lena suggested.

'Because they were unaccompanied.'

Lena pulled a face.

'Well, you mustn't run the risk of poor weak-willed women getting themselves into trouble,' Milly said in a voice laden with sarcasm.

'Angel drove an ambulance,' Lena said. 'That's how she first saw Pa.'

'I thought you said they met at the Findon Fair.'

'They did, but the first time they clapped eyes on each other, Angel was driving the ambulance that was taking Pa's best friend to 'ospital.'

Milly's eyes grew large. 'What happened to him?'

Lena shrugged. 'I never asked.'

Milly nodded. There was so much about her own family she didn't know. 'I don't think my mother did anything much,' she said. She turned her head, feeling slightly embarrassed. 'Apart from a bit of fundraising, maybe.'

'And now she wants you to get married,' said Lena.

'She says "it's a woman's duty to marry well",' Milly said, quoting her mother's favourite saying, 'but I'm not ready for that, for goodness' sake.'

Lena giggled. 'You sound like me. I want the chance to live a bit of life first.'

Milly pulled her shoes off and wriggled her toes. 'Does Rainbow George have anyone in mind for you?'

'Seebold Flowers.'

Milly blinked. 'Seebold!' She paused, aware that it might have sounded rude. 'He seems nice enough, and I'm certainly very grateful to him, but how does he feel about that?'

Lena shrugged again. 'Same as me, I suppose.' She sighed. 'He's all right, but I don't love him and he certainly doesn't love me. Anyway, I've got plans.'

It looked as if she was about to tell Milly what those were, but then they heard voices. Rainbow George was coming in and they heard Big Alice say, 'Go and wash up first and then you can go into the sitting room.'

Milly smiled to herself. Rainbow George might be cock of the walk outside on the field, but it was clear that here in the caravan, everybody danced to Big Alice's tune.

A few minutes later, Lena's guardian lumbered wearily towards his chair. 'How was your stint on the hoopla, little missy?' he asked Milly.

'I enjoyed it,' she replied.

'We made a mort of money,' said Lena. 'More than at Hurstpierpoint and West Hoathly put together.'

Rainbow George was impressed. 'Did you indeed?' he chortled. 'Looks like we'll make a showgirl of you yet.'

They all jumped as somebody knocked on the window and called out, 'Anyone at home?'

Lena jumped to her feet. 'That's my pa,' she cried and, racing to the kitchen door, she called, 'Pa, Pa.'

'Come on in, lovey,' said Big Alice as Charles came up the steps. 'Yer just in time fer tea.'

As her father came along the corridor, Milly leaned towards Rainbow George. 'Please don't tell my father about that awful man,' she whispered earnestly. 'He might stop me from coming to see Lena again.'

Rainbow George's eyes twinkled as he tapped the side of his nose. 'Mum's the word, little missy.'

Charles came into the room with Lena hanging onto his arm and chattering away nineteen to the dozen. Milly stood to give her father a hug, then they all spent a relaxed few minutes together drinking tea and swapping pleasantries. Charles was very apologetic that he was so late in coming. 'I had a little business that couldn't wait, I'm afraid,' he told them.

Milly couldn't help noticing that he looked a little pale, and when he started coughing, she felt a wave of anxiety.

But George came to the rescue. 'I got just the thing fer that cough,' he said, going to the cabinet and pouring a honey-coloured liquid into a small glass. He handed it to Charles. ''Ere, get that down yer neck.'

Her father held the glass aloft, as if giving a toast, then downed it in one go before another coughing fit overcame him. 'Good God,' he choked as he regained his breath. 'What the hell was that?'

Rainbow George grinned. 'My ol' granny's recipe.'

'It's got quite a kick,' said Charles.

Rainbow George grinned. 'But I bet yer throat feels better.'

Charles paused before giving him a nod. 'Either that, or it's taken all the bloody skin off.'

The two men laughed, and Milly could see there was a strong mutual respect between them. She was curious to know how her father had met these people. After all, Lena's mother and her father had clearly been poles apart when it came to their social standing.

The men began talking about the funfair and some

of the new regulations the government was putting into place regarding public safety, while the girls spoke of more interesting things like the Hitchcock film *The 39 Steps*.

'Is it based on a true story, do you think?' Lena wanted to know.

Milly shrugged. 'I know there's a book of the same name. It was written by John Buchan.'

'I remember reading about him in a magazine when I was a young girl,' said Big Alice with a dreamy expression. '*All-Story Weekly*.'

'I saw the film in Bournemouth,' said Milly. 'Mrs Tice took us.'

'I like Robert Donat,' Lena sighed. 'He's so good-looking.'

After a while, Charles made his apologies and said that he and Milly had to go back home immediately.

'Nothing wrong, I hope,' said Big Alice.

'No, no,' Charles said as they stood once more. 'My wife and Pearl have returned from London and Milly has a social engagement this evening. I'm sorry it has to be this way, but I promise we'll come back another time.' He kissed Big Alice on both cheeks, shook Rainbow George's hand then hugged Lena.

'Why did you say that?' Milly asked her father as they walked away. 'I don't have any social engagements.'

'I'm afraid you do,' he said, deliberately not looking at her. 'Your mother wants you to go to a country house ball tonight.'

Chapter 12

Lena watched her father and half-sister go with a deep sense of longing. From the moment her mother had died, Pa had given her what she had wished for. She'd had an education and then, when she'd left school, he'd allowed her to return to the fairground and its people, but she always felt torn. It was as if she didn't really belong anywhere. She respected Rainbow George, but being part of his patriarchal family structure was like living in a straitjacket and she wasn't allowed to step beyond boundaries which had been laid down in the year dot. She couldn't go out without an escort; she could work on the amusements but not have her own, and she would have to agree to a marriage before she was eighteen. Rainbow George didn't seem to realise that they lived in the twentieth century now.

When Angel died, Lena discovered she had been given her jewellery and a little money. It wasn't much, but twenty pounds gave her a small chance for independence. Pa had offered her some advice but, apart from insisting that she put the money into a bank account for safe-keeping, he had left her to choose for herself what she wanted to do with it. She'd kept quiet about it so nobody else knew about her inheritance. Good job too. She would have been coerced into a marriage pretty quickly had would-be suitors realised she had a bit of money. Lena had toyed with various ideas but, in the end, the twenty pounds had remained where it was . . . until last year. Having decided that she wanted something more permanent, something nobody could take from her and something that would give her a decent return, she'd asked Pa to help her buy a piece of land.

'You want to be a landowner?' Pa cried.

'I've found a place to the east of Worthing where some nurseries used to be,' she told him. 'It's near the station; well, it' a little halt really, but it means it has good transport nearby. There's a bus, some shops, a pub just up the road and, best of all, it's going quite cheap.'

'How cheap?' Pa had asked.

'The owner wants five pounds an acre.'

Pa had frowned. 'Oh, Lena,' he began, 'at that price, I'm not sure—'

'I know what you're going to say Pa,' Lena interrupted, 'but it's all right. I've listened to what Rainbow George does when he's shelling out with big money for something, and I've been careful to check up on everything. I'm sure it's perfectly kosher.'

'Lena, you're only fifteen,' Pa said, shaking his head.

'Almost sixteen,' she told him.

'But you're an innocent. You don't know how unscrupulous people can be. At five pounds an acre I find it hard to believe that it's a good investment. If I was you, I'd be very careful.'

'I'm not planning to sink all my money into it,' Lena said stoutly, 'but ten pounds will buy me two acres. All I want is for you to come with me to the bank. They tell me that even though it's my own money, I'm not old enough to make such a purchase without my father's consent.'

Charles Shepherd shook his head in disbelief, but what else could he do? He had never been a heavy-handed father, and wasn't going to start now. Amazed by her tenacity, and even more astonished by her decision, he agreed to help, providing that she took him to view the land for himself first. To begin with, he had wondered if she'd fallen for some fairy-tale purchase which didn't really exist, but when they visited the place he found the land was real enough. Back in Victorian times, it had been a nursery growing and selling tomatoes and grapes but, because so many young and fit men had perished during the Great War, the owner had soon gone out of business. He hadn't been able to find anyone who was interested in glasshouse work, and the bottom had fallen out of the market anyway.

But though real enough, the site was a tip. There was broken glass everywhere, the glasshouses were in need of serious repair, and the ground itself was completely overgrown. It had stayed on the books of the estate agent for a long time.

'You won't be able to use this ground for anything,' Charles said as the water squelched over his shoes. 'It's waterlogged. The owner seems desperate to sell even at five pounds an acre, so I can't help but wonder what else is wrong. It might look like a bargain but I'm afraid he saw you coming.'

'I know,' Lena said, 'but what he doesn't know is that I have the gift.'

Charles frowned, clearly puzzled. 'The gift?'

Lena grinned. 'When Angel was alive, people used to ask her to find water. She used a forked twig and walked up and down a field.'

Her father looked startled. 'She was a water diviner?'

Lena nodded. 'I was only a kid, but she taught me what to do and I have the gift as well. I have dowsing skills.'

Charles blinked. 'You're incredible,' he said, 'his voice choking with emotion.

'It's useful when we picks our part of the field for the fairs,' she grinned. 'We never gets stuck with the boggy patch.'

Her father grinned proudly. 'So you can find the source of the water and get it drained? Clever girl.'

'So will you help me?'

Charles nodded and, by the end of the week, Lena had been the secret but proud owner of two acres of East Worthing scrubland.

Now, as her father and half-sister reached the edge of the fairground, they turned round to wave one more time. Lena smiled. She ought to tell Milly about the field. They shouldn't have secrets from one another.

'Come on, girl,' said Rainbow George, coming up behind her and snapping her out of her daydream with a playful slap on her shoulder. 'You'm got a hoopla to run.'

Milly came home to find herself in the grip of an absolute nightmare.

Her mother was waiting in the hall, her feet tapping, arms folded, and, as Milly and her father walked through the door, she glanced anxiously at the clock.

'Where on earth have you been?' she said angrily.

'I'm sorry,' Milly said, 'but I had no idea that you would be here.'

Her mother hustled Milly towards the stairs, her beautiful silk dress rustling as she moved. 'I can't think why you were out today of all days,' she complained. 'You never go anywhere.'

Milly caught her breath. Why was her mother always like this? No *Hello, darling. It's lovely to see you. I haven't set eyes on you since Christmas. How are you?*

Agatha pulled at her arm. 'Hurry up.'

'Why? What's happening?'

'I've managed to get you a ticket for Lady Verity's charity drinks party,' Agatha told her irritably. 'They're absolute gold dust, you know.'

'Can't Pearl go?'

Her mother sighed impatiently. 'Don't be silly, Millicent. Pearl is already going.'

Milly swallowed hard. The thought of going to Lady Verity's (whoever she was) was scary to say the least. She felt so unprepared. She glanced back at her father for reassurance but he was having another coughing fit.

'Well, come on then,' Agatha snapped tetchily. 'There's no time to lose.'

Milly was dragged to the bathroom to have a quick wash. When she emerged, a woman who had been summoned from the village hairdressing salon was waiting to set her hair. Madam Irene wore far too much make-up and spoke with a fake French accent laced with the odd bit of Hampshire intonation. She also exuded a slight whiff of perspiration every time she lifted her arms. To be summoned to Muntham Court was clearly a great honour for her, and she positively gushed whenever Milly's mother appeared.

'I don't expect miracles, Madam Irene,' Agatha said, drawing hard on her cigarette as Milly sat in front of the mirror, 'but do your best.'

Milly was subjected to Mervin wave clips and a curling iron to get the effect her mother and stylist desired. While she was under the dryer, Madam Irene gave her a manicure and painted her nails.

Agatha, who had barely spoken to her daughter since she'd arrived home, sat with them, drink in hand, telling Madam Irene all about Pearl's coming out. It was all news to Milly.

'What was it like being in Buckingham Palace?' Madam Irene asked breathlessly.

'Och . . .' Agatha breathed. 'I can't tell you what an honour . . .'

Milly switched off. She'd just caught sight of an evening gown laid out across her mother's bed, reflected in the mirror. Who did that belong to? It was a dusty lemon (not a very flattering colour) and it seemed to have an inordinate number of frills. A light dawned somewhere in her head and Milly's heart sank. Surely her mother wasn't expecting her to wear that, was she? It was hideous. Like something out of the Edwardian age. No, of course not. That must be Pearl's gown. Milly relaxed. Yes, that was it. The dress was for Pearl. Milly suddenly frowned. Where *was* Pearl?

'Can you imagine,' Agatha was gushing, 'fifty girls floating across the ballroom floor, all dressed in white.' She paused for effect. 'Each of them had three Prince of Wales feathers on her head.'

Madam Irene clasped her hand to her bosom and sighed. 'Wonderful,' she agreed. 'Wonderful.'

Milly rolled her eyes.

'Of course,' her mother went on, 'my other daughter was among the very first debutantes to be presented to King Edward VIII.'

'Such a handsome man.'

'Do you really think so?' said Agatha, sipping her whisky. 'I thought him rather ill-mannered. As a matter of fact, he left the proceedings halfway through. Told the other girls to consider themselves "presented" because he wanted to play golf with that American woman.'

'Mrs Simpson.'

'Wallis Simpson,' Agatha sneered. 'I ask you, what sort of name is that?'

There was an awkward silence, then Madam Irene said, 'Me and my sister went up to London for King George's coronation.'

Agatha arched an eyebrow.

Madam Irene's face shone with excitement. 'Oh madam, you should have seen the procession . . . people came from all the dominions, and the gold state coach, it was magnificent.'

'We gave that a miss, of course,' Agatha said, haughtily. 'In a crowd like that, you could be rubbing shoulders with God knows who.'

For just a second, Madam Irene's cheeks flamed, but she said nothing. Eventually, the hairdresser patted Milly's hair one last time and stepped back admiringly. Milly swallowed hard. She'd never seen herself looking like this before and, quite frankly, she felt slightly ridiculous.

'Time to get dressed,' said Agatha, reaching for the overblown creation on the bed.

Milly's heart sank. 'Oh Mother,' she cried, 'I can't possibly . . .'

Agatha spun around and their eyes met. Milly had thought about wriggling out of it by saying the dress was too good for her, or that Pearl would look lovely in it, but by the look on her mother's face, she knew she was already defeated. 'It's lovely,' she said feebly, 'but it's not really . . . me.'

'Nonsense,' said her mother. 'I think it's perfect.'

With the zip done up, the two women 'oohed' and 'aahed' contentedly. Milly was lavishly sprayed with her mother's perfume and taken downstairs for her father's approval. Charles was at his desk writing something, which he hastily squirrelled away into a drawer as they walked into the room. Agatha pretended not to notice. He told Milly how beautiful she looked but she wasn't convinced. Her father was just being kind. She looked like an overgrown Christmas fairy.

To complete her ensemble, Milly was taken back out into the hall and given an old pair of scuffed and creased shoes belonging to Pearl.

'Nobody will notice them under that long dress,' her mother said determinedly as she whipped Milly's glasses from her nose, 'and you won't need those.'

'But I can't see without them,' Milly protested.

'Nonsense,' her mother snapped. 'No man will give you a second glance with those awful things on.'

'But . . .' Milly began again as she reached out for her glasses.

Her mother snatched them up again. 'Do that again and I'll break them in half, Millicent.' And Milly knew she meant it.

The door to the morning room was still open, and Charles was sitting at his desk with that same envelope in front of him. As his daughter came to say goodbye, he pushed the envelope into the drawer once again. Milly hardly noticed, but Agatha's sharp eye saw that it was marked 'Last Will and Testament'.

Moments later, they all went their separate ways. Madam Irene went back to the village with her fee plus a handsome tip. Agatha Shepherd headed for the ball, contented that she now had two daughters doing the circuit at the same time, along with Milly, who felt like a short-sighted lamb being led to the slaughter. As the car drove off, Charles Shepherd reached back into his drawer and took out the envelope again. Putting a line through the words 'Last Will and Testament', he wrote the name of his solicitors, May, May and Prior, in the top left-hand corner.

Chapter 13

Lady Verity's house wasn't far away. Deep in the beautiful countryside near Washington, West Sussex, and close to the Highden Estate, the house itself had been built in the early 1700s in the Queen Anne style. As Dixon drove them along a narrow lane, they suddenly burst into a wide-open space and the house dominated the scene. Without her glasses, Milly had to squint to see it in detail, but even she could tell it was magnificent. A red-brick building with long casement windows, eight on the ground floor, nine on the first floor and nine smaller windows at the top of the house, it was the perfect setting for such an occasion. The lawns were bedecked with tables and chairs and already people were milling about. There was a string quartet on the terrace, and black-suited waiters walked around carrying trays of hors d'oeuvres. The car park in front of the house was already quite full but luckily Dixon managed to find a space.

As Agatha stepped out of the car, they heard someone cry out, 'Yoo-hoo, Mother. Over here.'

'It's Pearl,' said Agatha, 'and look, she's with Friedrich, that nice German man.'

Agatha hurried off to meet them, and Milly, feeling horribly self-conscious, followed.

'Darling,' Agatha said as she and Pearl air-kissed each other's cheeks, 'you look fantastic.'

And she did. Her dress was a luscious gold silk with the most exquisite lace shift over the top. She wore her hair in an attractive bob and the pearl and diamanté slides in her hair glistened in the moonlight.

Milly and Pearl exchanged a perfunctory nod.

'Mother, you've met Freddie, haven't you,' said Pearl, but it was obvious from the way her mother gushed over him that she already knew him and really liked him. Milly thought he was more striking than handsome; with white-blond hair and perfect teeth, he appeared to be the sort of man who exercised regularly. He kissed Agatha's hand and gave them both a brusque nod of the head before clicking his heels together. When he grasped Milly's hand, she shook it vigorously before he could lean in to kiss her and she was surprised by his limp and sweaty fingers.

'Please excuse me,' he said in the most perfect English, 'I have to catch that fellow up there. We had a small wager and he lost, so now he owes me money.' He was pointing to the terrace but it was crowded, so Milly couldn't work out which man he meant. With a nod towards her mother, he bounded up the steps, two at a time. 'I say, Eustace,' he called out to no response. 'Eustace, old man.'

Milly suppressed a smile.

'What time did you get here?' said Agatha, noting the glass in her daughter's hand.

'About half an hour ago,' said Pearl and, pointing to a smart-looking sports car, she added, 'We came in Freddie's car. It's a bit draughty up on the terrace and, stupidly, I left my shawl on the front seat.'

'Why are you calling him Freddie?' her mother queried.

'In view of the growing anti-German feeling,' said Pearl, leaning towards her mother in a confidential manner, 'he wants to go by the name of Freddie now, and it sounds so much better anyway, don't you agree?'

Agatha patted her daughter's forearm. 'Absolutely.'

Freddie was back and looking very pleased with himself. He patted his inside top pocket and drew out his cigarette case.

'Millicent is nervous,' her mother whispered. 'Look after her, won't you, darling. I don't want her messing this up and embarrassing us all.'

'Of course I will, Mummy. We will make sure Milly has the best time, won't we, Freddie?'

Freddie was busy lighting a cigarette. 'Absolutely,' he agreed as he pulled a shred of tobacco from his bottom lip. He smiled languidly. 'In fact, I shall go and get her a drink.'

As he headed for the drinks table, Milly leaned forward. 'So, tell me more about him.'

'He's a German baron,' said Pearl, her eyes shining. 'Fabulously rich. He has a *schloss* in Bavaria.'

'What's a *schloss*?' Milly wanted to know.

'A castle,' said Pearl in a superior tone. She turned to her mother. 'Mother, you go off and enjoy yourself with the olds. Don't worry about Milly. She'll be fine.' She paused, then added, 'I'm pretty sure I saw Bunny Warren up there.'

Agatha hurried across the lawn to where the other chaperones and parents had gathered in comfortable-looking chairs. Pearl pulled her cashmere shawl up over her shoulders and linked arms with her sister.

'Isn't he divine?' Pearl said as they watched Freddie mount the steps ahead of them two at a time. 'He's from one of the oldest families in Germany. He knows all the best people . . . he's even met the German chancellor, Adolf Hitler. I keep asking Freddie about him, but he doesn't say much.'

Milly was impressed and, although she was feeling a tad nervous, for the first time, she was glad to be here.

Shame that Freddie didn't like talking about the German chancellor. It might have been interesting to hear about Adolf Hitler. Was he really as terrible as the newspapers were saying? Probably not – after all, King Edward VIII, before he abdicated, had been really impressed by him. She began to relax.

'I hardly recognised you at first,' Pearl said close to Milly's ear. 'My dear, who did your hair? It looks frightful.' She stifled a giggle. 'You look like one of those stuffy Edwardian mistresses. And as for that dress . . . Did you think it was a fancy dress party or something?'

'You're an intelligent man. I don't understand why you didn't come to me before.'

As the doctor glanced back at the X-ray, Charles began to cough violently again. When he'd finished, he wiped his lips with his already stained handkerchief as the nurse took the sputum bowl away.

He'd had a fraught evening. Almost as soon as Agatha and Milly had set off for the party, he had been wracked by a series of coughing fits which resulted in Mrs Cunningham, despite his protestations, ringing his GP. Dr Jennings was unequivocal in his diagnosis.

'I'm sorry, Charles,' he said, 'but there's no avoiding it this time. I'm phoning for an ambulance. You have to go to Worthing Hospital immediately.'

Charles tried to protest but Dr Jennings overrode his objections. 'Pack a bag,' he told Mrs Cunningham. 'Mr Shepherd may be gone for some time.'

'I want to stay here,' Charles said breathlessly. 'If I'm going to die, I want to be in my own home.'

Mrs Cunningham clamped her handkerchief over her mouth to suppress a cry as she hurried from the room.

'Listen to me, old man,' said Dr Jennings, leaning over him. 'Let the surgeon take a look at you before we decide on something like that. This is going to come as a tremendous shock to Agatha, not least because she has no idea how ill you are. I wish you'd let me tell her about your condition six months ago. You never should have hidden it for so long.'

Weak and breathless, Charles leaned back in his chair. 'I want you to do something for me,' he said, his breath coming in heavy gasps. 'It's important.'

'Anything, old man.'

'In my desk drawer,' said Charles. 'My will.'

The doctor shook his head. 'Let's not get ahead of ourselves.'

'No, listen,' said Charles, suppressing another cough. 'Please. I want you to take it with you.'

The sound of an ambulance pulling up on the gravel outside made Charles even more anxious. He tried to get up.

'All right, all right,' said Dr Jennings. 'I'll get it. In the desk drawer, you say?'

Charles sank back down onto the cushions with a sigh and a weak nod of his head.

Mrs Cunningham knocked and, putting her head around the door, said, 'The ambulance is here, sir.'

As Dr Jennings crossed the hallway, Mrs Cunningham was opening the front door. 'In the lounge,' the doctor told the St John Ambulance men as they came in. 'I'll be with you in a minute.'

He had to open several drawers before he found the document, and he felt a little awkward when he became aware that Mrs Cunningham was standing in the hallway watching him. It didn't look good rifling through drawers when his patient was so helpless. 'Mr Shepherd wants this,' he told her brusquely.

Back in the sitting room, Charles was being strapped onto an ambulance chair. He was very pale, and perspiration trickled down his face.

'Is this what you wanted?' Dr Jennings said in a loud voice, holding up the envelope for all to see.

'Give it to my lawyer,' said Charles, his voice weak and feeble. 'No one else, d'you hear me? Only my lawyer.'

Dr Jennings put the envelope into his bag and the sorry procession made its way outside to the ambulance. As it set off, Dr Jennings climbed into his own car. 'You'd better get hold of Mrs Shepherd,' he told Mrs Cunningham as his parting shot. 'Mr Shepherd is quite poorly.'

The doctors at Worthing Hospital put Charles into a private cubicle and ordered X-rays. The results came as no shock to him. Cancer. Advanced tumour in the right lung. He'd known for some time but had kept it to himself. It was stupid, but something had made him believe that if he paid it no attention, it might go away. He'd been a damned fool but there it was. He'd gone to see Dr Jennings about a month before, but by that point all the doctor could suggest was hospital and surgery, and Charles wanted neither. He'd seen enough of his old friends succumb to the disease. Surgery was still in its infancy and radical. It only seemed to delay the inevitable, anyway.

He'd done some careful thinking and the only change he'd made in his life was his Last Will and Testament. He'd done it some time ago, but it had only occurred to him tonight as he sat in his sitting room, gasping for breath, that his new will had to be protected. It was imperative that nobody took the opportunity to destroy it.

It was quiet in the garden. Milly found a seat near a sweet-smelling border containing phlox and night-scented stock. Old-fashioned honeysuckle and star jasmine had been encouraged to intertwine and climb along the wall of what Milly supposed were the kitchen gardens. It was quite dark now. She could hear the voices of lovers in other parts of the garden, and in the far distance, someone was smoking a cigarette. Every now and then the red glow of the tip grew brighter.

She was exhausted. The whole evening had been a nightmare. She'd entered the house in an optimistic mood, but Pearl's carefully crafted 'put-down' had changed all that. She hadn't seen her sister in months and, until that moment, she had almost forgotten how devastating her cutting remarks could be. Nervous and embarrassed in equal measure, her mood wasn't helped when Pearl had completely abandoned her and she'd been forced to stand alone for ages. She didn't know anyone and, without her glasses, she could hardly see anyone anyway. Thankfully no one seemed to notice she was there. Pearl and Freddie only had eyes for each other and everyone else seemed to be deep in conversation. At one point the crowd parted and, turning her head slightly, Milly saw a vaguely familiar figure on the other side of the room. She couldn't quite make out her features, but the person smiled so Milly smiled back. Thus encouraged, she walked towards the girl and the girl came towards her. Milly's hand was outstretched when, to her absolute horror, she suddenly realised that the person in front of her was, in fact, her own reflection in a long mirror. For a second or two the conversation in the room died. The silence was broken by the sound of Pearl's raucous laughter. Then the rest of the room erupted into laughter. Milly froze. Tears bit the back of her eyes but she managed to keep her dignity. Turning, she pretended she'd done it on purpose as a joke by joining in with her sister's laughter and, for a few very welcome minutes, people offered her a drink, or an hors d'oeuvres, and asked where she was from. Eventually Milly excused herself from the room by saying that she needed to get a breath of fresh air.

It was cold in the garden and Milly shivered. Unlike her sister, she hadn't brought a shawl. She was unused to soirées and posh-frock dos, and besides, the only shawl she had was wrapped around the doll in the bottom of the drawer in her room. The thought of it made the dark fingers of guilt worm their way into her thoughts once more. She shivered again.

'You look cold.'

Milly jumped and, looking up, she saw a man removing his dinner jacket.

'Oh no,' she cried, 'please don't.' But it was already around her, and she could feel the residual warmth from his body seeping into her cold shoulders. 'May I?' he said, indicating the spare seat on the bench.

Her heart already quickening, Milly nodded. She didn't know this man, but if he was at Lady Verity's, she supposed he must be all right, mustn't he?

'Eustace Henderson,' he introduced himself, holding out his hand as he sat beside her.

'Eustace?'

He shrugged. 'God-awful name, I know, but I'm stuck with it.'

Embarrassed, Milly added, 'Sorry. I didn't mean to be rude.'

'It's fine,' he said amiably. 'And your name?'

'Millicent Shepherd,' said Milly with a smile, 'but everyone calls me Milly.'

'Haven't seen you around the circuit before.'

'I haven't been,' she said shyly. 'This is my first event.'

He frowned. 'You're Pearl's little sister, aren't you?'

Milly was a bit embarrassed to be called 'little', but she nodded nonetheless. 'We were together but she's gone off with someone called Freddie.'

'Oh that blasted idiot,' Eustace said dismissively, then obviously thought better of his comment because he added, 'Excuse my French, but I take exception to someone barging up to me and demanding that I settle a wager in front of everybody. There are ways of doing things, you know.' He shook his head apologetically. 'Sorry to rant on like that,' he continued, 'but I'd be very careful if I were you. He's always sneaking around and watching people. I wouldn't trust him as far as I could throw him. I ask you, what sort of chap carries a little book around with him and spends all his time scribbling in it?'

'Really?' Milly gasped. 'What sort of things does he write?'

'No idea,' said Eustace, 'but it gives me the creeps.' He pointed to his jacket, indicating his inside pocket. 'I say, do you mind?'

She shook her head and he reached in for his cigarette case. He offered her one but Milly shook her head. He found his lighter in his trouser pocket and lit up.

'So, Milly,' he said, taking a deep breath, 'what do you do?'

'Nothing. I'm studying art at the moment.'

He smiled. 'Oh dear. Always sounds so awfully final, doesn't it?'

He didn't seem very old himself – maybe nineteen or twenty. He wasn't particularly handsome but he had a kind face. His wild ginger hair gave his head a sort of cone shape and, because they were sitting so close together, she could just make out the five o'clock shadow on his face.

'I hate these bloody parties,' he said, crossing his legs and leaning back on the bench.

'You and me both,' Milly blurted out. There was a short silence then they both laughed. She felt comfortable with him. They chatted for a while and she discovered that his father was a Member of Parliament and that his mother was dead. He had a brother at Oxford reading history and his little sister had been the victim of polio.

'She wears callipers now,' he said dully. He sighed. 'Because of her, I had ambitions to be a doctor, but I'm no bloody good at maths or Latin. Got to have both to be a doctor, d'you see.'

105

'I'm sorry,' said Milly.

'Added to that,' he said with an exaggerated sigh, 'I always faint at the sight of blood.'

Milly couldn't help laughing.

'Useless Eustace,' he said, picking some cigarette paper from his bottom lip. 'That's what they used to call me at school. Useless Eustace.'

'Oh, don't say that,' she chided. 'I'm sure you're really good at something but you obviously haven't found it yet. I think you're destined to walk a different path, that's all.'

He turned and looked at her, a smile beginning on his lips. 'Why thank you, Milly Shepherd. That's the nicest thing anyone ever said to me.'

She wasn't sure if he was teasing her, but someone was calling her name. Milly got to her feet and let the jacket slide from her shoulders. 'That's my sister,' she said. 'I have to go.'

Taking it, he gave her a mock salute. 'Nice to have met you, Milly.'

'You too,' said Milly as she turned to run.

Chapter 14

Milly was absolutely dog-tired when she got home. Surprisingly, Mrs Cunningham had waited up for them, even though it was one in the morning.

'Could I have a word with you, madam,' she said as Agatha headed for the stairs.

'It'll have to wait until the morning.'

'I'm afraid it can't,' said the cook. 'It's about your husband.'

Agatha turned with an irritated expression on her face. 'What about him?'

'I'm afraid Mr Shepherd has been taken to hospital,' said Mrs Cunningham.

Milly took in her breath noisily. Pearl pushed past her and continued up the stairs.

'He was taken ill and we telephoned for Dr Jennings,' Mrs Cunningham continued. 'After he'd examined him, the doctor sent for an ambulance. They took him to Worthing Hospital.'

Milly was deeply shocked. 'Taken ill? What does that mean? Will he be all right?'

Mrs Cunningham opened her mouth but Agatha cut her short. 'There's nothing we can do about it now,' she said, mounting the stairs. 'We'll see to it in the morning. Thank you, Mrs Cunningham, and goodnight.'

'But Mother, shouldn't we telephone the hospital to see how he is?' Milly cried.

'What difference would it make?' Agatha said without turning. 'Like I said, we'll see to it in the morning. Now come along. It's time for bed.'

Milly was rooted to the spot. She stared helplessly at Mrs Cunningham, who mouthed, 'He'll be fine.'

'I think . . .' Milly began.

'I shall not tell you again, Millicent!' her mother shouted from the upstairs landing. 'Get to bed.' She paused. 'And goodnight, Mrs Cunningham.'

Even though she was very tired, Milly spent a restless night. As soon as she was on her own, her tears flowed. Poor Father. It must be because of that cough of his. She was aware that it had got a lot worse and now she regretted not saying something about it. He probably thought that nobody cared.

Not wanting to face her mother or Pearl again, she'd struggled out of the flouncy dress on her own and, in the process, trodden on one of the frills. There had been a loud ripping sound but she didn't care. She had made a vow that she would never, ever wear anything like it again. Her hair, which hadn't moved an inch all evening, was like a rock. Whatever was that stuff the hairdresser had put on it? She sat in front of her mirror, desperately trying to brush it out as her tears flowed. Tears for her father but also tears for herself. She was being bullied and pushed into a way of life which she didn't want. No, more than that, which she hated. Some of the people she'd met tonight were all right. People like Eustace; she'd liked him. The rest were shallow. They had belittled her and made her feel as if she didn't belong. She thought back to the moment when she'd made that mistake in front of the mirror. No one, apart from Pearl, knew how much she needed her glasses, but the first sound of their laughter had been so humiliating, and even though she had redeemed herself, the thought of it still chilled her.

Her hair looking like a frizzy triangle, Milly climbed into bed and switched off the light. That's when she thought of Lena. Charles was her father too. Milly would have to let Lena know that he was ill. She owed her that much. Charles was the only parent Lena had left. Once again, the same old sickening memory filtered through her mind. '*May this doll bring a thousand curses upon the Jezebel who stole our father . . .*' If only she could turn the clock back. Why had she done it? How could she explain herself to Lena? Yet she had to. She just had to. Milly stared at the ceiling. *What are you, Milly Shepherd – a woman or a mouse?*

And another thing . . . She'd have to stand up to her mother. If she was going to make something of her life, she jolly well couldn't allow herself to be persuaded into a marriage with the first chinless wonder who made a pass at her, no matter how rich he was. Her father would understand. As she remembered her poor father, Milly could feel her tears coming again. 'Oh, please be well. Please, God, make him better.'

Lena got up with the lark. Her first job was to make some flags; that done, she looked for a suitable stick in the shape of a 'Y' to use as a dowsing wand. After breakfast, she caught a bus into Worthing, changing at the Dome cinema for a bus to East Worthing. From there she walked over the railway bridge to the old nurseries. The two-acre area of wilderness which now belonged to her had already been fenced off. It was the rest of the plot she was interested in. Just as the first plot had been, it looked bleak, untidy and unkempt. With her flags stowed away in her backpack, Lena held the ends of the forked stick under her thumbs, allowing the rest of the stick to lie across her palms between her second and third fingers. She held it slightly off centre because if she found something manmade under the ground, such as a copper pipe, the stick was likely to jerk upwards and smack her in the face. If she found water, the stick would pull itself down towards the ground.

Holding the dowsing wand in a horizontal position, she began a slow walk from one side of the field to the other. She did three circuits before she had a reaction and then the dowsing wand suddenly, and quite violently, jerked down towards the earth. After marking the position with a flag, Lena carried on.

It took about two hours to cover the whole area and, when she looked back, the flags were in a diagonal line across the field. After pulling away some of the vegetation, she had found the reason why the ground was so waterlogged. A small stream fairly near the surface had been allowed to become clogged with debris and earth. It would be a simple matter to clean it out and perhaps dig a larger channel or, better still, pipe the water away.

Lena stood up and put her hand into the small of her aching back. She wished now that she had been able to secure the whole of the nurseries site. Earlier this year, she had decided to use the rest of her inheritance to buy another two acres, which would mean she owned an area roughly the size of four football pitches, and now that she knew why the ground round here was so wet, she could sort out the problem. She'd already cleared the first two acres and, if the rest was drained, that would mean it was an even better investment. As she tucked into a sandwich, Lena decided that if she left the flags in the ground, someone else might get the same idea. No, it was better to pull them up for now and have another word with Pa and see if he could help her secure the rest of the site. She could offer him a partnership. Having eaten her lunch, Lena packed up her things and set off for the bus stop. She felt rather excited. If she acquired more of the land, it would go a long way to making her independent. She didn't need a husband, not yet. With some careful planning, she could become a woman of means, and then, in her own time, she could marry for love.

Milly's mother and sister slept late. Milly hung around downstairs for an hour or so but, after a quick breakfast, she knew she couldn't wait any longer. She thought about telephoning the hospital, but decided that as she was a minor, they probably wouldn't tell her anything, so she decided to go in person. Dixon was cautious about taking her in case Mrs Shepherd wanted the car, so there was nothing for it but to catch the bus. Mrs Cunningham told her the Southdown bus from Horsham would be leaving from the village at ten. A glance up at the clock told Milly she would have to hurry but, if she caught it, she could be at the hospital before eleven.

Worthing hospital was in Lyndhurst Road, a three-storey building within a neatly manicured garden and lawn. Most of the wards were on the ground floor, with a few rooms on the upper floors surrounding the turret over the main entrance. Milly was unsure as to where her father was, but the woman on the reception desk was most helpful.

'Visiting isn't until two this afternoon,' she explained, 'but I'll have a word with the ward sister.' And, as it turned out, Milly was allowed to see her father immediately because of his critical condition.

He looked awful. His skin was grey and his breathing laboured. He was awake but not very responsive. He wore an oxygen mask and he was connected to a drip. 'I'm afraid he's quite poorly at the moment,' said the sister.

Milly gave her a horrified look. 'He's not going to die, is he?' she whispered.

The sister hesitated. 'Not just yet,' she said in a low, cautious voice, 'but you must understand, he is very ill.'

Milly made a small sound.

'Now, now, my dear,' said the sister. 'Pull yourself together. We don't want to frighten your father, do we?'

Taking a deep breath, Milly managed a brave smile and walked towards her father's bed. 'Hello, Father,' she said brightly as she pushed her glasses up her nose, 'I was just passing and thought I'd pop in to see you.'

Milly's first visit was short. Her father wasn't up to talking, and the sister pointedly reminded her again that official visiting was from two until four and six until seven. She kissed Charles on his forehead, promising to come back in the afternoon, and left the ward in tears. She would have called her mother straight away, had the ward sister not mentioned that she had telephoned her just before Milly had arrived.

Milly glanced at her watch. It was almost noon. She had to let Lena know, although with her mother about, it would be tricky getting her half-sister to his bedside. Fifteen minutes later, Milly was on a bus heading for Findon.

She arrived at the fairground to find Lena and Rainbow George having a row. It appeared that Lena was late getting started on her stall, and Rainbow George didn't like it. He was even more grumpy when he discovered that Milly was there to take Lena to the hospital.

'We have to get the bus there straight away,' Milly told her. 'I don't know how long he'll last.'

Lena was immediately thrown into a blind panic.

Under the circumstances, Rainbow George wasn't hard-hearted enough to refuse to let her go, especially as he liked Charles, but they could tell he wasn't happy about the stall being left unmanned. Once again, Vera was called upon to take over the hoopla.

'Bus be hanged,' Lena said suddenly. 'Seebold, Seebold.'

He came from behind the carousel with a spanner in his hand. 'What's up?'

'My father is dangerously ill,' Lena said. 'Can I borrow your lorry to drive us to the hospital?'

Milly's eyes grew wide. She had no idea Lena could drive.

'If he's that bad,' said Seebold, 'you be in no fit state to drive. Give me two seconds and I'll take you.'

He wasn't gone long, but Milly was so anxious that it seemed like a lifetime. Once they had set off, Milly couldn't stop herself glancing at him as he drove the lorry. She loved his dark curly hair. He was like a big kid. One tendril fell across his forehead in an attractive way and his face was sun-kissed . . . He had turned his head slightly and now he was looking at her. Milly looked away quickly, but a moment later she was stealing another glance at him. She watched him as they went around corners, his strong arms turning the wheel, his muscular chest straining his shirt, the smell of him warm and manly. Part of her felt ashamed. She shouldn't be thinking this way about someone else when her father was so ill, but being in such close proximity with Seebold was . . . intoxicating.

'There you are, duchess,' he said as he helped her down from the lorry. 'I 'ope it's not as bad as you think.'

Milly felt her face heating up. She turned to go and it was then that she spotted Dixon sitting in the car near the hospital lawns. She tugged at her sister's arm.

'My mother is already here,' she whispered. 'You'd better not let her know who you are.'

Lena looked stricken. 'What are you saying?' she challenged. 'He's *my* father too.'

'I know, I know,' Milly said desperately, 'but you don't understand. My mother can be vindictive, and I feel sure that if she finds out who you are, she'll tell the hospital authorities not to let you in.'

'But she's got no right . . .' Lena protested.

'I know, but I promise you, that's exactly the sort of thing she will do.'

'We'll see about that!' Lena retorted angrily.

'She might be right,' said Seebold, chipping in.

Lena was furious. 'Who asked for your opinion?'

Seebold held his hands up in mock surrender. 'You're not thinking straight, girl,' he said. 'If she does what Milly says she will, you won't never see your father, will you. Hang on for a bit until the old lady's gone and then you can stay as long as you like.'

Frustrated as she was, Lena saw the sense of it. Milly could have kissed him.

When they arrived outside Charles's room, they could hear Agatha's angry voice. 'No, Charles, absolutely not!'

There was a sound of a scraping chair, so Milly nudged Lena towards a small recess in the corridor.

'We need the house for Pearl's engagement party,' Agatha was saying. 'This is to be a happy occasion. I can't have ambulances and nurses littering up the place. You must understand that.'

Charles made a reply, but Milly couldn't hear what he was saying.

'But we need the east wing for the guests, Charles.' Milly heard the click of her mother's heels on the tiled floor. 'I'm sorry, but it's just not possible. You must see that.'

Charles began coughing again.

'Anyway,' said Agatha, 'must dash. Get well soon. Bye.'

A second later, she almost bumped into Milly in the doorway. 'Talk some sense into your father, will you?' she said confidentially as she pulled on her white gloves. 'The man's an idiot.' And with that she swept away.

As soon as her mother had gone, Milly beckoned Lena. When the two girls entered his room, Charles was very distressed. 'Please don't leave me to die here,' he gasped. 'I want to go home.'

Chapter 15

Agatha and Pearl were in the throes of packing. Most of Pearl's best dresses were in the London flat, but there were quite a few things she wanted with her – like her pale blue Jeanne Lanvin cotton and silk evening dress, and her Schiaparelli jacket with the metallic decoration down the front and on the waistline.

The Coco Chanel dress she had worn at the party last night was damaged. It had ripped at the hem when she and Freddie had been walking in the rose garden. They hadn't been doing anything wrong but, when she'd heard Lady Verity calling, she'd panicked, and somehow or other her dress had got caught on a particularly thorny rose bush. It was a shame, but she consoled herself that she had already worn it twice.

After breakfast, Pearl commandeered the maid who was polishing silver in the dining room, and set about laying her things on the bed ready for her to pack. Pearl surveyed her wardrobe. Everything looked perfect but she was badly in need of a blue shawl. Of course, there was no time to buy one, but she vaguely remembered that her sister had one in her room. It was an age since she'd seen it and perhaps her memory was hazy, but she thought it might be just what she needed.

Halfway through the morning, her mother set off for the hospital. 'Do you want to come, dear?'

Pearl frowned. 'Whatever for?'

'To see your father.'

Pearl stared in disbelief. 'Mother, you know how I hate hospitals.' She handed Elsie another blouse to fold. 'Anyway, I have to get all this done if we're to be on our way by lunch time.'

As soon as her mother was gone, Pearl hurried to Milly's room. She'd heard Mrs Cunningham telling her mother that Milly had caught the bus into Worthing some time ago, so she knew she wouldn't be back any time soon.

The hideous frock her sister had worn last night was draped across a chair. How could she bring herself to wear such a ghastly thing? Honestly, she had no dress sense at all. Poor Mother. Getting such an old-fashioned frump ready for her coming-out ball would be an uphill job.

Pearl rummaged carelessly through the drawers but couldn't find the shawl. She stood in the middle of the room and looked around. The only place she hadn't looked was in the old chest of drawers where Milly kept her childhood toys. She wouldn't have a shawl in there, would she? But for some reason Pearl was drawn to the bottom drawer. She pulled it out and reached inside. Right at the back she spotted a blue fringe. There it was! Pushing aside the teddies, a stuffed rabbit and a jack-in-the-box, she pulled it out. It was heavy. Something was wrapped inside. Pearl pulled the shawl and something fell to the floor with a clatter. She let out an involuntary squeal. It was a doll. Not just any doll, but it looked like the doll she had used that time when she and Milly had cursed that trollop in the cottage. Pearl stared down at it in disbelief. Surely it couldn't be the same one? Yet it looked like it. But how on earth did it get here? Hadn't she'd thrown it to the back of the log pile? And the eye . . . hadn't she poked that out with her finger? She bent

116

down and picked it up. It had been repaired; repaired and dressed up. A white rage filled her whole body. Of course, now that she was older she didn't believe the curse could have done real damage, but back then she certainly did. Now it looked as if all those years ago her stupid sister had gone back to fetch the doll, despite her best efforts to get rid of her father's tart and save their family. How dare she? How bloody dare she! For a second or two, Pearl was sorely tempted to smash it on the floor, or stamp on its face but, after a short pause, she thought better of it. Calmer now and breathing normally again, she reflected that the shawl would be useful for tonight and, as for the doll . . . She nodded as a triumphant smile moved across her face. The doll would be useful on another occasion. She would keep it.

Milly and Lena were on the horns of a dilemma. It tore both of them apart to see their father so broken in body, and it was even worse to see him broken in spirit. As they left his bedside, they asked to see the ward sister, who explained that Charles had lung cancer. It had eaten away most of his left lung and already his right lung was showing signs of damage.

'Shouldn't we encourage him to give up smoking?' Milly asked.

'There is little point,' the sister said kindly. 'Thirteen years of forty or more a day is a hard habit to kick. He hasn't got long anyway. Let him continue to do what he enjoys.'

'What will happen to him now?' Lena sniffed into her handkerchief.

'I'm afraid there is nothing more we can do. We suggested to your mother that you take him home, but she says it's impossible. That being the case, we shall move him into a home for incurables.'

Both girls stared at her, aghast.

'*Is* it possible for a relative to look after him?' Milly said.

She suspected that her mother didn't want her husband at home simply because it wasn't convenient. 'I mean, what sort of care does he need?'

'Just to be made comfortable,' said the sister. 'You'll probably need a nurse to keep an eye on him, and someone to come in when the end is near, but other than that, all he needs is to be surrounded by his family and the people he loves.'

As they left the hospital and walked to where Seebold had parked the lorry, Lena was already weeping. Seebold jumped down and came to meet them. He helped Lena up into the cab. Ashen-faced, Milly climbed in after her and put her arm around her half-sister who sobbed on her shoulder.

'I'm guessing it's not good news,' said Seebold, climbing into the driver's seat.

'Our father is dying,' Milly said simply.

Seebold looked at her, sympathy written all over his face. 'I'm sorry.'

Milly felt her chin quiver as she battled her tears.

'I'm taking you both for a stiff drink,' he said, starting the engine.

Ten minutes later they were sitting in the Half Brick on the corner of Brighton Road and Ham Road. Under normal circumstances, Milly would have shared her knowledge of the public house, which dated back to the middle of the last century. It had been built to replace the original Half Brick, which had been washed out to sea in the days when it stood on an unstable salt-grass common, but what did she care for that now? She was far too upset about what was happening right now.

Seebold bought each of them a sherry (as strong a drink as Milly would allow, considering that Lena was under age) and half a pint of bitter for himself.

'So what can I do to help?' he said, looking directly at Milly.

She looked up at him, grateful for his genuine concern. 'Nothing,' she said sadly. 'The sister said we can take him home, but my mother is adamant that he can't be nursed in the house.'

'Is there no one else?'

Milly shook her head.

'No other relatives?'

Again Milly shook her head. 'He has a sister but she lives too far away. She lives in a village called West Moors, which is on the Hampshire–Dorset border. The journey would be too much.'

'Why can't your mother have him home?'

Milly was beginning to feel embarrassed. All this was typical of her mother. Milly was used to her stubbornness, but for an outsider it was difficult to understand. 'I'm not sure. She says she's going to London later today and I know there's to be a big party at the end of the week.'

Their angry and frustrated thoughts remained unspoken. Seebold sipped his beer. 'What about that place where you used to live?' he asked Lena.

'Nan would have him like a shot,' said Lena, 'but,' she glanced helplessly at Milly, 'I don't think . . .'

'My mother would never allow it,' Milly chipped in. 'What would the neighbours say and all that.'

'The man is dying,' said Lena. 'What event is so important that it can't wait?'

Milly sighed. 'It seems that my sister is getting engaged, once her future intended has proposed. Like I say, they're all coming back to the house for a stupendous party.'

'I can't believe your mother would put a party before her husband's last wishes,' Lena spat.

Milly felt her face colour.

'It's not Milly's fault,' Seebold said.

Lena looked contrite. 'I know. I'm sorry.'

'I hate it as much as you do,' Milly said helplessly, 'but

119

my mother is totally focused on making a glittering marriage for Pearl.'

Desperate to help them find a solution, Seebold frowned thoughtfully. 'Didn't you say Angel was hidden away somewhere around here when she was ill?'

'In a cottage in the grounds,' Lena said dully.

'Well . . .?'

There was a pregnant silence, then Milly said, 'He's right, you know. We could do it, Lena. You and I. Hide Father in the cottage. And even if my mother knows he's there, she won't come near the place.'

Lena looked up sharply.

'It wouldn't be quite the same as being at home,' Milly went on, 'but he'd be in the same place where Angel spent her last days, and we both know how much he loved your mother.'

'Your mother will be very angry with you,' Lena whispered cautiously.

Milly chewed her bottom lip thoughtfully. 'D'you know what?' she said defiantly. 'For the first time in my life, I don't really care.'

The next two days were hectic. With her mother and Pearl in London, Milly had a free hand to make all the arrangements. Nan mustered a couple of women from the village to spring-clean the cottage and, of course, Milly and Lena were there to lend a hand too.

The girls had already boiled water and they'd come with plenty of buckets, bleach, carbolic soap and brushes from the house.

'Thank you all for coming,' said Milly, tying her apron at the back, 'I think you all know my father.'

The women nodded.

'I'm afraid he's very ill and there is no hope . . .' she took a breath, 'but he doesn't want to die in hospital. That's why we're here. The cottage hasn't been used for some time, so everything will have to be cleaned to within an inch of its life.'

Everybody spread out and worked solidly all morning. Every cobweb, every patch of mildew and the dirty skirting boards were thoroughly scrubbed; before long, the cottage took on its bright atmosphere once more. There wasn't time to wash and dry the curtains, but Elsie found some spare pairs in an old trunk and, after beating them on the washing line, they were deemed fit for the job. Mrs Cunningham, bless her heart, had already set about cooking nourishing food in the kitchen, even though she knew there was little chance of Mr Shepherd being able to eat any of it.

While Seebold took Lena back to the fairground to tell Rainbow George she would be taking time off, Milly went to see Dr Jennings to arrange for the hire of a nurse. She was hoping that she might get the same nurse who had looked after Lena's mother, but sadly the woman had long-since retired to Eastbourne to live with her widowed sister.

'Nurse Revell is highly respected,' Dr Jennings assured her, 'and I myself shall pop in every day.'

An ambulance brought Charles home in the afternoon. He looked frail but they could tell that he was pleased to be out of hospital.

Milly guessed it must have been hard for Lena to see him in the same bed her mother had lain in. It would have brought back some bitter-sweet memories, but the two sisters took comfort from each other. Charles was getting the best of care and, thank God, they had managed to give him what he'd wished for. It also reminded Milly that she really needed to come clean to Lena and her father about what she and Pearl had done all those years ago. Looking at the two people she loved most in the world, she wondered if she could she really tell them now.

Perhaps not.

Later that same day, Agatha and Pearl returned from London. When Elsie saw their car pulling up she hurried across the ha-ha to tell Milly they were back. Although Milly had known this time would come, it was still an anxious moment when she went back to the house to tell her mother what was happening.

'You've done what?' Agatha spat. 'How dare you take it upon yourself to—'

'Mother, he's dying,' Milly interrupted. 'He wanted to come home, and it seemed only right that we should help him do that.'

'We have half the county arriving on Saturday,' Agatha began again. 'They don't want to see ambulances, and nurses running around the place. I won't have—'

'You won't see a thing,' Milly said firmly, as she mustered a courage she didn't know she possessed. 'The cottage is completely hidden from the house. We'll come and tell you when it gets nearer the time.'

'You needn't bother,' said Agatha turning to leave. 'I'll know soon enough.'

Milly blinked as she felt tears pricking the backs of her eyes at the depth of her mother's anger. But she wasn't going to argue. Not now.

'Fine,' she said quietly as she began to close the door behind them.

Her mother suddenly turned. 'We,' Agatha challenged. 'You said "we".'

Milly froze. If her mother found out that Lena was in the cottage with their father, there would be hell to pay. She looked to the floor so that her mother wouldn't see her scarlet face. 'Dr Jennings booked a nurse,' she said coolly.

They heard a footfall and Pearl was standing there, her face wreathed in smiles. 'You haven't seen my engagement ring yet, have you?'

She waggled her hand under Milly's nose. The enormous

rock on the third finger of her left hand glistened in the late-afternoon sunlight. 'Freddie proposed last night,' she cooed. 'I'm to be married to a baron. I shall have a title.' She paused. 'What is the wife of a baron called, Mummy?'

Neither woman spoke.

'Well?' Pearl demanded. What do you think?'

'Very nice,' said Milly.

'Very nice,' Pearl cried. 'Is that all you can say?'

'Our father is dying,' Milly said in a measured tone, 'and all you can think about is that ring.'

Pearl looked stricken. 'Oh no, he can't be dying. He can't.'

Surprised by her sister's reaction, Milly felt guilty. Perhaps Pearl hadn't taken on board what was happening. Maybe she hadn't understood just how ill Charles was. Milly moved to put her arm around her but Pearl turned to Agatha with a scowl on her face. 'Oh Mummy, this is too awful,' she cried out. 'I couldn't bear it if he died now. It would completely ruin my engagement party.'

Chapter 16

Charles Walter Peregrine Shepherd, a man who never liked to make a fuss, left this world quietly. The whole evening had been punctuated by the sound of loud music from Pearl's engagement party in the big house but, once the fireworks had finished, only the occasional sound of laughter drifted across the ha-ha. Although the girls were annoyed and upset by the frivolity, in all honesty Charles didn't appear to be distressed by it. In the small hours of the morning, silence descended.

Charles had been in the cottage for four days. Despite the sadness of the situation, he and his daughters had enjoyed precious time together. At first he had been lucid, so the three of them shared their memories and the little cottage had been filled with laughter.

'Do you remember taking me donkey riding on Bournemouth beach?' Milly had asked.

Charles had chuckled. 'How could I forget it, given that you rode through the bunting enclosure and took half a dozen fold-up chairs with you!'

'My fondest memory,' said Lena, 'is of you and my mother on the beach.'

Charles smiled. 'You mean the day when Angel ran up to

124

the water and shouted, 'Lena, Lena come out. It's raining. You'll get wet.'

On the day of the party, he suddenly deteriorated, and they sat silently by his bedside. Then, early on the Sunday morning, his breathing became more erratic. Milly was holding his left hand on the bed while Lena held his right hand against her cheek. Nurse Revell was standing at the end of the bed, filling in the charts, when Charles opened his eyes one last time. He seemed to be looking at something on the far side of the room and they saw a small smile forming on his lips. Milly turned her head to see who was there just as he breathed out a long sigh. His last word was little more than a whisper but all three of them heard it. 'Angel.'

The next few hours were a bit of a blur. The girls held each other close and wept in the little kitchen while Nurse Revell prepared him for the undertaker. Seebold, who had agreed to come in the morning to see if they needed anything, took his lorry down to the telephone box in the village. Dr Jennings came within the hour and the death certificate was signed.

As he left, Nurse Revell said, 'I'll stay until the undertaker comes, if you like.'

So Seebold took Lena back to Nan's house and Milly walked across the ha-ha to Muntham Court to give her mother and Pearl the news. It was a lovely morning. The air was crisp and it was a little chilly, but the birds sang and the subtle scent of asters, cyclamen, the purple emperor salvia and snapdragons wafted through the morning mist towards her. It struck her as the strangest feeling because – in the midst of all this beauty – there was such a sadness, for she knew she would never see her darling father again. She'd never realised before that grief brought on a physical change in the body. Milly had a tightness in her chest and an overwhelming headache in addition to a heaviness of spirit she'd never experienced before. How could life go on without him? He had been her one constant; her solid rock; the only member of her close family who truly loved her.

Once she was inside the house, the pungent smell of spilled wine and stale cigarettes stripped all her bitter-sweet memories away. It was no good telling her mother and Pearl what had happened. They were both still asleep in bed. In the kitchen, Milly told the staff the sombre news. Mrs Cunningham pressed her handkerchief to her mouth and turned away. Elsie, who was busy washing glasses and clearing up the party mess, stood by the kitchen sink with red eyes and her chin wobbling. Bodkin excused himself from the breakfast table and went outside, while Dixon sat staring into space and saying nothing.

After a while, Mrs Cunningham made Milly a cup of tea, which she drank before heading to her own room. She took off her glasses and lay on the bed but she didn't sleep. At around ten o'clock, she heard her mother ringing her bedside bell, but before Elsie reached her bedroom with the breakfast tray, Milly knocked quietly on the door.

'Come in.' Agatha seemed surprised to see her daughter, but before Milly had time to say anything, she'd guessed why she was there. 'So he's gone, has he?'

Milly nodded her head. 'At five this morning.'

Agatha sat on the chair by her dressing table. 'At least he had the grace not to spoil Pearl's engagement party,' she added coldly.

Milly felt a sudden wave of red-hot anger. 'That's all you think about, isn't it, Mother!' she snapped. 'Pearl, Pearl, Pearl.'

'Oooh,' Agatha said sarcastically. 'Listen to the green-eyed monster.'

For a second or two Milly was taken off balance. 'Not at all,' she said haughtily. 'I don't give a damn about coming out and all those endless and pointless parties. I was thinking of poor Father. He was so ill, but you didn't once show him an ounce of sympathy. He was your husband, Mother. He didn't have a mean bone in his body and now he's dead.'

Agatha said nothing.

'You must have loved him once,' Milly protested.

Agatha let out a bored sigh. 'I never loved Charles,' she said, picking up her hairbrush and turning to face the mirror. 'He was convenient, that's all.'

'Convenient?' Milly gasped. 'What does that mean?'

They were interrupted by Elsie bringing in the tray.

'I thought I told you to knock before you come into my room, you stupid girl,' Agatha said tetchily. 'Put it on the bedside table.'

Elsie, her face flaming, did as she was bid and left the room.

Determined to find out what her mother meant, Milly resumed their argument. 'What did you mean when you said my father was convenient?'

'I haven't got time for this,' said Agatha.

'I want to know, Mother. Just tell me. I hated the way you treated him. You and Pearl were quick enough to spend his money but you treated him like a dog.'

Agatha took in her breath noisily, her chest expanding and her face dark with fury. 'How dare you speak to me like that!' she shouted. 'Who do you think you are, you jumped-up little madam. Get out of my bedroom. Go on, get out.'

Milly's eyes blazed. 'Why do you always do this, Mother?' she complained. 'Why can't you just talk to me for once?'

Just then the door burst open and Pearl bounded into the room. 'What's going on?'

Milly and Agatha were still staring angrily at each other, until Agatha broke the spell by swinging her legs around her dressing-table stool and getting to her feet. 'Nothing,' she said in that same bored tone as she sat on the edge of the bed to pour herself some tea. 'Nothing at all. Leave the door open, dear. Your sister is just leaving.'

Pearl looked at Milly. 'Why are you here anyway?' she said contemptuously. 'I thought you'd be in that cottage with him.'

'Father died this morning,' said Milly, mustering as much dignity as she could.

Pearl's face crumpled. 'Oh God, no! Does that mean I have to wait ages and ages before I can get married?' Pushing past Milly, she knelt by the bed and laid her face on her mother's knee. 'You have to do something Mummy. If I hang around much longer, the baby will start to show.'

Milly's jaw dropped, but they didn't seem to be aware that she was still in the room. Her mother began stroking Pearl's hair. 'There, there, darling. It'll be all right, I promise.'

Milly felt sick. Desperate to get away, she headed out of the door, just catching her sister's muffled voice saying, 'How long is the official period of mourning, Mummy?'

Pearl's fiancé, Friedrich von Herren, now officially known as Freddie, was in London. He had gone to the German Embassy, located at Prussia House, 9 Carlton House Terrace. It was an imposing building, with four floors built in the Georgian style. Freddie had been there twice before, once when the previous ambassador, Leopold von Hoesch, had died in 1936, when he had been invited to be a part of the huge gathering for his funeral. The ambassador had been given full military honours, with a nineteen-gun salute in Hyde Park and various British dignitaries acting as mourners. The coffin, mounted on a gun carriage, had been draped with the Nazi swastika. Freddie hadn't travelled with it to Dover where it was put on board HMS *Scout*, but he had attended the wake in Prussia House. The second time he had been in the building had been earlier in the month, when he had told his Uncle Reinhard about Pearl and asked him for a special favour: money.

This time he was shown into a newly decorated room

where his uncle, seated at the desk, rose as he came in. 'My dear fellow,' he said with a wide smile. 'Do come in, but first just make sure we won't be disturbed, will you?'

Freddie slid the wooden slide on the outside of the door until the German word '*Privat*' appeared, then he entered the room and closed the door.

Charles was buried just over a week later, his funeral being held in the church of St John the Baptist in Findon. In days gone by, parish churches had been central to the community, but first the Black Death and then the new bypass meant that the church, which stood on a wooded slope, was now some distance from the village of Findon. However, people came from far and wide to mourn Charles and the service was well attended.

Agatha, Pearl and Milly arrived together in the same car just behind the hearse. All three women were dressed entirely in black. Agatha wore a satin dress with a scoop neckline. The bodice had black lace up to the throat, and she wore it under a coat with a heavily black-beaded front. She also had a large hat which was covered by a thick black veil. Pearl wore a dress with a square neckline. There were embroidered angel wings on the left shoulder and down the right side of the skirt, which had a chiffon handkerchief hem. Her hat was covered in the same kind of floating veil her mother wore. Milly had chosen a much simpler ensemble. Her undecorated black dress had been cut on the bias, which was very flattering to her figure. The dress had short sleeves and a cowl neckline with a belt and art deco buckle at the waist. To complete her outfit, she wore long black gloves and a plain cloche hat, and carried a small clasp bag. An usher showed them to their seats at the front of the church.

The coffin was lifted shoulder high by the pallbearers and the vicar asked everyone to stand. A moment later they could hear him reading from a prayer book.

'I AM the resurrection and the life, saith the Lord: he that believeth in me, though he were dead, yet shall he live, And whosoever liveth and believeth in me shall never die.'

The assembled congregation was silent. Milly wondered if Lena was here and where she might be sitting. She tried to look around, but Agatha nudged her in the ribs.

The service lasted about thirty minutes, and then the pallbearers came back to take Charles to the burial ground. It was raining outside. Someone gave Milly an umbrella and then she saw Lena. While her mother and Pearl followed the coffin, Milly hurried over to fetch her half-sister. 'You should be with us,' she whispered.

Lena shook her head. 'Your mother will go mad.'

But Milly wouldn't be dissuaded. Linking her arm through Lena's, she guided her towards the graveside. Agatha gave them a dark frown from behind her veil as the vicar began the age-old words:

'For as much as it hath pleased Almighty God of his great mercy to take unto himself the soul of our dear brother here departed, we therefore commit his body to the ground; earth to earth, ashes to ashes, dust to dust; in sure and certain hope of the Resurrection to eternal life . . .' Milly gripped Lena's hand tightly as the pallbearers lowered the body of their much-loved father into the earth.

Agatha stepped forward and threw a handful of dirt onto the coffin. Pearl did the same but, when it came to Milly's turn, she still had hold of Lena's hand. Agatha stepped between Milly and the grave and, taking her arm, pulled her firmly away from Lena.

Back at the car, Pearl was told in no uncertain tones to sit in the front with Dixon. 'I shall sit in the back with Millicent,' said Agatha.

As they moved off, her mother closed the glass partition and pulled off her veil. Judging by the thunderous look on her face, she was furious. When she spoke, her spitting voice was full of venom. 'What the bloody hell did you think you were doing, you idiot girl?' she hissed. 'Who was that person?'

'Her name is Lena,' Milly said, the firmness of her voice belying the terror she felt right now. 'And she had every right to be with us. Lena is his daughter.'

'His daughter?' Agatha spat. Her eyes flashed. 'His daughter!'

'Angel was her mother,' said Milly, her legs turning to jelly.

'You held hands at his funeral with his bastard daughter?' Agatha choked. 'How could you? How could you?'

Milly knew she was waiting for an apology, waiting for her to grovel, but she was done with that now. Lena should have been allowed to sit at the front with the rest of the family. What did it matter which side of the blanket she'd been born? Her grief was more genuine than Pearl and Agatha's.

'How long have you known about her?' Agatha snapped. 'Why didn't you say something?'

Milly didn't answer.

'She looks about the same age as you,' Agatha went on. 'Charles had a bastard child? I can't believe it!' There was a pause, then she added, 'Who else knows about this? Say something, you stupid girl; who else knows?'

'I don't know,' said Milly.

Agatha huffed and crossed her legs. 'Really, Milly. You are impossible.'

The two of them didn't speak for the rest of the journey. When they arrived at the house, Agatha swept in first. The hired maids were standing by the entrance with trays of wine for the mourners who had been invited to the wake.

Agatha slipped off her coat and Elsie took it from her. A large man with an equally large brown tobacco-stained moustache sidled up to her.

131

'Aggie darling,' he said huskily as he kissed her cheek. Milly was deeply shocked to see him slip his hand around her mother's waist and down to her bottom. 'This must be absolute hell for you,' he said, giving her buttock a gentle squeeze.

Agatha stepped away from his inappropriate caress and smiled. 'Bunny, dear, why don't you get yourself a little drinky-poo and I'll be with you in a minute.'

While 'Bunny' headed for the drinks cabinet, Agatha motioned to her older daughter. 'Pearl, would you mind seeing to our guests for a moment?' she said sweetly. 'Milly dear, please come with me into the morning room for a minute.'

Milly followed. Agatha closed the door then reached back her hand and slapped her daughter across the face with such force that Milly slipped and fell against the arm of the chair. Getting back up, Milly stared at her mother in disbelief as she held her hand over her stinging cheek.

'As soon as this is over,' Agatha snarled through gritted teeth, 'you can pack your bags and get out of this house and never come back.'

With that, she sailed out of the room.

Chapter 17

It took Milly a while to recover from what her mother had done. As soon as it was practical, she had hurried upstairs and away from the guests coming into the house. Shutting herself into the bathroom, she looked in the mirror. Her face was a mess. Her cheek was swollen and she had a large bruise appearing under her eye. She guessed her mother's ring had caught her cheekbone as she struck out. As she held a welcome cold flannel against the wound, the skin was painfully sore.

She didn't cry until she was in her bedroom. She had pulled her suitcase down from the top of the wardrobe and set about packing. The case was almost full when her mind cleared and she began to realise the extent of her loss. Her beloved father had gone, and now she was being turfed out of her only home. Where would she go? There was no time to write a letter to Aunt Betsy in West Moors, and she had nowhere else to go. She'd have to find somewhere for the night, maybe the next two nights, and by that time she might be able to work something out. She had a little money put aside, but there was no way she could support herself for any real length of time. Much as she hated being with her mother, she hadn't realised until this moment just how lucky she had been to grow up in the safety of Muntham Court. She wished Lena was here and wondered briefly if Rainbow George would let her join the travellers. But what did she have to offer him? And where would she sleep? When the tears finally came, Milly sat on the edge of her bed and lowered her head.

Sometime later, a sharp knock at the door made her jump. Quickly wiping her eyes and putting her glasses back on, she looked up and said, 'Come in.'

It was Elsie. 'The mistress says to come into the morning room, miss,' she began. 'The solicitor is here to read the will.' All at once Elsie gasped. 'Oh miss, what happened to your face?'

'I fell over a chair,' Milly lied as she blew her nose.

The maid was shocked. 'Can I do anything for you?'

'No, no,' said Milly. 'I'll be fine.' She managed a brave smile. 'But tell my mother I'm not coming.'

'The solicitor says they can't start without you.'

Milly knew better than to argue. 'Very well. I'll be down in a minute.'

When Elsie had gone, Milly powdered her face, although it didn't seem to make much difference to her bright red cheek. Putting on a pair of sunglasses, she made her way downstairs.

The guests had gone but the door to the morning room was open and she could hear her mother's strident voice. 'What is that creature doing here? This is for family only.'

As Milly walked through the door, Lena was standing next to Mr May, of May, May and Prior, her father's solicitors. She hurried to Lena's side and grasped her hand encouragingly.

'Miss Buckley has every right to be here, Mrs Shepherd,' Mr May was saying quietly. 'She is mentioned in your husband's will.'

Agatha harrumphed and sat down.

Milly and Lena sat side by side. 'I've got something to tell you after all this,' Lena whispered out of the corner of her mouth.

Milly chewed anxiously on her bottom lip. 'And I you.'

Mr May took a last look around the room before opening an envelope marked 'Last Will and Testament'.

'*In the name of God,*' he read from the title page, '*I, Charles Walter Peregrine Shepherd of the parish of Findon, investment banker, do hereby solemnly declare that I am of sound mind and perfect memory . . .*'

The reading went on for several minutes. Milly's father had left a request to pay any funeral expenses incurred and to settle any outstanding debts first. He also stipulated that he wished to annul his previous will, which he had written in 1919.

'And now for the bequests,' Mr May said, and the room settled into an air of quiet anticipation.

'*Item: To my daughter Millicent, I leave Muntham Court, along with all furniture and fixtures, its grounds and gardens. The property will be held in trust until she is twenty-one years of age. I also bequeath her an annual annuity of fifty pounds.*'

There was a shocked gasp from Agatha. Mr May paused for a moment and looked over the top of his glasses as she pressed her handkerchief to her mouth.

'*Item,*' he continued, '*I bequeath Lena Buckley the cottage in the grounds of Muntham Court and an annual annuity of fifty pounds.*'

Agatha turned to glare at both girls.

'*Item,*' Mr May began again quickly as he anticipated trouble brewing, '*I bequeath my wife Agatha and Pearl Shepherd an annual annuity of fifty pounds between them. If I die before Millicent is twenty-one years of age,*' Mr May looked up over the top of his glasses again before adding, 'which of course he did, *they are to be allowed to reside in Muntham Court until Millicent Shepherd reaches the age of twenty-one. Messrs May, May and Prior can discontinue this agreement without penalty if and whenever my wife should so desire before Millicent reaches twenty-one years of age.*

'*My assets, properties and monies, once my debts and bequests are paid, I bequeath to the following charities . . .*'

Mr May droned on with what seemed like an endless list of those who were to get smaller bequests. When it came to the house staff, Mrs Cunningham was to have twenty-five pounds a year, Bodkin and Dixon were bequeathed twenty pounds a year and 'the maid who is currently serving the house', which was Elsie of course, was to have a lump sum of five pounds. Considering the girl only earned ninepence an hour, it was a very generous amount, so much so that – when she heard the news – Elsie fainted clean away and the proceedings had to stop for a while until she had been revived and given water and a seat by the open window.

'Just a minute,' Agatha interposed haughtily as Mr May resumed the reading of the will, 'what is the date on that document? My husband was very ill before he died. I cannot believe he was of sound mind or understood what he was doing when he wrote it. He was extremely upset.'

Mr May turned to the last page of the document. 'It is signed, *In Witness whereof, I have hereunto set my hand and seal this 15th day of August.*' He paused because today was 30 September.

Agatha looked around the room with a triumphant sneer on her face.

Taking a new breath, Mr May began again. '*In the year of our Lord, one thousand nine hundred and thirty.*' And looking directly at Agatha he added, 'In other words, madam, your husband wrote this will seven years ago.'

There was a murmur in the room and Agatha's nostrils flared as she pursed her lips.

Pearl, who had been waiting patiently to hear what her inheritance would be, suddenly jumped up. 'But what about me?' she said tetchily. 'I was his daughter too. Didn't he leave anything to me?'

'As I said, Miss Shepherd,' Mr May repeated, 'under the terms of the will, you and your mother will receive the sum of fifty pounds annually between you.'

'But that means I get the same as the cook!' Pearl cried.

'I shall hear no more of this,' Agatha snapped as she rose to her feet.

'Before you go, Mrs Shepherd,' Mr May said in a raised voice. 'Mr Shepherd also left this envelope to be opened on the day his will was read.'

Recognising the envelope she'd seen Charles hiding in the drawer of his desk on the day of Lady Verity's party, Agatha lowered herself back into her chair.

As soon as he'd finished the formal reading of Charles's will, Mr May opened the other envelope. It was marked 'Last Will and Testament' but with the wording crossed out.

'How did you get that?' Agatha demanded. 'I saw Charles with that envelope the day he went to hospital. Who gave it to you?'

The room went very quiet, and Agatha glanced around, clearly embarrassed. It was obvious by the tone of her voice that she had searched for it, and the same thought was going through every head in the room – had she wanted to destroy it?

'It was me,' said a voice at the back of the room. 'Dr Jennings.'

'Then you should have given it to me,' Agatha said cuttingly.

'It was the master himself who asked Dr Jennings to fetch it for him, madam,' said Mrs Cunningham. 'I saw him do it.'

Agatha's face was red.

When Mr May opened the envelope, it contained four separate letters: one for Agatha, one for Pearl, another for Milly and the last one for Lena. There was also one piece of paper marked with Agatha's name. 'There is no need to read them here,' said Mr May. 'I received instruction that they are private to each of you.' After distributing the letters and the piece of paper, he began to pack up his papers and people started to drift from the room.

'This is preposterous,' Agatha said coldly as she turned to Milly and Lena. 'I shall of course contest this will. It's obvious that you both manipulated that man to your own advantage.' She glanced down at the slip of paper and sneered.

As Agatha stood to leave, the paper fluttered to the floor. She didn't appear to notice. 'Expect to hear from my solicitors,' she snapped.

Alone in the room, Milly and Lena looked at each other. Milly picked up the note with her mother's name and placed it on the table, but not before noticing what was written there.

Silence is golden. I remembered my promise.

The two girls looked at each other with a frown. 'What on earth does that mean?'

Lena shrugged. 'Haven't a clue. I never expected him to do that,' she whispered as Milly sat back down.

'Me neither.'

Both girls fingered their sealed envelopes, but neither of them opened them. A few minutes later, Lena rose to her feet.

'Are you all right?' she said. 'You look . . . very pale.'

'My mother has thrown me out,' said Milly. 'My suitcase is in the hall but I have nowhere to go.'

Lena squeezed her hands.

'Do you think Nan would let me sleep on her sofa?' Milly asked, adding quickly, 'It's just for one night.'

'Of course she will.' Lena shook her head sadly. 'It seems very unfair,' she said, looking around the room, 'when all this will be yours one day.'

'It might not happen,' said Milly. 'You heard her. Believe me, she is going to fight tooth and nail to get that will annulled. My mother is a very determined woman.'

They were both silent.

'You could use the cottage,' Lena suddenly said.

Milly frowned.

'There was no age clause on my inheritance.'

'Could I?' said Milly, her eyes filling with tears.

Lena gave her a sympathetic smile. Milly blew her nose.

'In fact, we could both go there.'

'What, now?'

'Yes, why not?'

Milly gave her half-sister a wobbly smile. 'Thank you. Oh, thank you.'

The pair of them struggled outside with Milly's suitcase and painting things until they came to Seebold's lorry parked in the drive. What a good job Lena had arranged for him to come and collect her. He dashed out of the cab and took the case. 'What happened?' he said, horrified.

'We'll tell you in a minute,' said Lena. 'Can you take us both to the cottage?'

Once the fire in the hearth was lit, it didn't take long to transform the cold, empty cottage into a warm and friendly bolthole. Lena made up the beds and Seebold brought in more logs. Milly unpacked some of her things and looked in the kitchen. There was no food apart from the basics like tea leaves, a little sugar and a few biscuits. The shops would be closed now.

'I'll go and get some fish and chips for now,' Seebold said.

'And I'm sure Nan would let you have a couple of slices of bread and stuff,' said Lena.

Milly struggled not to give way to her ever-persistent tears. After her mother's nastiness, their kindness was almost too hard to bear and, being in the cottage with Lena, her feelings about her betrayal so long ago were only exacerbated. With Seebold gone, she knew she ought to pluck up the courage to tell her sister about the curse, but she couldn't bring herself to do it. Lena threw herself onto the sofa and put her feet up. 'I can't believe Pa gave me all this.'

'You may have to wait a long time before you can safely call it your own, Lena,' said Milly. 'Like I said, my mother is going to fight us all the way.'

Lena shrugged nonchalantly.

'I'll go and see Mr May first thing on Monday morning and see what he says,' said Milly. She frowned. 'I just don't understand why she hates me so. What have I ever done to her?'

'Nothing,' said Lena. 'Look, I know she's your mother, Milly, but she's an absolute bitch. Whatever happened in the past between my mother and Pa, you didn't deserve to be treated like that. It's not your fault, so please don't let her pull your down.'

'I'll try not to.' She sat in the easy chair. 'By the way, what was it you wanted to tell me?'

'I've bought some land,' said Lena and, while her sister sat with an open mouth and raised eyebrows, she told her all about the old nurseries.

'I couldn't have done it without Pa's help,' Lena went on. 'There's still some more drainage to fix, but the agent told me this morning that he has a client who is very interested in renting.'

'That's incredible,' Milly gasped. She felt immensely proud of her half-sister. Imagine being a landowner at her age. It was amazing!

They heard Seebold's lorry pulling up outside. 'Not a word to Seebold,' Lena cautioned. 'I don't want him to get any more romantic ideas.'

'Especially now that you are a woman of means,' Milly added with a grin.

The fish and chips were wonderful. When they'd finished, the three of them relaxed in front of the fire with a cup of tea and talked a lot about Charles. After a while, the conversation drifted towards their personal hopes and dreams for the future; it seemed that all three had reached a crossroads in their lives. For Milly it was clear that her mother wasn't going to bother with her coming out, which was a great relief. 'I had thought that I would be able to continue with my studies at Worthing School of Art and Science,' she said, 'but it transpired that Father died before he'd paid the fees for next term.'

'Heavens above,' cried Lena. 'So what will you do?'

Milly shrugged. 'I suppose I'd better write to Aunt Betsy,' she said and, glancing up at Lena, added, 'Actually, she must be your Aunt Betsy too. She's lovely. I'll take you to see her sometime. Of all my relatives, she's the nicest. She may be willing to help. I guess my future rather depends on what she says.'

'What about Lena?' Seebold asked. 'Would she help her too?'

Milly looked a tad uncomfortable. Aunt Betsy was a sweetie but Uncle Neville was rather Victorian in outlook. In fact, she wasn't even sure if they knew of Lena's existence.

'I don't need anybody's help,' Lena said quickly.

'So you won't be marrying me then?' said Seebold.

'No, I won't,' Lena retorted.

Seebold appeared to be shocked.

'And you needn't bother looking at me like that,' said Lena. 'You don't want to marry me anyway.'

Seebold grinned. 'They do say that a man with a wife and children finds it hard to get on,' he admitted. 'But keep me in mind if you feels desperate.'

'And I would have to be desperate,' Lena chuntered. Milly jabbed her with her elbow, making her sister look up with an innocent expression. 'What?'

Milly changed the subject. 'I hope it doesn't sound rude,' she began, 'but I've always thought your name is very unusual. How did you come by it?'

'I found it on the road,' he quipped.

Lena giggled. Milly blinked.

'Na,' he went on, 'that's down to my old mum.' He took a deep breath. 'When she was a youngster, she was very taken with roller skating. There used to be a ring in the Dome. 'Course back then it was called the Kursaal, and the chap running it was called—'

'Seebold,' Milly interrupted. She frowned. 'So where did he get the name from?'

Actually he was called Carl,' said Seebold. 'Carl Seebold.'

They laughed. 'What about you now, Seebold?' Milly asked. 'Are you happy and settled with Rainbow George?'

'Seebold doesn't just work for Rainbow George,' Lena corrected. 'All the fairground folk like his work. He's in great demand.'

'But I think it's time I branched out on my own,' said Seebold. 'I'm planning to create a permanent kiddies' playground. I've been over to Bognor to take a look at the Centre of Happiness.'

Milly and Lena gave each other a quizzical look.

'It's run by a chap called Butlin,' Seebold went on. 'He's

created a funfair that goes on all year round. They've got swing boats, dodgem cars, ghost train, you name it.'

'But surely it would take a huge amount of finance to get something like that going,' said Milly. 'You'd need backers, wouldn't you?'

'I've got one,' said Seebold. 'Me. I've been saving like mad. I wouldn't be able to do what Butlin's done, but once I get it going, I intend to build it up year on year.'

'So how would you start?' asked Milly.

'I found a plot of land to rent,' Seebold said. 'It's well drained and it's near the sea in East Worthing.'

Fortunately for Milly and Lena, he was looking at a hole in the toe of his sock and rearranging it so that it didn't show, which meant he didn't notice the look of surprise, then the grin the girls shared between them.

'The agent seems to think he could persuade the owner to let me have it at a reasonable rent,' he went on.

'The agent?' asked Milly.

'Cooper and Docket,' said Seebold. 'They have an office in Broadwater.'

'Sounds good,' said Lena.

'But what about the rides?' said Milly. 'Have you got money for them?'

'Just a while ago, I heard that Mick Jackson is jacking it in,' said Seebold. 'He's let me have a few of his rides at a knockdown price.'

'Mick Jackson? Are you sure about the quality?' Lena cautioned.

'Maybe, maybe not,' said Seebold, 'but you know me. I'm a dab hand with a spanner.'

Lena couldn't sleep. She lay in the darkness listening to Milly's soft breathing but she was wide awake. She kept wondering what Pa had said to her in his letter. At three in the morning, she could bear it no longer, so she stole out of bed and went into the kitchen. Having lit a candle, she made herself comfortable in a chair and slid a knife along the crease of the envelope.

My darling Lena

I am writing this knowing that when you read these words I shall no longer be here. I consider myself a privileged man both to have loved your mother and to have had you as my child. I have so many happy memories of our times together. I wish things could have been different; that you could have grown up in the same home as your sister Milly, but it was not to be. I made some promises to her mother and if I had broken them, I would have lost her for good. You must never think you meant any less to me.

I am so proud of you, Lena. You are forward thinking and you have already surprised me with your business acumen. I am sure that you will go far. You are your own woman; a woman of the twentieth century, and I feel that you will one day be a trailblazer. Don't let anyone, even Rainbow George, make you do something you don't want to do.

It makes me so sad to think that at such a young age you have lost both your mother and your father but I am delighted that you and Milly seem to be genuinely close. I am comforted to know that when I am gone you have each other.

I wish I could have lived to walk you down the aisle, but something tells me that might not happen for a long while, or maybe not at all. Whatever you do in life, I shall be proud of you, my darling. Never forget that you were greatly loved by both Angel and me.

God bless you, my darling.

Pa

There was a stain at the bottom of the page. Lena couldn't see what it was but it had warped the paper and bleached the colour. She touched it lightly with her thumb, and in her mind's eye, she could see her father brushing his tear off the page. She hugged the letter to her chest and rocked herself gently until she felt the need for sleep.

Chapter 18

Milly found it hard to suppress a smile. Hiding behind the dustsheets hanging at the front of the shop window, she could see a huddle of people on the street outside. Mr Johnson, the store manager, standing beside her, gave her a nod of approval, and Milly let out a grateful sigh. Her little scheme had worked.

Ever since her father died, Milly had endured some really difficult weeks. She couldn't stop wondering what he would have thought if he had known that she and Pearl had heaped curses on poor Angel and Lena. Milly was mature enough to realise that they'd been childish and stupid, but still the guilt of what they'd done that night never went away. Four o'clock in the morning was the worst. She would stir in her sleep or wake to go to the toilet, and then her brain would play and re-play their actions over and over again.

Milly had been trying to find a job for ages but it wasn't easy. She had little savings and, until the will was ratified, no income. She had plenty of interviews but, as soon as she opened her mouth, she was told the job was 'already filled'.

'I don't understand it,' she complained to her sister. 'What is it about me?'

'You sound too posh,' Lena said.

With the new term under way, Milly had gone back to art school to explain to Mr Salt, the principal, what had happened. He was both sympathetic and understanding, but he told her that his hands were tied. 'This is tremendously disappointing, Millicent. You have a fine talent and it seems an almost criminal waste if you give up your studies now, but this school is not a charity.'

When Milly mentioned that she was hoping Aunt Betsy might help, he added, 'I'll hold your place open until Christmas, but if you cannot come up with the fees by January, I'm afraid we shall have to withdraw your name from the register.'

Milly suffered another bitter blow when Aunt Betsy replied to her letter. *I don't want to put a dampener on your plans, my darling*, she wrote, *but it is neither healthy nor decent for a young girl like you to be living on her own. Rather than risk sullying your reputation, we think it best if you come to live with your uncle and me in West Moors.*

Milly was deeply disappointed. She liked West Moors but her life was here, in Worthing. To be uprooted and transplanted somewhere else was too much to ask.

Her lucky break came when she'd gone into Hubbard's with an armful of magazines. With a reputation as Worthing's most prestigious department store, it had in some areas failed to move with the times, and window-dressing was one of them. The windows were so cluttered it was hard to find what you wanted. It seemed that the window-dresser put something from every department into the display. The row upon row of handkerchiefs, gloves, pillowcases, tablecloths, children's toys and men's slippers was completely overwhelming.

Milly asked to see the manager.

'I was so sorry to hear of your father's passing,' he began as she walked into the room. 'Mr Shepherd was a good customer of Hubbard's and a man I deeply respected.'

'Thank you, Mr Johnson,' Milly said, sitting in the chair he'd indicated. 'I appreciate that.'

Mr Johnson resumed his seat behind the desk. At first he treated her as an aggrieved customer, thinking she was here to complain that since Charles's death, her dress allowance had been withdrawn, but Milly explained that she was here on a completely different matter. 'I wonder if you wouldn't mind looking at these pictures of the best London stores,' she said in a voice loaded with a confidence she barely felt. 'Window-dressing has evolved, Mr Johnson, but sadly Hubbard's has not. I should like to offer you a week's trial.'

'A week's trial,' Mr Johnson spluttered. Until that moment he'd also been under the impression that *he* was in the driving seat.

'I will increase your shop's footfall if you allow me to bring your displays up to date.' She knew she was taking a huge risk but, Milly told herself, nothing ventured, nothing gained. If she was too posh for the shop floor, she would have to aim higher. Whatever happened, she had to be able to support herself and, if possible, find enough money to continue her studies.

Mr Johnson regarded her carefully as he made a tower with his fingertips pressed together. 'Have you been trained as a window-dresser, Miss Shepherd?'

'No,' Milly admitted, 'but I am an artist.' She hoped she sounded confident when in fact her heart was beating so wildly she feared it would leave her chest. Would he give her this chance? He had to. He must. Taking a deep breath and willing her voice not to wobble, she began again. 'In fact, I have been told more than once that I am a gifted artist.' She pulled her sketchbook from her bag and laid it on the desk in front of him. 'All I ask is one week,' she reiterated. 'If my ideas are not to your liking, you've lost nothing.'

Mr Johnson began turning the pages of her sketchbook. Milly held her breath.

Mr Johnson looked up with an empty expression. Sensing defeat, Milly gathered her things but, as she turned to go, she heard a sigh. 'Very well, Miss Shepherd. One week starting from Monday.'

She stared at him for a second then gave him a big smile. 'Thank you, Mr Johnson. You won't regret it, I promise.'

'I hope you are right, Miss Shepherd,' he said, rising to his feet and offering her his hand. 'I hope you are right.'

Milly had a very busy weekend making plans for the displays, but on Monday she was ready. The windows were large, so she divided them into four separate compartments. The main window had three dummies dressed in elegant party clothes in front of a painting of a great ballroom. When she'd gone back to the school and explained her plan, Mr Salt had allowed her the use of one of the studios after hours, where she had sketched then painted the ballroom scene.

Milly used the next window to display household items such as saucepans, roasting dishes and tea towels. She took great pains not to 'stuff' everything in there. The customer had to be able to make a choice before going into the store. A mannequin dressed in an apron and holding a box of Christmas crackers presided over the display.

The third window had a huge box which had once been tied with a red ribbon. Scattered around the box were bottles of perfume, men's handkerchiefs and ties, ladies' underwear and stockings. On the side of the box she had created a label saying 'With love from Father Christmas' and an invitation for the children of Worthing to come and visit him in the store. The final window, the one next to the entrance, was full of toys; everything from toy trains to dollies. She had created little scenes such as a dolls' tea party, spinning tops coming down a ladder, a teddy and a giraffe playing board games and an animal zoo.

The glass front of the windows overlooking the road had been covered with a dust sheet until Milly had finished her display. She had pasted notices on the outside, 'Grand Opening at Noon', and 'Don't Miss It'.

When Mr Johnson himself unveiled her creation, the small crowd gathered outside clapped enthusiastically. That drew a bigger crowd and, once the children saw the toys, everything gathered momentum. People started to come through the doors in their droves. Milly breathed a sigh of relief as Mr Johnson told her the job was hers. Once a week she was to change the window displays until further notice.

'I believe you live in Findon, Miss Shepherd,' he said as they walked back to his office. 'Were you aware that Hubbard's has its own staff accommodation?'

Milly had no idea about the staff accommodation, but she expressed an interest anyway. Mrs Everett – Hubbard's chief of staff – was sent for, and eventually she was shown a bright and sunny room at the back of the store in the next road, Marine Place.

'If you take the room,' Mrs Everett, a plump, matronly woman who had worked in the store for more than thirty years, said, 'the rent, which is nominal, will be deducted from your wages.'

Milly also discovered that the food in the staff canteen was subsidised so she could eat quite cheaply. Although her wage packet at the end of the week would be smaller than someone 'living out', it was a win-win situation. With no external bills, every penny would be hers to do with as she wanted. She had a day off on Sunday and a half-day off on Wednesday.

When she told Lena about the room later that evening, Milly went on to explain that on Wednesday she would go

150

back to the art school. If Mr Salt was amenable, she could pay her fees each week, with an agreement that when she'd finished at the school, she could carry on until the debt was paid. 'I shall miss being here with you,' Milly went on, 'but it would cut out so much travelling if I live in town.'

Lena told her she quite understood, and it was a bittersweet moment when her sister helped her to pack up her things and, because Seebold was 'up country', Nan's husband, Cyril, arranged for a mate of his from the pub to take everything over to Milly's new accommodation that evening.

'Have you decided what you're going to do?' Milly asked Lena when they were alone.

'My plans are put on hold at the moment,' Lena said with a sigh. 'I may ask Nan to put me up until I can be sure the cottage is mine.'

Milly nodded. 'You'll be company for each other.'

'I've looked for a job,' Lena continued, 'but I don't think I'm cut out to be a shop assistant or a live-in help. Being shut up in one place all day would drive me mad. It's my Romany blood, I suppose. I may end up going back to Rainbow George.'

Milly chuckled. 'And he'll have you married off in a trice.'

Lena's expression clouded. 'No way!'

'I've still got a few things at Muntham Court,' said Milly, changing the subject. 'What am I going to do about them?'

'Come back on Sunday,' Lena suggested. 'I'll get in touch with Seebold. I'm sure he'd be happy to drive you to the house to collect your things.'

Milly looked a little uncomfortable. 'What if my mother is there and makes a scene?'

Lena laughed. 'I can't see her wanting an altercation with Seebold hanging around, can you?'

Chapter 19

Milly was strangely nervous about returning to the house, and the driveway to Muntham Court had never seemed so long and forbidding. Seebold parked around the back of the house near the kitchen, and Milly knocked on the kitchen door. Mrs Cunningham was surprised to see her.

'Oh miss!' she cried. 'Why are you coming in this way?'

'I don't think my mother would be too happy to see me here,' said Milly, 'but I've come to collect a few of my things.'

Mrs Cunningham stepped aside and let her in. 'Does your friend want to wait in here?' she asked. 'I've just put the kettle on.'

Milly relaxed and smiled then waved Seebold in. 'Is my mother here?'

'She and Miss Pearl and Miss Pearl's future intended have gone to church,' said Mrs Cunningham. 'They came back from London last night to hear the banns being read.'

Milly frowned. 'The banns?'

Mrs Cunningham's cheeks coloured as she put her fingers to her lips. 'Surely you know that your sister is getting married next month?'

'Oh, yes of course,' Milly said brightly. 'How silly of me.' She paused. 'Well, I'll just nip upstairs then.'

Milly had planned to go up the back stairs, but if her mother wasn't at home, she might as well use the main staircase. She was still reeling from Mrs Cunningham's announcement. It had stung. Though aware of Pearl's engagement, Milly had no idea that her sister was getting married next month. Her own sister was going to be a bride and nobody had thought to tell her? She knew her mother was angry because of the will, but this made their estrangement seem so . . . permanent. As she reached her old bedroom, Milly asked herself, did she care? Well, yes, she did. Agatha was still her mother and Pearl was still her sister, even if they had disowned her.

The room seemed exactly as she had left it. Even the dip on the eiderdown where she had rested her suitcase was still there. As she stood in the doorway looking around, all at once the loss of her father slammed so hard into her chest that she could hardly breathe. Staggering towards the bed she sat down, pulled off her glasses and sobbed.

Downstairs, Seebold and Mrs Cunningham were becoming great friends. They chatted amiably as she poured him tea and he told her all about Milly's new position.

'She always was good at painting,' said Mrs Cunningham. 'The master used to say she'd be a great artist one day.'

'She's hoping to go back to art school after Christmas.'

Mrs Cunningham smiled. 'Are you two . . .? I mean, are you, like we used to say in my day, walking out together?'

Seebold chuckled. 'No, not me, missus. I like to be footloose and fancy-free.'

'Why? You like her a lot, I can see that by the way your face lights up whenever you talk about her.'

Seebold nodded shyly. 'I do. She's a beautiful girl.'

Mrs Cunningham nodded. 'You're right there,' she said. 'She and her sister are as different as chalk and cheese.'

'When does her sister get married?'

'On the eighth of January,' said Mrs Cunningham. 'It's going to be quite an occasion, from what I can gather. Half the county will be there, and the bishop of Horsham is taking the service.' As she reached over and put a plate with a generous slice of cake in front of him, Mrs Cunningham nudged Seebold's arm. 'You could make it a double wedding.'

The young man shook his head. 'Umm.' he said thoughtfully, 'I think I'm busy that day.'

They were interrupted by the sound of a car coming up the driveway. 'Oh lummy Charlie,' said Mrs Cunningham, getting to her feet. 'They're back already.'

Upstairs, it had taken several minutes for Milly to regain her composure. She blew her nose and opened the canvas bag she'd brought with her. There wasn't a lot left in the drawers in her room, but a photo album distracted her once again. As she turned the pages, childhood memories came flooding back. Walks with her father by the sea, a picnic on Cissbury Ring, that frisky dog they'd once had, a garden fête in the vicarage, playing in the garden with dolly . . . dolly! She hadn't thought about her doll for a while, not since she'd wrapped her up and hidden her in the back of the drawer. Well, she'd better take her now.

Pushing the album down the side of the bag, she knelt beside the chest of drawers and pulled open the bottom drawer. Milly caught her breath. Everything inside had been disturbed. Her neatly stored toys and games were untidy and jumbled up. She reached her hand into the back of the drawer where the blue shawl should have been and found an empty space. Dolly wasn't there! So where was she? As Milly began to pull everything out onto her lap, a voice behind her said, 'You won't find her. She's not there.'

Milly spun round. Pearl stood in the doorway. Milly's first thought was that her sister looked sensational. Dressed in a pale grey woollen dress with matching coat, the dress

154

itself was loose with a pleated front panel reaching to the hem. Round her neck her sister had a three-string pearl necklace which rested on a chevron design in a darker grey on the front of her dress. Pearl's eyes were covered by some fine netting on her small-brimmed black hat and, as she moved into the room, a waft of Chanel No. 5 accompanied her.

'What have you done with my doll?' Milly demanded. 'Where is she?'

'Oh, she's safe enough,' said Pearl, a malicious smile on her lips. 'You needn't worry. I won't be getting rid of your doll.' She sat on the bed. 'You're a sly one, aren't you? When did you get her fixed up?'

'I didn't,' said Milly. 'I thought I'd lost her forever down the back of that log pile, but Le . . .' She stopped, already realising it was too late to pretend that she hadn't been about to say her sister's name.

Pearl moved her head up and down slowly, her mouth in a sneer. 'I see. Now I wonder what Lena would say if she knew why the doll was there in the first place.'

The remark made Milly feel ridiculously panicky. 'You won't tell her, will you?'

Her sister simply raised an eyebrow.

'Oh Pearl, please . . . You can't!'

Her sister gave her a smug smile. 'I rather think I can,' she said.

Milly could feel tears pricking her eyes, but she was determined not to let her sister see she was upset. She turned her attention to the bag and began stuffing as much as she could inside.

'Oh, of course, you don't know, do you? We've all been to church,' said Pearl. 'Today was the third time the banns for my wedding were read out.'

'Congratulations,' Milly said quietly.

'You must come and meet my fiancé.'

'I already met him,' said Milly, beginning to regain her composure. 'You introduced me that night at Lady Verity's, remember? He seemed very nice.' She rose to her feet. 'I've almost finished packing. I'll soon be out of your way.' She zipped up the bag but, as she headed for the door, she bumped into her mother. 'Oh!'

'I've told Freddie to send that man with the lorry packing,' Agatha said coldly. 'Who is that dreadful creature, and what was he doing in my kitchen?'

'He's my friend,' Milly said defensively, 'and he came to help me collect the rest of my things.'

'Really?' her mother said with a sneer. 'Well, I wish you wouldn't bring people like that to the house. Types like him are just as likely to be back next week to rob us.'

'Seebold isn't like that,' Milly protested.

'Seebold,' her mother said scornfully. 'What sort of a ridiculous name is that? Honestly, Millicent, the company you keep.'

Pearl smiled. 'You don't know the half of it, Mummy.'

Milly bristled with indignation. She was about to make a suitable retort, but as she took in a breath, she paused. No, she wouldn't rise to the bait. That was what they both wanted – to start an argument, after which she would be the one in tears. Well, she wasn't going to go down that path again.

'Excuse me, won't you, Mother,' said Milly. 'Must dash.' And with that, she walked from the room with her head high. At the top of the stairs, she turned and said, 'I wish you and Freddie all the best on your wedding day, Pearl. I hope you both have a very happy life.'

Milly hurried down the stairs.

Pearl leaned over the banister. 'I don't need your good wishes; for all I care, you can go to hell,' she shouted after her before she burst into tears.

'Don't upset yourself, my dear,' her mother soothed as

Pearl laid her head on Agatha's shoulder. 'It won't be long before she's back with her tail between her legs.'

Pearl looked up with a startled expression. 'She's not going to turn up at my wedding in that awful lorry, is she?'

'Of course not, darling,' said Agatha. 'She's not invited.'

Seebold was waiting in the lorry. He had been as surprised as Mrs Cunningham when Milly's mother, her sister and a young man appeared in the kitchen doorway. Mrs Shepherd had looked him up and down, as if he was something disgusting attached to her shoe. 'Who are you?' she'd said sneeringly. 'Mrs Cunningham, you know better than to have your relatives in my kitchen.'

'We're not related,' Seebold said. 'We've only just met.'

'Then what are you doing in my house?' Agatha retorted.

Mrs Cunningham had looked uncomfortable. 'Mr Seebold came with Miss Milly.'

Agatha had frowned. 'Millicent? Millicent is here?'

'She's upstairs collecting her things.'

Pearl left immediately.

'We won't be long, missus,' Seebold said.

Agatha gave him a filthy look. 'Freddie, will you escort this . . . this person off the premises.'

Seebold had risen to his feet. 'No need,' he said curtly. 'Tell Milly I'll wait for her in the lorry.'

As he left the kitchen, he heard Milly's mother saying, 'I don't know what you were thinking of, Mrs Cunningham. You invite a complete stranger into my kitchen and give him tea! Freddie, make sure he goes straight to that lorry and nowhere else.'

Seebold had bristled. He would have turned back and given her a mouthful, but he was mindful of Milly and didn't want to cause her more trouble.

Freddie walked with him to the lorry. 'Go on, off you go,' he said, waving his arm in a superior fashion.

'I'm not going until Milly comes out,' Seebold told him.

'What would a scruff like you be doing with the likes of her?' Freddie asked. 'Are you planning something?'

'No, I am not,' Seebold retorted. 'I'm perfectly well aware that Milly is a respectable girl and so is her sister.'

Freddie's expression darkened. 'How do you know my fiancée?'

'I don't,' Seebold said. 'I was talking about Lena.'

Freddie seemed puzzled. 'Who is Lena?'

'Milly's sister.'

'Her sister is called Pearl.'

'Lena is her younger sister.'

'She hasn't got a younger sister,' Freddie said.

'Fat lot you know, then,' said Seebold. He was beginning to feel irritated.

Freddie's eyes narrowed. 'If she has another sister, where does she live?'

'At the moment she's with a woman down the road, but she used to live with the fairground folk. That's where I met her . . . when she was living with Rainbow George.'

Freddie's eyebrows had shot up. 'Gypsies!'

'No,' Seebold said patiently. 'We're fairground folk.'

'Then you're lucky to live here,' Freddie retorted. 'In my country, the Jew, the disabled and the gypsy are all being removed. They're being taken to camps.'

Seebold squared up to him. 'I told you before, we are not gypsies!'

'Whatever you call yourself,' said Freddie, poking Seebold's shoulder with a bony finger, 'come back here and you'll be in trouble.'

Seebold suddenly jerked towards him in a threatening way. He was sorely tempted to clock him one but, as Freddie took a step backwards, something in the man's eyes told Seebold that was exactly what he wanted him to do; to goad him into a fight and then he'd call the police. He'd seen his type often enough at the fairground. Well, he wasn't going to give him the satisfaction.

'You needn't worry pal,' Seebold had said as he opened the lorry door and jumped in. 'I shan't be coming back here.'

With a contemptuous sniff, Freddie stuck his chest out and marched away.

As Milly approached the lorry, Seebold jumped down and took her bag. She thought he seemed rather tight-lipped and he thought she looked upset. They drove in silence until they reached the road, then Milly suddenly burst into tears. Seebold pulled into a farm gateway and stopped the lorry. Handing her a handkerchief, he sat awkwardly waiting for her to pull herself together but, after a minute or two, he could bear it no longer. He slipped his arm around her shoulder and she laid her head on his chest until the tears subsided.

'I'm sorry,' she choked as she sat up.

'It's fine, duchess,' he said. 'Don't worry about it.'

Milly blew her nose. 'Was she terribly rude to you?'

'I've heard worse.'

'I'm sorry,' Milly repeated. 'I feel so embarrassed.'

'Please,' he protested. 'It doesn't bother me. I've got broad shoulders.' He gave her a grim smile. 'What about you?'

'She didn't say a lot,' Milly said, careful not to offend Seebold any further by relaying her mother's comments. 'It just hurts.' Her face crumpled. 'She's still my mother.'

Seebold held her close again. 'I don't know what to say.'

'There's nothing to say,' Milly said bitterly.

They sat for a while until Milly calmed down, then, blowing her nose, she said, 'We'd better go. It must be almost lunch time and I have to be in the canteen if I want any lunch today.'

Chapter 20

There was blood on her knickers. Pearl stared down in horror. She'd had a dull ache in her stomach all morning but had put it down to eating too much the day before. Yesterday, Freddie had bought some French langoustines from one of the East Worthing fishermen. They were a favourite of his and, much to the annoyance of Mrs Cunningham, he had commandeered the kitchen to cook them himself. It was a rare moment of genuine pleasure for her, Freddie and her mother. They'd enjoyed a delightful meal and then he'd gone back to London where he had some business to attend to.

Earlier in the week, when he had arrived at Muntham Court for the first time, he'd seemed very impressed. He had wandered through the house with Pearl, admiring the décor and furnishings. In one of the bedrooms he had pulled her towards him and kissed her ferociously. '*Sehr gut*,' he said huskily. '*Meine englische Schönheit*,' and when he saw her confusion he chuckled and said in English, 'You are my English rose, my perfect English rose.' He would have taken her there and then, but the moment came to nothing when they heard her mother calling in the corridor.

The blood was a bit scary but, she told herself, it was only a few spots. Perhaps that was normal. Whilst it was true that she wasn't that keen to be a mother, she and Freddie weren't married yet. If she lost the baby, there was a good chance he would call a halt to their wedding, and what would she do then? Her mother had called her a silly little fool for getting pregnant, but how on earth could she have prevented it? And she never would have got Freddie if she hadn't given in almost as soon as they'd met. That first time he had been so eager, so domineering, so rough.

Pearl changed her underwear and went back to the sitting room. Her mother had gone shopping in Worthing, so she was quite alone in the house – apart from Mrs Cunningham, of course. She lay on the sofa and cuddled a cushion. It was going to be so exciting to see the place where Freddie had grown up. He'd told her all about it. 'A palace,' he'd said. 'Berlin Schlossplatz was first built in the fifteenth century and the surrounding area was planned at the same time. It's very beautiful.' He chuckled. 'My home has a dome bigger than your St Paul's.'

She'd gazed up at him, dewy-eyed. It was the stuff of dreams. When they married, she would be a baroness and living in a real palace.

The pain seemed to be fading. Perhaps everything was settling down now. Pearl moved her position to make herself more comfortable, stretching her legs and rolling onto her back. To take her mind off things, she thought back to that day when she and Freddie had walked around the house and grounds. It had been quite an education. He knew far more about the house than she did! She had no idea that it was covered with Jacobean flint, or that the pointy bits were called Dutch gables. He'd wanted to walk through the gardens, something her mother had advised her to discourage because – since the gardener had gone – it was becoming unkempt and overgrown. She'd hastily explained that Mr Bodkin had retired through old age and her mother was actively looking for a new man. It wasn't true, of course, but Freddie accepted her explanation without question. He told her that whoever had created the garden with its dwarf box hedges, gravel walkways and seasonal flower beds had been trying to recreate a seventeenth-century garden. All news to Pearl, who hardly ever stepped outside the house except to go to London or Brighton.

She groaned. The pain was coming back. She wondered if she should say something to Mrs Cunningham but then thought better of it. Her mother would go mad if word got out around the village that she was to have anything other than the perfect marriage to the perfect man. Anyway, as far as everyone else was concerned, Pearl was as pure as the driven snow. She felt a gripping sensation at the base of her stomach, as if she needed to go to the toilet, but she didn't. She got up and walked to the window to see if she could see her mother's car. That's when it happened. She wet herself and her knickers couldn't contain it. Grabbing a small cushion, Pearl pushed it between her legs and headed for the stairs again. Halfway up, the gripping pain was back, only this time it was overwhelming. Clinging to the banister, she cried out loud as a wave of nausea swept over her and she felt her legs buckling beneath her. A voice behind her said, 'Are you all right, miss?' but Pearl couldn't answer. Just before her legs gave way, she felt a pair of strong arms around her.

'It's all right, miss,' Mrs Cunningham said in her ear. 'I've got you.'

Somehow or other, the pair of them managed to get to her bedroom and Pearl collapsed onto the bed, drawing her knees towards her chin in an effort to lessen the pain. Mrs Cunningham left the room but came back a couple of minutes later with some towels. Lifting Pearl's legs, she pushed the towels under her bottom and took the bloodied cushion away. 'Oh, miss.'

Downstairs, they heard the front door open. Mrs

162

Cunningham hurried to the top of the stairs and Pearl heard her saying, 'Oh madam, come quickly. It's Miss Pearl. I think she's losing a baby.'

It was another three hours before Agatha could speak privately to Mrs Cunningham. Dr Jennings had arrived only twenty minutes after Agatha had rung him, and confirmed that Pearl had indeed lost her baby. Mrs Cunningham had helped Agatha clear up the mess, and the cushion and towels were burning in the garden. Pearl, exhausted by the turn of events, was sleeping.

Now that Dr Jennings was on his way home, Agatha called Mrs Cunningham into the sitting room where they could be alone.

'I hope I can trust you to keep this a secret,' Agatha told her one-time cook, who now worked as a general help. With little money apart from her allowance, Agatha had had to let Elsie, Bodkin the gardener and Dixon go. Hopefully, with Pearl married to the baron, the money would flow in once more and they'd be back up to a full suite of staff before long.

Mrs Cunningham looked hurt. 'I am not one to gossip, madam, you know that.'

Agatha reached for a cigarette from the box on the table. 'Then we shall say no more on the matter,' she said, striking her lighter.

'Of course,' said Mrs Cunningham. 'Shall the baron be returning from London?'

Agatha drew on her cigarette. 'Why should he?'

'Well, I thought . . .' Mrs Cunningham began.

'Apart from we three,' Agatha said firmly, 'there's no need for anyone beyond these four walls – except, of course, Dr Jennings – to know what has taken place this afternoon. Do I make myself clear?'

'Crystal,' said Mrs Cunningham. She was appalled that

Miss Pearl's young man wasn't to be told, but later on, in the kitchen, she began to understand why. The poor bugger was prepared to do the decent thing by marrying the girl he'd got into trouble, but that conniving bitch wasn't going to let him off the hook, was she.

There was a tricky moment when Freddie telephoned that evening. Mrs Cunningham had picked up the receiver. She called Agatha and then went back to the kitchen, only she didn't close the door. Standing just inside the room, she heard her employer say, 'Darling, she's in bed. Poor girl, she's got the most frightful cold.'

There was a pause, then Agatha said, 'Well, apart from a raging temperature, she seemed all right, but I thought it best to call the doctor. He said because of her condition she should have complete bedrest. I will go and call her if you insist but . . .'

Another pause, then, 'I think it best, dear. Yes, yes, I'll tell her you called. Bye now.' Agatha replaced the receiver muttering, 'Stupid boy.'

The next day Pearl's physical pains had faded, but she felt very weepy and there was a hollow feeling in her chest. Dr Jennings had told her that her baby was gone. Gone, and she didn't even know if it had been a boy or a girl. Freddie had wanted a son, of course, but now his dream was gone as well.

Her mother had sorted everything admirably, but she was not one to show any emotion. That afternoon she had sat on the edge of Pearl's bed and given her what she called a 'pep talk'.

'You won't tell Freddie any of this, of course,' she began.

'But he must know, Mummy. It was his baby too.'

'Listen to me,' Agatha said firmly. 'Freddie doesn't need to know until after the wedding. If you tell him before that, he may well change his mind.'

'So what if he does?' said Pearl. 'I don't love him, you know.'

'Love,' Agatha said scornfully. 'You don't get a good marriage if you do it for love. Marriage is a business arrangement. That's why Freddie is so ideal. A rich man, a castle in Germany, the prospect of foreign travel to anywhere in the world, and even the possibility of meeting world leaders. My dear child, every woman in England would give their right arm for such a glittering prospect.'

Pearl blinked.

'That is why you say nothing, do you hear?'

Her daughter appeared to be struck dumb by her mother's calculating callousness.

'Do you hear me?' Agatha's tone was more aggressive.

'Yes. Yes, I hear you.'

'Now, when he rings this evening, you tell him you've had a bad cold but you're feeling much better now. Nobody but you and I and Dr Jennings need to know the real reason you're in bed.'

'What about Mrs Cunningham?'

'She'll do as she's told,' said Agatha dismissively. She rose to her feet. 'I suggest you stay in bed for now. The doctor said he would come in this afternoon to look you over but it seems as if you've come through all this without a problem.'

'Does this mean I can't have any more babies?'

'Of course not,' her mother said. 'You'll have plenty of babies. Freddie is a fine young man. He's got a wonderful pedigree and you'll be back to normal in next to no time.' She turned to leave the room, but as she put her hand on the doorknob she added, 'But if you'll take my advice, you'll keep your legs crossed until after the wedding. He mustn't know. Have you got that?'

Pearl nodded obediently. 'Yes, Mummy.'

Chapter 21

December 1937

Christmas had been busy and by the time the shop closed on the Friday, Christmas Eve, the last of the shoppers – all men frantically searching for presents for their wives – had finally made their choices.

'Why can't these men come out earlier in the day?' Gill, the girl behind the wrapping counter, muttered out of the corner of her mouth. She had been rushed off her feet since four o'clock and, although the doors were now shut, there was a queue a mile long waiting for her services. Milly, who was on her way out, stopped to help.

'Are you home for Christmas?' Gill asked as she put a ribbon around the umpteenth box of perfume she'd wrapped since the rush began.

Milly shook her head. 'I'm with friends.'

'Oh.' Gill sounded surprised. 'We'll be having a family Christmas. Mum's got everybody coming: my three brothers and their wives, my niece and nephew and my gran. It'll be manic.' She looked up at the anxious man waiting by the counter. 'There we are, sir. I'm sure your wife will love it. Happy Christmas.'

Milly smiled up at her customer. 'Red ribbon or green?'

The grey-haired man in front of her took his pipe out of

his mouth. 'Red,' he said assertively. 'No, green. Oh, I don't know. What do you think?'

'Tell you what, sir. What about the gold?'

'Yes, yes, the gold.'

Milly reached for some gold ribbon.

'I did all my presents three weeks ago,' Gill went on as they worked together. 'Do your friends live locally?'

'Findon,' said Milly. She was eternally grateful to Nan and Cyril. If they hadn't asked her to join them, she supposed she would have faced a lonely Christmas in the staff accommodation, living on cold tins of soup or something. Because Christmas Day fell on a Saturday this year, they didn't have to be back in the store until Wednesday, so everybody else was going away. Lena was in Kent, where Rainbow George had taken a pitch for the St Thomas's Christmas Fair. With no trains on Christmas Day or Boxing Day and a limited service on the two bank holidays that followed, it seemed sensible that she should spend her festive season with the fairground folk.

Milly knew her Christmas would be quiet, but she was determined to make the most of it. She and Nan began the festivities by going to the midnight service in All Saints, the Findon Valley church. Cyril was already there. In his capacity as verger, he had to be early, to make sure people arriving for the service had a warm welcome. He was also responsible for making sure the vestments were ready for the priest and choir members, as well as checking that the building itself was clean and tidy before the service. When it was over, he had to make sure that the church was safely locked up after everybody had gone home. Cyril took this role very seriously

On Christmas Day, Milly was surprised to see Nan laying the table for four people.

'Who else is coming?' Milly asked.

'Oh, didn't I tell you?' Nan said casually. 'I invited Seebold.'

Milly's heart did a double beat. She hadn't seen him since

that dreadful day when she'd gone back to Muntham Court to collect the last of her things. Flustered and embarrassed, she felt her colour rising as she recalled that moment they'd shared in the lorry when he'd put his arm around her shoulder and she'd leaned on his chest for comfort. Sometimes, when she put her head on her pillow in bed, she could still hear the thud, thud of his steady heartbeat. Why did she feel this way about him? It wasn't as if he'd made a pass at her. Far from it. Seebold was ever the perfect gentleman.

'I couldn't let him spend Christmas on his own,' Nan said as she bustled around the kitchen.

'Where is he now?' Milly asked.

Nan smiled to herself as she opened the oven door to baste the goose inside. 'Don't you know?' she said. 'He's got a caravan on that plot of land he rents in East Worthing; working day and night on getting his amusements ready, so I'm told.'

Milly knew about the caravan, but she'd been too busy at work to pop down to see her friend. She occupied herself polishing the glasses and putting them on the table.

It seemed like an age until he turned up at noon, when he walked into the kitchen with an armful of presents. After dumping them on the dresser, he turned to give Nan a kiss then nodded at Milly. 'Hello, duchess. I've brought you a special present.'

Milly was immediately thrown into a panic. A present for her? Oh no, he shouldn't have. She hadn't bought him a thing. She became aware of a shadow falling in the doorway and a voice said, 'Happy Christmas, everybody!'

'Lena!' Milly cried. 'How wonderful!'

Seebold took Lena back to Kent on Tuesday morning. Thanks to Nan and Cyril, they had all enjoyed the most wonderful Christmas. Nan had cooked enough food to feed an army: roast goose – one she had reared herself from a gosling – with all the trimmings, followed by Christmas pudding soaked in brandy and set alight; then later on, for tea, sandwiches and Christmas cake. On Boxing Day, Nan and Cyril went to church but Milly, Lena and Seebold decided to have a walk. They went up Bost Hill, passed the windmill, and turned right into Honeysuckle Lane, then walked all the way to Long Furlong and from there to the new bypass road and back to Nan's cottage. The day was crisp with some sun so the walk itself was very pleasant.

'Are you going to stay in Hubbard's?' Lena asked as she slipped her gloved hand through Milly's arm.

'For the time being,' said Milly. 'I'm pretty skint, but Mr Salt says I can pay my college fees in instalments, so I'm lucky enough to have the opportunity to get both teaching and practical experience.'

Lena nodded her approval.

'What about you?' asked Milly. 'I thought you were fed up with being under Rainbow George's thumb.'

'Oh, he's all right,' said Lena. 'Anyway, I won't stay there for ever. I have plans of my own.'

'What plans?' said Milly.

Lena tapped her nose playfully. 'I think I'll keep them under my hat for now,' she teased.

'Is Rainbow George still trying to marry you off?'

Lena turned her head and grinned at Seebold. 'As long as Seebold is still in the picture, he's happy for me to wait a while.'

'Oh dear,' said Seebold. 'Looks like I'll have to see the vicar before long.' And they both laughed.

Milly looked away and said nothing.

'So tell us about your amusement park,' Lena said.

Seebold was happy to spend the next twenty minutes telling them all about castles, hoopla stalls and the children's rides he was creating. 'Of course I can only do it in the evenings and on Sundays,' he went on. 'I still have to work for a living."

'So what do you do?' asked Lena.

'Anything and everything mechanical,' he said. 'Cars, lorries, tractors, you name it.'

'When will the amusement park be open to the public?' Milly wanted to know. 'And what are you calling it?'

'The Worthing Wonderland,' he said. 'And it's opening at Easter.'

As soon as Lena and Seebold set off in the lorry, Milly went back to Hubbard's. The shop wouldn't officially open until the next day, but she had plenty to do. With Christmas over, the shop windows would be out-of-date. It was her job to create a 'taster' of the New Year offers so that the customers would be queuing up before the doors opened for the beginning of the January sales on Thursday 6 January.

Some of the sales assistants were already hard at work by the time she arrived. Milly moved around the various departments collecting items for the window displays. Upstairs in the dress department, even though, technically, the shop wasn't open, the store's seamstress was expecting a very important visitor. 'Apparently she's getting married in a couple of weeks and wants her bridal gown altered,' Ivy confided. 'Mr Johnson says we have to pull out all the stops.'

Milly pulled a face. 'You'd better hope there's enough material in the seams to let it out.'

'Oh this one wants it taken in,' Ivy said. 'She's *lost* weight. It's very unusual. In most cases I have to alter their dresses because they're pregnant.'

Milly smiled. 'Can I have that frock?' she said as she pushed the dresses along the rail. 'Oh, and that one. Will they be in the sale?'

'Everything is along that rail,' said Ivy. 'Help yourself. It all has to go. The Spring collection comes in at the end of the month.'

Milly busied herself choosing from a range of colours, and eventually settled on the blue. She vaguely remembered a pair of navy shoes in the shoe department which would complement the dress perfectly. All she needed now was a coat or a cardigan. As she bent down to look through the bottom cardigan drawer, a voice said, 'Well, well. How the mighty are fallen.'

Milly froze. She didn't need to look up to see who it was. She would recognise that voice anywhere. It was Pearl. Milly felt her face colouring.

'Oh, good afternoon, madam,' said Ivy, coming out of the small office. 'We're all ready for you. My assistant and I have reserved a special place for you to put your gown on. Perhaps you would care to step this way.'

'I should like that girl to help me,' Pearl announced. She pointed at Milly. 'Her.'

'With respect, madam,' said Ivy, 'that girl is the window-dresser.'

'And I should like her to dress me.' Pearl's tone was strident.

Milly closed her eyes with a shudder.

'In fact, I insist.'

Milly rose to her feet. Her sister, her eyes bright, smiled triumphantly. 'Come along, girl,' she said in a superior tone. 'And bring my dress with you.'

By the time Pearl had gone, Milly was furious and trembling with embarrassment. Her sister had insisted that she put her gown on for her, and that she wait while Ivy and her team pinned and tucked the material more closely to her body. A couple of times, Milly made an attempt to leave, but Pearl soon called her back. She didn't once mention who she was or why she wanted Milly with her, which of course made the whole incident all the more intriguing for the other staff members.

The wedding gown was fantastic. It was obvious to everyone that it had been made by some fashionable London designer and that it must have cost an absolute fortune. Satin, with a cowl neck and plunging back, it had a fish tail which went from the edge of the back seam to the floor. There were seams under the bust, and a front panel, which could all be taken in to give the dress a much more slender look. The long sleeves had covered buttons and the whole dress had been cut on the bias of the material. When Pearl stood in front of the mirror, Milly couldn't help taking in a breath of admiration.

There was one moment when they were left alone. 'I can't wait to tell Mother I've seen you,' Pearl whispered slyly. 'How long have you been a shop girl?'

Hearing the venom in her voice, Milly fought the desire to justify herself. She wouldn't give Pearl the satisfaction of seeing her embarrassment. Anyway, why should she feel embarrassed? Working in a shop was an honourable profession. Her sister was such a snob. Fortunately, just at that moment, Ivy came back to tell Pearl that the dress would be ready by Friday morning.

'As you can imagine,' Pearl said loftily, 'I'm extremely busy at the moment. You can get your girl here to deliver it to me. She knows where I live, don't you, dear?'

Ivy seemed puzzled as, without another word, Pearl swept from the department.

'What was all that about?' Ivy gasped when she'd gone. 'How do you know her?'

Milly sighed. 'Believe it or not, she's my sister.'

On the big day itself, Milly was determined to see Pearl in the altered gown. She hadn't got an invitation to the wedding, of course, but she couldn't resist hovering around with the small crowd of villagers who had gathered in the churchyard outside St John's Church in Findon on Saturday 8 January

1938. Milly had worn a wide-brimmed hat and came with a small watering can and some flowers. If anyone asked, which they didn't, she'd planned to say she was changing the flowers on somebody's grave, although it couldn't be her father's, because he was buried in the cemetery across the bypass.

As the guests arrived, Milly hardly recognised any of them. Not even Aunt Betsy was there, which was a little puzzling considering that Pearl was the first of her nieces to marry. Freddie looked magnificently handsome in some sort of German uniform, and Milly felt a pang of longing when she saw her mother entering through the lychgate. Agatha was dressed in pale violet with a pretty matching Italian guipure lace coat. She had expensive white leather gloves and a small-brimmed hat with netting at the front and a bow at the back.

When the bridal car arrived, Pearl walked beside a rather portly man with a smoke-stained moustache. As they posed for the photographer, the woman standing next to Milly said to her companion, 'Who's the man giving her away?'

'That's Councillor Warren, don't you know,' her friend replied. 'Absolutely rolling in it, so they say.'

Milly recognised him now. He was the man who had squeezed her mother's bottom at her father's wake.

'Apparently,' the same woman continued, 'he adores the bride's mother. Would do anything for her, so I'm told.'

'Poor sod,' said her friend, and they both sniggered.

Pearl looked as beautiful as a film star, a cross between Joan Blondell and Loretta Young. There was a ripple of applause from the assembled crowd as she and Councillor Warren prepared to walk into the church arm in arm. Milly had a lump in her throat. Whatever had passed between them, she and Pearl were sisters. Weddings were a time when families came together – a time of celebration – but instead, she'd been left out in the cold. She should have been

Pearl's bridesmaid. Milly's chin quivered with emotion as her sister posed by the church door for her final photograph as a single woman. She looked fantastic, and Milly wished she had a camera because the alteration on her sister's dress did Ivy a lot of credit. The photographer's bulb flashed and the wedding party turned to go.

Milly thought about staying long enough to see the wedding party come out of the church, but she decided it was too upsetting. Considering how unkind both her mother and sister had been towards her, Milly was surprised how much she missed being a part of the family. But she did. So, leaving the flowers on a stranger's grave, she hurriedly left.

By the time Pearl and Freddie's wedding was over, they had danced well into the night. It had been agreed that they should have Muntham Court to themselves for a few days by way of a honeymoon, so Agatha had gone away to spend a couple of nights with friends.

Pearl was a little tipsy as her bridegroom took her upstairs. She wasn't nervous, of course. They had made love many times before, but this was the first time in their relationship that it wasn't a quick fumble in the linen cupboard or a hasty episode on the floor with an anxious eye on the doorknob in case somebody came in.

As they entered the bedroom, he kissed her hungrily. Pearl responded with sighs and encouragements until Freddie turned her around to undo the buttons on the back of her gown. It took an age, and then she felt his hands slide within the dress and onto her belly. She moaned slightly and leaned back against him, but he had stopped exploring her body. He pressed her stomach firmly.

'Where is it?'

'Where's what?' she said dreamily.

He spun her back. 'The baby!' His face was dark.

Pearl sucked in her bottom lip. 'Oh my darling, I'm sorry.' She swallowed hard. 'I lost our baby.'

He said nothing but continued to stare. She stepped out of her twisted gown and then it dawned on her that she was going to have to give the performance of a lifetime. Pearl's eyes filled with tears. 'I was so ill,' she bleated, 'and all I could think about was how could I tell you about our beautiful baby . . . I prayed to God that He would let me keep him . . .' She was sobbing now. 'But it didn't matter how hard I tried . . . he came . . . oh Freddie, he came too early.'

'When?' he said coldly.

Pearl blew her nose. 'What?'

'When did it happen?'

'Oh,' she said, struggling to remember, 'about a month ago.'

'A month,' he repeated coldly.

'Yes.' She grabbed his forearms dramatically. 'Darling, I did my best. I'm so, so sorry.'

'You lost our baby a month ago and you never thought to tell me,' he snarled.

'I wanted to, darling, really I did, but I couldn't find the words.'

His expression was terrifying. 'No, you thought if you told me, I wouldn't marry you.'

Her heart was thumping. He'd never looked at her with such anger in his eyes. 'Oh, Freddie . . . darling.'

His move was very quick. She didn't see his hand go back but she felt the full force of the slap he gave her. She fell to the ground with a thump. 'Bitch!' he cried. 'You bloody sodding bitch.'

Chapter 22

Easter 1938

The letter from the courts arrived just before Easter. As soon as she opened it, the judgement dominated Milly's every waking moment. Her first thought was to contact Lena who was back in Worthing, helping Seebold with the children's play park.

The Worthing Wonderland had finally opened on 2 April, but Milly had yet to see it. Just after her father had died, when she, Lena and Seebold had been together in the cottage, the girls had been convinced that Seebold wanted to rent the piece of land Lena had acquired near Bridge Halt, so it came as a surprise to realise that he had somewhere else in mind.

The plot was on the fringe of the Worthing and Lancing border. The beach was just across the road, and further up there was an area of wasteland. There was talk of a council development by the Teville Stream, but thus far it hadn't materialised.

Worthing Wonderland stretched from Onslow Court, the new block of flats adjacent to the seafront, towards the Lancing border, and it was already so popular it seemed that Seebold had pulled a master stroke. Everyone was talking about it. Easter Monday was on 18 April, and fortunately the weather was mild and spring-like, which meant the day-trippers would soon be pouring through the gates.

At its beginning, 1938 had promised to be a brighter year after the turbulent days of the two previous ones. Edward VIII had abdicated just before Christmas 1936 to marry the woman he loved, and now he was to be known as the Duke of Windsor. In May 1937, the new king, George VI, had been crowned, and everyone had settled down with the feeling that some order and contentment had returned, but now all of that was being challenged again. The country was still reeling from the news that Adolf Hitler had annexed the Federal State of Austria. People were glued to their radios or reading their newspapers, and the daily conversation was of little else. What did this mean for Britain? How far would he go? Was it true that he already had his eye on Poland? But while the public trembled, the British establishment pretended it wasn't happening. It was obvious that there was little they could do, short of waging war, and – given that it was less than twenty years since the end of the Great War – the appetite for another full-blown conflict just wasn't there.

Milly paid her one and six at the entrance. The children's playground stretched over a couple of acres, and she was amazed by what she saw. Seebold had worked hard to achieve a magical atmosphere. A castle dominated the centre space. Children could climb a winding staircase to drop 'bombs' – soft balls – from the battlements, and for an extra thruppence could try on some child-size armour. There were swings, roundabouts, slides and a climbing frame. For older children and adults, there was a shooting range, darts, hoopla, and a game where you rolled tennis balls uphill and into a hole. Milly saw a queue of small children waiting to have a ride in a Cinderella coach, which was pulled by a goat in harness, and little ones were leaning over low fences, fascinated by the white rabbits and guinea pigs running around in an enclosure which looked like a village from a fairy story. Their hutches were made to look like tiny houses and there was a small village green in the middle. All the staff wore smart blue shirts and blue trousers or skirts, and it struck her that none of them had pockets. That meant that none of his staff could craftily pocket the takings instead of putting the money into the tills. She smiled to herself. Seebold had thought of everything.

At the back of the complex was a small tea van which also sold ice creams. People sat around on the benches provided to eat and drink their refreshments.

Milly headed for the office which, to her surprise, turned out to be nothing more than a wooden shed on the edge of the site. Clearly he was more keen to create an unforgettable experience for his punters than catering for his own creature comforts.

'Knock, knock,' she said as she approached the door.

Seebold sat behind a small desk. As soon as he saw her, he leapt to his feet. 'Milly! You came!'

'Of course I did,' she said with a laugh, 'but I had to fight my way in. It's manic out there.'

'It's great, isn't it,' he beamed. 'You know I can hear the sound of the children's laughter in my dreams.'

He offered her a chair and turned towards a small primus stove. 'Tea?'

Milly nodded. 'I can't believe what you've done. It's magnificent.'

'I didn't manage to get everything I wanted,' he said, handing her a mug of dark brown tea. 'There's still more to come. I've only half-done the enclosure for the story of Little Red Riding Hood.'

'I think I saw that!' cried Milly. 'Was that where a child-size dummy wearing a bright red cloak was standing behind a fenced-off area?'

Seebold nodded. He was pouring himself some tea. 'I've

arranged for a wolf to come. It should arrive this afternoon, along with some more sheep and a snake to go in my Adam and Eve booth.'

Milly's eyes widened. 'A wolf? I thought they were hunted to extinction in this country. Are you allowed to bring a wolf over here?'

Seebold came closer and tapped his nose. 'Probably not, but don't tell anyone.'

'You naughty boy,' Milly said teasingly and Seebold grinned.

As they sipped their tea, someone knocked on the door and a swarthy-looking man with greasy hair and a sweaty face stepped into the office.

'Road train has arrived, boss,' he said, snatching off his flat cap.

'Good man,' Seebold said, rising to his feet. 'Milly, this is Alf.'

Milly and Alf exchanged a nod.

'Have the press turned up, Alf?'

'There's one chap from the *Gazette*, but nobody else.'

'Damn,' said Seebold. 'This was supposed to bring me some publicity.'

Lena suddenly burst through the door. 'Seebold, you'd better come quickly. There's a problem.'

Milly stood up and Lena gave her a quick wave. 'Sorry,' she said. 'I'll chat to you later.'

'What's happened?' asked Milly, as she tagged along behind them.

'The road train just came in,' Lena said over her shoulder, 'but one of the cages is damaged.'

Everybody hurried to the far corner of the field, where a collection of vehicles was parked up by the fence. Some boys no more than twelve years old were hanging around, trying to see what was going on. There was a lot of shouting, and people were gesticulating with their hands. She spotted a couple of men removing animals from their cages to put them into their new accommodation, but the boys weren't interested in that. As she came closer, Milly could see a couple of sheep, and a man who was heading towards the Adam and Eve enclosure, carrying a large box which she guessed must be the snake.

'Lena, what is it? What's wrong?'

Her sister swung around. 'Seebold ordered a wolf but it isn't there,' she whispered.

Milly frowned. 'Perhaps they forgot to put it in the cage,' she suggested. It was a little disconcerting, but there had to be a logical explanation – didn't there?

It was only when she set eyes on the wolf's cage that she understood everybody's panic. One bar was only attached to the cage at the top because the wood underneath appeared to be rotten. It was powdery and splintered. The bar next to it was bent in the middle, as if someone or something had pushed its way out.

Seebold was interrogating Alf, the driver. 'That cage couldn't have got damaged that bad without you knowing about it, man. You must have seen what happened.'

'No, guv, I just told you. I only took over in Brighton. Herb asked me to drive the wagon 'cos his missus is having a baby. They said the kiddie was on its way and Herb wanted to be there, though why 'e did I shall never understand. I saw my baby brother coming and I'm telling you it wasn't a pretty sight. Enough to put you off your dinner fer life.'

'Yes, yes,' Seebold interrupted. 'But that bar couldn't have got bent like that unless somebody exerted considerable force on it.' He put his hand on Alf's shoulder. 'Don't you see? Somebody must have tampered with it.'

'Well if they did, guv, I never saw 'em,' Alf insisted. 'I never saw nobody.'

'Did you stop somewhere?'

'No, guv. Upon my life.'

Seebold shook his head with a puzzled expression.

'Oh wait a minute,' Alf cried. 'Now I come to think about it, I did stop. I had to. It was near the river.'

'What do you mean, you had to? Are you saying somebody forced you to stop?'

The driver leaned towards him in a confidential manner. 'Nah. I needed a pee.'

'But when you stopped, you were seen?'

'Course not,' said Alf. 'I made sure of that, don't you worry.'

Seebold seemed confused. 'I don't understand.'

Alf moved closer and lowered his voice. 'I got out of me cab and went in the bushes,' he confided. Lena and Milly stifled a laugh. 'Bloody busting I was,' he continued, 'so don't worry, nobody saw me.'

Seebold rolled his eyes.

Someone pushed through the gathering crowd. 'Excuse me, excuse me. Archibald Crump, reporter, *Worthing Gazette*. What's going on?'

He motioned to a man with a camera and, a second later, there was a bright flash. Seebold froze and the driver looked like a rabbit caught in the headlights.

He turned away muttering, 'All this fuss for a bloody pee. If there was a wolf, I never saw the going of 'im.'

The reporter did a double take. 'What's this about a wolf? What wolf? Where is it?'

'Nobody knows,' Alf said solemnly. 'It ain't my fault the cage is broke.'

'And you are?' Crump asked.

'Alfred Penrose.'

The photographer was busy taking pictures while Crump slipped his arm around Alf's shoulders and drew him to one side. 'Mr Penrose, I wonder if you could answer a few questions for the *Worthing Gazette*. You'd like your picture in the paper, wouldn't you. Something to show your children and grandchildren . . .'

The two of them walked away from the others.

Lena looked around. 'Where did Seebold go?' she asked Milly.

'He said something about making an urgent telephone call to find out what happened to the wolf, so I guess he's gone back to the office.' Milly smiled at her sister and the pair of them held out their arms to one another and hugged. 'It's lovely to see you again. How long have you been here?'

'A week,' said Lena. 'Rainbow George gave Seebold a couple of old stalls for old times' sake, the darts and the hoopla, so he sent me down here with them.'

'It's amazing what he's done with it all,' said Milly.

'How many times have you been here?'

'This is my first visit,' Milly confessed. Lena seemed surprised so she added, 'I kept meaning to stop by, but you know how it is. I'm back at college and I do the windows for two other shops now. I've gone freelance.'

Lena squeezed her hand. 'Milly, that's amazing. Pa would be so proud of you.'

Milly gave her a shy smile. 'Lena, I need to talk to you about Pa's will.' *And I need to tell you something else*, she thought to herself. Now that they were alone, it was a good time to come clean about that curse . . . but already her stomach was falling away just at the thought of it.

Lena took in a breath. 'Has the court finally decided?'

'I've had a letter and this one is yours,' Milly said, handing her sister an envelope. 'They've upheld his wishes. There's no reason to believe Pa didn't know what he was doing.'

'So you get the house and I get the cottage?'

Milly nodded. 'The cottage is definitely yours, as from now. I still only get the house when I'm twenty-one.'

Lena sucked in her lips and looked away tearfully. 'I still can't believe he's gone.'

'I know, I know.' Milly squeezed her arm and they walked on in silence for a bit. She glanced at Lena's profile. *Tell her, tell her now . . .*

Her sister turned her head and caught her staring. 'What?'

Milly took a deep breath. 'Nothing . . . I was just wondering if . . .' And suddenly panicking, she blurted out, 'If you and Seebold are any closer to getting married?'

Lena gave her a quizzical look. 'I've already told you. Seebold and I aren't getting wed.'

'But you said Rainbow George was keeping on and on about it.'

Lena snorted. 'Oh Milly, we only let him think that might happen to get him off our backs. I told you once before, I shan't get married until I'm an old woman.'

'And how does Seebold feel about it?'

'He doesn't want to marry me either,' said Lena. She put her lips close to Milly's ear. 'Seebold loves somebody else.'

Her remark was like a hammer blow to Milly. She longed to ask who it was, but at the same time, she didn't want to know. Oblivious to her sister's thoughts, Lena giggled and nudged her in her side.

Archibald Crump and his photographer watched Alfred Penrose walking towards the office. He hadn't been much help anyway. 'There's a story here, Bert,' the reporter said. 'I can feel it in me water.'

'Na,' said Bert. 'It's just a misunderstanding, that's all. He thought the wolf was in the cage but turns out nobody put it in.' He began packing up his camera. 'Any road, where would you find a wolf these days? They'm all hextinct, ain't they?'

Crump shook his head. 'There's more to this than meets the eye,' he insisted. 'Let's follow Alfred and see what he's up to.'

They hurried in the same direction they'd seen the lorry

driver go, but it took a few minutes to track him down. Suddenly, they spotted him coming out of the office. Crump tugged at Bert's arm to prevent him from making their presence known, but Alf didn't notice them anyway. He was too busy counting a wad of notes.

'There must be ten pounds or more in his hand,' Crump whispered.

'What's that all about?' asked Bert.

Crump's eyes narrowed. 'Hush money,' he said.

Inside the office, Milly and Lena watched the driver leave. 'That was an awful lot of money you gave him,' Lena remarked.

'Only twelve pounds,' said Seebold. 'I haven't paid him for a month.'

'Did you telephone to find out what happened to the wolf?' Lena asked.

'Couldn't get through,' said Seebold. He pulled on his jacket. 'It'll soon be time to close up for the day. I'd better start shutting up the animals.' And with that he left the room.

Chapter 23

Agatha threw herself onto the sofa and swore out loud. 'Damn, damn, damn.' She was angry, furious, bloody livid. How could this be happening? For years she had planned, shaped and moulded her future. She had progressed from a penniless fifteen-year-old to a woman of social standing, someone respected in society, rich and well-heeled. Just a year ago, everything had been so perfect and now, despite her best efforts, it was all slipping through her fingers like water. She rose to her feet and, grabbing the open letter on her desk, she began ripping it into little pieces, the sound of her frustration growing from small grunts into a cry of anguish.

The door flew open. 'Mummy?' Pearl sounded very concerned. 'Whatever's the matter?'

Agatha took a deep breath. 'Nothing, dear.'

'But there is something,' her daughter insisted. 'I can see you're upset.'

Still trembling from her outburst, Agatha walked to the drinks trolley and poured herself a stiff drink. If it wasn't enough that the court had decided her stupid and weak-willed husband wasn't out of his mind when he wrote that will, now she had to face this as well.

'Mrs Cunningham has just handed in her notice. She leaves at the end of the week.'

Pearl frowned. 'But why? She's been here since the year dot.'

Of course Agatha knew perfectly well why she was going. On the day it was read, the will had been called into question. She knew that Mrs Cunningham had almost reached retirement age anyway, but the woman must have decided to stay long enough to make sure she would still be getting her twenty-five pounds a year. The morning post had brought news of the court's ruling, and her cook/housekeeper's notice had quickly followed. Agatha had been shocked. It was obvious that Mrs Cunningham didn't care about the inconvenience it would cause her mistress. True, Agatha hadn't actually paid her since Charles died. She would have done, had her challenge to the will been successful, but she wouldn't be doing that now. Why should she? It served the wretched woman right. She'd shown her no loyalty whatsoever.

Agatha took a gulp of her whisky. 'You can't rely on anybody these days,' she said acidly.

'Oh don't worry, Mummy,' said Pearl. 'We'll soon get someone else.'

Agatha glared at her as she patted the back of her hair.

'Honestly,' Pearl insisted. 'I'll go down to the village and put a notice in the post office window.'

'For goodness' sake,' Agatha snapped. 'Don't be so bloody ridiculous.'

Her daughter's eyes grew wide.

Her mother filled her glass again and went back to the sofa. 'And don't look at me like that,' she said. 'You tell me where the money's coming from to pay for a cleaner . . . and a cook . . . and a housekeeper.'

Pearl looked crestfallen. 'I was only trying to help.'

'Yes, yes,' her mother said quickly. 'I'm sorry. But all this on top of your father's will . . .' She gave Pearl an anxious glance. 'You haven't told Freddie the result of the court case, have you?'

'Not yet.'

'Then don't,' Agatha said, leaning towards her. 'He mustn't know. I don't want him thinking we're a charity case.'

'He wouldn't think . . .' Pearl began.

'I want you to promise me you won't say anything.'

'But . . .'

'Promise me!'

'All right, I promise,' said Pearl.

Agatha nodded and relaxed back into her seat. 'Where is Freddie anyway?'

'He's gone for a bike ride.'

'Another one?' cried Agatha. 'He's always out on that bike.'

'He loves being in the countryside,' said Pearl. 'He's got a whole stack of photographs: Pulborough, Steyning, Shoreham Harbour, Selsey . . . you name it, he's been there. He says he's going to write a book.'

Agatha frowned. 'It must be costing him a fortune to get all those photographs developed.'

'Oh, he does them all himself, Mummy. He's created a darkroom in the cellar.'

Agatha tut-tutted her disapproval. 'Has he mentioned taking you to see his castle yet?'

Pearl shook her head.

'Doesn't he want you to meet his family?'

Her daughter shrugged. 'He doesn't really talk about them.'

Agatha frowned again. 'Well, he can't stay here sponging off me for ever.

There was a pause, then Pearl said, 'Are we really so poor, Mummy?'

'There's only the small annuity Charles left,' said Agatha. 'Your husband will support you, so I hope you won't begrudge me having that.'

Pearl gasped in shocked surprise. 'But that means I get nothing.'

'Pearl, I have no other way to live,' Agatha said coldly.

Pearl swayed slightly as the colour drained from her face. 'It's not fair,' she cried. 'Milly gets all this,' she waved her hand expansively, 'that gypsy creature gets the cottage, and meanwhile I get nothing.'

Agatha stood up to pour herself another drink. 'I know, but that's just how it is. It can't be helped.' As she came back to the sofa with her glass refilled, she rubbed her daughter's arm. 'I'm sorry.'

'I hate her,' Pearl muttered. 'I hate them both.'

'I don't blame you,' her mother said dully. 'So do I.'

Pearl smiled wanly. 'There is one bit of good news, Mummy. I think I'm pregnant again.'

Agatha beamed. 'Oh, that's wonderful, darling. You clever girl. Have you seen Dr Jennings?'

'Not yet,' said Pearl, 'but when I lost the first one, he said there's no reason why I shouldn't carry another one all the way.'

'Of course, but you must be careful,' Agatha agreed. 'In fact, I think you should go and put your feet up right this minute.'

As soon as her daughter had gone upstairs to rest, Agatha tipped the bottle over the glass once again. What was she going to do? There was precious little money coming in. Pearl was used to spending it like water, and that husband of hers didn't seem to be very eager to put his hand into his pocket. Tight-fisted twerp. She looked around the room. That picture above the fireplace . . . could it be an original? And that vase . . . she'd always hated that thing. It had been a gift from her mother-in-law on their wedding day. Old Mrs Shepherd was rolling in it, but she wouldn't be putting anything Agatha's way. They'd crossed swords years ago. She couldn't even remember when they'd last spoken.

Agatha walked over to the vase to take a closer look. Called *Gold and Orange*, it was by Otto Thamm; it was probably worth a bob or two. She picked it up and something inside rattled. She tipped it over and some beads fell out. One of the girls must have put them in there when they were children. Agatha turned them over in her hands. Horrible black things. There wasn't even a hole in them to thread a string through. She threw them back inside.

A plan was forming in her mind. She had always thought Muntham Court was cluttered, but Charles had been far too sentimental to get rid of anything. The fashion now was simplicity. She would tell everyone she was redecorating. She would find some up-and-coming interior decorator (that would be cheaper) and begin to minimalise . . . tell everyone she was putting all this stuff in the loft, but instead, she'd sell it to the highest bidder. Mrs Cunningham could spend her last week washing all the dust off and wrapping everything up for her. She smiled to herself. It would kill two birds with one stone. That little minx Millicent might be getting the house, but Agatha would make sure she didn't have its treasures.

On her way to work a couple of days later, Milly noticed that the paper boy who stood next to the Old Town Hall was doing a brisk trade. 'Read all abou' it. Read all abou' it. Ferocious h'animal on the loose. Extra police drafted in. Get your *News Chronicle* 'ere.'

Milly bought a copy and fanned it out as she headed towards Hubbard's. Half the front page was taken up with a picture of Seebold and the driver of the road train. She stopped in the street to read the accompanying article with some sense of alarm.

> The inhabitants of the seaside town of Worthing were advised by the police to lock their doors and close their windows yesterday for their own safety when it was discovered that a vicious wolf-like animal was on the loose from the Worthing Wonderland entertainment establishment run by Mr Seebold Flowers. Local farmers have banded together with motor vehicles to scour the countryside around the River Adur. The mystery of what happened to the animal deepened when the driver of a road train told our reporter that he stopped to relieve himself somewhere along the A283. Although he was responsible for the animals in his care, he had failed to notice that the cage containing the wolf was damaged. "E must have broke out then,' said Mr Alfred Penrose, 52, of Jefferies Lane, Goring. Sergeant Littlejohn of the Worthing police force urged people not to panic. 'We have the matter in hand,' he said. 'We have alerted local animal trainers and we anticipate the beast will soon be apprehended.'

Milly felt a bit sick. This was obviously getting serious. Poor Seebold; he must be frantic with worry. Her eye was drawn to the Stop Press column at the side of the page. *Wolf spotted in garden. Police are investigating.*

Oh dear, oh dear. What could she do to help? He might be in love with someone else, but Seebold was still her friend and he'd always been kind to her. She glanced at her watch. If she could get the display in the big window finished this morning, then she could catch a bus along the seafront at lunchtime and be there by one o'clock. It was only right that she should support him in his hour of need.

Crump and his photographer exchanged a sly glance at each other as they looked at the *Worthing Gazette*. 'Got your story now, Archie,' Bert muttered from the corner of his mouth.

Crump suppressed a smile. 'Better than that, Bert. Got a bloody scoop, haven't we.'

It was four o'clock by the time Milly arrived at the Worthing Wonderland. The display had taken longer than she had anticipated. Then, just as she had been about to set off, Mr Johnson had called an emergency meeting of staff in the canteen, where he announced that Hubbard's would be closing early today and would not be opening tomorrow.

'The safety of you all is paramount,' he said gravely. 'I've no wish to alarm anybody, but we have no idea where this ferocious beast may be. It's been missing for over forty-eight hours and by now it must be hungry.'

Several of the younger assistants whimpered or cried out in distress.

'As soon as the store is closed,' he went on, 'every girl is to go straight home. Inspector Young has told me that extra buses will be laid on and the bus stop is right outside. Do not, I repeat, do not hang around. Go straight home.'

Milly knew Inspector Young quite well. He had been a friend of her father.

By now a couple of girls were in tears, and for the first time Milly felt nervous herself. This was becoming more and more alarming.

When she eventually arrived, the Worthing Wonderland was almost deserted. Milly made her way towards Seebold's office and, opening the door, she saw Lena sitting by the desk. As she rose to her feet, Milly ran towards her to give her a hug. 'You shouldn't have come,' Lena said. 'It's not really safe.'

'I couldn't leave you to face all this alone,' said Milly. 'Where's Seebold?'

'Sergeant Littlejohn took him to the police station this morning,' said Lena. 'He's not back yet.'

Milly frowned. 'Why? He hasn't done anything wrong.'

'I don't really know.'

Milly looked anxious. 'Has the wolf been found?'

Lena shook her head. 'Do you want some tea?' she asked, picking up the empty kettle to fill with water from a tap just outside the door.

Milly hesitated. If it was as dangerous as they said, was it worth the risk of sending Lena outside. Her sister tossed her head as if she could read her mind. 'Oh bugger it,' she said, opening the door again. 'I want a cup of tea. If I get eaten, I get eaten.'

Milly admired her bravado, but it was slightly disconcerting all the same.

Ten minutes later, they sat in the office sipping their tea in silence. What could they say? Each girl was going over every scenario she could think of, but really there would be no resolution until the animal was accounted for. Then the door burst open and Seebold tumbled in. 'Blimey,' he exclaimed. 'What a day. What a blinkin' 'orrible day.' He threw himself into a chair and put his head in his hands.

Lena busied herself pouring him a mug of tea. Milly laid her hand on his shoulder. 'We were worried that they'd arrested you.'

'They wanted to, but they couldn't pin anything on me. How could they? It wasn't my fault. I wasn't anywhere near that road train. All I did was buy the damned thing.'

'So, does anyone know what happened to it yet?' asked Lena, putting the mug on the desk in front of him.

'Search me,' said Seebold. 'As far as the police are concerned, there's a wolf on the loose somewhere and it has to be found.'

Milly nodded. 'I'm sure they'll catch it soon.'

'No, I'm afraid they won't,' Seebold said dejectedly.

Milly and Lena exchanged a confused frown.

Seebold took a gulp of his tea. 'You see, there never was a wolf. As soon as the bloke who sold it to me saw the condition of the cage, he never bloody sent it.'

Chapter 24

Milly took in a noisy breath while Lena stared at him with her mouth open. 'You mean all this has been a hoax?'

'Not exactly,' said Seebold. 'I honestly thought it had been sent. As soon as I saw the broken cage, I went and telephoned the seller but he was out. His wife said to phone back.'

'And all afternoon, when you were talking to the police,' said Lena, 'you didn't tell them? Do they know?'

Seebold shook his head. 'I've only just found out myself,' he said. 'They questioned me and sent me home at about three. There were no buses so I walked. When I got to Ham Road, I was so anxious I couldn't wait any longer, so I used the telephone box on the corner by the pub.'

'And that's when you found out?' Milly asked.

Seebold nodded.

'So why didn't you go back to the police station and tell them the animal had never even been sent?' Seebold didn't answer.

'Seebold!' Lena said crossly.

'I was afraid if I went back, they would arrest me,' he said, his face colouring.

'Why?' said Milly. 'It was obviously a misunderstanding.'

Lena frowned. 'You can't ignore this. They'll find out eventually.'

Seebold got to his feet and took off his coat. As he sat down again, Milly wondered if he realised how serious this had become. There was every possibility that he could be in big trouble. 'Seebold, the whole of Worthing is virtually shut down because of this,' she said. 'Everybody is so terrified they are going to be attacked by some ferocious animal. Even Hubbard's closed early. All the girls were sent home.'

'I know, I know.' He ran his fingers through his hair. 'But what can I do? If I tell them there never was a wolf, they'll say I made it up and arrest me. They'll shut the Wonderland down. The punters love the place but there's plenty around here who would be only too glad to see the back of an entertainer like me.'

Milly's heart went out to him. 'Did you know someone has claimed to have spotted the wolf in his garden?'

'What?' Seebold gasped. 'Where?'

'It was Stop Press in the evening paper,' said Milly.

'This is getting out of hand,' cried Seebold.

'Of course it is,' said Milly. 'That's why you have to come clean. You have to tell them.'

He leaned forward, his head in his hands. As much as she wanted to, Milly resisted the urge to put a comforting hand on his back. His heart belonged to somebody else. She was here purely as his friend.

'There is one way around it,' he said, suddenly looking up at them. 'We could produce the wolf.'

Milly was puzzled. 'What do you mean . . . produce the wolf? You yourself have just told us there was no wolf.'

'Yeah, but I've been thinking. A mate of mine has an old dog,' Seebold said excitedly. 'He's a bit doddery and grey, but he's the right size and shape. I reckon he could fool them.'

'Don't be so ridiculous!' Lena snapped. 'People aren't stupid. They'll know the difference between some old mutt and a wolf.'

'But don't you see?' Seebold said, rising to his feet. 'People won't believe me if I simply say there was no wolf, but if I can produce it and say it ran away, it'll be fine.'

Milly shook her head. 'No, it won't work. How would it know to come here? It's too much of a coincidence if it suddenly turns up.'

'Ah yes,' said Seebold, beaming, 'but what if we caught it out in the wilds somewhere . . .'

Lena looked thoughtful but Milly's heart sank. If they 'found' the wolf, everybody would start asking questions and she was no good at lying. She glanced at Seebold, who was becoming more and more animated at the idea. Much as she wanted to help, she couldn't do this. 'Count me out,' she said. 'I'm not lying to the police.'

'You won't have to,' said Lena with a sudden change of heart. 'Look, Seebold is right. If he gets on to his mate, he can arrange to borrow the dog. Then first thing in the morning, when he goes looking for it, he'll "find it",' she added, making quote marks in the air, 'and bring it back here in a cage. What's wrong with that?'

'You can't be serious,' said Milly. 'It's crazy.'

'It's the only answer,' Seebold said resolutely. He reached for the petty cash box then picked up the telephone. 'Don't go away,' he said as he dialled a number. 'I might need you both.'

Milly hadn't counted on being asked to get up at the crack of dawn. She set her alarm for four-thirty and was dressed and ready half an hour later. Having crept out of the house, she waited on Marine Parade for Seebold's lorry.

It was a wonderful, bright morning. Across the road on the beach, the gulls were gathering, waiting for the first fishing boats to land their catch. Milly leaned against the walled enclosure of a house and yawned. This was a crazy scheme, but if it worked Seebold would be in the clear. If it didn't . . . She shuddered. That scenario didn't bear thinking about. She paced up and down, but it wasn't long before she heard the rumble of Seebold's lorry.

'Good, you made it,' he cried as Lena opened the passenger door and gave her half-sister a hand to get in.

'I must be mad to do this,' Milly grumbled half-heartedly.

'You and me both,' said Lena, but they exchanged an excited grin.

They drove to the north of Shoreham and entered Mill Lane. It was beautiful up there. They drove past miles of chalk grassland, famed as a habitat for the Adonis Blue butterfly, and for the yellow horseshoe vetch plant. Years before, it had been the place of windmills, hence the name, but they were long gone. The views near the top were fabulous, with Lancing College in the distance, the River Adur just below them, and Shoreham Airport in between. A low plane flew overhead ready to land.

Just off the Steyning Road, close by Eringham Farm, they spotted another lorry waiting by the side of the road. The two girls stayed in the cab while Seebold got out to talk with his friend. Milly saw a brown envelope exchange hands, and then the other man opened the cab door and a mangy-looking dog jumped down. The two men shook hands and parted then Seebold brought the dog, which was on a leash, over to his lorry. Lena climbed out to help him lift it onto the back and into the cage. The dog seemed unperturbed by all the fuss and lay down for a sleep.

Milly got out of the cab to have a look at it. 'He's massive.'

'Danny says his mother was an Alsatian and his father an Irish wolfhound,' said Seebold.

'That'll account for his shaggy coat,' said Lena, 'but he doesn't look much like a wolf.'

'Beggars can't be choosers,' Seebold said crisply. He rubbed his chin. 'It's too clean. If it's supposedly been on the loose for two days, it's too clean.'

'You've got enough on your plate trying to convince people that poor old dog is a wolf,' Milly said bleakly.

'Thanks for that vote of confidence,' Seebold said sarcastically, and Milly felt awful until Lena said, 'You're right. It is too clean.'

They stood looking at the dog, each lost in his or her own thoughts, then they all climbed back into the cab. Seebold drove the lorry towards the river. The girls were wondering what he was up to but neither of them spoke. Seebold stopped the lorry and got out again. Putting the dog back on the leash, he took it from the cage, and walked towards the river bank. 'There's an old tin can in the back of the lorry,' he called out. 'Can one of you bring it down here? If someone keeps holds of his lead, I can slosh some of that muddy water over it.'

Seebold walked off to the river, looking for an accessible slope, and Milly and Lena were heading over to him when they heard some ducks quacking. The dog let out a deep throaty bark and all at once took off, dragging the reluctant Seebold with him.

Milly and Lena watched helplessly as the pair of them hurtled down a gentle slope towards the water, Seebold shouting, 'Whoa, stop. Come back you, stupid mutt.'

Then Seebold slipped on the mud. His legs seemed to go every which way, and a second or two later he was on his bottom, with the dog still dragging him towards the water's edge.

'Aaaaggh.'

Seebold tried to find his feet, but the dog was on a mission. Three ducks took to the air and flew away from them, and by now the dog was in the water, still barking. As Seebold slid on the mud for a second time, he landed with his rear end in the water. Milly and Lena burst out laughing.

The dog calmly lapped at the water as Seebold staggered to his feet once again. 'It's not bloody funny,' he snapped. 'I'm soaked to the skin.' Milly and Lena struggled to control themselves but it was hopeless.

Lena waved something in the air. 'Do you still want this can?' she called, and that started them off again.

As Seebold squelched slowly up the slippery slope, Milly saw something that made her blood run cold. About a hundred yards up the river, a swan, its neck outstretched, was advancing on the muddy pair. 'Seebold,' she cried, 'get out of there as quick as you can. There's a cob following you. There must be a nest nearby.'

Seebold looked behind him and did his best to hurry. 'You two get into the cab,' he shouted. Milly and Lena didn't need telling twice.

'How's he going to get the dog in the back?' Lena asked anxiously.

'I don't know,' said Milly. Her heart was already thumping and her mouth had gone dry.

They kept the cab door open and watched anxiously in the rear-view mirror and the wing mirrors. 'Come on, come on,' Milly whispered.

At last Seebold burst from the undergrowth, dragging the dog with him. He raced to the lorry and the three of them hauled the animal into the cab. Seebold climbed in after him and closed the door, seconds before the angry swan hurled itself towards him. Seebold, out of breath and panting hard, put his head onto the steering wheel. 'That was close. That thing weighs a ton.'

The dog had scrambled up from the footwell and began jumping up at the window, its barking reverberating noisily around the cab. The swan was still outside on the road, hissing angrily and with its wings outstretched. Eventually it folded its wings and waggled its tail indignantly as it turned around. It was with a sense of relief that Milly watched it waddle back to the river bank, but when it reached the grass verge, it began to hiss again,

'Now what?' Milly said quietly, peering out at the scene, but the other two were preoccupied. Seebold still had his head on the steering wheel and Lena was doing her best to push the dog's wet paws from her lap.

Milly watched in the reflection of the wing mirror next to her as the swan headed towards another part of the verge. All at once, a man emerged from the tall grasses. He had fair hair and wore an expensive-looking country suit and a deerstalker hat. There was something familiar about him but, as he kept looking back, she couldn't see his face clearly.

The swan had sensed a new threat. It raced towards the man, its head outstretched and its wings extended. The man didn't waste time. He charged up the road and a second or two later, Milly saw him pull a bicycle from the hedgerow. He fumbled a little as he threw something which looked like a camera into the bag behind the saddle. What on earth was he photographing? As he swung his leg over the crossbar, he almost lost his footing, probably through panic, and then he took off at top speed. Just before he turned the corner, he glanced back to see if the swan was still coming. It wasn't. The bird was now fluffing out its feathers and waggling its tail as it waddled back towards the river.

As soon as she saw the man's face, Milly took in a sharp breath, but just at that moment, the dog shook himself and everybody's attention was elsewhere. Cold muddy water rained down inside the cab. She and Lena squealed as their clothes were splattered. Seebold cursed. The dog stopped shaking and everybody looked at each other. Their faces were covered in large brown blobs; together with the splashes on their clothes, it looked as if they'd been painting.

Lena wiped her cheek with her sleeve and, looking down at the bedraggled dog, she said, 'Is he dirty enough for you, Seebold?'

They couldn't help laughing at themselves and, as soon as Lena had pushed the dog back down into the footwell, Seebold started the engine.

As they drove off, Milly looked out of the window. She was thinking about that man in the undergrowth. What on earth had he been doing, lying in the grass beside a muddy river? He preferred being smartly dressed and a cut above the rest. It was so out of character and so odd, but as soon as he'd turned around, she'd recognised him.

It had been none other than Freddie Herren, Pearl's husband.

Chapter 25

An hour later, Seebold was on the telephone. The press were on their way but Milly had to go back to her digs just behind Hubbard's and get ready for work. Even though the town was still officially a no-go area, she reckoned she might as well get the big window revamped for the new season, ready for when the public hysteria had died down. She had arranged to borrow a fishing boat for her 'Worthing by the Sea' display, and it was being delivered this morning.

She said her goodbyes to Lena and Seebold and took a bus back into town. The journey helped her to put a few things into perspective. She absolutely dreaded that this madcap scheme of Seebold's would backfire. It wasn't so much that she was scared that she would be in trouble, although that did come into it; it was more a fear that Seebold might end up in prison for lying to the authorities. Milly had made up her mind that – should she be arrested – she would ask Uncle Neville for help, but what hope did Seebold have, especially when there was so much prejudice against him?

Also, she had developed a keen determination to get to the bottom of why her mother was still so hostile towards her, and to visit her soon. Although Milly had glimpsed her, albeit surreptitiously, on Pearl's wedding day, she hadn't properly spoken to Agatha for a long time. As for her sister, Milly had guessed that when Pearl came to Hubbard's to have her wedding dress altered, that must have been because she had lost her baby. How sad for her, but she could well be pregnant again by now. Of course nobody would bother to keep Milly informed. She sighed. She and Pearl never had got on very well. Her sister was too bossy. Looking back, Milly realised she had been a bit of a doormat. She should have stood up to her years ago. And what had Milly done to her mother that had made her so angry with her all the time? She'd spent her whole childhood trying to please her, but it seemed nothing she did was good enough. Agatha always gave Milly the impression that she was a nuisance, and yet she doted on her sister. Why? Lena once asked her whether there had been an identifiable moment when it all started, but there hadn't. They had never had a close relationship but, even after all this time, there was something in Milly that still wanted to make it right.

Milly looked out of the window as the bus stopped by New Parade which was opposite Farncombe Road. A young mother was holding her daughter's hand as she climbed aboard. The conductress was upstairs taking fares.

As the bus reached Steyne Gardens and turned towards the sea front, Milly could see the council workmen building underground shelters. Nothing out of the ordinary there. They had been digging a deep trench for several days now, but what made her do a double take was a man lurking behind a tree taking photographs. She recognised him straight away. It was her new brother-in-law, Freddie Herren. There was nothing wrong with taking photographs. This was a seaside town, but he was doing his best not to be seen by the workmen. Why?

As the bus trundled on, Freddie turned and their eyes met as he dashed away. She frowned to herself. How odd.

The conductress came towards the mother and her child who were sitting nearby and Milly heard her say, 'Give the conductress the money, Hazel.'

The child handed over some coins and the conductress issued a ticket. 'There you are, lovey.'

'Say thank you, darling,' the child's mother instructed, and the little girl did just that. 'Well done,' the mother whispered as the smiling conductress moved further up the bus. 'You are a clever girl. Now you can tell Daddy you paid the fare all by yourself.'

Such a simple yet intimate moment, and one which brought tears to Milly's eyes. She couldn't remember one time when she and her mother had shared such an occasion. Now she was struggling to keep her tears silent. She pulled out her handkerchief and dabbed her eyes.

The woman behind her tapped her on the shoulder. 'You all right, love?'

'Yes, yes,' said Milly, turning slightly towards her. 'I'm fine. Just being silly.'

The woman nodded.

They had reached the pier and the woman stood up to leave. 'You take care, love,' she said. 'Life's a bugger at times, but there's always a better day coming.'

Swallowing the lump in her throat, Milly gave her a grateful smile.

The press had turned up at Worthing Wonderland in force. Seebold, still in his mud-splattered clothes, posed with the dog, and the press photographers from the *Worthing Herald*, *Worthing Gazette* and the Fleet Street newspapers snapped away. While he told the story of how they'd caught the beast, Lena was persuaded to change into a pretty dress for her photographs. Half an hour later she was posing next to the dog's cage, looking 'as lovely as a film star' as one man told her. 'You look like Madeleine Carroll,' said another. Lena was flattered. She'd loved Madeleine Carroll in Alfred Hitchcock's *The 39 Steps*.

The evening papers were full of the story. *Beautiful belle finds ferocious dog* was one headline. *Beast back behind bars thanks to beauty* was another. Not quite what Seebold was hoping for, but publicity all the same.

Twelve miles away in Slindon, Crump was drowning his sorrows in the Spur public house. His editor hadn't been that impressed with his latest story about a three-legged tortoise, but he had been really keen on the missing wolf story. That had brought a bevy of Fleet Street reporters down to sleepy Sussex, and they had hired local farmers to scour the countryside looking for the animal. Crump and his photographer had offered the *Worthing Gazette* the exclusive when the wolf had been found, but he didn't want to publish.

'That wolf looks more like a bloody dog!' he'd exclaimed. 'You're taking the Michael, aren't you?' And as a result, Crump's story was reduced to a few lines and put at the bottom of page eleven.

He sighed and swirled the last of the liquid in his glass. To think he'd been reduced to this: coverage of a bring-and-buy sale in the Coronation Hall. The only vaguely interesting thing about that was that the hall itself had been put up to commemorate the coronation of King George VI the year before.

The door burst open and a roughly dressed man stumbled into the bar.

What'll it be, Doyle?' the landlord called out. 'You look as if you've lost five bob and found a tanner.'

'Pint of best bitter,' his customer said moodily. 'I just found one of my best ewes stone dead.'

Nobody seemed that interested but, over in the corner, Archibald Crump pricked up his ears.

Now that Seebold was in the clear, people were coming to the Worthing Wonderland in droves. In fact, one coach company had even laid on a day trip. Things were looking up again, and Seebold was more than happy with his takings.

Later that afternoon, a car drew up outside his office and three men got out. Seebold recognised Archibald Crump and his photographer, but the third man was a stranger to him. Short and dressed in tatty clothes, he wore a flat cap.

After they'd exchanged pleasantries, Crump leaned forward in a confidential manner.

'This is Mr Doyle,' he said. 'He's a farmer over Slindon way.'

Seebold and Doyle shook hands cordially.

'It would appear that your wolf has attacked and killed one of his best sheep,' said Crump.

Seebold frowned. 'I don't think so,' he said.

'Really upset, so I was,' said Doyle, snatching off his cap and wringing it in his hands.

'Mr Doyle feels he should be compensated for his loss,' Crump went on. 'He was deeply shocked to find the body and he tells me his children helped to rear the poor thing when it was just a lamb.'

Seebold pursed his lips. 'The wolf was found near Shoreham,' he said. 'Slindon is a devil of a long way away from there.'

'No distance for a hungry wolf, I'm sure,' Crump said with a cunning smile.

'I can't afford to lose one of my sheep,' Doyle complained and, as he opened the boot of his car, a rancid smell seeped out, making Seebold turn his head in revulsion.

The photographer got two clear pictures.

'You needs to cover my loss,' Doyle insisted. 'I could've had good money at the abattoir for the meat, and the fleece would have brought me at least a couple of quid.'

When Seebold examined the carcass, it was obvious that a knife had been used to enlarge its wounds, something which he did not hesitate to point out.

'Come now, Mr Flowers,' said Crump, waving his arms. 'Looking around, I'm sure you can afford to help out a hard-working farmer. You wouldn't want this in the paper, now would you?'

'I reckon twenty quid might be fair compensation,' said Doyle.

'Oh, now I see what this is all about,' Seebold exclaimed. 'Well, I don't give in to blackmail. That sheep has nothing to do with me and you know it.'

'Don't do something you might regret, Mr Flowers,' Crump insisted. 'Think of your reputation.'

'I think you'd better clear off,' Seebold retorted, and a moment later they were all having a blazing row.

In the days that followed, the dog settled down in its enclosure where Red Riding Hood peered in through the cottage window. It was a little unfortunate when the dog cocked its leg against the little model in front of a party of children, but otherwise the idea was a success and Seebold was proved right. It was a real crowd-puller.

Agatha closed the sitting-room door. Pearl and her husband were in the house and she wanted privacy. The London papers were spread out on the sofa, all of them filled with the story of a missing wolf, Seebold Flowers and Worthing Wonderland. Agatha had turned the pages with disgust and contempt. The *News Chronicle* had four whole pages of pictures, no less. Front page, page two and a two-page spread between pages six and seven. *The Times* didn't go in for front-page pictures, but the correspondent had virtually filled page three, and the *Express* and *Mail* rivalled each other with their level of coverage.

The so-called wolf looked more like a mangy dog. It was big and it had pale eyes, but Agatha reckoned it was no more a wolf than she was the Queen of Sheba. In the newspaper picture, that dreadful gypsy man sat next to its enclosure, feeding it through the wire netting, while that Lena, all tarted up like a dog's dinner, looked on. Agatha curled her lip. Cheap. Like mother, like daughter.

She reached for the telephone. 'Number, please,' said the operator.

'East Preston six, nine.'

After a few minutes, a male voice answered. 'Chief Superintendent Davey speaking.'

'Hello, Reginald. Is that you?' she said quietly, her voice small and concerned. 'It's Agatha, Agatha Shepherd.'

'Agatha, my dear. How are you? We were sorry to hear about Charles. He was a good man.'

'One of the best,' Agatha agreed with a catch in her voice.

They exchanged a few niceties and then he said, 'What can I do for you, my dear?'

'I'm not sure how to put this, Reginald, but there's been a bit of a flap going on in Worthing and I'm worried.'

'Are you talking about the wolf debacle?'

'Yes.' Agatha hesitated. 'Look, Reginald, you know I'm not one to cast aspersions, but I've had dealings with that Mr Flowers, and quite frankly, I wouldn't trust him as far as I could throw him.' She caught her breath noisily. 'He came to the house and the next thing I knew, Millicent was in his lorry.'

'Good Lord!' cried the chief super. 'You mean he kidnapped her?'

'Not exactly,' said Agatha, 'but Millicent is completely besotted with him. The man is a thief and a liar, Reginald. I'm sure he's still not telling the truth about that animal, and he has practically the whole county in an uproar.'

'Really?'

'It says in today's paper that he caught the wolf himself and that it had been hiding in the bushes,' she went on, her voice now becoming shrill. 'But that can't be true, can it? I mean, a wolf wouldn't be sitting quietly in the shrubbery waiting to be caught! Why don't the police do something? I mean, a man like him wouldn't know the truth if it bit him on the bottom.' She stopped as if to gather herself before adding in a more compliant tone, 'Oh, I do beg your pardon. I didn't mean . . .'

'No, no, my dear. It's quite all right,' Reginald soothed. 'You're upset and worried about your daughter. I quite understand.'

'You are so kind, Reginald.' Agatha let out a small sob. 'It's just that, with Charles gone, I'm shouldering the responsibility for the girls all alone.'

'And I'm sure you're doing an admirable job, my dear. Leave it with me. I'll get my officers to look into it again, and be assured, if there is any wrongdoing, I'll throw the book at him.'

Milly decided to bike up to Muntham Court. She was a little nervous, so was almost relieved when she'd knocked on the door, and thought no one was in. The place looked deserted. The gardens were badly in need of weeding, and the fishpond outside the front door was overgrown with algae. She walked around the back and tried the French windows, but they were locked. When she peered through them, the sitting room looked rather bare. Most of the furniture was gone. Her mother must be having the room decorated. Milly turned back to fetch her bicycle. As she reached the front again, a first-floor window flew up and Pearl leaned out. 'Oh, it's you. What do you want?'

'I thought I'd come and see you, that's all,' said Milly.

'What for?'

'No reason. We're still family, aren't we?'

Pearl said nothing.

'Aren't you going to invite me in then?'

Her sister's head disappeared, and the window was slammed shut. A few minutes later, Pearl opened the front door. She looked unkempt and dishevelled. Her hair was badly in need of a wash and, despite the fact that it was four in the afternoon, she was still in her dressing gown.

'Are you all right?' Milly asked as she followed her inside.

'I'm fine,' Pearl snapped.

Milly knew she was going to have to stay calm if she was going to build bridges.

Pearl walked towards the kitchen. 'Do you want some tea?'

Milly was surprised at her sister's offer – she had no idea Pearl even knew how to make tea. 'That would be nice.'

Her sister busied herself filling the kettle.

'Mrs Cunningham's day off?' asked Milly.

'Mrs Cunningham left,' said Pearl. Her voice had an edge to it. 'So did all the others. We have to fend for ourselves now.' It came as a bit of a shock, but Milly kept quiet. If she responded, Pearl was bound to work everything up until they had a row. 'Mother and I are as poor as church mice these days,' she said, slamming the kettle onto the stove.

'How are you enjoying married life?' Milly said, changing the subject.

She saw her sister stiffen. 'It's all right. You know I lost a baby?'

'I guessed,' said Milly, 'and I'm truly sorry.'

She rose to her feet with the intention of giving her sister a hug, but Pearl deliberately moved away. Milly sat down again and fiddled with the tablecloth. 'I think I saw your Freddie on a bicycle near Shoreham the other day.'

'My husband is very keen on keeping fit,' Pearl said haughtily. 'He cycles all over the place, sometimes miles a day.'

'Very commendable,' Milly remarked.

'It's a German thing,' said Pearl. 'In his country, every young person is expected to exercise.' She placed the tea in front of Milly just as they heard the sound of a car coming into the driveway. 'That'll be Mother,' Pearl said casually.

Milly took a deep breath. Her heartbeat quickened as fast as her courage melted. This was a bad idea. A very bad idea.

An hour or so later, Milly was close to tears. She looked around the room. It was very dark, and the only furniture was a bare table and two tubular steel chairs with canvas seats. The room itself was quiet, but beyond the doors she could hear someone shouting and the sound of banging doors. This couldn't be happening. It was like some horrible dream and yet it was real. The room smelled damp and of stale cigarette smoke. Milly was in Thurloe House, the bleak Victorian building that housed Worthing police station.

When she'd heard the car on the driveway at Muntham Court, both she and Pearl had thought it was their mother coming back home. It wasn't. It was a police car and, what was more, the officers inside were looking for her. Apparently, they still had Muntham Court listed as her last known address.

Pearl had invited the two officers in, and they were in the process of introducing themselves as Milly came out of the kitchen. 'Which one of you is Millicent Shepherd?'

Pearl pointed to her sister and Milly said, 'I am.'

'Millicent Shepherd,' the more senior of the two began, 'my name is Detective Sergeant Bradley, and this is my colleague Constable Brown. We wish to question you in connection with the wolf at Worthing Wonderland.'

Pearl gasped. The detective ignored her. 'We can either do it here,' he continued, 'or you can accompany us back to the station.'

'You can't do it here,' Pearl said quickly. 'My husband would have a fit.'

'Worthing police station it is, then,' said Bradley.

Gobsmacked, Milly stared in disbelief. As they led her to the car, she heard Pearl snigger behind her back. 'Thanks so much for coming,' she said.

As soon as Milly arrived at the police station, she was brought into the room where she now was and, shortly afterwards, Detective Bradley and another officer, whose name she couldn't remember, had questioned her about the capture of Seebold's so-called wolf. Milly had answered their questions as honestly as she could, then they left the room, telling her to wait. So she'd waited. And waited.

She glanced up at the clock on the wall. Mrs Doughton, her landlady, would be wondering where she'd got to. A few minutes later, the door burst open, and Detective Bradley stood in the corridor. 'You can go now, miss,' he said curtly.

Milly rose to her feet. 'You're not charging me with anything?' she said weakly.

'Not at the moment,' said Bradley, 'but you are still under investigation. Inspector Young has vouched for you but we've got your sister, and her boyfriend has told us everything.'

'My sister . . .' Milly began.

'They've both been charged,' Bradley continued.

'Charged with what?' Milly cried helplessly. 'They didn't do anything.'

Bradley had a sceptical expression on his face. 'That will be for the courts to decide,' he said, 'but for now, we've charged them with wasting police time.'

Chapter 26

When Freddie saw the newspaper headline, his blood ran cold, but he managed to keep his rising panic under control. Pearl and Agatha were sitting at the breakfast table with him, and he didn't want to let them see that he was rattled.

'More tea, Freddie?'

'No thank you, Mother-in-Law,' he said casually as he shook the paper ready to fold it again. 'I'm going down to the darkroom to develop some more of my photographs.'

'I don't know why you can't send them to the chemist,' Pearl murmured in a disgruntled tone. 'It would be a lot less hassle.'

He reached out and patted her hand. 'But not nearly as enjoyable, my dear.'

He rubbed his forefinger along her palm before she managed to snatch her hand away.

Freddie rose to his feet. 'I shan't be in to lunch. I'm going for a bike ride.'

'Do you want some sandwiches?' Agatha asked languidly.

'No, no. I'll probably find a pub somewhere.' He kissed the top of his wife's head. 'Enjoy your day, my dear.'

Pearl seemed slightly surprised by his gesture but said nothing.

'You're not taking the paper with you, are you?' Agatha protested. 'I haven't looked at it yet.'

'I haven't finished reading it.'

'Really,' Agatha tutted as he closed the door behind him. 'That man!'

Down in the basement, Freddie closed and bolted the door. Clearing a space on the table, he spread the *News Chronicle* flat and switched on the Anglepoise lamp. Just lately he had enjoyed reading about the events connected with the Worthing Wonderland. The whole business gave him a sly satisfaction. Apparently the proprietor, a man with whom he had already crossed swords, had ordered a ferocious wolf as part of the attractions – although why anyone would want to see such an animal was beyond Freddie. The wolf had escaped from its cage en route, and a full-scale hunt had been launched to catch it. From there, things had progressed into something out of a music-hall farce. There were tales of people scouring the countryside in convoys of open lorries, loaded with men carrying guns and rifles. One newspaper had a picture of farm labourers forming a line across a field with a large fishing net. Each man held part of the net in one hand and a pitchfork, a spade or a beater in the other. How Freddie had laughed at that. Quite what would have happened if the animal had suddenly appeared and run towards them, he could only guess, but he was absolutely sure of one thing – not one of those men would have stood their ground. Oh no! They would have headed for the hills.

So up until now, he had regarded the whole incident as a joke. The papers had even made the gypsy girl the centre of attention. All that stuff about 'Beauty and the Beast' was typical of the British way of thinking. And as for photographing her next to the animal . . . how childish. How he despised them all. His mother-in-law with all her airs and graces was nothing more than a capricious snob;

his wife – his silly, frippery wife – had been a means to an end and nothing more, and the rest of the family were not much better. He had hoped that he would have been back in Germany by now, but the top brass thought he could be more useful here.

Of course, the English had no idea how he really felt. To them he was a displaced person grieving the loss of his beloved country to the tyranny of Nazism. They had no idea that he was the exact opposite. In fact, he'd already sacrificed himself for the Führer. And the day he met Pearl, he had been sharp enough to realise that if he became Pearl's husband, she would give him the perfect undercover opportunity. Living in a place like Muntham Court, who would suspect him of being anything other than the perfect English gentleman?

His brief had been quite simple; photograph and record anything which might be of interest to the German Luftwaffe should the worst come to the worst. 'Your English public school education is of great benefit,' his uncle Reinhard Heydrich had told him. 'We want you to blend in with the locals and gather as much information as you can. Nobody wants war,' Uncle Reinhard had assured him, 'but if the unthinkable happens, we shall really need that intelligence.'

It had been said pleasantly enough, but he knew that his uncle didn't suffer fools gladly. If he failed . . . well, he couldn't fail. It was unthinkable.

When he'd first arrived in England, Freddie had toyed with the idea of changing his name. Surely if he sounded more English it would be to his advantage, so he had arranged to drop the 'von' in his surname and he was now known as Freddie Herren on official paperwork, a name which sounded quintessentially English.

The English still clung to their belief that Hitler's Germany posed no threat to them, and of course it didn't, provided they didn't interfere with the Führer's plan, which was clear enough. The world was made up of different races, and each race had its own characteristics and traits, which in turn determined their appearance, creativity, strength and intelligence. That being the case, it followed that it was wrong to mix these up. All Germans were of the Aryan race and therefore, by definition, the master race. Just as a farmer weeds the ground to improve his crop yields, so they had to tend to their race, and anyone regarded as substandard had to go. Aryans were highly intelligent, learned, skilled beyond measure, so Freddie and others like him would help to create a perfect world. Pearl wasn't of German stock, but she was blonde and attractive to look at, and she was a member of the upper crust, so she suited him well for the time being, though he was quite content to get rid of her when she became of no further use.

Back in the Fatherland, his Uncle Reinhard had been elevated to head of Sicherheitsdienst, the German Security Service. Now he moved in exalted circles, even rubbing shoulders with Hitler himself, and Freddie was well aware that if he was to succeed in this life, it wasn't *what* you knew but *who* you knew that was important.

The newspaper he had been reading at the breakfast table was a broadsheet, so he had folded it in half. When he was ready to read more, he'd turned it over, and that's when he'd spotted the other article – 'German Boys Spy Cyclists'? It was about a party of Hitler Youth, boys who had once been members of the Boy Scout movement. In what was called a 'culturally inspired' visit to Britain, hosted by Mr Martin, the headmaster of Worthing High School for Boys, the visitors had been cycling all over the southern counties. They had been well behaved and polite, but they had secretly been taking photographs, some of which were in sensitive areas – Shoreham Harbour, Lancing Carriage Works, Portsmouth Dockyard, to name but a few. The paper was now bringing the visit into question, the implication being that the 'Boy Scouts' were more like men who had been recruited into a paramilitary organisation. Of course, the accusation was strenuously denied, but that didn't quell Freddie's fears. The last thing he wanted was to be put in a position of suspicion himself.

He had been on edge ever since he had spotted Milly and those gypsies on the Downs the other morning. Had they seen him taking photographs in the bushes? Nobody had mentioned it. Was that luck, or did they have something to hide too? Now that he really thought about it, there had been a lorry up there. Could that have been the moment when the so-called missing animal was 'captured'?

He leaned back in his chair and pondered. If Milly and the other two people with her were up to no good, he was reasonably safe. Would they risk going to prison for what they were doing, by telling the authorities that they'd seen him up there too? The answer had to be 'no'.

One thing was for certain. He couldn't carry on doing what he had been doing. A German cyclist would be the object of suspicion now. He would have to telephone his uncle for new instructions. He looked around at the jars of chemicals, dark bag, thermometer and developing tank. They would have to go. It was time to find a new hobby.

In the breakfast room, Agatha was feeling petulant. It was annoying not to have the morning paper in front of her, and now Freddie had squirrelled it away downstairs in the basement, she was sure that he wouldn't bother to bring it back. Did anyone ever have such an irritating and feckless son-in-law?

Pearl had been so keen to marry him, and of course when her pregnancy became obvious, Agatha understood why. Freddie himself had been a little too casual about the whole thing. She had expected protests and arguments, and had been prepared to threaten to destroy his reputation to get the pair married, but the fellow seemed happy enough to go along with it from the word 'go'.

She poured herself another cup of tea. Pearl had gone into the kitchen to fetch more toast, so Agatha was left alone with her thoughts.

Right from the start it was obvious that her son-in-law loved Muntham Court. He had spent hours and hours reading up about the history of the place. Until Freddie had told her, Agatha had never realised that the house dated from 1371, when it had been built by Thomas DeMuntham. She hadn't had a clue, either, that it had been remodelled several times. Apparently, Lord Montague developed it as a hunting seat in 1734, which was when the grounds were first landscaped. 'Did you know there's even an ice house in the grounds?'

'Really?' Agatha had done her best to appear interested. Her son-in-law was just explaining that the Gothic entrance lodge, the iron gates, and the half-mile carriage drive had been added during Victorian times, when she'd said, 'You must tell us about your family estate in Germany. My daughter tells me that you have a castle, no less.'

Freddie had puffed out his chest. 'My home was once used as the winter palace for Prussian kings and kaisers,' he'd said. 'I love its history. It dates back to the fifteenth century.'

'And where exactly is it?' Agatha asked.

'In the centre of Berlin, of course, near the Brandenburg Gate.'

Agatha's breath had caught in her throat. 'Can you describe it?

'Well, it has a fabulous portrait gallery, so many rooms I couldn't count them . . . oh, and it has a dome the size of your St Paul's in London.' He'd waved his hand languidly.

'My grandfather used to tell me that his grandfather said Peter the Great really admired it when he came to stay in 1717.'

Agatha's eyes had glowed with pleasure. Her daughter was married to a man who owned a palace where kings and princes had stayed. And it was in the very centre of Berlin. How marvellous. She knew Germany no longer had a monarchy, but Berlin was the place where everything was happening right now – it was the place to be. She could just imagine Adolf Hitler greeting vast crowds from a balcony. 'And when are you taking my daughter to meet your family?' she'd cooed.

'Soon,' Freddie had promised. 'Soon.'

Pearl returned with another rack of toast. 'Mrs Edwards has arrived.'

Their new general housekeeper only came three mornings a week. Agatha couldn't afford more. She looked up at her daughter.

'Has your husband said any more about when he's taking you to meet his family?' she asked tetchily.

'Oh, Mummy, please don't go on about it. Anyway, I'm not even sure I want to go to Germany right now.'

'Don't be silly. Why ever not?'

'Surely you know? Adolf Hitler and all that. It all looks a bit scary to me. They say we might even go to war with Germany.'

'Don't be ridiculous!' Agatha said stridently. 'Hitler strikes me as a man who gets the job done. Not like the lily-livered politicians we have in this country.' She bit angrily into her piece of toast. 'We could do with more of his ilk in our Parliament.'

Pushing her half-eaten toast to one side, Pearl sighed. She'd lost her appetite. Right now, she felt caught between the devil and the deep blue sea. She had a husband who, when he wasn't ignoring her, seemed to enjoy putting her down or hurting her, and a mother who wanted to get rid of her. Being married wasn't supposed to be like this. Being married was supposed to be romantic, beautiful, happy-ever-after. It wasn't fair. It wasn't right. She was her father's eldest daughter, and yet her younger sister had everything she wanted. Her eyes wandered to the window and towards the ha-ha across the lawn. She couldn't see it from here, but the little cottage lay beyond that. Pearl gripped her table napkin into a ball. Even her father's bastard daughter had more than she did. Why had he left Muntham Court to Milly and the cottage to that girl? Why had he left her nothing? It wasn't fair. It wasn't bloody fair!

She remembered the letter she'd been given the day the will was read. She'd been so angry she hadn't given it a thought since then. It was upstairs in her bedroom. Without bothering to excuse herself, Pearl left the room and took the stairs two at a time. All that time ago, she'd shoved the letter to the very back of the drawer. As she pulled it out, she felt a shiver of excitement. Perhaps he'd left her something after all.

Sitting cross-legged on her bed, she tore the envelope open and read her father's words.

Dear Pearl

I wish we could have got on a little better. I did try, but you made it so difficult to be a father to you. However, you have grown into a beautiful-looking young woman and I hope that you will soon find the love of your life. I am so sorry if I hurt you by loving someone other than your mother, but when you find your own happiness, you will understand that you never want to let that feeling go. As you will have this letter after my demise, and after you have heard the reading of my will, I think I owe you an explanation. You may not realise it, but I have followed your progress throughout your coming-out season and I am glad that you have been able to broaden your horizons. I should have loved to have known what you thought of Italy, France, and of course the United States of America. The bills coming in from haute couture designers and fashion houses tell me that you've made the most of the experience, which is why I thought that should be the bulk of your inheritance. Hold on to the memories, my dear, and I trust that you find a husband who can keep you in the new lifestyle you have created for yourself.

You may be feeling angry right now but I promise you, I do wish you well.

Charles

Her face flushed with anger. How could he? So bloody Milly really did get everything. 'I hate her,' she snarled. She glanced down at the paper in her hands then with a cry of rage, tore it into pieces.

Chapter 27

Summer 1938

After a very dry spring (Poole in Dorset had no rain at all for a whole month), June 1938 had seen high winds and gales which, according to Alvar Lidell on the BBC, 'were full of unprecedented violence'. The bad weather seemed to be going on for ever, which meant that the footfall in Worthing Wonderland was not nearly as high as Seebold had hoped. After the second round of bad press surrounding his indictment for wasting police time, things had picked up a little but, as the season wore on, although he hadn't lost money, he hadn't made much either.

The story in the newspaper had attracted publicity, but not the kind Seebold was keen to have. To begin with, mothers had been put off bringing their children to the Wonderland. It took him a week or two to discover that it was because the hungry 'wolf' was only a wire fence away from their little darlings.

'Supposin' it escaped from its cage again?' one anxious mother told him.

Of course, as soon as they saw the animal, everyone agreed that it was the most peculiar wolf they'd ever seen. That was quickly followed by angry murmurings and some customers even demanding their money back. As disappointing as it was, Seebold was forced to close down the Red Riding Hood enclosure and his mate, Danny, was summoned to come and fetch his dog.

Lena had stayed on at the Wonderland, putting together an attraction of her own. Once the land she had bought near Bridge Halt had been properly enclosed, she'd acquired three little ponies. Each day she would walk them to the Wonderland where they would spend most of the day giving small children rides around the park. Having three meant two could rest while one worked. The rides proved to be popular but, like Seebold, she suffered a reduced income because of the weather. Neither of them talked about the forthcoming court case but Lena had used some of her inheritance to get a good solicitor and barrister. Seebold had borrowed money from Milly (although she had told him not to worry about paying it back) for the same reason.

At the start of this sorry state of affairs, Seebold and Lena had only been accused of wasting police time, but by the time it came to court, the case had been further complicated by the farmer who had tried to persuade Seebold to compensate him for the loss of his sheep. His tale of woe, printed in full in the *Worthing Herald* and the *Chichester Gazette*, with graphic pictures of the dead sheep lying in a ditch, made good reading, but when the police saw it they were even more suspicious. To them it was beginning to look as if all three of them had colluded together with the reporter, Archibald Crump, solely for the purposes of publicity. The unfortunate sheep was dug up and an autopsy concluded that although it had probably died of natural causes, there were several severe knife wounds on its carcass. Seebold and Lena, along with the other two defendants, were charged with 'conspiring, combining and confederating and agreeing together to commit a certain misdemeanour, namely to commit a public mischief by their conduct and certain false statements, to wit, that a wolf which was being transported to Worthing, had escaped at Shoreham'.

While it was a relief to discover that they probably wouldn't be sent to prison if convicted, it could still result in a hefty fine. Lena accepted that if that happened she would lose most of her inheritance, but Seebold was afraid he might be made bankrupt.

Though Milly was very worried for them both, she was, in many respects, enjoying a season of success. Since she'd gone freelance she'd been extremely busy, so much so that it was hard to fit in her studies. As soon as her father's will had been settled, she paid off her debt to the college and made sure her tuition fees were up-to-date. With the examinations in July, Milly was destined to spend most of the lead-up to her exams swatting.

She'd also been thrilled when Principal Salt had hung one of her paintings in the school. It was of a nightjar. Milly had divided the picture into two halves. One half had the nightjar completely camouflaged by its woodland surroundings. If you looked very carefully you could just see the bird's eye. The other half of the picture showed the same bird in the same position but with a slight change in the light, so you could now see its whole shape and its grey-brown mottled plumage. Principal Salt considered it an excellent piece of work.

The only hiccup Milly had experienced recently was when she went up to Muntham Court to collect her bicycle. She'd been forced to leave it there the day the police took her in for questioning, and had been too busy ever since to fetch it. She'd walked from the bus stop one evening and found it round the back of the house, leaning against the greenhouse. Her intention was to ride it back to her digs, but she hadn't got very far before the whole thing fell apart. The handlebar went into her side, giving her a painful jolt, and she scraped her knee rather badly, though she'd been lucky enough to tumble off onto grass or it could have been quite nasty. She was very upset when, on closer examination, it became clear that someone had deliberately tampered with it by loosening the wheel nuts – but why? With the bike in bits, she'd had no alternative but to put it back where she'd found it and walk back to the bus stop. It took a couple of weeks for the pain and discomfort in her side to go.

Seebold and Lena had been sent for trial by Worthing magistrates. They had to go the Crown assizes in September, so they drove to Lewes in Seebold's lorry. Uncle Neville had advised Milly, and any charges they'd planned to bring against her had been dropped. Because she hadn't stayed to be photographed, it was concluded that she had only been a passenger in the lorry and not an active participant in the deception. Archibald Crump and James William Doyle had been remanded in custody because they had resisted arrest – Doyle had been so incensed that he'd knocked off a policeman's helmet. As a result, they arrived in police vans and both faced additional charges. Milly, who had been told not to contact her sister or Seebold before giving evidence, had arrived the day before the court case commenced and had taken a room in the Swan Inn. She was a witness for the defence, so she had to wait until she was called before being allowed to hear the proceedings. When she arrived at court, she and the other people who were to be called as witnesses had to wait in a specially designated room. The case had attracted a lot of press interest so the streets outside the courtroom were already heaving with spectators. It was all rather nerve-wracking, and she was terrified that she might do or say something which might make matters worse for her friends.

'Good luck,' Milly mouthed as she saw Lena and Seebold being escorted elsewhere.

The first two days were taken up with legal proceedings and the trial itself didn't get properly under way until Wednesday. Seebold, Lena, Archibald Crump and Farmer Doyle were together in the dock. Mr Bennet of the prosecution called the first witness.

Robert Knox, a small balding man, took the oath and told the court that he was a vet. Mr Bennet asked him about the animal in question.

Mr Knox laced his fingers through his braces. 'I was summoned to the Worthing Wonderland by the local police to look at a wolf,' he said, his feet rising a couple of inches as he spoke. 'They wanted me to ascertain its condition and confirm that it was none the worse for its experience.'

'Who owned the animal?'

'Seebold,' said Mr Knox, nodding towards the dock.

'C. Bold?' Mr Bennet queried.

Mr Knox sounded a little irritated. 'Mr Seebold Flowers.'

Several people in the public gallery giggled.

'And was the wolf in good health?' Mr Knox enquired.

'The animal in question was perfectly healthy,' said Mr Knox, 'for its age.'

'For its age, Mr Knox?' Mr Bennet repeated. 'Why do you say that?'

'I judged it to be well past its prime,' the witness said, turning his head for the benefit of all present. 'Looking at the few teeth it had left, I would say that it was at least ten years old or more.' There was a pause, then Mr Knox added, 'And it wasn't a wolf.'

There were audible gasps in the courtroom.

Mr Bennet looked up with a shocked expression, as if he had been taken completely by surprise. 'Not a wolf, Mr Knox?' he said incredulously. 'Then pray tell me, what sort of animal was it?'

'A dog,' said Mr Knox, his feet rising again. 'A crossbreed,

I would say. Irish wolfhound crossed with something like a German wire-haired pointer mix.'

'But not a wolf,' Mr Bennet added for emphasis.

'No, sir. Not a wolf,' Mr Knox agreed. There followed the sound of murmurings and laughter in the courtroom. 'And I must say that, in my opinion,' Mr Knox continued, 'if this was done in the name of entertainment, the man in the dock should be ashamed of himself.'

Seebold stared down at the floor, his face colouring with embarrassment.

'Confine yourself to the facts, please, Mr Knox,' the judge interrupted. 'We are not here to consider your opinion.'

The murmurings in the court increased again. The judge banged his gavel.

Having ascertained that a deception had already taken place, the testimonies of the next two witnesses Mr Bennet called were clearly designed to show the effect the fiasco had had on members of the public.

Jack Antell told the court he was a jobbing builder who worked in the Lancing area.

'You work outside?'

'I do . . . most of the time.'

'How did you feel about a wolf being on the loose?' Mr Bennet asked.

'I weren't too boffered. I had a gun—'

'A gun, Mr Antell?' the judge interrupted. 'And where did you keep this gun?'

'Under me bed, Yer 'Onour,' Antell said. 'But all me lady customers, they was all terrified.' He looked around the courtroom. 'They was all crying. So I took it wiv me.' He looked around the courtroom and licked his lips. 'I 'ad quite a job on that day.'

'I don't quite understand you, Mr Antell,' said the judge.

'You know, Yer 'Onour,' he said, giving the judge a wink

and a knowing smile. 'I 'ad to . . . you know . . . give 'em a bit of comfort like.'

A murmur of amusement ran through the court.

'You seem to have a rather flippant attitude to all this, Mr Antell,' the judge remarked as counsel sat down out of respect. 'Did you not understand the seriousness of a wild animal roaming the countryside and reportedly killing sheep?'

'Oh I did, Yer Worship, my lord, sir,' said Antell. 'When I was outside me van, I was pretty nervous meself.'

The judge nodded and counsel rose again.

'And had you encountered the wolf, Mr Antell, what steps would you have taken?'

'Very long ones, I reckon.'

The courtroom erupted into laughter and the judge banged his gavel until it subsided.

Mr Carstairs, who was representing Lena and Seebold, had no questions to ask the witness, neither did Mr Phillips, who was representing Archibald Crump, nor did Mr Heuvel, representing Farmer Doyle.

Next to take the stand was Euphemia Gordy. Euphemia informed the court that she was a widow who lived in an isolated spot near the Steyning Road. She had one daughter who was in the habit of cycling to school. 'When I heard about the wolf, I didn't want her to go to school that day,' said Mrs Gordy. 'I was nervous and upset.'

'And why were you nervous and upset?' Mr Bennet asked.

Mrs Gordy's eyes grew wide and she drew a lace handkerchief from her sleeve. 'Because she could have been attacked, sir.' She dabbed her eyes with the lace handkerchief and, turning towards the dock, she shouted at the defendants, 'She's my only daughter, the apple of my eye, and she could have been ripped to pieces by that ferocious mad animal; a creature which never ought to be let loose on the public.'

'Calm yourself, madam,' said the judge. But Mrs Gordy was already hysterical.

'I made her catch the bus that day,' she continued. 'One and thruppence it cost me, and me being a widow woman who can least afford bus fares, but what would I do if my daughter, the darling of my heart, had been attacked by that beast . . .' With that Mrs Gordy burst into loud tears.

Court proceedings were interrupted for a few minutes until both judge and counsel decided she'd said enough and needed medical attention. As Mrs Gordy was being escorted from the court, the judge looked up at the clock.

'Do you have many more witnesses, Mr Bennet?'

Mr Bennet rose to his feet. 'Two, m'lord.'

'Then I suggest we break for lunch. Court will resume at two-fifteen.' The judge got to his feet and the usher called, 'All rise.'

Seebold and the other defendants were taken to the cells below the courtroom and everyone dispersed. The usher hurried to tell the waiting witnesses that the court was adjourned.

Milly was glad of the opportunity to get some fresh air. So far she had spent every day cooped up in that stuffy room waiting to be called. Every time the usher opened the door, she had expected her name to be called, but it wasn't. She had brought a good book with her but she couldn't concentrate on the words. Why on earth was it taking so long? Surely it must be obvious to everyone by now that Lena and Seebold hadn't a malicious bone between them. She crossed the road towards the Swan Inn.

There appeared to be some sort of gathering in the main bar, then she heard the voice of an auctioneer. 'What am I bid? Two pound, two pound ten shillings. Any advance on two pound ten shillings, going . . . going . . . gone!' There was a sharp crack as his gavel went down.

As she was listening to this, the landlord came up behind her. 'I've put you in the ladies' snug, miss.'

Milly thanked him. The room was indeed 'snug'. It was small and nicely decorated with an open fireplace filled with summer flowers. The pictures on the walls depicted a bygone era when this had been a coaching inn. She could just imagine how nice it would be coming into the room in winter when there was a roaring fire.

The landlord served a hearty meal. Cottage pie, cabbage and carrots, with the promise of steamed treacle pudding to follow. Milly picked up her fork but she couldn't face it. She was far too churned up inside. Apologising profusely, she asked for a pot of tea.

When he came back with it, he left the door slightly ajar. A few seconds later, Milly was startled when a man's voice said, 'Milly? Milly Shepherd?' She turned her head and he said, 'It's Eustace. Eustace Henderson. We met at Lady Verity's party; do you remember?'

He was standing in the darkened corridor, so it took her a moment to remember that he was the man who had given her his jacket that night as they sat outside on the terrace.

'Why yes,' said Milly. 'I remember.'

He made to come in but the landlord put up his hand. 'Sorry, sir,' he said with emphasis. 'This is the *ladies'* snug.'

Eustace hovered in the doorway. 'I bumped into your sister, and she told me about the court case. I am so sorry that the showman has involved you in his deliberate attempt to deceive the public.'

'I'm not allowed to talk about it,' Milly cautioned.

'It's an absolute disgrace that a woman of your calibre and social standing should be abused in this way,' he went on.

Milly's nostrils flared. How dare he make assumptions. 'I'm sorry,' she repeated. 'I'm not allowed—'

'No, of course not,' Eustace interrupted. 'I'm the one

230

who should be sorry. That was clumsy of me. It's just that I should love to see you again once all this horrible business is cleared up.'

Milly was surprised. 'Oh.'

'My intentions are entirely honourable.'

Milly was puzzled. Had he come here especially to meet her? How did he know she would be in this particular inn?

'Believe me, this is a happy coincidence,' he added, as if reading her mind. 'I had no idea you would be staying here. I'm here for the auction.' He smiled. 'So can we meet again?'

Then someone called his name. He turned his head in the direction of the caller. 'Sorry,' he said quickly. 'Must go. My auction lot is coming up.'

When he'd closed the door, Milly was confused. He seemed a nice enough chap, but her heart wasn't exactly fluttering at the thought of a date with him.

But Pearl had been talking to him about her, hadn't she? Milly could only imagine what her sister had said. Just before she left the Swan, she asked the landlord for some paper and an envelope. Her note was hastily scribbled as she had to get back to court and she even surprised herself as she wrote, *Dear Eustace, It was nice to see you again. Thanks for the invitation. I should love to meet you again. All the best, Milly.*

Chapter 28

Agatha scoured the newspapers every day for news of the trial. She made sure she got hold of them before Freddie could get his hands on them. She couldn't pretend that she wasn't enjoying Millicent's discomfort. It was a ridiculous state of affairs when an educated middle-class girl got herself mixed up with showmen and gypsies – even worse when that girl was part of her own family. She had breathed a sigh of relief when she realised that Millicent was only to be called as a witness for the defence, but it was still unsavoury to have her name dragged through the courts. Part of her had wanted Millicent to be taken down a peg or two, but another part of her had dreaded the knock-on effect of the publicity and shame. Most of her friends had telephoned to extend their commiserations and sympathy, but Agatha was sure there was an element of smugness in their concern.

As the trial wore on, Agatha grew increasingly frustrated. The gypsy was being treated as nothing more than a harmless scallywag who had gone a step too far. The man should be locked up, and it was high time somebody stood up and said so. This was why she decided to drive over to Lewes towards the end of the week. With her head swathed in a headscarf which completely covered her hair, and wearing a pair of large sunglasses, she had hoped to sneak over to the assizes unobserved, but Pearl had spotted her before she left the house.

'You're going to the trial?'

Agatha turned to see if Freddie was coming downstairs behind her.

'It's all right, Mummy,' Pearl said. 'He's gone out.' She paused. 'You are going to Lewes, aren't you? Can I come too?'

Agatha hesitated. 'Oh all right then, but be quick about it.' Her daughter thundered back upstairs. 'And put on a headscarf or something which will mean nobody recognises you. I don't want anyone to connect us to this awful business.'

The court case lasted almost another week. Milly was called to give evidence on Thursday. When she had taken the oath, Milly glanced around the courtroom and froze as she spotted a familiar face in the gallery. Pearl's husband Freddie gave her a cold stare, and put his right index finger in front of his lips. Milly was frightened and confused. The only thing she could think of when she saw him was that he must also have spotted her the day the dog went into the river, and that this was a coded warning not to mention it. Although she tried not to look at him, there was something rather unsettling about him being there. What was he doing? And why did it matter so much that nobody knew? She shivered.

Mr Carstairs began. As part of the defence, she explained how she and Lena had gone with Seebold to collect an animal from a friend. 'We both knew that he was only doing it to allay people's fears,' she said. 'The whole of Worthing was shut down because people thought they would be attacked at any minute by a ravenous animal. No harm and no deceit was intended.'

There was laughter in the court as she described Seebold being dragged through the mud at the edge of the river by the dog because it was keen to chase ducks. Despite the hilarity in the courtroom, Milly could still feel her brother-in-law's cold stare. During a pause in the proceedings, her eye wandered back to the public gallery. This time he drew his right index finger across his throat. Milly's heartbeat quickened. So she hadn't imagined it, after all. He was threatening her. The judge called for order.

'Did anyone see you when you were in the lane?' asked counsel.

Milly sucked in her lips as she avoided the question. 'We were some distance from the nearest house and miles from civilisation.'

The rest of her time in the witness box passed by uneventfully, and when Milly was told to step down, she went to sit in the public gallery, although she was careful not to be near Freddie. To her great surprise, Agatha and Pearl were there as well, but they deliberately blanked her. There was a seat near the aisle. From up here, she could see the dock quite clearly. She was concerned for Lena who looked pale and tired. Even Seebold, sitting next to her, had an air of defeatism about him. Milly was filled with a longing to put her arms around him to comfort him, but Lena had told her he loved somebody else. Was she here in the courtroom? Milly looked around, but it crossed her mind that she'd never even seen his lady friend. Perhaps she was one of the travellers. Even so, she should be here to support him, surely?

When Lena was called into the witness box, she trembled as she held up the Bible and read the oath from the card. Milly wondered if Freddie might make the same threatening gestures to her, but Lena didn't look up towards the gallery anyway – her eyes were fixed on the floor. Her evidence was exactly the same as Milly's, but in his cross-examination of her Mr Bennet was far less gentle. At times, his quickfire questions had her flustered. 'You saw the sheep Mr Doyle brought to the Wonderland?'

'I glanced at it, yes.'

'That sheep had knife wounds.'

'I never saw them.'

'And one of its ears was cut off.'

'I don't know.'

'Do you think wolves are in the habit of killing their prey with a knife, Miss Buckley?'

'My lord,' Mr Carstairs protested languorously.

'Yes, yes,' said the judge. 'Don't badger the witness, Mr Bennet.'

'As Your Lordship pleases,' Mr Bennet said.

Seebold gave his evidence in a measured and clear voice. He said he had been shocked to discover the damaged cage and took steps to find out what had happened to the wolf. He had repeatedly rung the office of the place from which he'd bought it, but no one returned his call. In his opinion, he said, Mr Crump, in order to gain a newspaper scoop, had made a mountain out of a molehill, which had then taken off like a prairie fire.

'That's right, blame somebody else,' Agatha said loudly. Several people in the gallery turned to look at her. Milly saw her sister Pearl's face colouring.

Seebold looked up but continued his testimony. 'Later I discovered the thing had never even been sent, but there were fifteen or twenty newspaper men who had come down from Fleet Street on the doorstep,' he went on. 'That's when I realised no one was going to believe a word I said. I had to produce a wolf, even if there had never been one in the first place. Nothing else would do.'

'So you arranged for a dog to be brought to Worthing in its place.'

'Yes.'

'Disgraceful,' Agatha commented. Court proceeding were paused for a second or two as people's eyes were drawn towards the public gallery, but then Mr Bennet continued.

Milly glanced towards Freddie, who was sitting behind his wife and mother-in-law. Their eyes met and he mouthed a lion-like snarl. Milly looked away quickly. He was making threats again. She fixed her eyes on what was happening in the court and tried to concentrate on what was being said, but her heart was thumping. This definitely had to be because she'd seen him lurking in the bushes that day. Clearly he didn't want anyone to know he'd been there. But why? Bird-watching was an innocent enough hobby, so why be so secretive about it? She thought back. Freddie had only emerged from the reeds when the angry swan had come after him. Fair enough. That was perfectly understandable. After all, she, Lena and Seebold had all run from the same bird. Up until now she'd not given much thought to the incident but now she was suspicious. What had he been up to?

'When did you discover that a sheep had been killed by a wild animal?' Mr Carstairs was saying.

'I don't believe that sheep was killed by a wild animal. I think it was most likely already dead and somebody,' Seebold fixed his eyes on Farmer Doyle, 'took a knife to it.'

'Just give us the facts, if you please, Mr Flowers,' said the judge.

Seebold nodded and lowered his eyes.

'That's right, you tell him,' Agatha interrupted. 'Tell him to try telling the truth for a change.'

Pearl grabbed her mother's arm, but Agatha shook her hand away. The judge banged his gavel. 'Whoever is talking in the gallery,' he said sternly, 'be silent or I shall have you removed.'

All eyes were on Agatha who sat with a defiant pose. All eyes except Freddie's. She couldn't look, but Milly knew he was still staring at her. She could feel it! Why on earth was he intimidating her like this?

'When Farmer Doyle and Mr Crump arrived with the carcass of the sheep in the boot of his car,' Mr Phillips, Archibald Crump's counsel continued, 'did Mr Doyle ask for compensation?'

'Yes.'

'And did you give it to him?'

'No.'

'Did my client ask for money?'

'No, but they were very much working togeth—'

'Thank you, Mr Flowers,' Mr Phillips said as he sat down.

Up in the gallery, Agatha chuntered.

Mr Bennet was brutal in his cross-examination. 'Come now, Mr Flowers, this whole thing was nothing more than an elaborate publicity stunt, wasn't it?'

'No, it was not.'

'The four of you cooked it up together.'

'No.'

'You bet he did,' said Agatha. Pearl gave her a nudge and, turning towards her, her mother snapped, 'What?'

The judge banged his gavel again. 'I have warned you,' he said sternly. 'Stand up, madam, and identify yourself.'

Agatha would have stayed silent had not the rest of the people in the gallery turned to stare at her, indicating exactly where she was. She rose to her feet. 'I am perfectly entitled to my opinion,' she said haughtily.

'Madam, you are not. I am holding you in contempt of court,' said the judge. 'Bailiff, remove that woman from the court. I shall deal with her later.'

Milly gasped as her mother was dragged from the gallery shouting, 'How dare you! You have no right to do this. Unhand me. Let go of my arm . . .'

Despite herself, as her mother's voice faded, she glanced at Freddie. He smiled. Milly turned back quickly.

'Now I am warning members of the public,' said the judge, 'any more interruptions and I shall have the gallery cleared.'

Up in the gallery, Pearl was mortified. She turned to glare at her sister – it was her fault they were there in the first place! – but Milly was staring down at her hands in her lap. It was then that Pearl saw her husband was sitting just to the left of Milly. She was so shocked she could hardly breathe. She turned back, her face burning with embarrassment. What was he doing here? Why had he come?

'Please proceed, Mr Bennet,' said the judge.

'I put it to you, Mr Flowers, that this was an elaborate plot on your part; that, far from being the loveable buffoon you would have us believe you are, you machinated this whole scheme to enjoy cheap publicity.'

'No,' said Seebold.

'You badly needed to attract more customers to your Wonderland, and this lost so-called wolf was a gift.'

'No.'

'It not only gave you local publicity but, once it reached the national papers, country-wide publicity too.'

'That may have happened, but I had nothing to do with it.'

'And because of your deceit,' said Mr Bennet, raising his voice, 'you terrorised the whole of Worthing, sending frightened holiday-makers scurrying back home and anxious shopkeepers pulling down their shutters. Not to mention wasting hours of police time at a huge cost to the Worthing rate-payers.'

There was a pause then Seebold said, 'I didn't do any of this for publicity. What I did, I did to kill the story once and for all and to stop people panicking.'

The jury were sent out at three-fifteen. When the last of them had filed through the door, Milly had never felt so nervous. The next few hours could change Lena's and Seebold's lives for ever. Because of what Uncle Neville had said, Milly was confident that if they were found guilty, they would only get a fine. She had made up her mind to help Lena, but if the fine was big, Seebold might have to sell up and start again.

It took the jury just half an hour to reach their verdict. Lena – not guilty; Seebold – not guilty; Archibald Crump – guilty of wasting police time; Farmer Doyle – guilty of wasting police time and assault. Lena and Seebold were acquitted while Farmer Doyle was fined ten pounds and Archibald Crump was fined thirty pounds. Both Crump and Doyle were ordered to pay costs.

Once judgement was given, the judge told the usher he would be back in court in fifteen minutes to deal with the woman in contempt of court. Someone called 'All rise' and, after bowing, the judge left for his chambers.

Downstairs, Milly and Lena hugged each other. Lena was in tears, but they were tears of relief and joy. Pearl, still in the gallery, curled her lip with contempt. Seebold was shaking hands with just about everybody in sight until the usher called for the courtroom to be cleared.

While everybody filed out of the gallery, Pearl stayed where she was. What was going to happen to her mother? She felt someone sit beside her and turned expecting to see Freddie. She looked up and took in a breath. 'Milly!' Pearl's face soured. 'Come to gloat, have you?'

'Oh Pearl, please don't be like that,' said Milly, trying to take her hand. 'I thought you might need a little support.'

'I don't need anything from you.' Pearl snatched her hand away as their mother was brought to the dock. The judge came in and bowed. Apart from Agatha's family, only the court stenographer and a few other officials remained.

'Madam,' he said once he was seated, 'I hold you in contempt of court.'

Agatha puffed out her chest, 'Don't be so—'

'Madam, be quiet!' The judge's tone was authoritative. 'You seem to be a woman of good breeding and good education. You should know it is unlawful for you to express an opinion in open court; an opinion which might endanger the chances of a fair trial. Yet you deliberately made your comments loudly enough for the whole court to hear. I thereby fine you twenty pounds or one week in jail.' With that he banged his gavel and stood up.

Agatha's jaw dropped. 'But I don't have twenty pounds.'

Her protest fell on deaf ears. Everybody in the courtroom bowed and the judge left.

'This isn't right,' Agatha cried out, but the officers of the court were already taking her down the steps to the holding cell. 'Call this justice?'

Pearl burst into tears. Freddie came and sat on the other side of her, but his wife was so upset, she hardly noticed. 'What did your mother mean when she said she doesn't have the money?'

Pearl shrugged. She didn't dare tell Freddie that her mother was stony-broke. Freddie handed her his handkerchief and she blew her nose.

'What are you doing here anyway?'

'I was concerned about you, that's all. I got word of what happened to your mother, so I rushed over. Why doesn't she have any money?'

Milly stood to leave as Freddie was repeating the question.

'I don't know,' Pearl wept. In her agitated state, she didn't think to mention the fact she had seen her husband was already in the court. 'She forgot to bring her handbag, I suppose.'

Freddie had a puzzled expression on his face. He pointed to the floor. 'Isn't that it?'

Pearl dried her eyes and looked down. Sure enough, her

mother's handbag was under the seat in front of where she'd sat. It had tipped over, probably when her mother had stood up, and its contents had spilled. They spent the next couple of minutes picking everything up.

'Here's her purse,' said Freddie, and before Pearl could stop him, he opened it and pulled out a five-pound note and some change. 'There's not enough in here to pay the fine,' he began. 'I only have enough in my wallet for the return train fare home. Do you have any money?'

Pearl looked in her own purse and found three pounds, seven and six in loose change.

'I'll go to the bank,' said Freddie, pushing the handbag back into his wife's hands but taking the purse.

Pearl glanced up at the clock on the wall. It was ten minutes past four. 'All the banks will be closed now,' she said. 'They shut at three.' She gave her husband an anxious look. 'What are we going to do?'

'Find a shopkeeper willing to cash a cheque,' said Freddie, waving his cheque book in the air. 'You wait downstairs in the foyer.'

Still fighting back her tears, Pearl made her way downstairs.

Bad enough if her mother was in a cell all night, but if she was locked up for a whole week – well, it didn't bear thinking about. As she sat on a bench, Pearl spotted Milly holding hands with Lena. Pearl's lip curled.

This was all stupid Milly's fault. If she hadn't got mixed up with those dreadful fairground people, she and her mother wouldn't be in this mess. A wave of rage passed through her and Pearl swayed. Lena thought Milly was so wonderful, but what would she think if she knew that her perfect sister had cursed her mother to death all those years ago?

Just then, Freddie burst through the door and together they hurried to the bursar's office to pay Agatha's fine.

Freddie was called in and Pearl went back to her seat. A few minutes later, her mother walked out into the corridor.

When the others got outside, Lena and Seebold were immediately surrounded by a sea of newspaper reporters. Milly took charge of the situation, telling them to come with her to the Swan. When he opened the door, the landlord fended off the reporters and they all sat in the ladies' snug with a pot of tea. Because it was out of hours, the landlord made an elaborate gesture of generosity which meant that Seebold could sit with them.

'Thank God that's over,' said Milly, passing the cups around.

Seebold gave her a knowing look and grinned. 'Put the Worthing Wonderland on the map though, didn't it?'

Lena seemed shocked. Milly frowned crossly.

Seebold raised his eyebrows, feigning innocence. 'What?'

Chapter 29

As Pearl walked downstairs the next morning, she could hear angry voices coming from the breakfast room. Her mother was barking, 'How dare you? I have a good mind to telephone the police!' while her husband was doing his best to drown her out by shouting, 'It's not what you think, Mother-in-Law.'

Last night had been a strange one for Pearl – a lot better than she had come to expect from her husband, but strange. She had become used to him being distant and unresponsive towards her, but last night he'd been kinder, softer, almost considerate. After the trial, he'd wanted to pay her mother's fine and, back home and alone in their bedroom, he'd seemed keen for her body but he'd been a gentle lover. She'd lain in bed afterwards, staring at the ceiling. Why couldn't it be like this all the time? And why the sudden change? When she'd got up this morning, she was feeling happier than she had done in a long time but now it looked as if everything was spoiled. Why on earth were they so angry with each other?

When Pearl came into the room, her mother and her husband appeared to be arguing over her mother's handbag. As soon as they saw her, they both turned to her for support.

Pearl put her hands up. 'Don't shout at me,' she cried. 'What's going on?'

Her mother was the first to speak. 'I just walked in here and found him rummaging around in my handbag,' she said huffily. 'Can you believe that? The man is nothing less than a rogue and a thief.'

'You've misunderstood me, Mother-in-Law,' said Freddie. 'If you care to look inside your purse, you'll find all your money is there.'

With an angry glare at him, Agatha opened her purse. He was right. Everything was as it should be. Freddie turned to his wife. 'I was putting it all back when she crept up behind me.'

'So you have been taking my money,' Agatha said coldly. 'I knew it. I knew it.'

'No, Mummy, he wasn't.' Pearl almost buckled under the furious glare her mother gave her but, with her husband beside her, she was brave enough to continue. 'When the court bailiff took you away, you dropped your handbag on the floor. We picked everything up and after the judge said you were to be fined, I opened your purse and then we pooled all our resources.'

'So you took *my* money to pay the fine?' Agatha squeaked.

'We took it so that you wouldn't have to spend the night in the cells,' said Freddie.

'And the rest of the week in jail, remember?' Pearl chipped in.

Agatha suddenly looked deflated.

'There wasn't enough, so Freddie went to the shops for the rest,' said Pearl, her voice softening. 'He wrote cheques and the shopkeepers gave him the money from their tills.'

'After taking a commission,' Freddie mumbled.

Agatha seemed puzzled. 'But I don't understand. If you used my money to contribute to the fine, why is it now all back in here?'

'By the time I got back, the fine had already been paid,' said Freddie.

Agatha lowered herself onto a chair. 'So if you didn't pay the fine, then who did?'

'That's just it, Mummy. We don't know.'

The newsreels at the pictures at the end of September 1938 were dominated by the prime minister and the speech he had broadcast from Downing Street. The Munich Agreement – which had been signed by Adolf Hitler himself – made it clear that all future disputes between Britain and Germany would be settled by peaceful means. For weeks the whole country had held its breath as German expansionist policies grew ever more threatening. People were divided in their opinions. On the one hand, there were those who wanted peace at any price, while others felt that if Hitler decided to annex the Sudetenland, it would be nothing short of the thin end of the wedge.

After hearing the prime minister's promise that Britain and Germany would never go to war again, Milly and Lena watched with mixed feelings as Neville Chamberlain stood waving on the balcony of Buckingham Palace with King George VI and Queen Elizabeth beside him. Although the crowds below were happy and cheerful, somehow it didn't feel like the end of the matter.

Even in sleepy old Worthing there was a lot of preparation going on. The bomb shelters in Steyne Gardens were finished and Worthing museum was relocating many of the town's artefacts. Principle Salt from the art school had asked Milly if she would accompany Miss Gerard from the library while she hid a couple of the school's most valuable pictures. The hiding place turned out to be on the Gallops where a tunnel had been created in the rock face on the hill. They had carefully stored several items belonging to the art school along with the cases already there and Milly had taken a picture of Miss

Gerard outside the entrance before the workmen sealed it up. That photograph would be locked in the library vault for future reference in case something happened to them.

As she'd turned to leave, Milly had spotted her brother-in-law striding along the Gallops. She was puzzled as to why he was there, but she'd said nothing. He was a fit man and used to bicycling or walking across the Downs so perhaps it was just a coincidence.

Now, when the advertisements came on, Milly was wondering what would become of them all. She'd heard the stories of the privations and hardships of the last war. So many men had been called up that the women had had to step up to keep the country running. They'd become railway porters and delivery drivers. They'd gone to France to nurse the wounded. Would it come to the same thing if war came again? Supposing some of her friends got killed? She closed her eyes and forced herself to think of something else, but now her mind was in overdrive. Where would she go? Would she and Lena be able to do something together? And if they did, who would look out for her mother? Despite their difficult relationship, she still cared about her.

Milly leaned back in her seat. It had felt so good when she'd paid her mother's fine before Pearl and Freddie got back to the courtroom. One little thing she'd done to show there were no hard feelings on her part. Of course, it would have been nice to tell her mother and have her say thank you for all that she'd done, but something told her that – even if Agatha knew – a grateful response from her would be highly unlikely.

The film they had chosen to watch didn't lighten their mood. *The Lady Vanishes*, starring Margaret Lockwood and Michael Redgrave, was set on a train journeying through the continent. It was a thriller about a rich girl who realises an elderly woman is missing from the train. This story of spies, false imprisonment and secret codes only heightened their nervousness about the world around them.

After the film, they stopped for a cup of tea in the café next door to the cinema before making their separate ways home.

'I haven't told you,' Milly began, 'but I have a date.'

Lena's eyes grew wide. 'A date? With who? Do I know him?'

Milly shook her head. 'We met last year, before Pearl got married.' She went on to tell Lena about Lady Verity's party and meeting Eustace in the garden, and that he happened to be in the Swan hotel for an auction at the same time Milly had been there.

'Eustace . . .' Lena said cautiously.

'I know, I know,' said Milly. 'The poor man told me his friends call him Useless Eustace. I think there should be a law against parents calling their children dreadful names.'

Lena laughed. 'So what's he like?'

'To be honest,' Milly confessed, 'I hardly remembered him. But he seems very nice, kind, considerate, friendly.' She held back from telling her sister that she was only really going because she now knew there was no chance with Seebold.

'You've made him sound like Prince Charming himself,' Lena giggled. 'When do you meet him?'

'Next Wednesday,' said Milly.

'Well, have a wonderful time,' said Lena. 'And let me know how you get on.'

'I will,' she promised.

They lapsed into talking about Lena's plans for the future. She was still at the Wonderland but – with winter coming on – she needed to think of something else. Nobody would be wanting Shetland pony rides in December.

'Will you go back to Rainbow George?' Milly asked.

Lena shook her head. 'I don't know what to do. I always feel caught up between two different worlds, you see. I love the fairgrounds and entertaining people, but with no real specialist talent, it's hard.'

'You still have the cottage,' Milly reminded her.

'I was thinking of moving my caravan from East Worthing down there,' said Lena. 'Do you think they would mind?'

'It's your property,' Milly said stoutly. 'I think it sounds like a good idea. You'd be closer to Nan as well.'

'You see, I've been offered a place for the ponies at a stable on the Horsham Road,' Lena went on. 'It's only a stone's throw from the cottage and, actually, if I lived in the cottage, I could become a pigeoneer.'

Milly's eyebrows shot up. 'What on earth is that?'

'Someone who trains homing pigeons,' said Lena. 'You know, looks after them, houses them, feeds them, makes sure they're fit and healthy, then sends them away and waits for them to come back home.'

Milly frowned. 'As a sort of hobby, do you mean?'

'Yes and no,' said Lena. 'People do race them against one another but if we do go to war, carrier pigeons could be very useful. They used them quite a lot in the Great War – you know, sending messages from the front and all that. I thought that if I was accepted by the War Office, or whoever decides these things, it would be my way of doing my bit.'

'Then go for it,' Milly said stoutly.

Back home and in her own bed, Milly pondered her own future, as her conversation with Lena had given her much food for thought. Quite simply, Milly empathised with her half-sister's feelings. She enjoyed doing the windows of the big stores, but it was a job with no real purpose. She longed to get her teeth into something which really mattered.

'Do you think there will be a war?' she'd asked as they parted.

Lena had shrugged. 'Your guess is as good as mine,' she'd said, adding darkly, 'but it doesn't look good, does it?'

* * *

Milly and Eustace ended up meeting the following week. He'd cancelled on her twice, as his other commitments seemed to get in the way.

He picked her up from Hanningtons in Brighton where she had been giving a 'class' to some new window-dressers who were just about to start in the shop. Once again, she had excelled herself, this time with an autumnal scene. A mannequin dressed as a farmer was raking up leaves, while a display of autumn fruits and produce from Hanningtons' grocery shop was arranged on a barrow behind him. As soon as the window had been revealed, crowds had gathered outside the shop to admire it, and the footfall inside the store had rocketed.

Eustace was parked outside when she emerged. He hailed her and leapt out of the driver's seat to hold the passenger door open for her. As they greeted each other, he raised his hat.

Once in the car, she was able to look at him more closely. At Lady Verity's party, Milly remembered being struck by his gingery complexion and the downy fuzz on his face, so had been under the impression that he was not much older than she was. Sitting next to him in broad daylight, she now she realised how wrong she had been. He looked about twenty-three or maybe a little older and, far from having teenage fluff on his face, he sported a close beard.

'It really is lovely to see you again,' he said as he threw the hat on the back seat and started the engine. His light brown eyes twinkled as he gave her a winning smile.

Milly blushed. 'And you too.'

They both laughed and exchanged the usual pleasantries as he motored out of town. He took her for a walk along the River Adur near Shoreham. The weather was getting cooler and Milly was glad of her coat and gloves. She was also glad that she had treated herself to a new pair of pixie boots with fur around the ankle.

Eustace looked really handsome in a naval-style duffel coat with a tartan lining. He walked with his hands stuffed in his pockets.

They began by asking each other about their lives. She discovered that his father was 'something in the Foreign Office', and it seemed that his mother centred her life around the home and the local golf club. 'Right now they're skiing in the Austrian Tyrol at a place called St Anton to celebrate their silver wedding anniversary,' he said.

Milly was slightly puzzled. She thought he had told her his mother was dead, but perhaps she'd got it wrong.

'It was my mother's lifelong dream to go, after she saw the German film *The White Ecstasy*,' he continued. 'They're having the time of their lives, but I don't mind telling you, I shall be glad when they're safely back home.'

Milly could understand the sentiment. Things on the world's stage were gathering pace. Although the 'peace for our time' Munich Agreement was supposed to bring an increasing sense of calm, it seemed that every government in Europe was saying one thing but preparing for quite another.

Eustace was interested in what she had been doing and Milly felt slightly awkward telling him that most of her time of late had been taken up by the events in the courtroom.

As they came towards the river itself, Milly brought up the subject which had been puzzling her for some time. 'Are there a lot of bird-watchers around here?'

'The odd one or two, I suppose,' he said, adding with a chuckle, 'although I haven't come across very many. Why?'

'It's just that when Seebold, Lena and I were collecting his friend's dog up there on the hill, I saw a man hiding in the undergrowth.'

Eustace gave her a puzzled frown.

'You remember I told you that Seebold was chased by a swan,' she continued, 'well when he managed to get back into the lorry, the swan turned back and then it suddenly spotted the man coming out of the long grass and chased after him instead. I've often wondered what he was doing up there.'

'Probably watching the swans,' Eustace suggested with a shrug. 'Or maybe butterflies. You get a lot of Clouded Yellow butterflies and the Dusky Sallow up there on the grassland. Did the man have a net or a camera?'

'I don't think so.' Milly shook her head. 'Anyway, he was facing that way.'

Eustace followed her pointing finger then pulled a face. 'The only thing over there is Lancing College and Shoreham Airport.'

Milly said no more but it struck her that Pearl's husband didn't seem to be the type to be interested in butterflies. And come to think of it, yes, he had had something in his hand that day. She had seen him throw it into the bag on the back of his bicycle. Could it have been a camera or perhaps some binoculars?

So what was the true reason for him being up there? Was he bird-watching, or was it something more sinister? She shivered. Could he have been looking at Lancing College or the flight path to Shoreham Airport?

As they walked on, they bumped shoulders and Eustace reached for her hand. After spending such a lovely afternoon together, it seemed the most natural thing in the world and it gave Milly the most delicious feeling.

Chapter 30

Freddie dropped his bombshell at the breakfast table a week later, leaving Agatha and Pearl completely stunned.

'We've done nothing at all this year. It's about time we started some proper socialising in the run-up to Christmas,' he told them. 'I want you to organise a dinner party for the local gentry.'

Agatha opened her mouth to say something, but Freddie put up his hand. 'I know what you're going to say, the expense will be too high. Well, it may be considered vulgar, but I want to help.' He rolled a wad of notes along the table towards her.

'I can't possibly . . .' Agatha spluttered.

'Please consider it as a gift, Mother-in-Law,' he said, helping himself to another egg. 'I have not made much of a contribution since I've been here and, after all, I am family.'

There was a moment of bemused silence, then Pearl said, 'How exciting. Who shall we invite, Mummy?'

It had been so long since Agatha had entertained, she could hardly think. 'Major Chipping might be a good option,' she began, adding by way of explanation for Freddie, 'He's the chairman of the local hunt.'

'Excellent,' said Freddie.

'What about Lady Verity?' said Pearl. 'After all, we did go to her party all that time ago.'

'If we invite her, we should have Sir Maurice as well,' Agatha said. 'And if they come, maybe His Grace the Duke?'

'Oh Mummy, he's a bit of a bore.'

Agatha nodded. 'You may be right. Let's stick with fun people.'

'No, no,' said Freddie with a wave of his hand, 'invite the duke. Old bores are fine. In fact, invite the whole bloody gentry!'

'We need to write this down or we shall forget,' said Pearl, going to the dresser drawer and taking out a writing pad. 'You must ask Bunny Warren.'

'Who is Bunny Warren?' said Freddie.

'Oh darling,' Pearl scolded. 'He's the man who gave me away at the wedding.'

Freddie turned his attention back to his toast. How could he have forgotten that stupid old buffoon? His raucous laughter had near driven him mad at the reception. What on earth his mother-in-law saw in the man was anybody's guess – unless it was his money. He made a mental note to put Bunny Warren at the top of his list; after all, he'd look quite fetching hanging from a lamppost.

Just the day before, Freddie had been up to London and the German Embassy with his photographs and a few picture postcards of the local area. Prussia House was a magnificent building which only last year had hosted a party with a thousand guests to celebrate its reopening after a £100,000 renovation. The guest list included royalty: Prince George, the Duke of Kent and his wife Princess Marina. Freddie's dinner party might not reach such lofty heights, but the type of people Agatha wanted to invite sounded just perfect.

As his wife and mother-in-law put together an impressive list of the great and the good, he smiled to himself. Little did the British know that the German Embassy had been used as a base for the Gestapo ever since its formation.

When he'd handed his little treasure trove into the office, he had been told to wait for further instructions.

'You have done a good job,' Christoph, his superior said, as he sifted through the photographs. 'Good shot of that plane coming in to land at Shoreham.'

'I thought so too,' said Freddie, careful not to mention being chased by an angry swan in full view of Pearl's sister Milly. 'It gives you a really clear idea of the flight path.'

'And nobody suspects you?'

'Absolutely not,' Freddie said emphatically. 'I've done everything possible to make them believe I have no time for the Führer. To them I am the perfect English gentleman.'

'*Sehr gut.*' Christoph put the photographs and cards to one side. 'We have had a communiqué from your uncle. He wants you to contribute to the *Sonderfahndungsliste.*'

Freddie gave him a confused stare.

'We are collecting the names of everyone who is antagonistic towards the Fatherland and those who are sympathisers. When we invade these shores, all traitors will be immediately arrested and deported to Germany.'

'What about gypsies?'

'It goes without saying,' said Christoph, 'that they will be rounded up with the Jews and the imbeciles. No, the people we are looking for are those who speak out against us, people of influence; the sort of people the British call the upper crust.'

'I shall need money,' Freddie had said. Hence the roll of notes he'd given Agatha.

Now he looked over Pearl's shoulder. His wife and mother-in-law were rejigging the names on their list. There were plenty of upper-crust-sounding names in the mix. Good, good. He couldn't wait to rid the world of these snobbish bores.

'What about the members of the local Masonic Lodge?' he suggested. 'Or perhaps one of the local clergy or a Boy Scout leader?'

Agatha looked up. 'Okay, why not?'

Freddie gave her a nod of approval. And you, my dear mother-in-law, will be the very first on my list, he thought savagely.

Seebold, Nan, Cyril and Milly had spent the day helping Lena to move into the cottage. Milly had been busy cleaning while Nan had changed the sheets and washed the curtains. The men had been working outside, building a chicken run and setting up the pigeon loft while Lena had taken her Shetland ponies to the stables on the Horsham Road. By the time evening came, the cottage was looking cosy once more.

Nan had prepared a hotpot which only needed to be heated through to be ready to eat. Milly laid the table.

'Does she know what she's going to do?' Nan called from the kitchen.

'I don't think so,' said Milly. 'One thing is for certain: she doesn't want to go back to Rainbow George.'

Nan put her head round the door. 'Tell her I can get her daily work in service anytime she wants,' she confided. 'There are a lot of well-to-do people in Findon Valley who are crying out for domestics. They pay good wages too.'

'I'll mention it,' Milly promised as Nan went back into the kitchen.

For Milly, being back in the cottage brought mixed feelings. She'd enjoyed some happy times here but also some very sad ones. A couple of times, as she'd turned quickly, she thought she could still see her poor father sitting in the armchair and doing his best to be jolly when it was obvious that he was in a lot of pain. It also reminded her of that night when Angel had been here and she and Pearl had been outside in the dark. Milly shuddered. She had never got around to telling Lena what they had done, and there were times when, even after all these years, it still weighed heavily on her mind. As she put the condiments onto the table, Milly heard the sound of voices and the door burst open. Lena was the first to come in, her face wreathed in smiles, but she was quickly followed by someone else. 'Look who I found on the doorstep,' Lena cried.

It was Pearl. Milly almost fainted with the shock, especially when she saw what her sister was holding in her hand. It was the doll. Milly's heart went into her mouth. Pearl was going to tell Lena what they had done all those years ago, wasn't she? Oh, why-oh-why had she put it off for so long? By the time Pearl was finished, Lena would hate her. A lump was forming in Milly's throat and her eyes were already pricking with unshed tears.

'Come in, come in,' Lena told Pearl. 'Sit down. Make yourself at home.'

Pearl nodded regally and placed herself in the armchair. Nan popped her head around the kitchen door. 'Oh, it's you, Miss Pearl,' she said in a measured tone. 'How nice to see you. Can I get you some tea?'

'That would be very kind of you, Mrs Martin,' Pearl cooed. She smiled up at Milly but Milly didn't return the smile. She felt sick. Although it was all done, she turned her attention back to laying the table. Her hands were trembling. Was Pearl going to do this in front of everybody or would she ask to speak to Lena in private? Stupid question – Pearl would want to have her revenge in public. Milly sucked in her lips and struggled to control her sense of panic.

Cyril came in, stamping his feet on the mat and taking his coat off. 'There's going to be snow before long,' he said then, spotting Pearl, he touched his forelock. 'How do?'

Nan brought in the tea tray.

Lena chatted away, telling Pearl that she was going to stay here permanently now but she wouldn't bother them up at the house. Politely she asked after Milly's mother. Pearl, all smiles, spoke about the upcoming parties at Muntham Court, clearly waiting for her moment. Milly was in agony. Cyril might consider what she'd done as a childish and foolish superstition, but what would Nan and Seebold think when they heard that she had cursed Lena's mother to death? And more importantly, how would Lena react? She would be horrified to know that her own sister had been so cruel.

'May I ask,' Lena enquired eventually, 'what are you doing with that old doll?'

Pearl looked down at her hand as if she'd quite forgotten the doll was there. 'Oh,' she said, 'is it yours?'

'It's Milly's really,' said Lena. 'When she was a little girl, she left it in the wood pile.' And turning to her sister she added, 'Don't you remember?'

'Lena . . .' Milly said helplessly.

'I found it after I saw you and Pearl arguing under the window,' Lena went on.

Milly's jaw dropped. So she'd seen them? It must have been Lena who she had seen moving behind the curtain that night. Had she heard what they'd said? A deep sense of shame overwhelmed her.

'It had a broken eye,' Lena went on cheerfully. 'Pa and I got it repaired and you made some lovely new clothes for it, didn't you, Nan?'

'That's right,' Nan smiled.

'Then Pa left it in Milly's bedroom for when she got back from school.'

'What the devil was it doing in the wood pile?' asked Cyril.

'Milly threw it there,' said Pearl, a note of triumph in her voice.

'Really?' said Lena. 'I thought *you* threw it there.' There was an ominous silence, then Lena added, 'It was the night you said all those terrible curses over my poor mother, don't you remember?' Her tone was soft, innocent.

Pearl's face flushed. 'Milly was there too,' she cried.

'Only because you made her stay,' said Lena, her voice becoming firmer. 'I heard you. You were right under my bedroom window and I heard every word.'

The room was filled with an awkward silence.

'Have you come to confess?' Lena asked. 'To say sorry?'

Pearl jumped to her feet and threw the doll in the chair. 'No, I haven't,' she said, tossing her head. 'I found the doll in the house and thought you might like it back. I was only trying to be friendly.'

'Oh, I don't think so,' said Lena. 'You came here to try and make things difficult for Milly, didn't you?'

Pearl made for the door, but just at that moment it was flung open and Seebold burst into the room. 'Flippin' heck, it's perishing out there,' he said, undoing his scarf. Then seeing Pearl he added, 'Oh excuse me, miss. I didn't mean to get in the way.'

'Don't worry, I was just going,' Pearl said through gritted teeth.

'So soon?' Lena trilled. 'But you haven't drunk your tea yet.'

Without another word, Pearl barged past Seebold and slammed the door behind her. Milly turned to Lena with tears in her eyes. 'I am so sorry,' she whispered. 'I'm so ashamed. I didn't know how to tell you.'

Lena put her arm around Milly's shoulders. 'There was no need.'

'I can't believe you heard it all and didn't say anything,' Milly said. 'It must have hurt you so much.'

Lena shrugged. 'It didn't really understand at the time,' she said, drawing her to one side so that the others wouldn't hear, 'so I asked Angel. She explained what curses were but she told me yours wasn't a real one. She said it was just a stupid childish prank. Pa said the same. Angel told me I had to forgive you . . . which I did, and then Pa and I got the dolly mended. Pa told me you would talk to me about it one day. He said I should be patient and I just had to wait.'

'He never said a word,' Milly said. 'And I did try so many times to tell you, but I couldn't bring myself to do it. I didn't want you to hate me.'

'I would never do that, you silly goose,' said Lena. 'You're my sister. And anyway, it wasn't you, was it? It was Pearl.' She smiled then threw her head back and laughed. 'She really thought she was going to put the cat among the pigeons, didn't she? She was dying to cause trouble between us. What a joke. Did you see her face?'

The two sisters laughed and hugged each other.

Nan put the big pot onto the table. When she lifted the lid there was a collective cry of delight as the wonderful aroma of lamb hotpot filled the room. While Nan dished it up, Lena said, 'This has been a wonderful day. Thank you all so much.' As they waved away her compliment she added, 'Oh, I didn't tell you, did I? I've got a new job. Next week I start work at the stables. I shall be giving horse-riding lessons and helping to run the livery side of the business.'

Pearl was in such a rage she could hardly breathe. Her plan, so carefully thought out, had seriously backfired and, what was even worse, that gypsy girl had made her look a complete fool. By the time she'd arrived back at the house, she had a headache and she was shaking with rage. Coming in through the French windows, she grabbed a wine glass and helped herself to a stiff drink. How dared they; how dared they laugh at her?

Pouring herself another whisky, she threw herself into the armchair. She would get her own back on them. She would get that dreadful woman out of the cottage somehow or other. It wasn't fair and it wasn't right. As the oldest girl, that property should have been hers. How she hated Lena.

Unknowingly, she was squeezing the stem of her glass. It broke. She had cut her little finger – not badly, but enough to draw blood. With whisky and glass in her lap, she vowed her revenge against Milly as well. They would pay for this. They would all rue the day they had crossed the Baroness Herren.

When they were alone at last, Lena could hardly wait to hear all about Milly's date with Eustace. Milly told her everything.

'So, are you seeing him again?'

Milly smiled happily. 'He asked me if we could meet again,' she said. 'Oh Lena, he's lovely. Such a gentleman, so kind and considerate.'

'It's taken you long enough to get there,' said Lena, giving her a playful nudge. 'He sounds right up your street.'

Chapter 31

Agatha and Pearl were basking in a warm glow of recognition. Their parties had fast become the talk of the county, and invitations to other people's soirées, tea parties and card evenings had already filled their diaries up until the spring of 1939. Freddie kept the money flowing for them, and Agatha was thrilled that her son-in-law had finally started living up to her expectations.

Freddie's superiors in London and Germany were more than happy too. The last time he'd gone to Prussia House, Christoph had been delighted with the names in Freddie's little red book, but he'd explained that from now on, things were going to become difficult. MI5 were keeping a close watch on embassy staff, so frequent visits to London could result in Freddie himself being arrested. For that reason, he was to be given a radio receiver set.

Christoph handed him a railway left-luggage ticket. 'In one week, you are to go to Worthing Central to pick up a case,' he said, handing him a set of suitcase keys. 'The radio will be inside.'

Freddie felt excitement and trepidation in equal measure. He wet his lips. 'Supposing someone follows me from here?'

'That is why you must wait a week,' Christoph said tersely.

Freddie nodded.

'You must keep us informed,' Christoph told him, 'so you will have to find a place of secrecy when using the radio.'

'I have the perfect place,' Freddie assured him, as he thought of the ice house he'd stumbled across in the grounds. He hadn't been there since he'd first discovered it way back when he'd first married Pearl, and he was pretty sure that his wife knew nothing about it. Hidden far from the house but still on the private estate, and overgrown with ivy and brambles, it would be the perfect hiding place.

Just before Christmas in 1938, Eustace took Milly to the Grand Hotel on Brighton's seafront for afternoon tea. As he pulled up, the concierge opened the car door and a young man took the car keys. Milly guessed that he would be taking the car to the hotel car park. The hotel, perhaps the best known in Brighton, had six floors of rooms, plus two more floors above – most likely where the live-in staff were accommodated. The rooms faced the sea and every single one had its own balcony. Milly took in her breath when she walked into the foyer where a huge Christmas tree dominated the space. Tall enough to reach the third-floor staircase, it gave off a wonderful aroma of fresh pine. It was heavily decorated with large baubles, and Milly guessed that they must have been put in place using long poles. There was no other way anyone could have reached across the lengthy branches. A glittering star graced the top, while silver tinsel and fairy lights added to the sparkle. The staff had put an array of Christmas presents around the huge tub holding the tree in place. A small notice in front told hotel patrons that any gifts left on display would be taken to the local children's hospital for the patients who had to spend their Christmas apart from their families. Even as she walked through the door, the pile of presents was growing.

Eustace told the person on the desk that he had booked a table, and a maître d' showed them to their places next to the window. Milly had been slightly surprised that he was so confident. At Lady Verity's, although he'd been gallant enough to offer her his jacket, he hadn't come across as quite so sophisticated. Milly loved the snowy-white tablecloths and the beautiful silver cutlery. Even though it was not yet four o'clock, dusk was gathering as the waiter pulled out her chair, so she could watch the streetlights going on and the people hurrying to catch the bus at Pool Valley. Others came from the opposite direction, perhaps heading home after leaving the entertainments on the pier. Tapping a cigarette on his silver case, Eustace offered Milly one as well but she shook her head. He leaned back as he lit his, inhaling deeply and puffing the smoke out over his head. A black-waistcoated waiter came to the table with a tea tray and sandwiches, and Eustace indicated that Milly should pour.

'I see you are still drawing the crowds with your windows,' he remarked as he inhaled once more.

Milly looked down. She never really knew what to say when someone complimented her like that. If she agreed with them, it might sound arrogant; if she disagreed it might look like false modesty. 'I enjoy what I do.'

As he extinguished his cigarette and they turned their attention to the sandwiches, he said, 'What have you been doing since I last saw you?'

'Nothing very exciting, I'm afraid,' she said. 'What about you?'

He smiled. 'Much the same, although I have found it awfully hard to get you out of my mind.'

Milly felt herself blushing. No one had ever said anything like that to her before. She was flattered, but there was still a part of her that couldn't help wishing he was another person. But no, she had to get Seebold out of her head. He was in love with someone else.

She was about to pour them both another cup of tea, but it looked a bit stewed. Eustace waved the waiter back and asked for a fresh pot. After he'd put it onto the table, he said, 'Would you care to look at the cakes, madam?' A moment later the maître d' was wheeling a dark brown trolley towards them. Milly's mouth watered. It positively groaned with chocolate éclairs, pastries, strawberry gâteaux, frangipane tarts and the inevitable Christmas cake. Milly chose a tart and an éclair. Eustace had a piece of Christmas cake and a pastry. Using some silver tongs, the waiter put them onto their personal cake stand.

'Last time we met,' Eustace began, 'you said you had studied art. I have some friends in London who are artists, and I wondered if you would like to meet them.'

Milly dropped the cake fork onto her plate with a clatter. 'Really? Oh yes please,' she cried. 'It's always good to meet fellow artists. Thank you for the suggestion.'

'You're welcome. They are surrealists,' said Eustace, 'which is probably why I can't understand their paintings.' He grinned. 'They have a studio in London and they are people at the cutting edge of modern-day art.'

Milly's eyes grew wide. 'I know very little about surrealism,' she admitted. 'I've heard the name but . . .'

'Apparently it's a way of letting the unconscious mind express itself,' he said, 'which is why their paintings can be unnerving – or perhaps illogical.'

'I see,' she said.

Eustace laid his hand over hers. 'It'll be fun, darling.'

Milly looked out of the window. *Darling*, he'd called her *darling* . . . A trip to London to meet some real artists sounded wonderful, but was she right to encourage him? She was really enjoying his company, but she still wasn't completely sure about him. But then she turned and his soft expression made her smile. She needed to give him a proper chance.

'I quite understand if you're not keen,' he said.

'No, no,' she said. 'It's fine and I'd love to meet them, and I really do appreciate the offer. By the way,' she added, 'did your parents get back safely from Austria?'

'They did,' he said, although he sounded a little surprised that she should remember.

'I imagine your sister was glad to have them back home.'

The sound of laughter distracted them. Two small children had just discovered the Christmas tree in the foyer and were dancing and clapping with delight at all the presents. The maître d' went over to them and crouched down to their level. Milly guessed that he was telling them that the toys were for children who were very sick. As he stood up, he handed them a lollipop each and they skipped away happily.

'My mother adores Christmas,' said Eustace.

Milly smiled.

Eustace reached for his cigarette case again before continuing. 'She spends months getting ready for it, so we are guaranteed a wonderful time.'

Milly felt a pang of envy. Her mother always spent a lot of time preparing for Christmas, but Milly was never really included. In fact, she was hard pushed to remember a Christmas she had spent with her mother.

When they had finished their afternoon tea, Eustace drove her back to Worthing and parked the car close to her digs.

'I've really enjoyed today,' he told her. 'Next time we'll go to London and meet my friends.'

Milly smiled back at him. He leaned towards her and kissed her lips. His kisses were gentle and – to her great surprise – left her wanting more. When Milly walked through her door later, she felt as if she was floating on air.

Chapter 32

January 1939

After talking things over with her sister, Milly decided to give up her digs in the centre of Worthing and move into the cottage with Lena. Seebold was still at the Wonderland, where he had been using the winter months to repair and revitalise the amusements. The animals were all gone – some given away as presents to local schools and others to the relatives of the people working for him. He knew they couldn't be properly looked after if they stayed, and this was the best way to ensure that none of them suffered. The only animal left on the property was Nipper, a mongrel, who acted as a rather soppy guard dog. Now that he was free from animal husbandry, Seebold was working all hours, principally on a model village of Worthing itself, but he still found time to help the girls. Milly was pleased to see him again but she couldn't help noticing that he seemed rather unwell.

'Are you all right?' she asked after she saw him shivering.

'Got a bit of a headache, that's all.'

Milly and Lena got on well together, and it didn't take long to settle into a routine. There was a good bus service which passed the end of the drive twice every hour, so there was no problem for Milly getting to work. It also meant that she was on hand to help Lena with the animals when needed and, although they couldn't see the house from the cottage, Milly was strangely comforted to be nearer to home. Yes, she had some bitter-sweet memories and her mother's attitude towards her was still not resolved yet somehow being in the cottage made her father seem closer,

Milly had expected to go to London with Eustace when they met again but, as soon as she got into the car, he was apologetic. 'I'm so sorry, darling,' he said. 'I have to be back in Hove this evening and there's just not enough time to take you. We'll do it next time, I promise.'

Milly smiled bravely but she was hugely disappointed. He drove her instead to a place called Rottingdean, a picture-postcard village that had become part of the borough of Brighton and Hove in 1928. Famed for its association with the Quaker movement in one century, and for the smuggling of tea, spirits and tobacco in the next, when farming collapsed after the Great War it had become popular with celebrities. The village also boasted some really good home-grown talent. The Copper family had been singing traditional Sussex folk songs in the Black Horse public house since Victorian times. Mostly farm labourers and shepherds, they usually sang in the evenings, but today they were singing in the afternoon.

It was a charming setting, and it wasn't long before Milly got over her disappointment about the London trip and was joining in with some of the refrains.

> 'Twas of a brisk young ploughboy, come listen to this refrain
>
> And join with me in chorus and sing the ploughboy's praise . . .

'You've given me such an education,' she quipped as they left.

'All part of the service,' he said, bending to kiss her lips.

'Tell me about him,' Lena said when she got back home. 'What does he do for a living? Where does he live?'

'Not much to tell.' Milly changed the subject. It wasn't that she didn't want to tell her sister. She'd enjoyed being with him, but she couldn't shake the feeling that she was being disloyal. Silly really. It was Seebold who was in love with somebody else, so she owed him nothing. And another thing, she still genuinely didn't know much about Eustace. He preferred to ask questions rather than answer them – and he did it so cleverly that it wasn't until she got home that she realised he still hadn't told her anything about himself, and the little he had told her about his family didn't add up. His mother was dead – but she was in Austria. His father was an MP – but he was in the Foreign Office. His sister wore callipers – but she still didn't know the girl's name.

It was February, and at long last Milly was on her way to London with Eustace. At first she hadn't been sure if she should go, but in the end she reasoned that it would make a welcome break from her normal routine. She enjoyed the ride in his MG TA Midget sports car, stopping off at Box Hill to use the toilets. It was enormously satisfying to see heads turning as they pulled into the public car park; he certainly kept the car looking in tip-top condition with its polished red leather seats and black wet-weather soft top. 'Enjoying yourself?' he asked as they climbed back in.

Milly nodded happily.

'Next time I take you for a drive we'll go in the warmer weather,' he said. 'It's even better with the top down.'

The engine was quite noisy so they didn't talk very much during the drive. His friends' art studio was in Bedford Square, Bloomsbury, and it turned out to be inside a beautiful Georgian terrace. They parked opposite the square itself, where the trees waved their branches gently in the breeze. Milly loved it. An oasis of green calm in the middle of the bustling city.

As they headed towards the door, Eustace told her that the house next door was once the home of Frederick and Norman Warne. She must have looked slightly bewildered because he added, 'They published Beatrix Potter, you know.' He chuckled. 'I'm full of useless information like that!'

There were several people working on different projects in the studio and they seemed a little surprised to see her. Milly was introduced to a few but quickly forgot their names. The leading light was Stanley Richardson, a man who had apparently had a number of his paintings hung in the smarter London galleries.

'Eustace tells me that you are an artist,' he said. 'Have you had any exhibitions?'

Milly shook her head. 'My portfolio is a little thin at the moment,' she confessed. 'I studied for two years at Worthing School of Art and Science under Principal Salt,' she said, 'but since I left I've been working as a window-dresser in several large department stores.'

'A window-dresser?' Stanley seemed taken aback.

His tone was such that Milly flushed with embarrassment.

'She's frightfully good,' said Eustace. 'In great demand in both Worthing and Brighton.' Stanley excused himself and went back to his easel. Milly felt like a fish out of water. She shouldn't have come. She didn't belong here, that much had been made very clear.

At Eustace's invitation, Milly glanced over Stanley's shoulder. The painting he was working on was rather confusing. In the centre was a woman's face, but the eyes were missing, and the top of her head ended just above her eyebrows. The woman's chin rested on a barrel and her left foot (missing the big toe) was emerging from the ground beside her. The sky was blood red as if it were sunset. As he picked up his paintbrush again, Stanley began working on the face of a clock in the top right-hand corner of the canvas. As she watched, he painted the two hands of the clock to say ten past five.

Milly was dying to ask what the picture represented but, after Stanley's icy reception, she didn't dare.

'Roland old boy, said Eustace, moving on, 'I'd like you to meet Milly. Milly, this is Roland Rotherford-Smuts.'

She shook hands with the tall, distinguished-looking man with deep-set eyes and dark slicked-back hair.

Roland's painting was far more recognisable because he was painting a model who lay in a relaxed position on a couch on the other side of the room. Her name was Wanda and, as soon as she spoke, Milly knew she was an American. Her face was familiar but it wasn't until a little while later that she realised that the face in Stanley's picture and Roland's work was one and the same.

Roland and Wanda took a break and shared some tea with Milly and Eustace.

Watching the artists at work fuelled Milly's desire to pick up her paintbrush again. It had been ages since she'd had the time to paint.

'What sort of art do you do?' asked Wanda, as she joined them at the table.

'Nothing as avant-garde as this,' said Milly. 'Landscapes mostly, but I also enjoy painting wildlife. I'm fascinated by anything in the natural world which can make itself look like something else; for instance, a stick insect that looks like a twig or a deer that blends so well with its natural surroundings that it becomes invisible.'

Wanda seemed impressed.

'Do you paint?' Milly asked.

'Me? Lord no. I'm a poet.'

Milly smiled. 'I don't think I've ever met a real live poet before.'

'She's brilliant,' said Roland. He put his arm around Wanda's waist and drew her close to him. Milly looked away as they started kissing.

After they'd spent about an hour in the studio, Eustace suggested that they leave. Milly excused herself to go to the toilet and freshen her make-up. As she walked to the sink, Wanda came out of one of the cubicles.

'Enjoy yourself?' she said as they stood side by side.

Milly nodded. 'You're all so talented.'

Wanda grinned. 'I'm only the model, darling.'

They heard a commotion out in the corridor, then Stanley's voice said, 'Don't do this again.'

'Oh for God's sake,' Eustace retorted crossly. 'Get a hold of yourself.'

'This place is not a peep show,' said Stanley. 'If you want to impress your tarts, do it somewhere else.'

Milly felt her face heating up. Wanda moved to the towel rail to dry her hands.

'Let me remind you who found you this place,' they heard Eustace say.

'That doesn't give you the right to bring all and sundry here for a cheap thrill,' Stanley hissed.

They heard the sound of two sets of footsteps and, just before a door slammed, Eustace said, 'Now look here, Stanley, if you . . .' Their voices faded.

Milly's eyes were already pricking with tears. The artists didn't want her there, so why had Eustace brought her? All she wanted now was to go home.

'I'm so sorry, darling,' said Wanda.

Milly smiled. 'It's all right. It's not your fault. Anyway, it's I who should apologise. I had no idea we were gate-crashing.'

'Men can be such pricks at times,' Wanda went on. 'I for one loved having you here. Take no notice, darling.'

Milly blew her nose into her hanky. 'Please don't worry. It's fine.'

271

Eustace was waiting by the door. They said their goodbyes and left.

'I think we should have something to eat before we go back,' said Eustace.

Milly would have preferred to go straight home, but he was probably right. They had had nothing all day and driving all the way back to Worthing on an empty stomach was probably not a good idea. He didn't seem to realise that she'd heard every word that had passed between him and Stanley, and Milly preferred to keep it that way. She smiled. 'A meal would be just perfect.'

'I would offer to take you to a show, but virtually all the theatres are closed now.' He sighed. 'We're living in momentous times.'

He found them a small hotel nearby. The restaurant was open to non-residents and the menu was à la carte. As soon as she sat down, Milly realised how hungry she was. She ordered the lamb cutlets while Eustace asked for the steak. He ordered wine, and when an old woman came round the table with some stem roses, he bought Milly three. A crooner sang as they sat. It was a pity their visit to the studio had been such a disappointment because Milly thought this was the most romantic thing that had ever happened to her.

'What did you think of today?' he asked as they waited for their meal. 'Can you imagine being in a studio like that?'

'I think it would be fascinating,' she said, not wanting to be drawn into a conversation about Stanley and his rudeness. 'I enjoy doing the windows but this has rekindled my passion to be even more creative.'

He gave her a satisfied grin.

The waiter arrived with some bread rolls in a basket.

'I really liked Roland's wife,' said Milly, taking one.

'Roland's wife?'

Milly was puzzled. 'Wanda.'

'Oh, I see,' said Eustace. 'Wanda isn't his wife. His wife is . . . well, I haven't a clue where she is these days.' Eustace leaned forward and whispered confidentially, 'Roland and Wanda are both married, but not to each other. Wanda is his mistress.'

Milly did her best to look as if she already knew that, but she knew she had failed when he grinned at her. 'You're so innocent, darling,' and taking her hand in his he added confidentially, 'They all do it.'

Of course she knew that artists were notorious and in their private lives were often . . . different, but she'd never met anyone like that before. Eustace was still watching her.

'You're laughing at me,' she accused.

'Of course not, darling.' He shook his head. 'It's just that one gets so used to something, one hardly even notices it any more.' He reached for her hand across the table, but she snatched it away. 'You're angry with me,' he remarked.

'I'm angry with myself,' she said. 'I feel such a complete idiot.'

'Not at all, darling,' he said gravely. 'You're lively, fun to be with, you're beautiful and you make the whole world light up when you come into a room. Don't let this spoil our evening.'

The crooner was back again and Milly looked up at him. 'Isn't that . . .?'

'Jack Buchanan,' Eustace whispered.

Milly stared at the tall, suave man in a dark suit. Famed for his shows in London and on Broadway, he looked totally relaxed – some said almost lazy – in his performance.

Eustace held out his hand over the table. 'Dance with me, darling?'

He led her onto the small dance area in front of the orchestra. His arm was gentle yet firm around her waist, and he held her hand close to his chest rather than extended. His head rested tenderly against hers and she breathed in his aftershave, only faint now that it was the end of the day, but still perceptively there. Gradually, she began to relax. It was odd being this close to such a famous musical star such as Jack Buchanan, and being in the arms of a man like Eustace was even more wonderful.

Later, much later, on the way out, the man who had parked their car was nodding his head. As Milly approached she thought she saw Eustace slip him something and the man touched his forelock.

'The damned car has a flat,' Eustace growled.

Milly stared aghast. 'Oh no! What are we going to do?'

'The fellow can get it fixed,' said Eustace, 'but not until tomorrow.' He hesitated. 'Look, my flat is only just around the corner. Let me take you there and then I'll come back and do it myself.'

Milly felt a little uneasy. 'I do need to get back,' she said cautiously.

'I will get you back tonight, I promise.'

His flat was literally only just around the corner. It was surprisingly roomy and he had a great taste in décor. As she relaxed on the sofa, he put the kettle on for some tea.

The tea made, he came towards her and bent to kiss her lips. It was wonderfully exciting and Milly could feel her heart banging away in her chest.

'Oh Milly . . . darling.'

She never wanted it to end but, as the minutes ticked by, she was thinking about how she was going to get back home. Supposing he couldn't fix the wheel – where was the nearest station? It was still reasonably early, so she guessed there would be no problem in finding a train, but would she have to go to Brighton first or could she get a train direct to Worthing? His kisses were wonderful, wonderful, but she had to be sensible.

'Hadn't you better go?' she whispered.

'Go?'

'To fix the wheel.'

'In a minute.'

It was getting very late. 'Please, Eustace,' she whimpered. Reluctantly, he broke away. 'I'll be back as soon as I can.'

As soon as he'd gone, Milly went to the bathroom. He was out of loo roll, so she looked for a new one in a cupboard. When she opened the door, several things fell out. The shelves inside were filled with nail varnishes, talcum powder, perfume and face creams. Milly was startled. After putting them all back, she opened the door next to it and found fancy soaps and a lady's bath cap. Her heart sank. He had someone else living here. A woman.

When she came out of the toilet, she stared at the other doors in the corridor. There were obviously two bedrooms. She opened one door. The master bedroom had two massive wardrobes. Milly hovered by the door. She wasn't one to snoop, but now she felt compelled. One wardrobe was full of men's things. Eustace's. She recognised the duffel coat he'd worn when they had gone walking by the river. The other wardrobe was full of ladies' clothes. Milly felt sick. He had joked about his friends having loose morals, and yet it was obvious that he was married. Even more disturbing was the fact that he'd gone to great lengths to hide his wife's things. That's when it dawned on her. There was no flat tyre, was there. He'd planned this from the start. He was going to come back in a minute and tell her he'd tried to fix it, but he'd have to get a mechanic to look at it in the morning.

Milly went to the window and looked out. The flat was on the first floor but there was a fire escape on the side of the building nearest the window of the second bedroom. There was no apparent access to it, but she could stand on the low roof immediately in front of the window and easily reach it from there. She would have to climb under the handrail to get onto the stairs, but it was doable.

After a few minutes, Milly had gathered her things and gone into the smaller bedroom. There was no lock on the door but a fairly large chest of drawers stood to the right. It took some effort, but she pushed it in front of the door. There, that would stop someone getting in in a hurry.

It only took a few minutes to reach the ground, and then she headed for the bright lights of the busy street. Something told her to be cautious and sure enough, when she put her head around the corner, she had a terrific shock. Eustace was standing just a few feet away from her, outside the front door, smoking a cigarette. Milly jumped back. She was livid and could have easily given him a piece of her mind, but she also wanted to steer clear of him and get home, so there was no other option but to wait for him to go back in.

As soon as the coast was clear, Milly came out onto the street and hailed a taxi. With a bit of luck, she would be able to catch the last train from Victoria. If not, she would wait on the platform for the milk train in the morning. As luck would have it, she was in time for the last train to Worthing and scrambled aboard just as the guard blew his whistle.

On the way back home, she had a little smile to herself. How she wished she could have been a fly on the wall when he realised his quarry had flown.

Chapter 33

After a couple of days, Milly and Lena had both expected Seebold to roll up and see how they were doing, but when almost a week had passed with no sign of him, Milly was getting worried. Whilst it was true that she sometimes felt awkward around him, he was still her friend and she missed him.

'You know Seebold,' said Lena, when Milly remarked that they hadn't heard from him. 'Once he gets focused on something, everything else goes out of the window.'

She was right of course, but Milly couldn't shake this feeling of unease. She decided to make her way over to Wonderland after work. It was already dusk as she alighted from the bus, but the first thing that struck her was that there were no lights on anywhere in the Wonderland. The gate was locked, but she knew of a weakness further along the fence, so she climbed in that way and headed for Seebold's caravan.

Milly was even more concerned when Nipper, looking rather bedraggled and miserable, came out from under the caravan. 'Hello, old fellow,' she said, waggling his ear. 'Where's your master?' Although she knocked hard on the caravan door and called his name, Seebold didn't appear.

Now Milly was really worried. She tried the caravan door and, much to her relief, found it open.

It was the smell that told her something was very wrong. The whole place reeked of vomit. The lights were run off a battery but, when she reached for the switch, it didn't work. She remembered that he kept an old oil lamp on the table, so she searched for matches. Once the pale yellow beam filled the room, she could see stacked-up dishes in the washing-up bowl. That was odd because Seebold was a tidy person. Nipper, who had followed her in, was making a yipping sound, so she poured some water into a clean bowl and put it down for him. The dog lapped at it greedily.

'Seebold?' The only sound Milly could hear was that of her own heart thumping. 'Are you there, Seebold?'

His sleeping quarters were at the other end of the caravan, behind the heavy curtain. Taking the oil lamp with her, Milly made her way cautiously towards it, her thoughts growing darker by the minute. What if he had left? Supposing he was . . .? When she pulled back the curtain, it came as a relief to see the outline of his body in the bed, but then she realised he wasn't moving. 'Seebold!'

She held up the lamp and was shocked by the colour of his face. His skin was grey. Beads of perspiration stood out on his forehead and yet when she touched his bare arm, it was cold and clammy. Dried vomit was stuck to his pillow and in his hair. His eyes were half-open and he was shivering. His breathing was shallow. When he saw her, he let out a soft moan. She lifted his head gently and turned the pillow so that he wasn't lying in the goo.

'Listen, Seebold,' she said, firmly yet not wanting to alarm him, 'you're ill. I have to go for help. You need a doctor, okay?' She pulled another blanket over his naked chest. 'I have to go to the phone box in Ham Road.' She patted his arm. 'I'll be as quick as I can.'

Seebold did his best to smile. 'Bad pain. Chest.'

'I know, I know.' There were tears in her eyes, which she fought to hold back. Nipper pushed his nose towards his master.

'I'm going to leave Nipper in here with you. I shan't be long.'

It was only as she stepped out of the caravan that Milly remembered the telephone in the office. Where were the office keys? Dashing back into the caravan, Milly searched until she found a big bunch of keys in a drawer, but which was the one for the office? For a second she hesitated. What if it took her ages to identify the right one? What if it wasn't on this bunch at all? It might be quicker to run to the kiosk, after all. Three minutes, she told herself. If she hadn't found the right key in three minutes, she would run to Ham Road.

As luck would have it, it was fairly obvious by the size of the lock which key was the one to the office. Once inside, she found the switch, and electric light flooded the room. There on the desk was a black GPO telephone. Picking up the receiver, she waited for the telephonist to answer. If she had been in London, she could have used the new 999 service everybody was talking about, but it wasn't yet available in all parts of the country.

A few minutes later, a doctor was on his way. Now all she had to do was find the key that opened the gate.

By the time the doctor arrived, Milly had heated some water and put it into a bowl. She'd found a flannel and was washing the dried vomit from Seebold's face and hair. It seemed strange to be touching him so intimately. Apart from that one time when he'd put his arm around her and drawn her close to him after her mother had been so nasty, they had never really touched each other. As she washed his dark curls and cleaned his ear, Milly felt oddly emotional – close to tears. Her heart was thumping. He was such a wonderful person. She swallowed the lump in her throat as she washed his torso. She had begun by thinking of him as like a brother, but now that those strong arms were limp and his clear blue eyes (lapis lazuli, she had once told Lena) were dull and empty, Milly was afraid. He had a dry cough and it was obviously hurting him a lot. As she did her best to comfort him, she felt painfully tender towards him.

Nipper sat up and barked as the doctor came through the door. The doctor wrinkled his nose. 'Has the patient been drinking?' he said curtly.

'No,' said Milly. 'I thought the same at first but there's nothing here. No bottles at all but he's been dreadfully sick.'

The doctor came towards the bed. Milly stepped to the other side of the curtain and left him to examine Seebold. She was washing her hands when the curtain flew back again and the doctor came out.

'I'm glad to see you're washing your hands,' he said. 'Make sure you do a good job of it. It looks as if he may have pleurisy and he's also got hypothermia.'

'What's pleurisy?' Milly asked as she dried her hands.

The doctor took her place at the bowl to wash his own hands.

'It's a lung infection,' he said. 'As soon as I've finished, I shall ring for an ambulance. He may have to have the fluid drawn from his chest.'

Milly caught her breath. That sounded really serious.

'I suggest you get rid of those sheets,' said the doctor. 'Burn them if necessary, and you should sleep elsewhere tonight until this caravan is thoroughly cleaned.'

'I don't live here,' said Milly. 'I'm just a friend.'

'Ah,' said the doctor. 'Then I apologise for my presumption.'

Twenty minutes later, Seebold was on his way to hospital. Milly didn't want to stay in the caravan any longer than necessary, so she stuffed his washing into a holdall she'd found at the back of the cupboard, ready to be burnt back at the cottage. She then put an old belt through Nipper's collar to make a lead, and the pair of them headed for the bus stop.

As she reached the driveway of Muntham Court, it seemed that there was some kind of party going on at the house. Several big cars were snaking their way down the driveway as Milly and Nipper made their way towards the little lane which took her to the cottage. At one point, the passenger in a large chauffeur-driven Bentley wound down the window. 'Milly!' she cried. 'Oh my goodness, it *is* you.'

Milly turned her head to see Sarah Whitmore, her old school friend. She hadn't seen her for years. 'Sarah!' she cried. 'How are you? Where have you been? I did write ages ago but your letter was returned.'

'Stop the car a minute will you, Jackson,' Sarah said. The chauffeur pulled the car over and Sarah climbed out to walk beside her old friend. 'We went to Austria,' Sarah continued. 'You remember my father was in the diplomatic service.'

'Gosh,' said Milly. She frowned. 'You said "was". He's not . . .?'

'No, no,' said Sarah with a chuckle. 'He's in the car. I'm sure you know things have hotted up a lot lately. My father has been recalled to the UK.' She gave Milly a hard look. 'I say, you don't exactly look ready for the off. Can I give you a lift to the house?'

'No thanks, Sarah,' said Milly. 'I'll be fine. I'll catch you later. I'm just giving the dog a bit of a walk.'

The driver of the car behind the Bentley tooted his horn abruptly. A man, Milly presumed Sarah's father, wound down the back-seat window. 'Darling, we have to get going.'

'Sorry, Daddy,' said her friend.

'Look, you go on, Sarah,' said Milly.

'Well if you're sure?'

'Absolutely,' said Milly as they air-kissed each other's cheeks. She watched Sarah climb back into the car and for a brief moment she missed her old life. The Bentley drove on and, as she turned into the lane, Milly had already changed her mind again. No, she didn't miss those ghastly parties or the dressing up. She just missed having lovely friends like Sarah.

Chapter 34

On 15 March 1939, the Czechoslovakian president was intimidated into signing away his country's independence. That meant that one of the world's most modern, developed and industrialised economies – and one of the world's largest food producers – had toppled into Hitler's lap without so much as a cross word. Everybody said that Poland would be next.

Though internationally the situation was becoming increasingly worrying, matters closer to home were starting to look up. Seebold had spent a week in hospital before it was deemed that he was ready to be discharged. 'The doc tells me it was a really close call,' he told them. 'Good job you turned up when you did, duchess. You're my hero!'

Lena rolled her eyes as Milly shook her head and waved him away.

'They say they want me to go to some sort of convalescent home,' he complained bitterly. 'I don't want to be locked up indoors with a load of old men.'

Nan was willing to help, but Cyril's brother who lived in Horsham was very unwell and the girls felt that she had enough on her plate. How could they convince the powers-that-be that Seebold could live with two unmarried girls, though? In the end, Lena solved the problem at a stroke.

'He's got to come with me,' she told the doctor, as if there was no argument. 'He's my brother. I can't leave my brother out in the cold, can I?' She sighed and looked down at the floor. 'No, I'll look after him. It's what my mother would have wanted me to do. It's my duty.'

So a week later, an ambulance brought him to the cottage.

Once the ambulance had driven off, the three of them had a good laugh, and then Lena laid down some ground rules. 'I know you are itching to get back outside, but you're to stay in the warm for a few days. Milly can see to you in the mornings, and I'll make your tea when I get home in the evenings. We've decided you can sleep in the bedroom. Milly and I can bunk up together in the boxroom.'

Seebold gave her a mock salute.

It was lovely to be together again although, for all his bluster, Seebold was still quite weak. He tired easily and he went to bed much earlier than the girls. Nipper, now recovered from his own trauma, was delighted to be reunited with his master. Milly and Lena didn't mention that the poor dog had been half starved when Milly brought him home. They both knew it wasn't Seebold's fault anyway.

In the evenings they played cards, or Seebold showed them a few tricks. His cough was slow to go, and it was obvious that he still had a pain in his side. Being unwell frustrated him. 'I've already been ill for too long. I need to get the Wonderland ready for the season.'

'You will,' said Milly brightly. She looked up and noticed that he was giving her a long hard look. 'What?'

'If there is a war,' he said gravely, 'I wonder how long I can keep it going. Now that Czechoslovakia has capitulated, things look pretty bad.'

'It'll be fine once the dust has settled,' Milly tried to reassure him.

Seebold shook his head. 'If push comes to shove, I shall join up. I shan't wait to be conscripted.'

'What brought that on?' she said with a chuckle.

Seebold looked away. 'Cyril came up on his bike this afternoon. He heard on the radio that Neville Chamberlain has promised to help Poland if Hitler invades.'

Milly frowned. 'You don't think Hitler would really do that, do you?'

Seebold turned towards her. 'I think he might, you know,' he said quietly.

Milly felt her eyes stinging. 'But that really would mean war.'

Seebold nodded.

'And if you join up, what will you do?'

He shrugged. 'Probably something like the Royal Engineers. I'm not going yet. I just wanted you to know, that's all.'

Milly had a sick feeling in her stomach but she didn't say anything. Everything pointed towards war, but there was a part of her that kept hoping all the signs were wrong. If war did come, everything would change. Come to that, what would she and Lena do if the country went to war? Sussex was right next to the continent of Europe. It would be on the front line if there was an invasion. She glanced over at Seebold again. What if they sent him abroad? What if he was injured . . . what if he was . . .?

'Sorry, duchess,' he said softly. 'I've upset you with all this talk of war, haven't I?'

'No, no,' she said with a shaky smile. 'Just me being daft, that's all.'

Agatha stood by the ha-ha and strained her eyes to see if anyone was about. Should she cross over and take a look at the cottage? She was fairly sure the girl would be out at this time of day. Her new live-in housekeeper (employed since her son-in-law had given her some money to get the house in a fit state for socialising) had told her that Lena helped out at the stables nearby during the day, so it was a reasonably safe bet that the cottage was empty.

Spring had been extremely cold, and although it was a rare occurrence this side of the Downs, there had been a significant snowfall. Everything was late this year. Agatha pulled her collar up and trudged on.

She'd forgotten how attractive the cottage looked. She couldn't remember the last time she had been here, but it must have been when the girls were small. Hadn't she had some renovations and improvements done before she'd allowed them to play here? It suited her to have her children out of the way, but she wasn't a neglectful mother. She had made sure the cottage was safe for Pearl's sake. Millicent was easy to please. She always enjoyed dressing up, but Pearl liked to . . . Agatha stopped in her tracks. What did Pearl like to do? She hadn't a clue, but the two of them had spent hours down here, their only other company the cat. Good Lord, she hadn't thought of that wretched cat for years. It had scratched Pearl's arm, hadn't it, and she'd had it put down. Quite right too; poor little Pearl. Yes, she'd been a good mother.

Wandering around the outside of the fence, Agatha was disturbed to see rabbits in hutches and chickens running around behind a fenced-off area. And wasn't that a pigeon loft? She pursed her lips angrily. Really! That wretched girl had turned the place into nothing more than a squalid farmyard. Agatha could only imagine the vermin those creatures would attract: mice, foxes, even rats. She shuddered at the thought. Not only that, but it lowered the tone of a grand country house. She only hoped that Freddie had never seen it. What would he think? And what of her illustrious visitors when they came? What would they think? How would she explain it? She would never have thought of coming here had it not been for Sarah Whitmore telling her she'd seen Millicent walking with a dog in the drive on the night of the party. Her daughter hadn't turned up at the house, so Agatha reasoned that she must be in the cottage with her husband's bastard child. And now just look at the state of it! Oh really, it was too bad! After all the work she had done to make Muntham Court the place to be, they'd turned this into a squalid camp!

She clenched her gloved hand into a fist in a wave of fury. Agatha was sorely tempted to open the chicken run and shoo them all out. Ha! That would be a prize and a half for the fox's lair. But as she came closer, she heard the deep throaty bark of a dog and then a man's voice called out, 'Quiet, Nipper.'

Agatha froze and her eyes nearly popped out of her head. A man! The little tart had a man living in there. Agatha let out a disgusted snort as she felt her face go pink. Well, she was her mother's daughter all right. She couldn't begin to imagine what was going on in there. Well, she could, but that was not the point. How dare the creature turn the cottage, Pearl's cottage, into a place of ill-repute. It was tawdry and revolting and it had to be stopped.

'Can I help you?' a man's voice called out.

She looked up and saw him standing by the door with the dog beside him. She recognised him at once. He was that dreadful man from the court case who Freddie had removed from the kitchen when Millicent came to collect her things! Speechless and appalled, Agatha spun on her heel and headed for home.

As she strode back to the big house, Agatha came to a conclusion. It didn't matter if Charles had bequeathed the cottage to her, the girl must be persuaded to leave. After the failed court appeal, clearly she couldn't be evicted by fair means, so it would have to be done by foul. Well, if needs must . . . All that remained was to dream up some plan that would achieve the desired effect . . . and it had to be something permanent, very permanent.

Chapter 35

As Milly was throwing out an old newspaper, an article caught her attention.

The Ministry of Home Security's Camouflage Directorate are looking for artists, designers, architects and craftsmen for a special project. Government-funded and of national importance, applicants are invited to submit their work with references to this address . . .

Milly felt a flutter of excitement. Here at last was something she could relate to and, should there be a war, it would feel wonderful to do her bit to help her country. She'd been angry and humiliated by Eustace, but that trip to London had done one thing she hadn't counted on. It had rekindled her desire to paint. And the thought of being in a studio with many other like-minded artists appealed to her. When she re-read the advertisement, Milly knew she desperately wanted to apply for this, but there wasn't enough time to do something from scratch. Then it occurred to her. Principal Salt had some of her work in the college. She would go to see him as soon as possible, today if she could, and ask him if he would send it for her and give her a reference.

* * *

Milly's sister had been very supportive when she'd finally got round to telling her about Eustace.

'You mean you had no idea he was married?' Lena gasped.

'Not until I saw all her things,' said Milly. 'Can you believe the brass neck of the man! He was so bloomin' sure I'd simply melt in his arms.'

'I guessed things hadn't gone well when you didn't mention anything, but I didn't want to pry,' said Lena. 'I'm so sorry.'

'I was so angry,' Milly went on, 'that I pulled his wife's things out of the drawers and piled them on the bed and then I climbed out of the window.'

'What, all of them?' Lena gasped again.

'Too right,' said Milly. 'Underwear, blouses, jumpers, shoes, coats, handbags . . .'

'You didn't.'

'I flippin' well did,' said Milly.

The two of them looked at each other and then they fell about laughing. 'I wish I could have seen his face when he found them,' said Lena, wiping her eyes.

'Even if he spent all night putting them back, she would have known they'd been disturbed,' said Milly. 'Men never can put things back properly.'

The two girls couldn't contain themselves. They laughed and laughed.

Milly fell against her sister's shoulder. 'Why can't all men be as nice as Seebold?'

Lena pulled a face. 'You can't be serious.'

'Why not?' said Milly. 'Oh, I know he does daft things and nothing ever seems to go right for him, but he's kind and he's funny and he's . . .'

She stopped because Lena had laid a hand on her arm. 'Milly, you silly goose,' she said with a chuckle, 'Seebold makes a muck of things and he gets all flustered because he's in love with you. He's always trying to impress you.'

Milly's jaw dropped.

'Surely you knew?' said Lena. 'In fact, I remember telling you once. That time when you were asking me if I would marry him.'

'But that was when you said he was in love with someone else,' Milly accused.

'Yes, *you*, you ninny!'

Milly sat down with a bump. 'Why didn't he say something?'

Lena gave her a sympathetic smile. 'Because he thinks you're too good for him.'

'I don't understand,' said Milly.

'Think about it,' said Lena. 'Your father was a rich man and you grew up in a big house. You've been educated in the best schools and you've carved out a career for yourself. What's Seebold got to offer? An amusement centre which takes a lot of hard work to keep going; something which the government will most likely close down anyway if we go to war.'

Milly was struck dumb. Seebold loved her?

All at once, Lena glanced up at the clock. 'Time to shut up the chickens.'

Having spent most of the spring receiving invitations to other people's parties, on the day of Agatha's fiftieth birthday party, a small army of workers, caterers and suppliers had arrived at Muntham Court. Most of the food came in a Fortnum & Mason's van.

'Don't tell me that's Fortnum & Mason of London?' Freddie gasped when he looked out of his bedroom window as he heard it pull up outside. 'Does your mother realise that will cost her an arm and a leg?'

'You said you wanted the best, darling,' Pearl cooed. 'My mother never does anything by halves.'

'I'm beginning to see that,' Freddie muttered. He frowned darkly. At this rate, she'd use up all his money in no time.

For the whole day, the house became a hive of activity. People seemed to be everywhere, all doing their best to get everything ready before seven, the time the guests were to arrive. It seemed that everywhere he looked there were snowy-white tablecloths, the family silver was polished to a mirror shine, chairs were dusted and brushed, and just about every vase in the house had been filled with flowers and brought into the dining room. Before long, the heady scent of fuchsias and roses filled the air, and Freddie was left wondering where on earth they could have come from so early in the season. More expense!

Agatha supervised it all magnificently, until five-thirty when she disappeared upstairs to get ready. Pearl had already been up there for hours with a local hairdresser. Freddie changed in his dressing room and, as soon as he was ready, he came back downstairs and poured himself a stiff drink. He was a bag of nerves. He'd better not fail this one. Christoph depended upon him, and there had been murmurings because he was giving them the same names over and over again.

As the guests arrived, waiters and waitresses mingled around them with trays of canapés and wine. A quartet tucked into the alcove played classical music as the great and the good wandered through the downstairs rooms.

When she finally came downstairs, Agatha wasted no time in introducing him to their illustrious guests.

'Darling, you haven't met my son-in-law, have you,' Agatha would say. 'This is Freddie. Freddie, this is Colonel Peregrine Fosset (or His Worship the Mayor of Worthing, or Dr Frasier, the Medical Officer of Health for Sussex),' and Freddie would shake hands before offering the colonel, or His Worship, or the doctor a drink. By the time the dinner gong sounded, Freddie had been invited for a game of golf, to look around the council chambers of the New Town Hall and to visit the local hospital. It was wonderful.

Agatha was the perfect hostess, and the meal that followed was the best that money could buy. The guests could choose from chicken breast basted with lemon and herbs, herb-rolled loin of pork, or roast sirloin of Richmond beef with Yorkshire pudding. For dessert the choices were French parfait, Manchester tart or summer fruits pudding with lemon cream and raspberry coulis, each one looking more tempting and delicious than the one before. Afterwards they were served coffee with handmade chocolate truffles. When the meal was over, people began to move around again; the women went off to the drawing room and the men to smoke a cigar.

Freddie had many useful conversations. For instance, he found out that the local scoutmaster was vehemently opposed to Hitler, calling him a 'jumped-up nobody', and the colonel was already putting in place a scheme to pull down a large estate of bungalows to hinder the invasion in Shoreham. Someone else mentioned a plan to blow up Worthing Pier to prevent alien troop ships from using it to bring their tanks and heavy armour ashore, should war be declared. He'd also been delighted when the leader of the Freemasons hinted that he might be able to secure him a meeting at the local Lodge. People like him had good contacts in the world of business. It was all going well. Who knows what else he might uncover.

As the evening wore on, the local folk club arrived with their instruments. The chairs were pushed back, and those who knew the old dances began with the 'Bridge of Athlone' before moving on to the 'Cumberland Square Eight' and the 'Gay Gordons'.

By the time the party ended around three in the morning, everyone agreed that the gathering at Muntham Court had far outshone every other.

Agatha went to her room, tired but contented. She had done them all proud, and everyone had been so appreciative that she couldn't help feeling smug about it. This was truly her forte, and she had missed being able to host lavish gatherings. It was what she was born to do.

Pearl was already asleep when Freddie finally came to their room. He sat at her dressing table for a while, jotting down a few pointers in his little red book to remind himself of what he had heard and overheard during the evening.

It had been decided that Seebold would return to the Wonderland on Monday. By then he would have spent almost three weeks in the cottage, and was anxious to get back to work. Lena would make sure he had enough food in his caravan larder, while Milly would take the bus over on Wednesday, her half-day, to check that he was managing all right. The pair of them had already spent the previous Sunday giving the caravan a spring clean, so they were confident that they had covered everything, which was why they all decided to make their last Sunday together a little bit special.

Nothing more had been said about Seebold between Milly and Lena, for which Milly was glad. Lena's revelation had come as a surprise – a nice one, but what could she do about it? A lot of water had gone under the bridge by now. How could she broach the subject? Perhaps she had left it too late and missed her chance.

Lena was a fantastic cook, so she prepared a roast dinner, and Milly made an apple pie. To walk off their meal, the three of them took Nipper along the lane over the hill and towards Long Furlong. It was a beautiful late afternoon and already the days were getting even longer. As they chatted about the Wonderland, Milly realised that Seebold was behaving as if this would be his last season. She sighed. An air of doom and gloom seemed to be hovering everywhere. The girls in Hubbard's talked about the prospect of war all the time in their tea breaks. Mary from accounts and Sonja from the beauty counter had both brought their wedding days forward. They were concerned that their fiancés might be spirited away by the navy and the army respectively, and who knew when they would see each other again? It was all very unsettling.

'What will you do if there's a war?' Milly asked Lena.

As a matter of fact, Lena had been finding out about what she could do. She didn't want to be in the battle arena, and she was too squeamish to be a nurse. She would definitely find out about homing pigeons, but she had also toyed with the idea of joining the RSPCA, because some propaganda was already making the British public aware of what bombing raids might do to beloved family pets. Leaflets had also been circulated advising people that 'in the event of war, a women's Land Army will be organised'. It went on to say that it would be a mobile force of women who would undertake farm work anywhere in the country. Although they would be employed by individual farmers, the organisation would supervise their accommodation and welfare. As Lena shared her scant knowledge about the scheme, Milly said indignantly, 'And so they should. I mean who would want some lecherous farmer wanting to share your bed?'

'Chance would be a fine thing,' Lena quipped.

Milly and Seebold laughed.

'What about you, Milly?' asked Lena. There was a twinkle in her eye. 'Are you still seeing Eustace?'

Milly shot her a look. Her sister knew perfectly well that her relationship with Eustace was well and truly over, and she certainly didn't want to talk about him – especially in front of Seebold.

'When do we get to meet him?' Lena continued as she raised her eyebrows.

Milly glared at her. 'You won't.'

'Who is Eustace?' Seebold wanted to know.

'Nobody,' said Milly. She was uncomfortable with this. Why on earth had Lena mentioned him? She knew very well that hell would freeze over long before she would see that creep again. Seebold was staring at her. 'I told you,' she said stiffly, 'nobody important.'

Seebold kicked at a broken branch.

They walked on in silence. The lane went through a small wooded area which was overgrown through lack of use. Just beyond the trees they could see the back of Muntham Court, and Milly felt the old familiar and distressing pang again. Why did her mother hate her so? What on earth had she done to make her feel that way? Even if her mother didn't want a mother–daughter relationship, they could still have some sort of relationship, couldn't they?

As the lane veered to the left away from the house, Lena suddenly pointed her finger and said, 'What on earth is that?'

Milly turned to look at something rather odd in the bank. Someone had cleared the brambles and ivy away from part of a door, but only the huge handle was visible. There didn't seem to be any brickwork, or perhaps that was behind the brambles, and the door seemed to be built into the hillock. If Lena hadn't had such a sharp eye, they would have walked past it, none the wiser.

'It looks to me a bit like an ice house,' said Milly, as Nipper came back and sniffed around.

'An ice house,' Lena repeated.

'In Victorian times every big house had one,' said Milly. 'They used to fill it with huge blocks of ice and store food inside. Funny, I thought I knew every inch of this place like the back of my hand, but I never knew this was here. It can't have been used for years.'

'Well, somebody's been here,' said Seebold. 'Look at all the footprints by the door. They're everywhere.'

'They're ours,' said Lena.

'That one isn't,' Seebold said stoutly, pointing to a large print just ahead of them.

'I guess somebody else must have come across it,' Milly suggested. 'That's probably why some of the ivy has been pulled away. It's no big deal. The people in the village sometimes walk across the hill as a shortcut.' She tried the door but it was locked.

They looked around for a key but couldn't find one. Milly tried the door again but it wouldn't yield. Nipper began to bark excitedly.

'I think we should turn back now,' said Lena. 'We don't want Seebold to get overtired.'

Also concerned that the sound of the dog barking might bring someone from the house, the three of them turned around and headed back to the cottage.

Inside the ice house, Freddie let his breath out slowly. Hell's bells, that was close. What a good job he'd bolted the door, and how fortuitous also that he'd heard them coming before he'd fired up the radio. If he'd had the earphones on, he might not have done so, and the sound of his voice would have given the game away. He could still hear the people outside, but their voices were becoming faint. He threw the monkey wrench back into the toolbox. As soon as he'd heard voices he'd snatched it up, knowing that if they had come into the ice house he would have had no hesitation in using it as a weapon. He waited a while to calm his breathing before he reached up and slid back the bolt. Opening the door silently, he stepped outside and looked down the lane. There they were. They all had their backs to him but he recognised them at once: his sister-in-law, the man he'd seen off the premises that time and the gypsy girl. He hurriedly pressed himself into the overhanging ivy as he saw one of them begin to turn

296

around. What should he do? They were a danger to his plans and much too close for comfort. He slipped back inside the ice house. From now on he would have to be more vigilant. For the first time in his life, he was doing something very important. Nothing and no one must be allowed to get in the way.

Chapter 36

Worthing was in a state of organised chaos. People were being kept well away from the centre of town because Captain Bailey of the Worthing Home Guard had instigated a full-scale exercise using personnel from Air Raid Precaution Group 2. The exercise area was between George V Avenue and Heene Road, up as far as the railway station at one end and down to the beach at the other. One hundred and sixty men and women gathered at 2.30 p.m. to play-act a major disaster. Imitation mustard gas bombs were set off at regular intervals. Fire engines raced to the scene and special constables patrolled the streets. On Goring Road, the pavement outside the newly built Sainsbury's food store was littered with 'corpses' while, a little further up the street, living 'casualties' with realistic-looking injuries were slumped at the bus stop and on the grass verge in various agonising-looking poses.

Along with several other employees from Hubbard's, Milly had volunteered to be a victim. A girl from Worthing Connaught Theatre had created a terrible 'open' wound on her leg and she was supposed to be in shock. Another girl had a 'broken arm' with the bone sticking through the skin. It was all cleverly done with nothing more than plasters, plasticine and cochineal, but everybody's injuries were so horribly realistic that – for the first time – Milly was confronted with the reality of what they all faced. God forbid, but if the Nazis should invade Poland and Britain declared war, she and the other inhabitants of Worthing might experience this for real, and most likely a lot worse.

'It's all a bit scary, isn't it,' said the girl with the 'broken arm'. 'The thought of going to war, I mean.'

Milly nodded grimly. 'Let's hope it doesn't come to that. Hitler could still make peace.'

The girl from the Connaught snapped her make-up box shut. 'And pigs might fly.'

Just after one o'clock, Milly and her companion were taken to an area near the end of Heene Road where they were told to lie on the edge of the gardens opposite Heene Terrace and wait to be found. 'A warning will sound.' The parting words of the officer who dropped them off were vague. Did he mean a warning would sound when the exercise started, or would it come when it ended? And did they still have to wait to be found if no one had come by that time?

As she lay in the shrubbery by an upturned seat, she rehearsed the rhyme which had been issued by the Home Office to help residents to understand what was going on.

Wavering sound – go to ground
Steady blast – raiders past
If rattles you hear – gas you must fear
But if hand bells ring – then all is clear.

But Milly had no idea which one to listen out for. She had the feeling it was going to be a long afternoon. A few passers-by paused to stare, and some people on the top deck of the bus waved but, apart from that, she was alone. The other girl had been left further up the road beside the pavement, next to an upturned pram which, fortunately, had no baby in it. At one point a man on a bicycle, alarmed to see the awful state of her 'broken arm', stopped to ask if he could help her to hospital. Milly heard the girl explaining that she was part of an exercise and the man rode off. Sometime later, the same girl was bundled into an ambulance, but still no one noticed Milly.

It was a little while later when Milly saw him. Pearl's husband. He was strolling along the walkway between the beach huts and the road. There weren't many people walking about today because there was a stiff offshore breeze which made it chilly. At first, he appeared to be just another visitor to the town, except that every now and then, he stopped to write something in a little notebook and then he'd put it back into his pocket. How strange. What was he doing? She frowned as a vague memory resurfaced. When she'd first met Eustace at Lady Verity's party, hadn't he said something about Freddie scribbling things into a notebook? Come to think of it, Eustace had a little rant about the same thing when they were out walking. So what did Freddie do all day? As far as she knew, he didn't have a job, and he certainly wasn't part of the exercise, and yet there he was, writing quite a lot into that notebook of his.

In the tranquillity of the garden, Milly started going over a few things in her mind. For a start, there was that business when he was chased by the swan. Eustace thought Freddie might have been photographing butterflies but the more she thought of it, the more Milly was convinced that his interest lay elsewhere. When he emerged from the undergrowth and headed for his bicycle, he had thrown something into the saddle bag. It had to have been a camera. Why else would he be making threatening gestures while she was giving evidence in court? Then there was that ice house. As they had walked away, she'd had a feeling they were being watched, though she hadn't mentioned anything to the others. The door was locked but somebody could have been inside and as she had glanced back, she thought she'd seen movement. At the time, she convinced herself she had imagined it, but now she felt differently. Milly cast her mind back to the first time she'd met Freddie at that party. She'd been impressed by his physique; even though he was covered by his shirt, she could tell that he exercised regularly. Could that mean that he was a member of some military movement? He was too old to be one of the Hitler Youth, but there were plenty of other Nazi groups. She frowned crossly. There was something else. Something niggling away at the back of her mind but she struggled to remember. What was it? And then it dawned on her. He'd clicked his heels, military style. She shivered. Surely that must make him . . .? No, she was being ridiculous, over-dramatic. He was just a polite German. They all did that, didn't they?

She forced herself to calm down. Things were bad enough between her and her sister. It would only make things a whole lot worse if she waded in with a half-baked idea that Freddie might not be all that he seemed. Perhaps she should speak to her mother first? She lay perfectly still as her brother-in-law turned from the seafront and walked up Heene Road. Where was he going? Milly was dying to get up and follow him, but she couldn't, could she? She was supposed to be a casualty.

Finally, after a long, cold wait, a car drew up and a man climbed out. 'Has anyone seen to you, love?'

Milly felt a bit of an idiot because she was in the middle of groaning with pain and holding her leg. The way he spoke made her sit up. 'No. I've been here for ages.'

'Okay,' he said. 'Hop in. We're done now. They're all having a cup of tea in Marine Gardens.'

Freddie dropped his wife at the junction of Oxford Street and Regent Street.

'I'll be back in a couple of hours,' he told her. 'Don't be late.'

Pearl gave him a perfunctory wave and disappeared

into the crowd. Freddie set off down Regent Street towards Piccadilly Circus. From there he headed towards Carlton House Terrace and Prussia House, which was close to Pall Mall. As he parked the car, he couldn't help noticing the smell of burning, and that the air was filled with small pieces of charred paper. It seemed to be coming from one of the chimneys. He mounted the steps and rang the bell twice before he pounded on the door.

It was several minutes before anyone opened the door, and even then the person on the other side only opened it a crack. 'Yes, what do you want?' he said in German.

'It's me,' said Freddie. 'I've come to see Christoph.' The door opened fully and he stepped inside. 'And you might like to know that the whole street is covered with burnt paper. I think your chimney is on fire.'

'It isn't,' said the man, whom Freddie recognised as Gunther, one of the junior secretaries. 'We are getting rid of papers.'

'But why?'

'You know how it works,' said the man. 'The British tell their people to leave Germany and then we tell ours to get out of the UK.'

Puzzled, Freddie followed him down the corridor. As he opened another door, for a second or two the people in the room froze. One of them was Christoph. The room was filled with smoke and the floor was covered with files. As soon as they saw it was only Freddie, the men continued to systematically empty the files and rip up the papers inside. The ripped-up documents were then piled next to the fireplace, where Christoph was throwing them onto the fire and stoking it, but the flat pieces of paper were reluctant to burn. Busy with their tasks, no one looked round at him. Freddie started coughing.

Christoph snapped his neck around. 'What do you want?' he asked irritably. 'Can't you see we're busy?'

'I need to talk to you,' Freddie spluttered. Christoph gave him an impatient glare. 'In private,' Freddie insisted.

His handler rose to his feet and another secretary took his place. The two men walked from the room and went next door.

'Well?' Christoph demanded as he helped himself to a whisky.

'I need to get away,' said Freddie. 'I must have diplomatic papers.'

'Don't be an ass,' said Christoph. 'I can't give you that.'

'But you have to,' Freddie cried. 'I've put my life on the line for you. If I stay here and they find out what I've been up to, I shall be arrested, put in prison – perhaps executed as an enemy agent.'

Christoph shrugged. 'You knew what you were doing,' he said coldly. 'Just sit tight. You'll be fine.'

'I don't think so,' Freddie said desperately. 'Look, I think someone may know about the ice house, and now that I've got all that stuff in there, what the hell am I going to do with it?'

Christoph downed his drink. 'I've told you. Just sit tight. Say nothing. Now, I have to get back to work. We've got to get rid of that lot before we go, and we've only got a few hours left.'

'You're leaving?' Freddie gasped.

'Tonight,' said Christoph, turning to leave the room. 'The bloody balloon's gone up. The announcement will probably come sometime tomorrow or maybe on Sunday.'

Freddie leapt in front of him. 'You can't leave me here,' he said desperately. His eyes were wild. 'You know who my uncle is. What's he going to say if you arrive in Berlin and tell him you left me to my fate?'

'I'm sorry but it's too late, old man,' said Christoph, his voice softening slightly. 'We've only got hours to get out ourselves. We're sailing from Harwich first thing in the morning.' He took Freddie's arm and ushered him towards the door. 'Look, if you want to come with us, go back home and tidy up any loose ends. There's a couple of ships heading for Holland tomorrow. We might be lucky enough to get you on board.'

'But I'll need tickets,' Freddie said desperately.

Christoph took in a breath as his nostrils flared. 'Gunther,' he shouted and, as the junior secretary appeared in the doorway, he added, 'You see to this, will you? Just give him what he wants.'

Out on the street, Freddie was so angry it took a few moments to collect his thoughts. He kicked himself that he'd left all his paperwork and his passport back home. If only he'd had them in his coat pocket, he would have simply left his wife and gone. Even now he toyed with the idea of going straight back to Worthing and telling his mother-in-law he was just popping out for a minute before disappearing for good. But then it occurred to him that she'd probably set up a hue and cry, which could mean he'd be stopped before he even boarded ship. Besides, Christoph said he should tidy up any loose ends, and he had one which was more than an irritation. Once that was sorted, he would be free to leave. Harwich was about three hours from London and the return trip to Worthing about the same. He glanced at his watch. There was still time to do it, if he could find Pearl quickly enough.

As luck would have it, when Milly knocked on the door of Muntham Court, her mother was alone in the house. After a lot of thought, Milly was sure she should tell her mother and sister of her suspicions. They might not listen; in fact they would most likely be horrible, but Milly knew she would never forgive herself if something happened to them because of her silence.

Agatha seemed far from pleased to see her daughter. 'What do you want?' she said curtly.

'I just wanted to see how you are.' They stood motionless, just staring at each other. 'Can I come in?'

Reluctantly Agatha stepped aside. The hallway was littered with suitcases.

'Going away?' Milly asked.

'Pearl's husband is taking us to his ancestral home in Germany.'

'Is that wise?' Milly blurted it out without thinking. Her mother gave her a cold glare. 'I'm sorry,' she added quickly. 'I didn't mean to interfere.'

'Then don't,' said Agatha, turning towards the sitting room.

'It's just that I worry about you and Pearl,' said Milly, following her. 'What with all this talk of war . . .'

'Freddie assures us that's just what it is. Talk.'

'When do you go?'

'Tonight,' said Agatha, pouring herself a whisky. 'We sail from Harwich in the morning.'

Milly stood with her mouth open. They were leaving the country and they hadn't bothered to tell her? How could they? 'When will you be back?' she asked faintly.

'Oh, we shan't,' Agatha said as she sat down and gracefully crossed her legs. 'Why should we? This country is finished.'

'How can you say that, Mother? This is where you were born. You do realise that Germany will soon declare war on Britain.'

'Don't be a fool, girl,' said Agatha. 'Herr Hitler has said on more than one occasion that if Britain rests with Germany, war will not come again.'

'What does that mean?'

'If we don't interfere,' Agatha snapped irritably, 'Hitler will not declare war.'

Milly closed her eyes. It was no use. Her mother was adamant.

'Anyway,' Agatha continued, 'we shall be fine. We shall live with Freddie. Did you know that he's a baron?' She paused, then added, 'Of course you did. So you can have your damned house back right now; no need to wait until you're twenty-one.'

Milly's throat tightened as she lowered herself down into a chair. 'Why, Mother?' she asked. 'Why do you hate me so much? What did I do to make you feel this way?'

Agatha gulped her drink in one go.

'Please, Mother,' said Milly. 'I have to know. Whatever it is, I deserve to be told.'

Agatha leaned back in her chair. 'I never wanted you in the first place. You were a means to an end, that's all.'

Milly blinked and pushed up her glasses. 'I-I don't understand.'

Agatha sighed. 'I married your father to secure a future for Pearl and me.' She reached for the cigarette box and took one out. 'I made sure I was already pregnant with you before we got married. I never loved Charles and he knew it but, fool that he was, he still took me on.'

Milly's heartbeat quickened. 'But you had Pearl before me. Why didn't you marry my father before she was born?'

Her mother put the cigarette between her lips and lit it. Blowing the smoke above her head she said, 'Since you've asked me, I may as well tell you everything.'

Milly could feel herself beginning to tremble inside. She was afraid and yet she had to know the truth.

'I was in love with Charles's best friend; the most wonderful man who ever drew breath. We were going to marry but the war came. He was killed.' Agatha's eyes moistened as she smoothed down the folds of her skirt. 'The army sent Charles to tell me. I was devastated, not only because Simon had died, but because by now I knew I was pregnant. I was well aware that my parents would disown me if they found out, so I went away to have Pearl. But when she was born, I knew I couldn't give her up. There was too much of Simon in her, you see. Charles kept in contact, but I needed more than that. I needed support, financial support, marriage.' Agatha rose to her feet and went to the window. With her back to Milly she said, 'So I let him seduce me, and when I was pregnant with you, Charles being Charles, he offered to do the decent thing.' She snorted. 'He always was a bit of an ass, wasn't he?'

Milly was staring at the floor. It all sounded so cold and calculating; so loveless. Her mother turned slightly. 'I loved Simon. I only ever loved Simon. When you were born, I made it clear I didn't want your father ever again, but I told him that if he wanted to be a part of your life, he would have to accept it.' She turned back to face Milly. 'And there you have it. You want to know why I was distant towards you? I only ever wanted it to be Pearl and me. I never wanted you in the first place. You were, as I said, simply a means to an end.'

A tear rolled down Milly's cheek and fell into her lap. In that moment she honestly thought her heart would break into a million pieces.

'I can't help what I feel, Millicent, but perhaps when I'm gone you can put all this behind you. After all, you will be a very rich woman.'

'Life isn't all about money, Mother,' Milly snapped.

'Oh, but to me it is,' said Agatha. 'Now you came here for something. What do you want?'

Milly rose to her feet. 'Nothing,' she said with what little dignity she could muster. 'Absolutely nothing.'

'Then I think it best if you leave now. We have nothing more to say to each other.'

Agatha followed her to the door. 'Goodbye, Millicent,' she said as Milly went through. 'Oh, and if you're going down to the cottage, tell that scruffy gypsy friend of yours to keep his dog under control, will you?'

Milly turned to retaliate, but the door was already closed.

Chapter 37

Seebold and Lena were both startled when Milly burst into the cottage. She was incandescent with rage, an emotion which they had never seen in her before.

'Whatever is wrong?' Lena cried.

Milly began to tell them but it took some time before they understood. As soon as she knew what had happened, Lena put her arms around her sister's shoulders, while Seebold sat staring into space. Both of them struggled with how horrible Agatha had been to her.

'Oh, Milly,' said Lena. 'I'm so, so sorry.'

All at once, Seebold got to his feet and dragged on his coat.

'Where are you going?' Lena asked.

'Up to the house to have it out with her,' he said angrily.

Lena followed him to the door. 'Best not,' she said calmly and in a low voice. 'Let it go.'

'Best not!' he shouted. 'That woman can say all that to her own daughter and you say to let it go?' He pulled the door open but Lena held onto his sleeve.

'You'l only make things worse,' she said desperately. 'Right now, your friend needs your comfort not your anger.' She felt the tension in his arm relax. 'She's hurt,' Lena went on. 'Stay with her. Help her, Seebold. We'll work out what to do afterwards.'

So he sat next to Milly and, trembling, took her hand, while Lena did her best to say something which might comfort her sister and make her mother's cruel words hurt a little less. Later, when things had calmed down a little, Lena made a point of reminding Milly how much their father had loved her; that he'd even given up a chance of marriage to the woman he loved to be able to have her in his life. Little by little, Milly began to look at things in a different way. The agony was still there but her two friends finally managed to convince her that Agatha was the one with the problem.

'She's a bitter, stunted and cruel woman,' Lena counselled. 'Don't let her rule your life any longer.'

'You deserve better,' Seebold said sagely.

For Milly the greatest torment was not being able to change anything. For years she had dreamed of the day when her mother would take her in her arms and say, 'Oh Milly, I've been so unkind to you and I am really, really sorry. Please forgive me. You are my daughter and I love you so much.' But now, of course, it was blindingly obvious that that would never happen. In one sense it was painful, but in another it was strangely liberating. She didn't need to spend any more time trying to make her mother love her, as now she knew for sure she never would.

Lena grasped her sister's hands. 'Just remember how much Pa adored you,' she whispered.

Milly looked up. 'Did he?' she said, her tone harsh and unbelieving.

Lena gave her a wounded look. 'Of course he did.' She paused. 'Surely he must have told you that in his letter.'

'I never read his letter,' said Milly.

'Why ever not?' Lena gasped.

Milly shrugged. 'I don't know. It never seemed to be the right time.'

'Look, why don't we talk to Nan?' Lena suggested. 'She's known you since we were just kids. You know how much she loves you. You're like a daughter to her.'

As soon as she'd said it, Milly longed for Nan's comforting arms around her. 'And bring Pa's letter with you,' said Lena. 'I haven't a clue what he might have said but I'm sure he would have been loving and kind.'

A little later, Seebold took both girls to Nan and Cyril's cottage at the bottom of Bost Hill in his lorry. Cyril had taken the bus to Horsham to see his sick brother and wouldn't be back until Sunday but, as usual, Nan was more than welcoming, and the two girls spent the late afternoon and early evening talking with her. 'All girls together,' the older woman said as she poured them tea. Milly was pleased to have Nan's wise counsel. And now that everyone was being honest, Nan admitted that there was no love lost between herself and Agatha but, for the sake of the girls, she had done her best to never let it show.

'It was the same with Mabel Cunningham,' she said. 'As far as we were concerned, your dear father was our employer. We always did our best to be there for his sake.'

'I had no idea,' Milly admitted.

'Of course, Mabel was better than me,' Nan confessed. 'She stuck it out a lot longer than I did.'

As they raked over the past, Milly began to understand why she had always been so close to Nan. The reason was quite simple, but it had never dawned on her before. Dear, sweet Nan had become a sort of surrogate mother, and now she understood that, Milly loved Nan all the more for it.

After they had comforted her, Milly decided to sit in the orchard where she could read her father's letter in private. They took a chair out for her and Nan made sure she was comfortable. As they left her, Lena gently rubbed Milly's arm and Nan squeezed her hand. 'It'll be all right, my dear,' she promised.

It was peaceful in the orchard. The dappled late afternoon sun was welcoming and only the sound of birdsong or the buzzing of an occasional bee broke the silence. Nan and Bodkin, the gardener from Muntham Court, were brother and sister, so when her father had arranged a new home for Cleo, the cat who had scratched Pearl all those years ago, this was where she had come. Every time Milly visited Nan in her school holidays, she and the old cat spent some precious times together until Cleo had died of old age the previous year. Nan's husband, Cyril, buried her under the apple tree in the orchard, the spot where she liked to sleep during the day. Now Milly sat under the same tree and leaned against the trunk as she finally opened the envelope she had been given the day they had buried her beloved father.

My darling Milly

I hardly know how to begin this letter because I know that if you are reading it, I am dead. Things will be difficult for a while but I don't want you to grieve too much for me, my darling. I had a good life and you were such a joy to me. I loved every moment I spent with you and I am so proud of your achievements. Something tells me that you will one day use your artistic talent in ways you never even dreamt of. But don't rest on your laurels, will you? Always work hard and aim for the next level, whatever that may be and wherever it takes you.

I am so sorry that your mother has been less than kind to you and I am also sorry that I didn't do more to stand up to her. But you must understand, my darling, that she has suffered too, and although it's wrong and hurtful to take it out on others, I hadn't the heart to cause her more grief. I am confident that you can be generous of spirit but, whatever happens, I counsel you not to become bitter or resentful. You have a sweet nature and I love your honesty and your openness. Please don't allow yourself to become harsh or vindictive.

You made me a very happy man when you welcomed your sister Lena so warmly. I leave this world content that you have each other and that your family ties are strong. I pray to God that, when the time comes, you will marry well. I may not be able to walk you down the aisle in person, but I will surely be with you in spirit. Tell your children of me, my darling. Say that as your father, I loved you with every fibre of my being.

May God bless and keep you.

All my love, Father

Lena had been right. Her father had loved her. Nan had been right too. It was all right. How blessed she was to have been loved by her father and now Lena and Nan. She would go back to them in a minute and say thank you. But for now, clutching the letter to her chest, Milly felt her anger dissolving as she finally gave way to her tears.

* * *

Later that evening, she had ridden Cyril's bike to the cottage. The chickens needed to be shut in the hen house and the rabbits put into their hutches. If he'd still been there, she would have asked Seebold to give her a lift but – exhausted by all the trauma – he'd already gone back to his caravan. As she arrived, it started raining, so she pulled a raincoat from the hook in the porch. Grabbing a handful of chicken feed to encourage them in, she put on the raincoat, the hood falling over her hair. As she tied the belt tightly around her waist, she didn't hear the person coming up behind her. The second she knew that she wasn't alone was when the heavy piece of wood came down on her head, but by then it was already far too late. The door of the cottage closed softly as her lifeless body fell to the floor.

Chapter 38

It was the low blue haze which first aroused curiosity. The driver of the Horsham bus noticed it as he drove past the end of the driveway, but of course being in his cab he was unable to mention it to anyone else until he reached the bus station.

A man on a motorbike turned his head towards the wooded area and smelled the smoke as he rode by. He would have stopped and investigated, but he was already very late for work. If he was hauled in front of the boss again, he'd be sacked for sure. Someone must be having a bonfire, he thought as he journeyed on.

The girls in the riding stables noticed that the horses in the top field were jittery and spooked, but again no one questioned the smoke. Perhaps the gardener in the big house was doing some woodland clearance. Lena hadn't come in that morning so they couldn't ask her.

'Better stick to the bridle path going west,' the riding instructor told their early morning customers. And when the group got back to the stables, they spoke of hearing the sound of animals in distress somewhere in the woods, which was why one of the girls decided to walk up the driveway towards Muntham Court. She returned a little later, running and shouting, 'Fire, fire. Lena's cottage is on fire,' and that's when everyone knew something was terribly wrong.

The people from the stables found the cottage well alight. The roof was ablaze, and tongues of fire filled the kitchen area. While someone ran back to telephone for the fire brigade, the other people from the stables set about moving the animals to safety. The chickens were crated up, the rabbit hutches were moved away from the smoke, and someone opened the pigeon loft. The birds flew out en masse and soared over the trees. As for the cottage itself, a couple of the men looked for a way to get in, but it was too risky.

'Do you think anyone is in there?'

No one had the answer, but a bicycle that they knew to be Cyril's leaned against the wall at the back. Could he be inside? The fire brigade arrived shortly after and everybody stood back as they turned on the hoses. When one fireman broke through the locked door, he found a body in the porch. They brought it out and covered it with a blanket.

'Who is it?' someone asked.

'No idea,' said the fireman. 'But it's a woman.'

The girls from the stables looked from one to the other, but nobody voiced the question on their lips. Was it Lena? Or Milly?

Someone said, 'You'd think someone would come down from the big house to see what was going on, wouldn't you?' So one of the younger girls ran to the ha-ha and on towards the house. She came back about twenty minutes later.

'There's nobody there,' she said breathlessly. 'I've been all round, but the place is shut up. They're all gone.'

'Go back to the stables and ring for the police,' the fireman said. 'There's sommat funny going on 'ere.'

Once the fire was under control, his men searched the cottage, but thankfully there was nobody else inside. All they had to do was the damping down and making sure the body was taken to the mortuary. As the sorrowful little group of mourners made their way back to the stables, Seebold's lorry thundered towards the cottage. He was distraught when he saw the state it was in, even more so when he saw the blanket-covered body being put into a hearse. 'Who's that?' he cried as he tried desperately to fight off the men who held him back. 'Who's under there?' he yelled.

'We don't know, lad,' said one of the fireman. 'You'll find out soon enough. The police will handle it from now on.'

The undertaker was driving off.

Seebold put his hands onto his head. 'No, no, wait a minute. I need to know. Is it Lena or Milly?'

PC Manville, who had biked up from the village, came over to him. 'Do you know who lives here?'

'Two girls,' someone else said. 'Sisters. Lena and Milly Shepherd.'

They all heard footsteps running along the path, then a woman burst through the clearing and screamed. As soon as he saw that it was Lena, Seebold sank to the floor, completely overwhelmed by his grief.

It had been a long and tiring journey, but when Agatha, Pearl and Freddie arrived at Harwich at eight-fifty in the morning, they hurried straight over to the waterfront. At the end of the previous year, Harwich had been in the public eye when 196 unaccompanied Jewish children fleeing the Nazi terror were brought to Britain for safe haven. It was an unusual place because no locomotives were allowed so, even in this modern day and age, goods were ferried about by horse-drawn trucks. The railway lines themselves went from Harwich Quay up to the Angel public house (a favourite meeting place for naval officers) and then on to Church Street. The Quay itself was the place where day-trippers took pleasure boats from the Ha'penny Pier.

Freddie had arranged that his wife and mother-in-law should have breakfast in the Great Eastern Railway Hotel, a Victorian building which dominated the waterfront. A sprawling edifice with fourteen or fifteen rooms on each of the three floors, the hotel had a dining room, coffee room, smoking room and a billiards room on the ground floor. As soon as his family were comfortably seated, Freddie went to the garage to sell the car, and from there to find their ship. There was plenty of time, he told himself. It didn't sail until noon.

The chap in the garage haggled the price down. Yes, it was a good car, but it was expensive to run. In the end, Freddie only got a third of the asking price. He wasn't very happy about it, but he had no other choice.

The whole quayside was teeming with people, so it took a while to find the ticket office. When he finally spoke to the clerk, Freddie had a terrible shock.

'Sorry, mate,' said the man, a flattened cigarette hanging from the corner of his mouth, 'there ain't no more ships.'

'What do you mean, "no more ships",' Freddie said indignantly. 'I have tickets. I booked them all yesterday. Look, look. You told me on the telephone. Sailing at noon.'

'They's all been can'sold,' said the man doggedly.

'Don't be ridiculous!' cried Freddie. 'They can't have been cancelled! I only booked them yesterday, I tell you.'

'Look, there's no need to get shirty wi' me, mate. I told you. Everyfing's been stopped on account of Adolf Hitler. If you ask me, there's goin' to be a war, so there's no way, not never, not no-how that you're goin' to get to 'Olland from 'ere.' And with that, the man pulled down the shutter with a bang.

One hundred and forty miles away in Findon, events at Muntham Court were moving on apace. Although a post mortem had not yet been conducted, the police suspected that the victim had been hit over the head, probably by

316

a piece of fence panel found on the grass near the front door. This, of course, made the cottage a possible murder scene. The body had been taken to the local mortuary, which was a pity because the girl who lived in the cottage turned up a few minutes after the hearse had gone and she might have been able to identify her sister. The chap with the lorry, a man with the inexplicable name of Seebold, agreed to take her to the mortuary, but now that would have to wait until tomorrow. The people from the stables had taken her in for the evening while the police began combing the area for clues.

Inspector Young and Constable Cox had walked up to the big house. It was all locked up and, as there was no sign of a key-holder, they forced the lock on the back door. It was clear that the owners had left in a hurry. Upstairs the wardrobes were empty, the doors flung open wide and articles of clothing scattered all over the place.

'Looks like they've done a runner,' said Cox. 'Who lives here anyway?'

'Charles Shepherd's widow,' said the inspector. 'And according to the women from the stables, her daughter is married to some German bloke.'

'Ah,' said Cox, as if that explained everything.

Everything in the house was perfectly normal, apart from one thing. An envelope marked *Two tickets for a ferry to the Hook of Holland* rested next to the condiments on the kitchen table. When the inspector opened it, inside he found a hastily scrawled note which said, *Thanks for the memory*.

The inspector glanced up at his constable. 'What the hell does that mean?'

Constable Cox shrugged. 'Buggered if I know, sir.'

Chapter 39

When the shutter went down, Freddie was left standing with his mouth open. He couldn't believe what had just happened. He had no intention of taking Agatha and Pearl with him, because the plan was that he should meet Christoph in Harwich, then Christoph would try and get him aboard a ship. So where was Christoph? Come to think of it, there was no sign of anyone from the embassy. Had they already gone? He could feel a rage welling up inside of him. Had they deliberately left him? That he was going to do the self-same thing to Agatha and Pearl was one thing, but to leave him behind after all that he'd done for the Fatherland – it was monstrous; unthinkable!

For a moment or two he was completely stunned. What should he do? Where should he go? He was on the horns of a dilemma. He couldn't stay in England. What would happen to him if they did declare war? If they found out what he had been doing, he'd be in big trouble or, worse still, hung. He felt sick to his stomach. Right now, he was so upset he couldn't even think straight. He had to make some other plan. Drive somewhere perhaps – Scotland or maybe Wales. Bloody hell – he'd just sold the car!

Back at the garage, the mechanic was unsympathetic.

'Sorry, mate, I already had a buyer lined up. He came almost as soon as you'd left. The car's already gone.'

With nowhere else to go, Freddie was forced to return to the hotel. What was he going to tell Agatha and Pearl? He'd only brought them along to humiliate them. When they all got to the gangplank, he would have turned to them and said, 'Show them your tickets then.' He'd enjoyed thinking about their expressions as they said, 'But you've got them, haven't you?'

'No,' he would say, 'I left them on the kitchen table for you. Don't tell me you didn't pick them up.'

It would have been a sweet moment.

Oh, why the hell had he let them come with him? It had delayed him, and now he was well and truly stuck. He should have just set off straight away alone in the night, then he wouldn't have had to face their questions either.

His wife and mother-in-law were sitting on a comfortable settee in the foyer when he got back. They were both looking up at someone. Freddie couldn't see who it was until he came round the side of a huge flowerpot with a massive aspidistra and by then it was too late. His heart sank as Agatha turned to him and said, 'This police officer says we have to go back home. There's been an incident.'

Freddie's face paled. 'An incident? What incident?'

'There's been a fire on your property, sir. A cottage has been badly damaged.'

Freddie decided to leg it. The policeman was the wrong side of fifty and very overweight. He turned sharply, but found himself facing another, much younger police officer. 'That's too bad,' he said, regaining his composure, 'but it doesn't really concern me. I'm sure my mother-in-law has already told you the property belongs to her.'

'To Millicent,' said Agatha.

Freddie blinked. 'You never told me that.'

'It was none of your business,' Agatha snapped.

'That may well be the case, sir,' said the constable, 'but that doesn't account for the body. It looks like there's been a murder.'

Freddie's jaw dropped. Agatha took in a noisy breath and Pearl fainted.

Seebold and Lena were still in a state of shock when they arrived at the mortuary in Broadwater. There was some paperwork that needed to be done and a police officer accompanied them down a corridor as they set off to view the body. As they drew nearer to the door at the end of the corridor, Seebold began to drag his feet. He stopped walking and shook his head apologetically.

'Sorry, Lena love. I know I'm being a wuss, but I can't. I can't look at her all dead. Not now . . . not yet.'

Lena was desperately upset as well, but she was clearly made of sterner stuff. She simply nodded and continued to follow the undertaker and the policeman.

Seebold sat on a chair in the corridor and, leaning forward, put his head in his hands. He closed his eyes. His chest felt like lead. He could hardly breathe. She'd died never knowing how much he loved her. He should have told her. Lena told him to tell her, but he was too afraid. What an idiot he'd been. He always thought having her close just as a friend was better than not having her at all, but now he wished he'd told her. He sensed a movement above him but he didn't look up. Then a soft voice said, 'What's going on, Seebold? Why are we here?'

The voice was hers, but it couldn't be her, could it. She was behind that door, under a sheet, all cold and dead. I'm hallucinating, he told himself. It's the grief.

But when he felt a light touch on his shoulder, he started. His head shot up and, as soon as he saw her, he cried out in shocked surprise.

320

At the same time, the mortuary door opened and closed and Lena came running towards them. 'Milly!' she said, her voice choked with emotion. 'Where have you been? Dear God in heaven. The body – we thought it was you.'

Seebold rose to his feet. 'I thought I'd lost you, duchess,' he said, grasping her hands. 'I couldn't bear it if I'd lost you.'

Milly frowned. His eyes were red-rimmed and puffy. He'd obviously been crying. 'I'm sorry. I stayed with one of the girls in Worthing last night.' She paused. 'I don't understand. Inspector Young came to Hubbard's and told me I had to come and identify a body. They said we'd had a fire and someone had been found dead. For one ghastly moment, I thought it was you.' She was looking at Lena. 'I've been out of my mind with worry. So who is it? And what were they doing in the cottage?'

They both turned towards Lena. By now she was visibly upset too. Milly's heart was thumping.

Seebold put his hand gently onto Lena's shoulder. 'Did you recognise the person?'

Lena nodded her head. 'It was Nan.' She gave an involuntary shudder. 'Oh Milly, poor Nan is dead. Someone banged her on the head and then set the cottage on fire.'

The next few hours were terribly painful for all of them. The girls spent the night with the people at the stables, then Seebold drove them back to Nan's cottage the next day. The worst thing was going to be having to tell Cyril. It was obvious that he was completely unaware of what had happened because he had been in Horsham visiting his sick brother.

When they all walked in, they knew Cyril was already back home. 'Come in, come in,' he said. He was twiddling with the radio knobs. 'Sit down. I'll soon have this thing working.'

'Cyril—' Milly began.

'Shh, girl,' he said. 'Mr Chamberlain is about to speak. Tell me what you've got to tell me when he's finished.'

The familiar voice of the prime minister came through the crackling radio.

'I am speaking to you from the cabinet room at 10 Downing Street. This morning the British ambassador in Berlin handed the German government a final note stating that unless we heard from them by 11 o'clock that they were prepared at once to withdraw their troops from Poland, a state of war would exist between us. I have to tell you now that no such undertaking has been received, and that consequently this country is at war with Germany.'

Cyril turned the radio off. Nobody spoke until he said, 'So that's it then. We thought it was coming and now it's here.'

Milly stared at her feet. War. What did it mean? How scary. She half expected to hear the thundering roar of aeroplanes overhead, but an uneasy silence filled the room. Now that there was a war, what should she do? Perhaps she should join up? She quite fancied the WAAFs but as yet she didn't know that much about them. She glanced at Lena and Seebold. If there was a war, they would be separated. They might not see each other for ages. She rubbed her forehead. There was too much going on right now to think clearly.

Lena felt a sense of relief. She had been wrestling with indecision for so long and now what to do with her life had been settled for her. The country was at war. She would have to do her bit. All that remained was to decide which bit. Should she join one of the forces or go for some sort of civilian post? She'd heard that the National Pigeon Service was recruiting people with homing pigeons, and she'd already contacted them. In fact, the official was coming to see her next week. Then she remembered the fire. Had the birds survived? And what about the hens and the rabbits?

Her breath caught in her throat. And what about poor old Nipper?

Lena glanced across at her sister and Seebold, and a cold shudder went through her body. War. People died in wars. Supposing . . . Dear God, it didn't bear thinking about, especially now that Nan had gone. She sighed. At least poor Nan had been spared that.

Seebold was filled with new resolve. He hadn't told the girls but he'd had a letter from the Home Office a couple of days ago. It was ironic really. All that plotting and planning around the wolf, all that ducking and diving, and now they'd written to tell him that all places of entertainment were to be closed forthwith. He'd been an idiot, of course. He knew that now. He'd risked the girls' reputations and nearly ended up in jail himself, and for what?

He'd already arranged to put everything into storage for the duration, and then he'd do what he'd always promised himself he would do. He'd join up. He'd prefer to do something involving an engine, spanners and oily rags, so maybe the Royal Engineers, or RAF ground staff, or maybe as a ship's engineer. That would be good. Ship's engineers worked on everything from ships to aircraft and submarines.

'I only just got back from Horsham,' said Cyril, breaking into their thoughts. 'My brother has been ill. Nan will be so pleased to see you, and she'll be right glad when I tell her my brother is on the mend at last. Sorry she's not here. She'll be at church, I expect. Never misses church, does my Nan.'

All at once Milly felt ashamed. Here she was thinking about herself and how the war would affect her when she still hadn't told Cyril why they were here. She took a deep breath. 'I think you'd better sit quietly for a minute, Cyril,' she said gently. 'We have something to tell you.'

* * *

323

Later, much later, they all sat in the kitchen, hardly knowing what to say. Soon after they'd told him, Cyril had gone to his room a broken man. Lena had got up to follow him, but he'd put his hand up. 'Just give me a minute, lass. Give me a minute.' And he closed the door.

Milly blew her nose. Seebold laid his hand on her arm and she gave him a weak smile. Cyril and Nan had been married for more than forty years, and they all knew he'd be completely lost without her. On top of all that, it didn't help matters to know that the country was at war.

Lena rose to make yet another pot of tea. She wondered, vaguely, why everyone thought a cup of tea would make any difference at a time like this; but they did, herself included.

'Why was she at the cottage anyway?' Seebold asked.

Milly shrugged. 'All I know is that she wasn't here when we got up Friday morning.'

Lena pushed a cup and saucer in front of Seebold. 'We thought she might have gone into the village.'

'I feel really bad about it now,' said Milly, 'but I didn't give it much thought. I had to go to work.'

'And I went to Frampton's to buy some chicken feed,' said Lena.

'Is there sugar in this tea?' asked Seebold.

Milly rose to get the sugar bowl and, as she did, she noticed a piece of paper which had fallen onto the floor by the dresser. Picking it up, she let out a gasp. 'Nan wasn't even here that night,' she said. She put the slip of paper onto the table in front of them.

Gone to shut up the hens.

'I suppose she could have left that before we got up,' said Lena.

Milly shook her head. 'If she wrote it in the morning, she would have said, "Gone to let the hens out." No,' she added bitterly, 'she left the note that night and we never even noticed it.'

'Don't be so hard on yourself, Milly,' Lena said gently, 'you were very upset about the conversation with your mother.'

'That must be why Cyril's bike was leaning against the fence,' said Seebold, having a lightbulb moment. 'She wanted to get there and back again before it got dark.'

They sipped their tea until Seebold said, 'Are you two staying here tonight?'

Milly looked at Lena and chewed her bottom lip. 'We forgot to ask Cyril. Do you think he'd mind?'

'You stay as long as you like, my dears.' The voice in the doorway made them all jump. Cyril stood there, red-eyed and looking exhausted.

Lena rose to her feet. 'Would you like some tea, Cyril? I've just made a fresh pot.'

'No, my dear,' he said. 'If you don't mind, I'm going to bed.'

Twenty minutes later, Milly walked with Seebold to his lorry. 'I'm sorry if I made a fool of myself at the mortuary,' he said sheepishly.

She squeezed his forearm. 'We've all had a very traumatic couple of days.'

It wasn't until he was at the Offington roundabout that it occurred to him that she might be thinking that he didn't mean what he'd said at the mortuary. He thumped the wheel in frustration. What an idiot. Why did he get so tongue-tied when he was with her? Why did he always mess things up?

Chapter 40

The letter had been addressed to the cottage so it was a couple of days before Mr Sewell, the postman, found out where Milly was staying and was able to deliver it to her. When she opened it, she had to sit down. It was from the Ministry of Home Security's Camouflage Directorate. Principal Salt had sent her painting, the one of the nightjar, along with a letter of recommendation, and she had been short-listed for an interview. If she was successful, they would contact her for a person-to-person meeting. Her hands were trembling. She felt elated and terrified at the same time. It would be hard to leave Lena and Seebold, but what an amazing opportunity this would be! She sighed. If only poor Nan had been here to see it. Milly felt her eyes stinging, but then she seemed to hear Nan's voice. 'Make the most of your opportunities, girl. They don't come round often.'

Milly took a deep breath. Yes, she would. This opportunity was too good to miss.

Agatha, Pearl and Seebold arrived back in Worthing two days later. Much to Agatha's disgust, they had been formally arrested on suspicion of arson and manslaughter when the Worthing police arrived in Harwich. The officers were too tired to drive all the way back the same day, so they had to wait in a police cell until the next morning. When they arrived back in Worthing, they were taken straight to Thurloe House in High Street and each put into a police cell. By the time they were interviewed the following day, Agatha was beside herself with rage. This was an affront to her dignity like no other.

'How dare they treat me like a common criminal!' she screeched when her solicitor arrived. 'Where's Inspector Young? He knew my late husband. Get Inspector Young here, this instant.'

But her solicitor was more circumspect and did his best to calm her down.

'It's no good going in there all guns blazing,' he said. 'Just answer the questions.'

'Don't be ridiculous! I had nothing to do with it,' Agatha shrieked.

'Then simply tell the truth.'

It was a harrowing day but, by four o'clock, she and Pearl had been released. Freddie was still in custody.

Agatha's main problem was where to go. Because she had been on her way to Germany, she had formally vacated Muntham Court. When she mentioned this to her solicitor, he had explained that – because the owner and her friend had lost their home – they would be moving into Muntham Court next week. 'Under the terms of my husband's will, she's not supposed to have that property until she's twenty-one,' Agatha spat.

'Under the terms of that self-same will, should you vacate the property, it's up to the Trustees to determine what happens next,' the solicitor reminded her. 'They have deemed that – under the circumstances – your daughter can make it her home.'

There was no way Agatha wanted to be under the same roof as Millicent and that creature, so she had no other choice but to find somewhere else – and she had less than a week to do so. Thus, Warnes Hotel along the seafront became her and Pearl's home while she worked out what to do. It was time to call in a few favours.

It wasn't until the following Wednesday that Bunny Warren offered her a workman's cottage on his estate for as long as she wanted it. It was a bit of a climb-down but Agatha accepted it as graciously as she could and, seeing as Pearl would be with her too, she was relatively safe from Bunny's advances. She even submitted herself to one of his wet kisses and allowed him to knead her breast to seal the deal.

Back at the house, she and Pearl were collecting the few things they had left behind. Her daughter seemed strangely quiet but that was hardly surprising with her husband still being held in a police cell.

It came as a shock when they found Freddie's note on the kitchen table. '*Thanks for the memory*,' Pearl read aloud.

'Can you believe the audacity of that man!' Agatha fumed. 'I wish I could wring his bloody neck.'

The note brought tears to Pearl's eyes. 'He had no intention of taking me with him, did he?'

'Well, he's locked up now,' said her mother. 'Let's hope they throw the book at him.'

The doorbell rang but, before she opened the door, Pearl peered through the glass. She came running back to her mother. 'It's Milly,' she gasped.

Agatha strode down the hall and swung the front door open. 'What do you want?' she said coldly. 'The solicitor says you don't move in until Monday.'

'Hello, Mother,' Milly said pointedly. 'I thought out of common courtesy I would ring the bell rather than walking straight in.'

'What do you want?' Agatha repeated coldly.

'I just came to say that you can both still live here if you want to,' Milly said calmly. 'There's plenty of room. Things have changed and I shall be moving myself shortly—'

'We don't need your charity, thank you very much,' Agatha interrupted spitefully.

Behind her back, Pearl looked crestfallen. 'But Mummy . . .'

Agatha was already closing the door.

Milly shrugged. 'Please yourself,' she said as she turned to go.

They buried Nan in Durrington cemetery. There was a large turn-out. Nan had been a friend to so many people. The hearse was so full of flowers that the undertaker had to ask the mourners themselves to take them up in their cars to the graveside.

The service had been held at All Saints Church in Findon Valley. Nan and Cyril had been going there ever since it had opened in 1934 when, alongside a small band of churchgoers, they had attended services held in what was a storeroom at the Highfield Dairy on Findon Road. The pair had been part of the group that had set about raising money for the building of a more permanent church, something that had been completed a couple of years later in 1936 when it was dedicated by the Bishop of Lewes. It was now packed with mourners but, even though he was surrounded by his friends, Cyril seemed to be a lonely man.

At the wake which took place in Cyril's cottage, Milly and Lena played hostess. When it was over, Cyril looked a shadow of his former self. It had been arranged that his recently recovered brother would take him back to Horsham with him for a few days' rest away from the cottage's memories.

Once Milly and Lena had cleared up and Seebold had taken borrowed chairs back to their owners, the three of them sat at the kitchen table over the inevitable pot of tea.

Milly took the opportunity to tell them about the Camouflage Directorate.

'Sounds amazing,' said Lena.

'You deserve it,' said Seebold.

They were both delighted for her, but she could still see their sense of loss.

Seebold stared into the depths of his half-empty cup. 'They tell me that Freddie has been charged with Nan's murder,' he said eventually.

'See, I don't understand that,' said Milly. 'Why on earth would Freddie want to kill Nan? He hardly even knew her.'

'Perhaps she found out something about him,' Lena suggested.

'Like what?' said Milly.

Lena shrugged.

Milly chewed the side of her cheek. 'There was always something about that man that made me feel uneasy, but I could never quite put my finger on it.'

'Like what?' said Seebold.

'Oh, I don't know,' said Milly. 'Little things, but they all added up.'

'Okay,' said Seebold, 'let's write them down.'

'Well, the first thing was that I saw him the day we collected your friend's old dog to take the place of the wolf,' said Milly. 'He was chased by the same swan.'

'I never saw him,' said Seebold.

'Because you were driving,' said Milly. 'The thing is, and I've asked myself the same question over and over again, what was he doing up there?'

'He could have been bird-watching,' said Lena. 'Maybe the swan had a nest nearby.'

'But he wasn't facing the river, was he?' said Milly. 'I'm pretty sure I saw him chuck something into the bag on the back of his bike. Could it have been a camera or some binoculars? I can't say for sure, but it looks like he could have been watching Lancing College, or maybe the flight path leading to Shoreham Airport.'

Seebold jotted this down on the back of an old envelope he'd found lying on the table.

'Then there was the incident with my bike,' said Milly. 'I nearly broke my neck when I fell off.'

'I agree that was strange,' Lena agreed, 'but how can you be sure it was anything to do with Freddie?'

Milly sighed. 'I can't, but I had spotted him taking photographs of the council workers in the Steyne. He couldn't get away fast enough when he saw me.'

'You never mentioned that,' said Seebold.

'Sorry, I thought I had,' said Milly. 'It was when they were building the underground public shelter and, although it's public knowledge, it just seemed a bit odd that he should take such a close interest.'

Lena pulled a face but didn't seem convinced. 'I may be playing devil's advocate, but aren't you reading a little too much into this?'

'I think it was the way he darted away that made me think it was a bit fishy.'

'Not much to go on so far,' said Seebold, making another note. 'He could have simply wanted to avoid you because of his mother-in-law.'

'He was scribbling something in his notebook when I was doing that Home Guard exercise the other day.'

'Something about you?'

'No, I don't think so. He didn't actually see me,' said Milly. 'I was in the gardens at the end of Heene Road trying to look as if I'd been horribly wounded by a mustard gas attack.' She paused. 'I suppose I've always been suspicious of him because I remember Eustace saying something really odd when I first met him at Lady Verity's party,' Milly went on. 'He said, "I wouldn't trust him as far as I could throw him."'

'What does that mean?'

'I don't know, but it wasn't exactly flattering, was it,'

said Milly. It crossed her mind whether to mention that she thought Eustace was nothing more than a pathological liar but decided that would only make Seebold dismiss the whole idea that there was something fishy about Freddie. 'Oh, and I've just remembered, I saw him on the Gallops when Miss Gerard from the library was showing me the tunnel they excavated.'

'A tunnel?' Lena gasped.

'They're hiding some of the town's historical treasures,' said Milly, 'in case of invasion. There's another secret hiding place in Carnegie Road Cemetery.'

'Well, they can't be much of a secret if both you and Freddie knew about them,' Seebold said with a chuckle.

'I was asked to help because my old art school want to protect a couple of their pictures,' Milly said stoutly. 'What Freddie was doing there was anybody's guess.'

'The evidence is very circumstantial,' said Lena, 'but, you're right, it is all adding up.'

'There's another thing,' said Milly. 'When we were walking near Muntham Court that time and we saw the old ice house . . .'

'Yes, and some of the brambles had been cleared,' said Seebold.

'And I tried the door, remember?'

'I remember,' said Seebold, 'but it was locked.'

'That's just it,' said Milly. 'The more I think about it, the more positive I am that it was locked from the inside.'

'Locked from the inside?' said Lena. 'What does that mean? If a door is locked, it's locked.'

'When I tried that door,' said Milly patiently, 'the lower part of it moved. I think we couldn't get in because it was bolted on the inside at the top of the door.'

'Which means . . .?' said Lena.

'Which means someone was on the inside,' said Seebold.

'Look, I know you're sceptical,' said Milly, 'but when we

were walking back, I turned around and I thought I saw something.'

'What?' said Lena.

Milly frowned awkwardly. 'I'm not sure – a movement. It was only for a second, but it was definitely something – or someone – moving by the ivy around the door.'

They were quiet for a minute or two, each trying to digest what was being said.

Seebold glanced up at the clock. 'There's nothing to stop us going back up there and taking another look.'

'What, now?' asked Lena.

'Why not,' he said. 'We've still got three, four hours of daylight left. Let's take another look and find out if Freddie is hiding something up there once and for all.'

It was a pleasant evening. Nipper came too, glad to stretch his legs. Seebold drove them as far as Long Furlong and then they hiked over the hill towards the back of Muntham Court. When they reached the track leading to the ice house, it was noticeable that there had been a lot of recent traffic. Not motor vehicles, but there were a great many more footprints and scuff marks.

The door was still partly covered in ivy and brambles, but now they only hung over it from above. Seebold tried the handle but the door was firmly locked.

'The bottom of the door didn't move that time,' Lena observed.

Milly had to agree. 'Maybe I imagined it.'

'Where's the key?' he said dully.

They hunted around, under stones and in nooks and crannies, but to no avail. The girls turned to go.

'Hang on a minute,' said Seebold. 'Milly, now that your mother has moved out, you own this place, right?'

'It was always her place,' said Lena. 'Just not officially until she turns twenty-one.'

'And I'm not twenty-one for a couple of years yet,' Milly reminded them.

'But the Trustees say you can live here if you want now that your mother has vacated it,' said Seebold.

Milly nodded.

'So I'm asking you, as the owner of this land: do I have your permission to break this door down?'

Despite being extremely old, the door didn't yield easily. Seebold had to use a stone to bash the lock until part of the frame splintered, then at last it swung open.

It took a moment or two to get used to the dim interior, and then they began to look around. On a small desk, they found writing paper, envelopes and pens. In a drawer there were some photographs but, without light, it was impossible to see what they were. Seebold walked around the perimeter of the room, searching for a light switch. There didn't appear to be one, but there was a Tilley lamp and some matches on a shelf. As soon as he lit it, the room was flooded with a low yellow light and the girls continued to sift through what was on the desk.

Seebold put the lamp down and went to the back of the room. There, on top of a wooden crate, was a radio receiver. Milly took in her breath noisily.

'Oh, my Lord!' Lena cried. 'Is that what I think it is?'

Seebold nodded. 'It bloody is. It's a radio. You're right, Milly. The man has got to be a spy.'

He ran his fingers over it and, as soon as he'd worked out how to switch it on, he began fiddling with the knobs. 'See what else you can find.'

The first thing the girls noticed was a little red book at the back of the desk. Lena flicked through the pages. 'It's just names,' she said. 'Loads and loads of names.'

Milly leaned over her shoulder. 'Kressman Dryden, he's the local verger,' she said pointing her finger. 'Sir Maurice Shearsby, that's Lady Verity's husband.'

'There's a little star next to his name. What does that mean?'

Milly shook her head. 'There's another star next to that name. What's that written underneath?'

Lena turned the book around. 'Jew lover.'

The two girls looked at each other in horror. 'You don't think . . .?' Milly gasped.

'I think perhaps I do,' said Lena.

Seebold was working his way along the wall. Whoever had been in the ice house had also been using it for storage. There were several bulky-looking objects under dustsheets. Seebold pulled off a cover to reveal an oil painting. 'Just look at this.'

Because there wasn't much light, the painting was unrecognisable. There were others behind it.

'Why are these in here?' Lena asked. 'Do you think they could be part of some sort of eighteenth-century smuggling haul?'

'They're much more recent than that,' Milly cried. 'I recognise the picture behind that big frame. It comes from the art college. It's one of the treasures I helped to put in the secret hiding place on the Gallops. Somebody obviously found it and nicked it – it was definitely put into the tunnel before it was sealed up. I was there when they did it.'

Milly and Lena stared at each other with the same name unspoken on their lips. They all jumped as the radio suddenly crackled into life. They had no idea what was being said, but the voice was guttural and distinctly German in origin.

All at once a shadow fell across the doorway, blocking the light. 'Right, you lot,' a man's voice said. 'Come on out of there. This is the police.'

Chapter 41

'Is that you, Inspector Young?' said Milly, recognising his voice. 'It's Milly and Lena Shepherd and Mr Flowers. Before we come out, you might like to come in here and see what we've found.'

The inspector and Constable Cox stepped into the ice house, and Milly wasted no time in explaining what the three of them were doing, and in showing them the notebooks, the photographs and the stolen paintings.

'Go back to the house and get on the blower, Cox,' the DI said curtly. 'Tell them to send a couple of cars and get someone from Scotland Yard to come down here. I hate to think what this man's been up to.'

'Anyway, what are you doing here, Inspector?' asked Milly.

'We had a telephone call from your mother,' he said. 'She and your sister heard intruders in the grounds.'

'My mother is in the house?' Milly gasped.

'Come to collect the last of her things before she and your sister move.'

If Milly was irritated by that, she didn't show it. She thought her mother had cleared everything out before Nan's funeral, but it didn't really matter.

They secured the door of the ice house as best as they could, although no one was really worried that anyone would tamper with the things inside. Nobody came this way, unless they either lived or worked in the house, and Freddie was still under lock and key. After that they went down to Muntham Court.

As soon as Pearl opened the door, the inspector walked in. 'No need to worry, miss. The intruders turned out to be your sister and her friends having a wander round.'

As the others walked in with Nipper trailing behind them, Agatha leapt to her feet.

'What do you want?'

'If I could have just a moment of your time, madam,' the inspector began. 'I should like to ask a few questions, then we can all be on our way.'

Agatha pointed at Nipper. 'I won't have that thing in the house,' she said, opening the French doors. 'Tell it to get outside.' Nipper was banished to the outside patio.

Agatha wasn't very pleased to see Milly either, and she made it plain by completely blanking her. Once upon a time it would have really upset Milly, but now, although it was still painful, she was in a better frame of mind. She made up her mind not to let Agatha get under her skin. Easier said than done, but she would give it a go. Her mother sat in a languid pose in the armchair, smoking a cigarette, while Pearl, who had just put a cake onto a small table, stuck her nose in the air. The cake knife clattered from the plate onto the floor, but Pearl ignored it and, deliberately standing with her back to Milly and Lena, looked out of the window.

'Now,' the inspector began again. 'Perhaps you wouldn't mind clearing up a few things?'

Agatha sighed impatiently.

'Can you tell me what your husband did all day, Mrs Herren,' the inspector asked Pearl. 'Was he in the habit of meeting with any enemy aliens?'

'Certainly not!' Turning abruptly, Pearl continued, 'I don't know what you mean, Inspector.' And glaring at Milly she added, 'What's she been telling you?'

'Nothing,' said Inspector Young. 'I just asked you a simple question. Your husband didn't work, so what did he do all day?'

'He did the sort of thing any gentleman would do,' Agatha interrupted as she straightened the folds of her skirt. 'He went to his club, he met important people, and he sometimes went up to London on business.'

'What sort of business?'

'I don't know,' Agatha said irritably.

The inspector turned back to Pearl. She shrugged. 'Sometimes when we went up to London he would have an appointment at Prussia House,' she said, adding smugly, 'My husband knows some very important people.'

'Prussia House?' the inspector said softly. 'That's the German Embassy, isn't it?'

'What of it?' Pearl snapped. 'My husband's business is my husband's business,' she protested. 'He never took me there, if that's what you mean. He would drop me off in Oxford Street to do some shopping, and then meet me later on.'

'Hmm.' The inspector looked unimpressed.

Agatha sat up. 'Look here, Inspector. I don't know what you're implying, but my son-in-law was the equivalent of royalty back in his own country. A baron, no less. He had what they call a *schloss* in Berlin. That's a castle, you know. Berlin Schlossplatz. It's very well known, so I'm told. It was once the winter palace to all the old kings and kaisers.'

'The Berlin Schlossplatz,' Constable Cox spluttered.

'I don't suppose someone like you would have even heard of it,' said Agatha cuttingly. 'It dates back to the fifteenth century.'

The constable puffed out his chest. 'Oh, I've heard of it

all right, madam,' he said. 'My old dad talked of nothing else when I was a kid. He was in the Great War and stationed in Germany after it finished, and I can tell you now, your son-in-law, Mrs Herren's husband, never lived there.'

Agatha's face clouded. 'How dare you! You jumped-up little so-and-so! What are you insinuating?'

'I'll thank you to tone down your language, madam,' the inspector cut in.

'I'm not insinuating anything, madam,' the constable continued, 'but your son-in-law never lived there because when Germany lost the war and the Kaiser abdicated, Berlin Schlossplatz became a museum.'

The room went very quiet.

'And you're sure of this, Constable?' the inspector said.

'As sure as I'm standing here, sir. My old dad never wanted to go to war. He was a pacifist at heart. For him, making a museum out of a palace was the best thing that ever happened to him.' He turned to Pearl. 'So you see, your husband never lived there, not unless he was the janitor's son, of course.'

Agatha bristled. Pearl lowered herself into a chair.

'Oh dear,' said Lena, suppressing a grin.

'And you needn't look so smug,' Pearl snarled. 'There's obviously been a mistake.' She turned her head, muttering, 'What would you know about anything anyway? You're just a common gypsy.'

'Now just a minute,' Lena flared, but when Milly put her hand on her arm, she held back.

'You make me sick,' said Pearl, rounding on the pair of them. 'Rubbing my nose in it just because you've got that cottage. I'm the oldest. It should have been mine.' She tossed her head. 'Well, you haven't got it any more, have you.'

The inspector raised his hand. 'That's enough, ladies. There's no need for a spat, but I am going to have to ask you all to come back down to the station for questioning.'

'What, *now*?' Agatha squeaked.

'Considering the time of day,' he began, 'I think perhaps you and your daughter could come tomorr—'

'It was you. You did it,' Milly interrupted as she pushed up her glasses. She was staring at her sister. 'You killed Nan and started the fire.'

'Don't be ridiculous,' said Pearl. 'Why on earth would I want to kill Nan?'

'You didn't.'

With an exasperated expression on her face, Pearl threw her arms in the air and appealed to her mother. 'Mummy . . .'

Agatha sat up straight. 'Do we have to listen to this nonsense, Inspector?'

Milly looked at the puzzled faces around her. 'She didn't want to kill Nan. She didn't know Nan would be there. That part was an accident. But she started that fire. I'd stake my life on it.'

Pearl scoffed. 'You're mad.'

'So if she didn't deliberately set out to kill Nan,' Lena interrupted, 'why did she hit her violently?'

Milly looked at Pearl steadily. 'Because she thought Nan was me.' Her sister didn't flinch. 'She was jealous of my inheritance. She wanted her revenge.'

'Now that I think about it,' said Lena, 'Nan was wearing your old coat, so if she had her back to Pearl . . .'

'I tell you, I wasn't even here,' Pearl protested angrily. 'I was on my way to Harwich when the fire broke out!'

Milly turned away. Yes, she was right about that. Seebold had said when he and the fireman had talked it over, they'd all agreed that the fire must have burned for some time before anyone noticed, but the three of them – Agatha, Freddie and Pearl – would have left Findon hours before.

'Did the firemen say how the fire started?' Lena asked.

'Not really,' said the inspector. 'I haven't had the official report yet but there was some discussion that it might have been a childish prank gone wrong.'

'I heard that,' said Seebold.

'Well, there you are then,' said Agatha. 'It can't be one of us. It must have been someone from the village. We don't have any children around here.'

'Hang on a minute,' said Seebold. 'The arsonist didn't need to have been here when the fire broke out.' He looked directly at Agatha. 'What if he – or she – had set up some kind of delayed fuse?'

'And why would you say that, sir?' said the inspector, his eyes narrowing.

'Because I saw the firemen with a tin they'd found under the eaves,' said Seebold. 'I didn't give it a thought at the time, but now it makes sense. You stuff some old rags in a tin with some linseed oil; give it a few hours to warm up, and poof!'

'Well, that lets me out,' said Pearl. 'I wouldn't know where to start with that one.'

'I remember you mucking about with something like that when we were little,' said Milly idly.

There was an ominous silence. Everybody stared at Milly. 'Didn't Daddy have an old book warning of the dangers of fire?'

'What book?' said Lena.

'I don't remember the name of it,' said Milly, heading for the big bookcase, 'but I'll know it when I see it.'

'Don't be stupid,' Pearl snapped, as she put herself between Milly and the bookcase. 'Our old books were chucked out years and years ago.'

'Oh my goodness,' said Milly, pointing over her sister's shoulder. 'There's that book of spells you used when we were kids.'

'Stop making such a damned fool of yourself, Milly,' Pearl spat as she batted her sister's hand away from the shelf. 'I said leave it!'

The inspector went behind her to reach up and pulled down a leatherbound book. 'Is this the one you mean?' They saw him looking carefully at the title. '*Witches, Spells and Folklore*. Ummm, interesting.'

The book next to it had fallen down. He went to set it upright, but then a lacrosse stick perched on top of the books slid towards the floor. Pearl seemed agitated. Something had attracted the inspector's attention. 'Give me your handkerchief, Constable,' he said, standing over the stick so that no one could touch it. 'That looks like dried blood to me. Looks like we might have found the murder weapon.'

Milly gasped, while Pearl gave her a stony look which would have curdled milk.

Between the two of them, the inspector and the constable wrapped the handle of the lacrosse stick in the clean handkerchief. 'When we get back to the station, get that finger-printed,' the inspector said, 'and check the blood.'

Constable Cox nodded.

Everyone was distracted by the sound of a car pulling up on the gravel outside and Nipper, who had been lying with his head between his paws on the patio, stood up and barked. Leaving the lacrosse stick in the care of his constable, the inspector went into the hallway and opened the front door, as a policeman climbed out of the car. 'Only one car, Hawes?'

'Detective Sergeant Drummond is just behind me, sir.'

They were interrupted by a bloodcurdling scream coming from the sitting room. The inspector rushed back inside, closely followed by Hawes and DS Drummond. At the same time, Nipper had come through the front door and pushed his way into the hall between their legs. Constable Cox was lying on the floor. He was out cold, and Pearl, the lacrosse stick in her hand, stood over him.

Seebold had positioned himself in front of her and stood

with his hands outstretched. 'Calm down, miss,' he was saying. 'Give me the stick.' Nipper rushed into the room and began to bark.

Pearl dropped the stick with a clatter.

'She just hit the poor man and knocked him out,' Lena gasped as she grabbed the dog's collar.

As the other policemen piled into the room, Pearl grabbed the cake knife she had dropped earlier and launched herself at Milly. Lena shouted, 'Look out!'

All at once, Milly was pushed violently against the chest of drawers by Seebold's bulk as he put himself between the two girls – which meant that Pearl plunged the knife into his shoulder rather than Milly's chest. He let out a yell and his body curled downwards but he didn't fall. Nipper barked like mad as Pearl brandished the knife again, this time aiming for Milly's throat. Before they knew it, the dog had broken free and hurled himself at her, knocking her off balance and giving the other constable a chance to grab her arm and pull her away. As she dropped the knife, the policeman swung her across the small table, knocking the cake to the floor. Having pulled Pearl's other arm behind her back, the policeman locked on his handcuffs. 'You are under arrest for attempted murder,' he began. 'You do not have to say anything . . .'

Pearl threw back her head and began to laugh; a high-pitched cackle that sent shivers down everyone's spine. They were all stunned by what they'd just seen, then Milly let out an anguished moan. Seebold had crumpled to the floor, the blood seeping across his shoulder blade and soaking his jacket. Milly grabbed a cushion and pressed it over the cut, while Lena reached for the telephone to ask for an ambulance.

Apart from lifting her legs slightly to get out of the way of tumbling figures, Agatha remained in her chair, watching the proceedings, apparently devoid of all emotion.

She was the only one of them to notice the dog making short work of the cake.

It was two in the morning. Seebold appeared to be asleep. They had taken him to Worthing Hospital and, after examination, the doctor deemed his wound was largely superficial. However, one part of the cut across his shoulder had needed stitches. After he'd been patched up, they decided that he should stay in overnight. While Lena returned to Nan's cottage to look after her animals, Milly waited in the corridor until the nurse came to say he was back from the treatment room and on the ward.

He looked very peaceful. It was unusual for her to be able to look at him at such close quarters without him seeing her. Someone had pushed his hair back off his forehead and she found herself coaxing a tendril towards his face. It always looked so much more attractive that way. She was looking at his mouth. What would it be like if . . .?

When he opened his eyes and looked at her, Milly felt her cheeks flush. 'You saved my life,' she whispered.

'I would gladly die for you, duchess.' His voice was croaky, as if his throat was dry. He turned his head towards the locker by his bed where there was a jug of water and a glass.

'Do you want a drink?' she asked.

He nodded and heaved himself up on one elbow. As she gave him the drink, his hand covered hers on the glass. Her heart was racing, and a feeling she had never experienced before almost overwhelmed her.

'Thank you,' he said, sinking back onto the pillows. 'I think they've given me something. I feel very sleepy.'

She forced a smile. 'I'll leave you to rest.'

She had begun to rise but then he opened his eyes and said, 'No, please don't go. I like having you here.'

She lowered herself back into the chair and he took her

hand in his. They looked at each other but neither of them spoke.

Eventually he murmured, 'I don't know what to say.'

'Neither do I.'

'I love you, duchess,' he whispered. 'But I have nothing to offer you.'

'Do you really think I care about that?' she said, her head close to his.

'I want you to have good things,' he said sleepily. 'I want to give . . .'

She put her finger over his lips. 'Shh,' she whispered. 'You've already given me something wonderful. Something I haven't had, or at least, not for a long, long time.'

He seemed puzzled.

'You've just told me you love me,' she said. 'I didn't know. I've been so blind. It never occurred to me that you felt the same way I do.'

He tried to pull himself up on his elbow again but failed miserably. 'You mean . . .?'

'Yes, yes, my darling, she whispered. 'I love you too.'

The moment was magical, but soon Milly heard the sound of Seebold's snores as he had drifted back to sleep.

Chapter 42

October 1939

Milly went over and over the letter when it arrived from the Civil Defence Camouflage Establishment. She had made it through the selection and had been offered a face-to-face interview on Friday 13 October, but now that it was something concrete, part of her held back. It was obvious that if she acted upon this, her life would be changed for ever. It would mean a move far away from Worthing and her sister. Now that she and Seebold were together, she couldn't bear the thought of being away from him either. And yet, even as she pondered the problem, she knew in her heart of hearts that – because of the present situation – they couldn't be together in the conventional sense of the word. The country was at war. Any moment now Hitler might send his mighty army across the Channel to smash all that was near and dear to them. Now that Poland had fallen, it seemed there was no stopping him. Of course France and the Netherlands would be the first in line, but if these fell then he would set his sights on the British Isles. Everyone in the country was holding their breath. What future now for a young couple hopelessly in love?

She and Seebold had talked for hours. 'I reckon it'll be all over by Christmas,' he'd said.

'Then perhaps joining the unit is not worth the bother.'

'It's up to you, darling, and I'll totally support whatever you decide, but I think we all need to show Hitler we mean business. He's less likely to go that one step further if we're all ready to meet his threat.'

It was for that very same reason Seebold had joined the army, and right now he was in Durham, doing his basic training. It had been agony saying their goodbyes, and even now Milly felt teary as she remembered the moment his train pulled out of the station. She knew at the time that they wouldn't be together for at least six weeks, but seven and a half weeks had passed already and he still wasn't back. She'd written every day, but he'd only managed to scribble the odd note to say that he still loved her. He was so busy he barely had time to think, the army demanded so much from him. His all too short letters had been censored, but from the bits that had escaped the black pen, she gathered that his days were taken up with learning to use a rifle, lots of marching and not having a lot to eat. She'd smiled at that last bit. Poor Seebold. He always enjoyed a healthy appetite.

Milly's letter was an invitation to go to Leamington Spa for an interview. Her geography was woefully lacking, but it didn't take long to discover that she had to go to Warwickshire. She set off from Worthing Central. The journey took four hours and involved lots of changes: Worthing to Barnham, Barnham to Southampton, Southampton to Leamington Spa. The trains were packed, mostly with service people or young men who were joining up. She was lucky enough to get a seat with each change, but some poor souls only had their kitbag to sit on in the corridor. Left to her own thoughts, she relived some of the wonderful times she'd had with Seebold before he went for his basic training. Long walks up Cissbury Ring and the Gallops; early evenings sitting on the beach before they started putting up barbed-wire sea defences;

bumping along in the passenger seat of his lorry while he took the last of his fairground equipment to a prospective buyer. She closed her eyes as she recalled the warmth of his kisses and the times when her heart raced if he touched her hand or interlaced his fingers with hers. *Oh Seebold. I miss you so.* She dozed for a while but, as the day wore on, she had to fight her sleepiness. All the station signs had been taken down in case of enemy invasion, and so she needed to be alert or she'd miss her stop. At around midday they pulled into a station, and to her relief she heard one of the station staff shouting, 'Leamington Spa, this is Leamington Spa.'

The station itself was beautiful. Completely refurbished only a couple of years before, it was a refreshing change from the old Victorian stations she was used to. Built in an Art Deco style with clean lines and geometric shapes, the waiting room had parquet flooring and a simple marble fireplace under a GWR mirror. Before she set off for her appointment, she sat in the ladies' waiting room and ate her sandwiches. There had been little opportunity to eat on the journey. How could she, when there were seven of them wedged on the carriage seat made for five. She could hardly move her arms. Having taken a minute or two to freshen up, Milly went on her way with the map she had been given to find the HQ of the Camouflage Unit in the Regent Hotel on the Parade.

She was surprised to find it was only a stone's throw away from the station. From there she was taken by taxi to another location, which was in a two-storey building with a flat roof. All the windows were boarded up and to any passers-by it looked as if it was ready for demolition. When she knocked on the door, Milly was totally taken aback when it flew open, and she was facing none other than Stanley Richardson.

'Oh!'

'Miss Shepherd,' he said kindly. 'I'm so pleased you could come.'

As Milly shook his hand, she was more than a little taken aback by the warmth of his welcome, especially when she considered how unpleasant he had been when Eustace had taken her to his studio in London.

He must have noticed her trepidation. 'Firstly, I feel I owe you an apology,' he began. 'The last time we met, I was annoyed that Eustace had brought you to the London studio. Constant visitors disturb the artists' concentration and, quite frankly, I had had enough of it. That said, I was rude to you, and for that I am truly sorry.'

Milly gave him a courteous nod.

He continued. 'I had no idea of your talent, but when Principal Salt sent your portfolio, I must say I was very impressed.'

Milly felt her face colouring as she thanked him.

'So . . .' he said, letting out a satisfied sigh, 'without further ado, let me show you around.'

He took her along a corridor and into a larger room which, though dimly lit, was a hub of activity. The people inside, mostly men but she spotted two women, were huddled over their desks, either model-making or apparently experimenting with colours on large canvases.

'We're still relatively new to this game,' Stanley continued, 'but our designers and technicians work on all aspects of civilian camouflage. The sole aim of this unit is to find ways of disguising key bombing targets should the worst come to the worst. When I first met you, you had mentioned your understanding of camouflage in the natural world, and since seeing your work on this, I am sure you would be a great asset to the team.'

As they walked around the building, Milly saw people working on things like giant nets which would be draped over buildings, and model-makers who were working out the best colours to use when painting fake road markings onto rooftops. They were obviously hoping to fool enemy planes into believing they were flying over the countryside rather than an area littered with factories. Though the gravity of the work was a bit scary, it was also exciting and inspiring, and everybody seemed friendly and helpful.

'If I come here to work, Mr Richardson,' Milly eventually asked, 'will I be asked to sign the Official Secrets Act?'

'Oh no, my dear,' he said. 'We want the public to understand what we are doing. Up until now there has been an unholy clamour to include buildings which it is not necessary to protect, so the powers-that-be feel that the more the public understands about camouflage and why we do it, the better. We want them to be supportive rather than critical.'

She hesitated. 'I shall need somewhere to stay.'

'We have a house just down the road,' he went on. 'You would have your own room and board. And while we're on the subject, we will pay you £200 a year, less thirty bob a week for board and lodging.'

Of course, the men in the room would most likely be getting at least a third more (that was the way of the world), but she would still be getting a good wage. If she came here, and it was until Christmas, she could save quite a bit towards her marriage.

They had reached the door.

'Do you have a place to stay tonight?' he asked.

'I'm catching the train back home,' she said, glancing up at the clock. 'There's one at five-ten and the last one is at six-fifty.'

'Then I shall run you to the station myself,' he said with a smile. 'We can't have you stumbling about in the pitch black on your own, can we?'

She arrived at the station in good time.

'I hope you enjoyed your visit, Miss Shepherd,' he said as she climbed out of the car.

'I certainly did, Mr Richardson,' she said and, as she went to close the car door behind her, Milly hesitated for just a second before she added, 'and I should very much like to work with you.'

Strangely enough, Lena was in Horsham having an interview herself. In the capital in September there had been an air of panic. Although the National Air Raid Precautions for Animals Committee had produced a leaflet advising people that if they couldn't send their pets to the country, the kindest thing would be to have them put down, there were still plenty of pets who needed help. However, as time went on, more and more RSPCA inspectors were being called up, so for the first time in its history the charity had looked to women to fill in the gaps. They were not allowed to be inspectors (that was too large a pill to swallow), but they could learn the basics of animal husbandry and how to drive an animal ambulance. Lena saw her chance to make a difference at last. Her interview went well. She was invited to learn how to drive and, once she'd mastered that, she could be trained in animal first aid. All that remained before she made a start was getting a medical, the usual requirement when joining a uniformed service.

Lena was already working with her pigeons. Most of the birds she'd had at the time of the fire had returned to the cottage, but of course she now had to retrain them to 'home' to Cyril's cottage. He helped her build a new cage with a small drawbridge opening which would allow the pigeons in while deterring predators. She spent whatever spare time she had off from the stables in encouraging the young birds – aged six to eight weeks and called squeakers – to get used to being handled by hand-feeding them. The slightly older pigeons, five to six months old, were being trained to home. That meant she had to take them a mile, then two miles, and anything up to ten miles from home and release them.

'They say the way to a pigeon's heart is through its stomach,' Cyril told her in the beginning, so Lena made sure the birds were ready for a meal when she set them free. Usually, they would circle for a few minutes until they got their bearings, and then they were off and, more often than not, they beat her back home. By the end of September, she was sending them on long train journeys to have them released, and most of them made it back to the cottage. All that remained was to ensure that her pigeons were registered with the armed forces so that – should the war escalate – her birds could carry vital messages from conflict zones.

Lena felt contented at last. She was still living with Cyril, and the arrangement suited them both. He still treated her like a daughter and enjoyed her company; she had a roof over her head and someone to care about. Yes, they were living in perilous times, but so long as she felt useful and she was with her beloved animals, life was good. Nipper had joined them and grown very close to Cyril. As for Cyril himself, he regarded the dog as his, even if Seebold was still around.

Lena's piece of land by Bridge Halt had been requisitioned by the army. They didn't seem to be doing much with it at the moment, but it was rumoured that it might become an ammunition dump, or maybe a camp site for some of the hundreds of Canadian servicemen believed to be on their way. Lena had been given some war bonds in exchange for the land, and they'd told her that as soon as hostilities ended, she would be compensated. Her hopes and dreams were on hold right now, but the country was at war and that had to take priority.

Cyril was out when she got back home; nothing unusual about that because he always played skittles in the Black

Horse at Findon with some of his old World War I comrades on a Wednesday. Nipper lay contentedly on the path leading to the back door; however, as she came round the cottage, she realised something wasn't quite right. The pigeons were spooked, and Lena thought she could hear someone moving about in the big shed. Who could it be? And what were they doing there? Were they after Cyril's tools, or maybe some of Nan's preserves? She'd bottled just about everything and, even though she'd been gone a couple of months now, the shelves were still stacked. Lena thought about calling out, but as her heartbeat quickened, she decided to go for the element of surprise instead. Why hadn't the dog reacted? He was old and she had long suspected that he was a bit deaf, but surely he should have guarded his domain?

Picking up the garden fork which leaned against the wall by the kitchen window, Lena crept towards the shed as quietly as she could. As she drew closer, she could make out that it was a man – he had his back to her, but he looked quite hefty and she was only a slip of a girl. She chewed her bottom lip anxiously and then decided that as Nipper was right behind her, as soon as she cried out, the dog was bound to leap into action.

Taking a deep breath, Lena shouted, 'Hey you! Come out from there, whoever you are.'

The person jumped and she heard the sound of something, a tool perhaps, falling with a loud clatter, then a man's voice said, 'Oh, for heaven's sake. You frightened the life out of me!'

Milly arrived back in Worthing at seven-thirty. She was exhausted but happy as her train pulled into Worthing station. In her last snatched conversation with Stanley Richardson, it had been arranged that she would receive a formal letter, and probably travel back to Warwickshire later in the month. She was also famished, so her first thought had been to dash over to North Street and Worley's fish-and-chip shop. Hurrying out of the station, she ran down the steps and crossed the road when someone called her name. She stopped in mid-track and turned around slowly. It couldn't be, could it? It was!

'Seebold,' she cried; a moment later, she was in his arms.

He had taken her to Worley's, and from there to the seafront, where they ate the best fish and chips on the planet. Milly was blissfully happy.

'It's so good to see you again. How did you know I would be at the station?'

'Lena told me. I was checking the lorry over in Cyril's shed when she crept up behind me and gave me the fright of my life.'

Milly laughed aloud as he told her what had happened. 'I bet she was just as scared as you were.'

'I think she was,' he said, screwing up the newspaper that had kept their food warm. Taking her into his arms, he kissed her tenderly, then hungrily. 'This isn't very romantic,' he apologised, 'but I think I shall remember this moment for the rest of my life.'

She gently tugged at his hair at the front until the curl, much shorter now, fell onto his forehead. 'So will I,' she whispered, 'and you're wrong. This is the most romantic place in the whole world.'

Chapter 43

With the last of the boxes almost empty, and most things where she wanted them to be, Agatha sat down and reached for her cigarettes. It was pretty decent of Bunny Warren to offer her a place to live for as long as she wanted it. She knew he thought she was wonderful, and he'd made no secret of his affections ever since Charles had died. That's why it was easy to ask him to give Pearl away on her wedding day. He'd been over the moon to have the honour, and he'd thrown in a couple of crates of champagne as well, which of course she knew he would. Agatha smiled to herself. She had always been a good judge of character.

Bunny had asked Agatha to marry him more than once, but he really was the most irritating man with a rather silly disposition, and she knew she couldn't live with his ridiculous laugh. She shuddered at having to submit to those puffy wet lips daily, and the thought of his podgy fingers seeking out her private parts made her feel positively queasy. As time went on, he was becoming bolder. When he pressed himself against her and kissed her, for her the earth never moved but for Bunny something definitely did. On the plus side, he was very rich, and before the Great War his passion for big-game hunting had often taken him abroad. Not so now.

This war which, like the last one, was supposed to be over by Christmas, was clearly going to be a long-drawn-out job. He was at least twelve years older than Agatha, and she wondered vaguely if she could bear to live with him for the rest of his life, even if he didn't last that long. Probably not. In order to have a secure and comfortable life, marriage was very tempting, but not unless she could work out a way to spend as little time with him as possible.

If Pearl had been with her, the cottage would have been rather cramped, but right now her daughter was incarcerated in a mental institution. As terrible as that was, Agatha knew that it was a blessing in disguise. Had the doctors decided she was in her right mind, Pearl would have been indicted and most likely hanged for her crimes. The murder of Nan had indeed been unintentional, but the attempted murder of Millicent was deliberate and – with four policemen as witnesses in the room – could not be denied. Some said she was wicked, but Agatha put it down to the stress of her husband's betrayal. She was relieved, though, when the doctors decided that her beloved daughter was insane and put her in a secure unit.

As for Freddie himself, he was in prison. He might have been simply interned, as were many of his ilk, but for the fact that he had left so much evidence of what he'd been up to in the ice house and downstairs in the basement. MI5 had gone through every list, and realised that he had not only collected the names of people who were Nazi sympathisers and others who were against Hitler's regime, but he had also photographed key installations and put together a detailed account of the workings of the surrounding ports and airports. All of that could have been very helpful for the enemy. The only thing which saved him from being executed as a traitor was the fact that he'd carried out his plans *before* the war started. He had been tried and found guilty of aiding and abetting an enemy, and sentenced to twenty years, with ten years hard labour. Of course, Agatha wasn't in the least bit sorry for him. She had treated him with respect, had him in her house, and allowed him to court her daughter, but all along he had duped them with his lies. She had thought of him as a member of the aristocracy, when he had been nothing more than a dirty little spy.

Surprisingly, most of Agatha's 'set' had sympathised with her rather than ostracising her. She was no longer young, but she was still an attractive woman and, as such, she got plenty of invitations to parties. There weren't so many now, but she belonged to a group of 'haves' who were sitting it out and carrying on as if the war didn't exist. Agatha was sure they talked behind her back, but she didn't care. She still managed to have a decent social life, and that was enough for her.

Millicent never did go to live in Muntham Court. Soon after Freddie's trial, the house was requisitioned by the government and was now a base for army officers, but quite what went on there was anybody's guess. At the beginning of November, Agatha read with disgust in the local paper that Millicent had joined the Camouflage Directorate unit in Leamington Spa, Warwickshire. Apparently two hundred and fifty artists, designers and technicians worked there and, according to the newspaper, her daughter had been one of two thousand applicants for the position. The article went on to say that her gift with a paintbrush was truly exceptional. Agatha scoffed at that idea, although she did wonder vaguely what they actually did in the directorate. Probably more window-dressing, or some such useless occupation.

She'd seen that dreadful showman Millicent was so keen on a few times. He was in uniform. He'd joined the Royal Engineers. Well, what did you expect? There was a war on, so she supposed the army would be forced to take on any old riff-raff. And as for the whore's daughter . . . she couldn't come back to the cottage until it was repaired after the fire, and that wasn't very likely to happen any time soon. She wouldn't have the money. Agatha had heard that she was living with Cyril. Apparently she'd been with the old man when she was a child and he treated her like a daughter. More fool him, that's all she could say. The girl had gone there with her menagerie, and someone had said she would soon be wearing an RSPCA uniform. When she heard that, Agatha had cancelled her subscription to the charity. In her opinion, if they were employing the likes of *her*, the organisation was definitely going downhill. As for the girl herself – well, she was no better than she ought to be.

Finishing her cigarette, she went back to the boxes. The last thing at the bottom of the box was an old handbag. Heavens above! She hadn't seen that thing in years. Agatha held it out in front of her. Did she like it? She wasn't sure. Would she use it again? Probably not. She was about to throw it in the bin when she thought she'd better open it to make sure there was nothing inside. To her surprise it contained a letter. An unopened letter. Agatha frowned. What on earth . . .?

It turned out to be a letter from Charles. As she rotated it in her hands, she realised it was the letter the solicitor had given her on the day Charles's will was read. Good Lord, all that time ago and she'd never even looked at it. She'd been far too angry with how little he had left her. All she remembered from that day was that silly little note. *Silence is golden. I remembered my promise.* She scoffed. She'd known what he'd meant, of course. He'd kept her secret about Pearl. Charles had never adopted Pearl; Agatha wouldn't allow it because the fact that she had never married Pearl's father would have become public knowledge, so the girl remained illegitimate. Agatha knew people would call her 'second-hand goods' had they known and so she had made Charles promise to never tell.

And now she had this letter. What on earth had he said

to her? She lowered herself into a chair and unfolded the paper.

My dear Agatha

I am so sorry we didn't manage to make a real go of things. I fear we only clung to each other because of our grief over the loss of Simon. He was your fiancé and my best friend. When I married you, all I wanted to do was honour his memory and make you happy. I'm so sorry it didn't work out that way. You gave me the most wonderful joy when Milly was born, so personally I have no regrets. You may feel I have been unfair to you with regards to my will, but you are still a very attractive and much sought-after woman so I have no doubt that you shall probably be married again before the first year of my passing. Be happy, my dear. Don't look back. Embrace life in all its fullness.

I have left you something which I hope will make you smile. It is just between you and me, and may remind you of our honeymoon. If you look inside Aunt Felicity's vase, the one you hated so much, you will find some black beads. They are not what they seem. They are, in fact, black pearls and, as such, very valuable. I didn't include them in the will, because I felt sure that if Pearl knew about them, she would want them for herself and would have persuaded you to give them to her. I always thought that you were far too soft where she was concerned. I want you to have them, Agatha. Do with them what you will. Sell them or have them made into a necklace. Don't be fooled by the slightly off-white ones. They are still black pearls, despite their colour, and actually much more valuable than the rest. Together they are worth a small fortune.

I hope you have a happy life, my dear.

With great affection and gratitude,

Charles

It took Agatha a few seconds to recall the vase, and then it came to her. It was one of the ones she had sold. She had found them herself, and then later Mrs Cunningham had heard the pearls rolling around inside when she'd come to clean it. Oh God, and she'd thrown the damned things into the bin! They were long gone. *Worth a small fortune*. She screwed the letter up in her hand as the tears smarted her eyes.

Oh Charles. You fool. You bloody fool!

Mabel Cunningham stood by the entrance to the jeweller's shop clutching her handbag close to her chest. Her life savings were inside. She knew it wasn't much, but it was all she had, and she wanted her daughter to have something very special for her birthday.

Life hadn't been easy since her husband took ill. She'd worked hard all her life and just about got by. It had been a blessing when dear Mr Charles had given her a small annuity, but when the mistress contested the will, she had been terrified that Mrs Shepherd would move heaven and earth to stop her from having it. When the rest of the staff left, Mabel stayed on, not out of loyalty but to make sure she got her fair share. And as soon as the terms of the will had been verified, she had left Muntham Court without a backward glance.

In her last few weeks, the mistress had had a clear-out. Mabel had been asked to wash some valuable pieces ready for the auction house. Inside a vase, the one that stood in the sitting room, she'd found some black beads. She'd shown them to Mrs Shepherd. Later on, when she'd emptied the waste-paper basket, Mabel had found the beads inside. Well, if Mrs Shepherd didn't want them, Mabel was sure her daughter would enjoy them. Only it never happened.

When her Harold died, the beads were tucked away in a drawer and forgotten. She'd found them again just a week ago and taken them to the jeweller.

'Can you make them into a necklace,' she'd said. 'There's no hole for you to thread them and they're a little bit dull, but perhaps you could add a few coloured beads on the string to brighten them up?'

The jeweller had promised he would make them into a necklace to remember, and Mabel felt content.

As she put her hand on the doorknob of the shop, a young couple were coming out of the jeweller's. They only had eyes for each other and didn't notice Mabel, not until they bumped into her.

'Ooh, sorry,' said the girl, and then she added, 'Mrs Cunningham!'

It was Miss Milly. Mabel was delighted to see her again, and she looked so different. Her eyes were shining; Mabel had never seen her looking so happy.

'I haven't seen you for ages, Miss Milly,' Mabel said. 'How are you getting on?'

'Oh, now you make me feel so guilty,' said Milly. 'I've been meaning to come round to see you. I'm going away, you see. I'm leaving Worthing.'

'I can see by your uniform that you've joined the ATS,' said Mabel.

'Yes, I'm going to put my artistic skills to good use. I have joined a camouflage unit.'

'Oh,' said Mabel. She hadn't a clue what that might be, but she knew better than to ask more. 'And your young man?'

'You should remember me, Mrs Cunningham,' he said. 'I'm Seebold Flowers, the man the baron sent packing all that time ago.'

'Oh, I'm sorry, dear,' said Mrs Cunningham. 'I hardly recognised you in your uniform. Royal Engineers, isn't it?'

'It certainly is,' said Seebold.

'You seem content with that,' Mabel added with smile.

'What could be better?' said Seebold with a chuckle. 'I'm up to my armpits in engines and oily rags all day long.'

Mrs Cunningham chuckled. 'Aren't you the young man who caught a wolf up Shoreham way and ended up in Lewes Crown Court?'

Seebold laughed. 'The very same.'

'Funny business that,' Mabel remarked with a puzzled expression.

Milly and Seebold looked at each other and grinned. 'Well, we'd better be going,' said Milly. 'Nice to see you again, Mrs Cunningham.'

Mabel hesitated. 'Miss Milly, when I worked for your mother,' she began cautiously, 'she threw out some black beads. I thought my daughter would like them, so I've asked the jeweller to make them into a necklace.'

'What a lovely idea,' said Milly. 'How is your daughter?'

'She's doing well, thank you, miss. She's left school now and she's training to be a hairdresser.'

'Good for her,' said Milly. 'Please give her my best wishes.'

Milly would have moved on, but Mrs Cunningham was looking a tad uncomfortable. 'Is everything all right?'

'You don't mind if I keep the beads?' she asked. 'I mean, if you want them back . . .'

'Absolutely not,' said Milly. 'Especially after all you did for my family.' She turned to leave but then paused and turned back.

'Mrs Cunningham,' Milly began again. 'Can I share something with you? I should like you to be the first to know, we've just got engaged.' She held out her left hand and the sweetest little opal ring twinkled on her finger.

'Oh miss!' cried Mabel. 'I'm so happy for you. So happy.'

Mabel admired the ring, then Miss Milly kissed her cheek and Seebold, his face wreathed in smiles, shook her hand vigorously.

As they parted, Mabel watched them cross the street. She was delighted for them both and she hoped they would be as happy as she and her Harold had been. In these difficult days, she thought to herself, we all need a little bit of good in our lives. Milly's mother had never treated her right. Such a shame that poor Mr Charles had died. She sighed. Far too young as well.

What a blessing that he'd given her that annuity. Back then, it had saved her bacon. Even though she had been the only member of staff who had worked for Mrs Shepherd all those months after Mr Charles had died, she was still owed a lot of money – Mrs Shepherd had never paid her a penny.

She turned around and pushed open the shop door.

'Ah, Mrs Cunningham,' said the jeweller, coming up to the counter. 'So glad you've come in. About those beads. I think you will be pleasantly surprised. I haven't made them into a necklace yet because I have something to tell you . . .'

Author's Note

The stories I write are entirely fictional, but I do use real-life settings and draw on historical facts. In this story, some of my readers will not be slow to recognise that I have unashamedly used parts of a real event, a story I came across some twenty years ago; one which still makes me laugh. It involves one of this country's greatest showmen, Sir Billy Butlin.

When he died, Billy Butlin was a much-respected man, and to this day his name is still synonymous with holiday camps and family entertainment. But there was a time when the people of Bognor Regis weren't too happy with him and neither, for that matter, were the police. The blip in his popularity was caused by a 'missing' lion called Rex.

In 1931, Billy Butlin acquired some land just a few hundred yards from Bognor Pier, known locally as 'the cabbage patch' because it had been used for allotments during World War I. He set about creating Billy Butlin's Centre of Happiness, with 'dodgem cars, water speed boats, roundabouts and automatic amusement machines, all brilliantly illuminated with hundreds of coloured electric bulbs'. The crowds flocked in.

The secret of Butlin's success was that he was never one

to rest on his laurels. In 1933 he decided to open a menagerie as well, so he gave instructions for certain animals to be transported from Skegness down to the south coast. These included a brown bear, a panther and an African lion. Billy Butlin made the same journey from Skegness to Bognor but not with the convoy. When he arrived the next day, the whole place was buzzing with rumour.

Following a slight accident at Clymping, a few miles from Bognor, staff noticed three bars from the side of one cage were missing. All the animals were accounted for . . . except the lion.

Butlin's quick phone call to Skegness proved that because of the damaged cage, the lion had never actually been sent. However, the manager of the Bognor Amusements, Clifford Joste, had already informed the authorities about the missing lion. Not surprisingly, the police immediately made this their top priority. Although he was never a party to deception, Billy Butlin was not slow to see the publicity potential of keeping mum.

When a zealous young reporter called Proctor picked up the story, the *News Chronicle* had a front-page exclusive. The next day, twenty reporters from Fleet Street arrived in Bognor and light-hearted lion hunts were organised around the Sussex villages.

However, things took a serious turn when John Wensley, a local farmer down on his luck, reported a dead and half-eaten sheep. As soon as Proctor published this story, near panic swept through the area. Terrified parents kept their children indoors and schools closed. Campers and holiday-makers left Bognor in droves, and hoteliers suffered a sharp downturn in takings. And all this at the height of the holiday season.

Billy Butlin realised that the public would only be put at ease if they could see the captured beast for themselves, so he arranged for another lion to be sent from Kent under cover of darkness. When the animal arrived in Bognor it looked bedraggled and was covered in green muck. Butlin told reporters and photographers it had been found in a local ditch. The following day, national newspapers carried pictures of Billy and Rex sitting side by side in one of the dodgem cars on the front pages, and everyone breathed a collective sigh of relief.

The whole thing might have been forgotten except for one thing. The police had spent many hours chasing a non-existent lion and public money had been wasted. As a result, four people were arrested, the reporter Proctor, farmer Wensley, Billy Butlin and Clifford Joste. After a magistrate hearing in October, they were sent for trial at Lewes Crown court.

Back in the day, newspapers reported court cases verbatim, and the 1933 reports of the trial read more like the script of a Whitehall farce. The defendants were accused of conspiring 'to commit a public mischief . . . and putting the public in fear' – serious stuff. The court was told of how a policeman on a bicycle was sent to escort sixty girl guides marching from their camp site to the railway station two miles away. Quite what that lone policeman would have done had the lion suddenly appeared out of the undergrowth is a mystery. The national papers carried pictures of a long line of farmers with pitchforks and carrying a fishing net, walking across a field as they searched for the lion, as well as people riding shotgun on the backs of lorries and cars as they roamed the Sussex countryside. There were accounts of a lion eating tomatoes in somebody's greenhouse but, as it turned out, Rex himself had no teeth at all. Had he been cornered, all the poor lion could have done was gum somebody to death! Even the green muck from the ditch turned out to be distemper, thrown over the animal to make his capture appear authentic.

Eventually, it was proven in court that although the

sheep had died, it had been wilfully mutilated by the farmer, and that he and Proctor had colluded together in the hope of making money.

The trial ended with the two men being found guilty of attempting to deceive the public (Wensley was fined £10 and Proctor was fined £30), but Billy Butlin and his manager, Joste, were exonerated and acquitted.

Despite the small setback of a court case, the publicity had the desired effect. Billy Butlin's popularity grew greater than ever. In the 1960s, he negotiated with Bognor Council to sell the cabbage patch. Using the money as capital, he set up a holiday camp on the thirty-nine acres of an area now known as South Coast World.

In this book, Seebold might have had the same kind of dream as Billy Butlin, but it remains to be seen if he succeeded!

Acknowledgements

With my grateful thanks to all the team at Avon: Raphaella, Katie, Rachel, Maddie, Sarah, Amy, Helen, Ella, Elisha and Kate. I shall miss you dreadfully . . .

**Three sisters torn apart by war.
Can fighting for peace bring them
together again?**

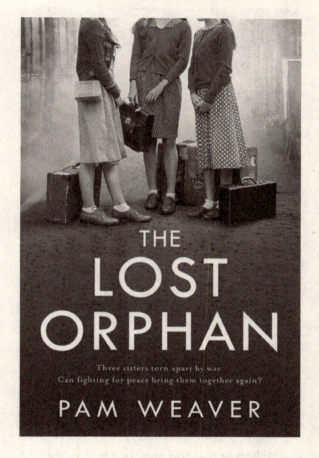

THE
LOST
ORPHAN

Three sisters torn apart by war.
Can fighting for peace bring them together again?

PAM WEAVER

A heart-breaking tale of the bond between sisters and the
courage of women in wartime.

Two sisters.

One secret.

A daring wartime journey . . .

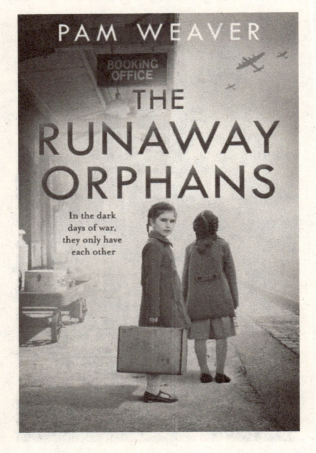

PAM WEAVER

BOOKING
OFFICE

THE
RUNAWAY
ORPHANS

In the dark
days of war,
they only have
each other

Will they find the strength to confront
what they have been running from,
when their past finally catches up with them?

Can she be brave enough to follow her heart?

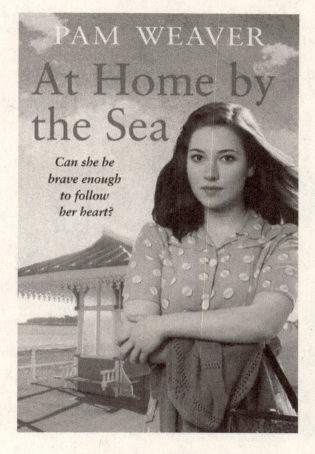

Can a second chance heal their broken family?

Can love find a way to overcome hate?

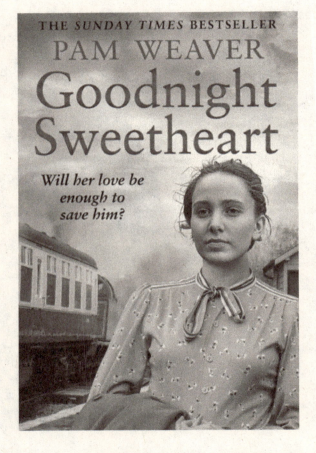

A moving, thought-provoking story, perfect for fans of Katie Flynn and Maureen Lee.

**An unexpected letter will change
her life forever...**

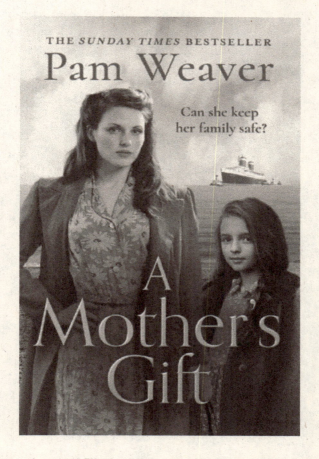

A dramatic story filled with family, scandal and friendships
that bring hope in the darkness.